Blame it on the Beatles

...and Bill Shankly

BLAME IT ON THE BEATLES

...and Bill Shankly

John Winter

Matador
9 Priory Business Park,
Wistow Road, Kibworth Beauchamp,
Leicestershire. LE8 0RX
Tel: 0116 279 2299
Email: books@troubador.co.uk
Web: www.troubador.co.uk/matador
Twitter: @matadorbooks

ISBN 978 1789014 549

British Library Cataloguing in Publication Data.
A catalogue record for this book is available from the British Library.

Printed and bound in Great Britain by 4edge Limited
Typeset in 11pt Minion Pro by Troubador Publishing Ltd, Leicester, UK

Matador is an imprint of Troubador Publishing Ltd

This book is dedicated to my wife, Susan, a passionate Liverpool supporter and listener to the music of The Beatles, who patiently provided coffee, tea, and endless encouragement during the writing of this book, and who offered invaluable advice upon the various drafts of the manuscript.

Grateful thanks for their comments are also due to my son, Robert Winter, who lives in London with his wife Lucy, my brother, Philip Winter, and his wife, Rhona, who now live in Nailsea, just outside Bristol; and to very good friends Janet and Andrew Baker from Abersoch in North Wales, Karen and Jim Kendig from Lancaster in Pennsylvania, Diane and Steve Adam from Seattle in Washington State, and Gill and Rob Klottrup, along with Alexander, Francesca, Sam and Juliet, from Newby in the Yorkshire Dales.

The photograph on the front cover is of the bronze statue of The Beatles, which stands on the Pier Head in Liverpool in front of the iconic Liver Building, Cunard Building and Port of Liverpool Building. It is used by kind permission of the sculptor, Andrew Edwards, to whom I offer my grateful thanks. The statue was commissioned by The Cavern Club and unveiled by John Lennon's sister, Julia Baird, on the 50th anniversary of the band's final concert in Liverpool.

And finally.
    To The Beatles. Thank you for the music.
    And to Bill Shankly. Thank you for making the beautiful game even more beautiful.

DISCLAIMER

This book is a work of FICTION. There are however well-documented historical facts interwoven with the otherwise fictional story. Real persons, both living and dead, who are named in this story including, but not limited to, The Beatles and their families, George Martin, Stuart Sutcliffe, Tony Sheridan, Paddy Delaney, Jim Gretty, Mr T.V. Williams, Bill Shankly, Ronnie Yeats, Ian St John, Roger Hunt, Gerry Byrne, Ian Callaghan, George Best, Bobby Moore, Geoff Hurst, Martin Peters, Kenneth Wolstenholme, Gerry and The Pacemakers, Cilla Black, Rory Storm and The Hurricanes, 'Kingsize' Taylor and The Dominos, The Undertakers, Pete Best, Mona Best, Brian Epstein, Eric Clapton, Little Richard, Craig Douglas, Patti Boyd, Bruce Welch, Phil Spector, Alan Williams, Sam Leach, Bill Harry, Ray McFall, Alf Geoghegan, Roger McGough, Adrian Henri and Mike McCartney, did not interact with any of the fictitious characters, or participate in any of the fictitious events, described in this story. The inclusion of their names within this story does not imply that they have approved, or that they endorse, any of the contents of this book.

All names, characters, places and incidents in this story are either a product of the author's imagination or are used fictitiously. Any resemblance to the actual statements, opinions or actions of real people, living or dead, at past or existing locations is entirely coincidental.

One

LIVERPOOL – 1960

I suppose you could just blame it on The Beatles. But, to be fair, Bill Shankly probably had quite a lot to answer for as well.

The thing is, we all thought it was normal. We were young. In our mid-teens when it all started. And when you're that age you don't think too much about what's happening around you. In the places where you hang out. You don't know any different. What happens is what happens. And it's normal. You think that's just the way things are.

Only it wasn't normal. It wasn't anywhere near normal. For a fairly ordinary city like Liverpool it was about as far from normal as it could possibly be.

But, as I say, at the time we all thought it was normal.

And we thought they were normal as well.

Well, no, we didn't actually. In fact, we thought at first they were from Germany. It wasn't that long after the war, but for us teenagers the war was like ancient history even though there were still loads of derelict bomb sites all over the city. In Liverpool we didn't get to see many people from Germany. So that made them a bit unusual.

But the sound they made, and the way they looked. All dressed in well-worn, black leather. That was something else. It's difficult now to describe the way it felt, watching them, listening to them. That first time.

It was Litherland Town Hall in 1960. A few miles north of Liverpool city centre. The day after Christmas. There were three well-known Liverpool bands on the bill that night. The German band were a last minute booking and we'd never heard of them. On the poster outside the hall, advertising The Del Renas, The Deltones, and The Searchers, someone had added, in a big, black, hand-written scrawl, *Direct from Hamburg – The Beatles*.

***

The opening line of *'Long Tall Sally'* hit us like a thunderbolt as the bass guitarist screamed the words into his microphone and hurled them out across the dance floor. It was electric. The hairs on the back of our necks stood on end. We'd gone out for some fun and a bit of a dance and then, all of a sudden, nobody was dancing. We stood there, heads turned towards the stage, mesmerised by the sound, and by the look, of the four, leather-clad figures. This was different. This was exciting. It was just a shame that they were from Germany so we'd almost certainly never see them again. Don't get me wrong. Some of our local bands were good, but these lads from Germany were like some sort of primeval force coming at you.

There was a loud roar as the song came to an end. The singer waved to the cheering crowd.

"Thanks for that. It's great to be playing fer yer all tonight."

One of the girls I was with turned to me.

"Jesus Christ. You'd almost think 'e was from round 'ere the way 'e speaks."

Before I could reply she was gone, heading towards the stage.

Just under an hour later, as they ended their set, the whole place erupted. I was cheering along with everyone else and most of the girls were, by now, packed together in a tight, little scrum, pushing to get as close as possible to their new idols.

Over the noise I could just about hear one of the guitarists, shouting into his mike.

"Ta very much. You've bin great. We'll be back 'ere soon. See yer then."

With that they started packing up their gear, and we all settled down to enjoy the rest of the evening. We never guessed for one moment that we had just witnessed something very special. Something that was going to change almost everything.

All we knew was that after hearing that German band we were on a real high.

And to make it even better, Liverpool Football Club had beaten Rotherham United at Anfield that same afternoon.

We'd not long got a new manager, you see. Bill Shankly his name was. A dour, but canny, Scotsman who'd previously been in charge of a team called Huddersfield Town over in West Yorkshire. There was something special about him. Everyone was saying he was a bit of a renegade. Once he'd got the job he refused to take a blind bit of notice of the directors at the club, who'd been picking the team each week, saying they didn't know the first thing about football. And he was right. They didn't. With a bit of luck, he'd shake the place up a bit.

It definitely needed shaking up. Seven years it was since we'd been relegated from Division One. Seven years. You probably can't understand what that felt like. The thing is football really matters in Liverpool. It's sort of like a religion. And Everton, the other football club in the city, were riding high. That really hurt, I can tell you.

We'd been close to promotion a couple of times, only for our hopes to be dashed. Sometimes it felt like we'd be down there, trapped in the misery of Division Two, forever.

But not that evening. As we left Litherland Town Hall, what with the music and the football, we were buzzing. It didn't last long though. Next day Liverpool went to Rotherham, the team they'd just beaten at Anfield, and lost. Down to third place. Out of the promotion race again.

So there we were. Living in a city that had been half-destroyed by German bombs. Supporting a football team that seemed to be going nowhere. And listening to a band who'd come over from the country which, not that long ago, had been doing its best to beat the shit out of us.

Was that normal? I've no idea. I'm just telling you what happened.

"They're from Liverpool, not Germany."

My mate, Steve, grabbed hold of me two days later outside the newsagents. It was a typically cold, grey, wet and miserable Wednesday morning and I was feeling pretty low.

"That band on Boxing Day. The Beatles. They all live down the south end of the city, somewhere 'round Speke and Allerton."

"But the poster said they're from Hamburg. That's Germany."

"Honest to God. I'm not havin' yer on. They're from round 'ere. Dave told me. 'E knows one of their mates. Apparently they was over in Hamburg, playin' at a club near the docks for a few weeks, but they got kicked out. Somethin' to do with bein' too young or not 'avin' work permits. I dunno. Anyway, they're back in Liverpool now. So maybe we can get to see 'em again. Dave's gonna find out where they're playin' next. He thinks they might be doin' somethin' on New Year's Eve."

For some reason that cheered me up. And anyway, in a few days there was another football match coming up. Hope springs eternal, as they say.

"Are you coming to Anfield on New Year's Eve?" I said. "We're playing Middlesbrough."

Steve shook his head.

"Nah. Liverpool's rubbish. They couldn't kick their way out of a bleedin' paper bag. I'm not wastin' any more money on 'em. They'll only lose again. I'm seriously thinkin' of givin' up on Liverpool an' supportin' Everton. At least they know how to play football. Goin' to Anfield at the moment's doin' me head in."

To be honest with you I couldn't argue with him. He had a point. But I was young. I was still an optimist back then. So on New Year's Eve I made my way up the steep steps which led up to the Kop at Anfield on my own. It was a long climb which took me to the back of a roofed terrace behind the goal at the south end of Liverpool Football Club's home ground. It was standing only. Match-day seats were reserved for the toffs who had tickets for the Main Stand which ran along the side of the pitch. The Kop, though, was where all the most fanatical supporters congregated. For a big match there'd be as many as twenty-five thousand people crammed onto the steep slope which overlooked the pitch.

An old guy once told me some soldiers from Liverpool nicknamed it the Spion Kop because it reminded them of a big hill in South Africa where they'd fought a battle way back in 1900. During the Boer War I think he said. He might've been having me on, I suppose. But the way he told the story it sounded like it could be true.

I reached the top of the steps and looked down into the stadium. A thin, drizzly rain was falling and the pitch looked dark and gloomy. In those days the floodlights didn't get switched on until half-time. Until then we'd all have to peer through the gloom of the mid-winter afternoon as best we could.

I made my way down the terrace to grab my usual spot behind one of the steel safety barriers just above and to the right of the goal. You need to be close enough to feel the action, but high enough above the pitch to be able to appreciate the tactics and see the shape of the game.

By kick off there were over thirty thousand of us in the stadium. The Kop wasn't packed, but the crowd was big enough to generate some noise and hopefully put a bit of fear into the opposition. The pitch was a typical mid-season mud-bath, which was generally the way of things back in the nineteen sixties, and Liverpool were three-nil up by half-time. With the floodlights on and the crowd behind them they should have walked it in the second half, but instead of making the most of their three goal advantage they started to play like rabbits in headlights. Their defending was abysmal and Middlesbrough scored four times to sneak back home with both points.

Steve was waiting by the bus stop when I got back. I broke the bad news.

"They lost. Four – three. Against Middlesbrough for God's sake. They're bloody pathetic. We'll never get back to Division One."

He just laughed.

"I decided to spend me afternoon with a copy of Reveille. There's some crackin' birds in there. An' believe me they're a lot better lookin' than the Liverpool players."

He'd definitely made the right decision. But it's hard to abandon your team. Being a football fan is ninety percent pain and suffering. Even when your team's winning you're always waiting for the next thing to go wrong. I suppose it's like being on drugs. You forget about the lows because the highs are so brilliant.

We stood in silence for a couple of minutes, hands in pockets and jacket collars turned up against an increasingly cold wind which drove the damp drizzle into the bus shelter. Steve blew into his cupped hands to try and warm them up a bit. He had some news.

"Here's somethin' that might cheer yer up anyway. Dave spoke to 'is mate, Robbo, and that band, you know, The Beatles. They're playin' at a place called The Casbah in West Derby tonight. We're gonna go along there an' see in the New Year. Fancy comin'? Me an' Dave are meetin' up at his place at about half eight. If you've got nothin' else on you should give it a go. It'll be good."

It didn't take me long to make up my mind. I definitely didn't want to miss out, and I thought it'd probably cheer me up. So, at just after eight forty-five that evening, I joined Steve and Dave on the Number 60 from Stanley Road, north of the city centre, for the twenty minute ride along Queens Drive which would take us out to West Derby, a smart, tree-lined suburb to the east.

We shared an untipped, Woodbines cigarette up on the top deck of the bus while Dave told us about The Casbah.

"It's in a big house which belongs to this Mrs Best. Her son Pete's the drummer with The Beatles. Accordin' to Robbo they've tarted up the basement an' made it into a sort of club. They called it The Casbah. To make it sound a bit exotic, I suppose. Robbo said it might've been Pete's Mum who came up with the name. She's from India."

Steve passed him the Woodbine and he took an extra deep pull on it.

"Eh! Come on, Dave. That's about 'alf an inch you've used up there. We've only the one Woody. So it's a third each. Fair's fair."

Dave shrugged his shoulders and handed the cigarette on to me before continuing his brief history of The Beatles and The Casbah.

"They used to be called The Silver Beetles. Apparently they weren't that good until they went off to Hamburg. There was this guy called Alan Williams who fixed it up for them. He had some contacts over there, and none of the other Liverpool groups much fancied the idea of headin' off to Germany. Probably worried they mightn't get too friendly a welcome. What with us havin' won the war an' all that."

Dave didn't know any more. So that's all I can tell you for now. But it gives you something to be going on with.

We got off the bus at The Jolly Miller. That's a well-known Liverpool pub on Queens Drive. Luckily the rain had stopped or we'd have got soaked. We headed off down Mill Lane towards West Derby Village and after about ten minutes Dave spotted a street sign on the left, half-hidden by a hedge that was badly in need of a trim.

"Hayman's Green. That's it. The Casbah should be down there on the right. Number Eight."

The house didn't look much different from the rest of the big, Victorian dwellings in the road. Like all the others it was slightly run-down and surrounded by mature trees. There was nothing to suggest there might be a club in the basement. But Dave said it was definitely Number Eight we were looking for so we walked up the drive.

The front garden was overgrown and a couple of girls were leaning against the side wall of the house. Short, tight skirts. Heavy, black make-up around their eyes. Hair piled up into beehives.

It looked like we'd found the right place.

As you'll realise when you get to know him better, Steve's main interest in life was sex. The fact that he'd not, as yet, succeeded in getting much in the way of practical experience just seemed to make him more obsessed about the subject.

He walked up to the two girls with a big smile.

"Hiya. You two okay? We're lookin' for The Casbah."

One of them removed a cigarette from her mouth and blew a cloud of smoke at him.

"It's down there. Round the back, on yer right."

"Ta. See yer inside."

"Yer might. But don't be gettin' any fancy ideas. Yer not on."

As we pushed the door open Steve gave us a wink.

"She's playin' hard to get. But I think the one in black might fancy me. You two can fight over 'er mate."

Dave looked at him and shook his head.

"Steve, my friend. I love you like a brother, but you're completely deluded."

We made our way down a couple of steps into a short, dark corridor. Opening off it were several, small rooms, each done in a different style. Some of the basement walls had been lined with thick, wooden planks which were decorated with stars and dragons, while one part of the ceiling, over a sort of stage area, had been picked out in rainbow colours. A huge, white spider stared at us from a large web, painted onto the back wall of the stage. Peering into the semi-darkness, we could just make out two guitars leaning against the planks, alongside a drum kit. A couple of microphone stands and some rather battered amplifiers were lined up in front of them.

The three of us stood in the doorway. The sound of Roy Orbison singing his first UK hit, 'Only The Lonely', emerged from a little Dansette record player. Some girls were crowded around it. The Dansette was turned up to full volume, but it couldn't drown out the chatter as they argued over what they were going to put on next. Cliff Richard's Christmas Number One, 'I Love You', seemed to be a hot contender, along with 'It's Now Or Never' by Elvis.

It didn't look like there was much happening so we wandered to the far end of the corridor where there was a small bar with a Coca-Cola sign alongside it. The words 'Casbah Coffee Club' on the bottom of the sign told us that we had indeed found the right place. It was almost nine-thirty and the bar was already crowded. A dark-haired lady with a smooth, brown complexion stood at the counter.

"Don't think I've seen you lads here at The Casbah before. I'm Mona Best."

It was Pete Best's mother. And she wasn't bad looking.

Steve winked at me, but I ignored him.

"What are you going to have to drink lads? There's no alcohol I'm afraid. We haven't got a licence. So it's coffee or Coca Cola. Personally I'd recommend the Coke."

"Okay. Three Cokes then, please."

As we sipped our drinks the two girls who had been hanging about outside wandered in with a couple of lads. Dave immediately recognised them as being two members of the band we had come to watch.

"Tough luck, Steve. Didn't I say you were deluded? Looks like you're gonna have to find yerself a guitar if you wanna get off with that one. I might be wrong, but I think she's taken."

In the background the sound of 'It's Now Or Never' could be heard, coming from the room down the corridor. The speaker on the Dansette lacked any real bass, but it was clear that Cliff had been out-voted and Elvis was singing his latest hit. His early records, like 'Heartbreak Hotel' and 'Jailhouse Rock', were brilliant but I could never really get into the big ballads. I have to admit, though, that diehard Elvis fans thought they were great. They probably still do.

We stood there, drinking our Cokes and watching the two Beatles larking around with the girls. There was no sign of the other members of the band, so it didn't look like they'd be playing any time soon.

I joined the queue which had built up at the bar to order another three Cokes.

"Any idea what time The Beatles'll be playing?"

Mona Best shrugged her shoulders.

"Shouldn't be long. They're just waiting for John to turn up. He's supposed to be on his way. Pete's upstairs in his room."

Even as she spoke a leather-clad figure with a guitar slung over his right shoulder entered the room and went over to the other two Beatles.

"Okay. I'm 'ere. Fetch Pete an' we'll get on with it."

They played for nearly two hours, joking with the boys and flirting with the girls between each number. It was all very relaxed and easy-going. The four Beatles obviously knew most of their audience well. But, although they were very laid back, they didn't let it affect their music. In the small space the sound was exhilarating, and very loud. The bass notes, which the Dansette so noticeably lacked, bounced off the walls and shook the whole of our insides.

When we finally left the club at just after twelve-thirty, having seen in a memorable New Year, our ears were ringing. It had been a great night. The last bus had long gone but, as we wandered back home along Queens Drive, it seemed that 1961 might turn out to be interesting. Things were looking good.

So that's how it all started. It didn't seem like much at the time. We were just happy we had something to look forward to.

But before we carry on maybe I should tell you a little bit about myself?

As you've probably guessed by now, I'm a Scouser. That means I'm from Liverpool. They call us Scousers because we eat Scouse. That's a sort of stew. You lob whatever bits and pieces you happen to have in the house into it. That's lob Scouse. Usually it's just spuds and veg, which is blind Scouse. But sometimes, if you're lucky, there's a few scraps of meat chucked in there as well. Back then, with wartime food rationing not long finished, we ate a lot of it. Blind Scouse that is. It was cheap to make. And if it wasn't all eaten it tasted even better warmed up next day. If you haven't tried it you should give it a go. I can definitely recommend it.

What else? Oh yeah. My name. I'm Tony, but most of my mates call me Tone. Scousers like to shorten names as much possible. Saves time when they're talking fast. Which mostly they do.

At the start of the sixties I was living in a place called Waterloo. Right on the River Mersey about five or six miles north of the city centre. Not far from the docks. My family moved to Liverpool just after the war from a place called Ruthin in North Wales. So I guess we're what they call Liverpool-Welsh. Which is why I've not got that much of a Scouse accent. A good job really. Otherwise you might struggle to understand me.

Some of my mates say I'm not a proper Scouser, cos I was born in Wales. But I wasn't more than about twelve months old when we left Ruthin and I don't remember a single thing about it. So by my reckoning I'm more of a Scouser than anything else.

My Dad decided on the move to Liverpool when one of his mates said he could fix him up with a job on the docks. It was good money but after about twelve years his back went when he was lifting some heavy, cotton bales. At fifty-five he was getting too old for such hard, physical labour. The docks were slowly dying anyway and the jobs were disappearing. With a bad back he struggled to get work a lot of the time.

Then came a stroke of luck. The shop where he picked up his newspaper every day, in South Road not far from the station, came up for sale so he decided to take a chance. He was generally quite cautious, my Dad, so it wasn't really like him, but he felt like he had no choice. That was just after Easter in 1958 and we moved into the flat above the shop. It was definitely a bit of a gamble, but it worked out okay.

Will that do? For starters I mean. I can tell you a bit more later but we need to move on or the story'll never get finished.

Where were we? Oh yes, the start of the sixties. As I was saying, Liverpool was still getting over the war. A lot of the city was just bomb-sites and rubble. You've probably seen some of the early pictures of The Beatles, perched on abandoned motor vehicles in their leathers. With guitars slung over their shoulders and shattered buildings all around them. That was what the place was like then. Gritty. Defiant. And broken. Sad really because the city was once pretty wealthy. Richer than New York. There were still a few grand buildings down at the Pier Head. Overlooking the river. Somehow or other the German bombs had missed them.

The war had changed things. All the money had disappeared. Or maybe been quietly salted away. By the nineteen sixties Liverpool was just another northern city, not that different from Manchester, or Leeds, or Sheffield.

So why, as were walking home along Queens Drive, did we think the future was looking good? To be honest, I can't tell you. I was only just past my seventeenth birthday. And maybe when you're young the future always looks good. But I don't really think that was it. So what was going on? I don't know. I'm not even sure we realised anything was going on. Nothing felt particularly different. At least not until things really started happening.

Two

THE THREE EXILES

"Jesus Christ, I'm depressed."

Steve sat there with his head in his hands. It was the middle of January and the two of us were listening to the Top Twenty on a small transistor radio. His G.I. uncle, who'd married his mother's sister at the end of the war, was still serving in the U.S. Army in Tokyo. He'd brought the radio over from Japan as a Christmas present for Steve. Pocket-sized transistors weren't that easy to get hold of in England back then. And the few that were available cost at least a month's wages. So it was a brilliant gift. The sound through the tiny speaker wasn't much to write home about, but with its light blue, plastic case and shiny, gold volume and tuning knobs, it was Steve's pride and joy. It never left his sight.

Through the windows of the flat above the shop we could see a slushy mixture of rain and snow falling from grey clouds which seemed to press down hard on the rooftops of the surrounding houses. It was as if Litherland Town Hall and The Casbah had never happened. About the only thing that stopped us going completely off our heads with boredom was Radio Luxembourg. At least they played some decent records. All you got on the BBC was David Jacobs and his 'Pick of the Pops' on a

Saturday evening. And with Elvis taking yet another ballad, '*Are You Lonesome Tonight?*', to the top of the charts it was getting even harder to believe that he'd ever sung anything as brilliant as '*Jailhouse Rock*' or '*Heartbreak Hotel*'.

"If they play that Johnny Tillotson singin' '*Poetry in Motion*' again, Tone, I might 'ave to top meself. Life's bad enough without 'avin 'to listen to that sort of garbage. I can't believe how anyone would want to waste their money on it."

I nodded in agreement but didn't say anything. Between you and me I quite liked Johnny Tillotson's hit record, even though it certainly wasn't rock and roll. Steve did sort of have a point though. Life was pretty depressing. You see the thing is we were teenagers. And in England that didn't really mean very much. In America teenagers lived these fantastic lives, hanging out at drive-ins with stunning blonde girls and taking surf-boards down to beautiful beaches under permanently blue skies. We'd see them, laughing and joking on screen in full Technicolor, almost every time we went to the pictures. It was another world. And it left us wide-eyed with amazement. America was the promised land. In Liverpool it was mostly grey skies and grey lives. There was nothing down for us. Our future was all mapped out. We'd follow in our parents' footsteps and end up slaving away at some boring job to pay for the wife and kids we'd accidentally picked up along the way.

It's a miracle we weren't all suicidal.

Then, at the beginning of March, Steve collared me with some news.

"'Ere's somethin' to cheer yer up, Tone. Bill Kelly's puttin' on a dance at The Institute on Saturday night. The Beatles are playin' an' we're all goin'. They're sellin' tickets on the door. Dave's bringin' 'is new girlfriend along. Yvonne she's called. I've not met 'er yet, but accordin' to Jacko she's a cracker. Jet black hair an' a figure like Elizabeth Taylor. God knows what she sees in a short-arsed bugger like Dave, but apparently 'e's gonna be bringin' 'er along. So we can take a look for ourselves. We're meetin' outside The Black Bull at seven."

After two months of nothing happening I needed a bit of cheering up. So I went along.

The Aintree Institute was in Walton, about five miles north-east of the centre of Liverpool and not far from the Grand National racecourse. It was a tall, red-brick building with typical Victorian embellishments around the windows and main entrance. Originally a religious mission hall, it had been built with charitable money with the idea of keeping the workers on the straight and narrow. But by the early sixties it had been turned into a dance-hall. The Beatles were booked in for an early evening session. Then they'd be heading into the city centre for an all-nighter at The Iron Door Club with Gerry and The Pacemakers.

As soon as I arrived Steve grabbed hold of me and pointed towards the stage. "Dave's over there. With Yvonne."

I took a good look. Jacko wasn't wrong. Wearing a low-cut, white blouse and a flared, polka-dot skirt, together with a wide, patent-leather belt, she looked stunning. Steve wasn't the only one who couldn't keep his eyes off her.

The Beatles went down a storm. Their music was different and exciting. It had a raw energy which the watching girls were unable to resist. Sex and rock 'n' roll. It seemed they just naturally went together.

And Steve had noticed. Standing there in his black shirt, tight trousers and grey winkle-pickers he had a sort of wild, evangelical look in his eyes.

"We're gonna form a group, Tone," he said. "You an' me. An' Dave as well. If 'e can tear 'imself away from what's inside Yvonne's blouse, that is. We're not that bad lookin'. An' if we're in a band the girls'll be all over us. We'll be able to take our pick."

I looked at him and shook my head. "Dream on, Steve. Dave's right. You're deluded."

"Come on, Tone. What've we got to lose?"

"A whole load of time learning how to play guitars for a start."

"Forget it then. You've got no imagination, Tone. Yer just can't see it. That's yer problem."

I shrugged my shoulders, which I knew would annoy him. I definitely wasn't going to admit he could be right until I'd had a chance to give it some thought. But it was an interesting idea. Maybe, just maybe, Steve might have hit on something.

Along with pretty much everything else I'd had enough of school by this time. So I got myself an apprenticeship with a small electrical firm based in Bootle, near the docks. The boss was a decent enough bloke and on my first day he took me along to a club called The Cavern. It was in a cellar beneath one of the old fruit warehouses in the commercial heart of Liverpool. Not a bad way to start a new job you must be thinking. No such luck. As I say, the boss was a decent enough bloke. But he wasn't soft. It was work, not play.

"This club we're going to. It belongs to a mate of mine," said the boss as we headed along the Dock Road towards the city centre in the firm's Bedford van. "A chap called Ray McFall. 'E got it a few months back off a lad who'd started it up as a jazz club. But it wasn't makin' any money. So Ray started puttin' on these rock 'n' roll groups. That's what brings the kids in these days. 'E rang me over the weekend cos 'e's been 'avin' some sort of problem with the lights. I told 'im we'd sort it out."

We parked the van right outside the entrance to the club in Mathew Street, a narrow, cobbled alleyway lined with warehouses, the exteriors of which had been stained and blackened over the years by the smoke and pollution of the industrial revolution. Tall and grim, they blocked out a good deal of what little light found its way through the thick, grey clouds overhead.

The boss and I made our way down a steep flight of stone steps which led to a slightly gloomy cellar with a curved roof, supported by a line of sturdy, brick-built columns and archways. A cleaner was hard at work, mopping the smooth, concrete floor.

"I'll be done in a sec," she said, picking up a large bottle of Dettol and splashing it about the place. "The drains keep blockin' up. This stuff helps kill the smell."

While she was finishing off the boss set up a step-ladder and started poking away at the lights with his screwdriver. As I said, we were there to work.

"These units are corroded to hell," he said as the tip of his screwdriver disappeared through the rusty metal cover on one of the lights. "There's no ventilation down 'ere. With a load of sweaty bodies crammed inside it must be like the black hole of bleedin' Calcutta." He threw down a set of keys. "They'll all 'ave to be replaced. Nip up an' get me four new ones from the van, lad."

In just under an hour the job was done.

"While we're down 'ere we'd better take a look at the mains." The Dettol wasn't going to stop the boss sniffing out a bit of extra business. "If the lights are anythin' to go by the rest of the electrics'll be shot as well."

I followed him as he walked over to a small, wooden stage which stood in front of a slightly grubby, white-painted wall at the far end of the club. On one side of the stage, where an amplifier and record turntable were still plugged in, there was an untidy jumble of extension leads, all plugged into a single socket.

He turned to me and shook his head in disbelief. "Look at

that mess. I'm gonna 'ave to tell Ray the whole lot needs sortin' out. Otherwise the fire brigade are gonna end up with a job on their hands."

I gazed at all the wires. I could see what the boss was on about. But I could also see them supplying power to amplifiers, electric guitars and microphones. The Cavern wasn't that big. The noise, bouncing off the brick walls in such a confined space, must be deafening. In front of the small stage there were rows of wooden chairs. They'd be taken by groups of excited teenagers. Mostly girls I guessed, driven wild by the loud music and screaming for the uninhibited boys playing just a few feet in front of them.

Steve would be in his element. The Cavern was something special. It made The Casbah look ordinary. I'd never seen anything like it.

"Come on, lad. Stop day-dreamin' an' wake yer ideas up." The boss wasn't for hanging about. "It's time we were off."

It was around that time that a smartly dressed chap, wearing a black, turtle-neck sweater, corduroy jacket and pressed blue jeans, turned up at our shop. He wasn't that old. Early to mid-twenties at most I guessed. But he was obviously out to impress.

"I'm Bill Harry," he said, holding out his hand as he approached the counter. "I don't know if you'll be interested, but we've just started a paper called 'Mersey Beat'. We're gonna be bringin' it out once a fortnight. It's about what's happening on the local music scene. I was wonderin' if you might like to stock it."

Luckily I was keeping an eye on things while my Dad was out picking up some supplies. He'd have sent this Bill Harry chap packing. My Dad didn't have any time for rock and roll.

The Billy Cotton Band Show and The Black and White Minstrels were more his thing.

"I'm Tony," I said, shaking his outstretched hand. "I'm just looking after the shop while my Dad's over at the wholesalers. He'll be back in half an hour or so if you want to hang on and have a word with him."

"No problem. It'll be kids your age who'll be buying '*Mersey Beat*', not your Dad." As he spoke Bill Harry reached into a large satchel which was slung over his shoulder and gave me a copy of his new paper. "This is our first issue. Take a look. You're the expert. You'll be able to tell if anyone round here'll want to buy it."

That was a smart move. Telling me I was the expert. I liked him straight away.

I flicked through the pages. It wasn't as big as the usual broadsheet, more the size of a magazine, but it looked interesting. There was stuff about the local groups. Like who'd be playing at the various clubs each day. And on page two there was an article by John Lennon, one of The Beatles. That definitely had me interested.

"John was a mate of mine at Art College here in Liverpool," said Bill Harry, "so I got him to do a piece for us. He fancies himself as a bit of a writer anyway. He was always scribbling away on scraps of paper, coming up with weird little cartoons and poems. When I told him we were going to be printing five thousand copies he was more than happy to help out. He said it'd be good publicity for his band."

He paused for a moment, watching me as I leafed through the paper. "It'll be in all the record shops in town. You know. Like N.E.M.S. and Rushworths. And Frank Hessy who's got the guitar shop off Whitechapel. He's taking it as well. I've not got many copies left. You'll be the only newsagent round here to have it on your shelves if you give me the nod."

"Leave it with me. I'll see what my Dad thinks when he gets back."

Bill Harry shook his head. "Can't do that I'm afraid. I need an answer right now. While I'm here. I've got to shift these last few copies today. If you don't want 'em I'll have to try some of the other newsagents in the area and see if they're interested. I called in here first because you're nearest the station. I reckon the kids'll want to read it on the train into town."

As I continued to look at the paper, trying to decide what to do, a couple of girls wandered into the shop. They were heavily made up, and dressed in fashionably tight pullovers and skirts, their dark hair piled-up in the latest style. After taking a quick look at the newspapers and magazines in the rack by the door, one of them came over to the counter.

"There's a new music paper just come out called '*Mersey Beat*'. We was in town this mornin' an' they 'ad it in N.E.M.S., but we didn't 'ave any money on us. 'Ave yer got a copy?"

I pointed to the paper in my hand. She grinned and called out to her friend.

"Eh, Doreen. 'E's got a copy over 'ere."

Doreen, who had been waiting by the door, joined her and produced a handful of coppers from her bag. I passed the paper to her in exchange for the coins.

"That's great. Ta."

Bill Harry gave me a wink as he watched them leave. "So you'll be stocking '*Mersey Beat*' then?"

"Looks like we better had. How many've you got left?"

He looked in his satchel. "A couple of dozen."

"Okay. I'll take the lot and see how they go." We had just become the first stockist of '*Mersey Beat*' in the Waterloo area.

"Thanks, mate." Bill Harry shook my hand and smiled.

After taking some money out of the till to settle the account he'd scribbled onto the top sheet of a cash book, I watched as Bill Harry made his way out of the door. The two girls had stopped on the far side of the road. He walked over and started talking to them. Were the three of them in cahoots? Had he pulled a fast one on me? No way, I thought. He was probably just trying his luck and chatting them up.

I pushed the door closed to keep out the wind. *'Mersey Beat'* looked good. But I knew that if two dozen copies were left on our hands it'd be me paying for them.

I needn't have worried. Half a dozen had gone before my Dad got back from the wholesalers. And by the time we shut up shop we'd sold eight or nine more. I picked up one of the remaining copies and took it to my room. As I put my feet up on my bed and looked through the paper again I was pretty sure it'd do well. On the front page there was a picture of the American rock and roller Gene Vincent. Not that long ago he'd been in Liverpool, playing a concert at The Rialto Ballroom, just south of the city centre. The photograph showed him signing some autographs for local fans.

The article by John Lennon was headlined *'On the Dubious Origins of The Beatles, translated from the John Lennon'*. It was a brilliantly surreal account of the band's beginnings, and how they'd got their name. According to Lennon he'd had a vision. A man on a flaming pie had appeared to him and said from that day on his band would be called The Beatles. Spelt with an 'a'.

And, best of all, on the page which listed upcoming gigs by Liverpool bands, there was an announcement. The Beatles, who'd built up quite a fan base during their previous residency at The Star Club in Hamburg and had gone back there for a few weeks, would be playing two Friday sessions at The Cavern as soon as they returned from Germany. At lunchtime they'd be the only band. But in the evening they'd be joined by a couple of other local outfits. Ian and the Zodiacs. And The White Eagle Jazz Band. It was just two weeks away.

I'd be telling the lads. And with a bit of luck we'd be there.

Three

LOUISE

"We've got ourselves a bookin'." Dave was smiling broadly as he gave me a thumbs-up. "A chap Eric knows at work was lookin' for a warm-up band for an end-of-term, dance down the south end of the city. Eric told 'im a load of cobblers. Said we was gettin' quite well known round Waterloo an' we was lookin' to get a few gigs in other parts of the city. The bloke fell for it an' 'e wants us to be the warm-up band for The Undertakers."

"The Undertakers! What the heck's Eric playing at? I saw them a few weeks ago at St Luke's in Crosby. They're bloody brilliant. When is it?"

"The fifteenth."

"But that's a week on Saturday. We'll never get our act together by then. And we're supposed to be going to The Cavern the night before."

It was July 1961. With me and Dave having nothing better to do we'd gone along with Steve's idea about forming a group. He'd got himself a Hofner violin bass. Like Paul McCartney's. Mainly because he reckoned it'd be a girl magnet. I was on guitar. And Dave was our drummer. We'd come up with what we thought was a decent name – The Three Exiles – and we'd been practicing hard. Sticking to just three chords, D, G and A, which is pretty much all you need to play basic rock and roll, we reckoned we'd got numbers like '*Be Bop A Lula*', '*Johnny B. Goode*', '*Roll Over Beethoven*', '*Rock and Roll Music*' and '*Sweet Little Sixteen*' pretty much sorted. But now, thanks to Eric, it looked like we were going to be playing our first gig alongside The Undertakers. I wasn't altogether sure it was the wisest of career moves.

"Eric's promised we'll do it," said Dave. "We can't let 'im down. 'E's only tryin' to help."

Eric had been a good mate of ours for a while. He was a fanatical Liverpool supporter and we'd first met up on the Kop. He was a couple of years older than us, and he'd been working as a legal assistant in a solicitor's office in the city centre for two or three years. That meant he knew people. And some of them were club owners. When we'd told him we were getting a band together he'd said he might be able to get us some bookings.

"Ten per cent be okay, lads? I'm keen to help you out if I can. But I can't afford to do it for nothin'. There'll be expenses I'll need to cover."

We'd laughed at him and sort of agreed to his fee. But there was no way we'd expected him to come up with anything quite so quickly. Sharing a bill with The Undertakers could easily make us look like idiots. And being made to look like an idiot definitely wasn't part of Steve's plan.

Dave and I weren't looking forward to passing on the news, but to our surprise Steve didn't seem that bothered.

"No problem. The girls down at The Cavern'll just 'ave to wait. We can give The Beatles a miss on Friday an' get a bit of extra practice in." He winked at Dave. "You're stuck with Yvonne, you jammy bugger. But yer never know. If we put on a really good show me an' Tony here might be able to persuade a couple of nice South Liverpool girls to give us an even better time than you've been havin." He pulled a bottle of Old Spice after-shave out of his pocket. "Special offer at Boots. The ads on the tele say women can't resist it."

Dave shook his head. "You're wastin' your time with that stuff, mate. Me grand-dad's been usin' it for years, an' I can't say I've noticed 'im 'avin' to fight off me Nan."

Steve laughed. "Yeah. But they're gettin' a bit old for that sort of thing."

"Who ses? Picasso was still at it when 'e was well into in his eighties."

"Maybe," said Steve, making a face. "But not with yer Nan."

* * *

The school where we were doing the gig was just off Queens Drive, not far from Sefton Park. The land for the park had been purchased by the council in the 1860s and kept, since then, as a welcome recreational area for the residents of the city. It was a good ten miles from Waterloo and, with all our instruments, drums and amplifiers to carry, we'd have struggled to get there by public transport. So, after a bit of arm-twisting, Steve's Dad had agreed to drive us there in his van.

"I'll be back for yer at ten sharp," he said as we unloaded the last of our gear. "An' don't keep me waitin'."

After lugging everything into the school hall we went outside and sat on the pavement for a quick smoke, hoping that a dose of nicotine would help calm our nerves. We'd not been sitting there long when we caught sight of a vehicle driving sedately towards us along the road.

"Bloody 'ell!" shouted Dave. "Look at that."

For a minute I thought he was going to choke on his Woody as a highly polished, black hearse pulled smoothly to a halt by the school gates. The glass-sided space behind the driver, where a coffin would once have sat, was packed full of drums, guitars and amplifiers.

A couple of young lads, wearing smart, black tee-shirts and jeans, jumped out.

"Is there a dance on 'ere tonight? We've got the stuff for The Undertakers. We're their roadies. D'you know who's in charge so we can check we're at the right place?"

"We're the other band, The Three Exiles," said Steve. "Yer okay. This is the place. We've taken our gear in already. There's a lad called Jeremy in the hall. He seems to be the one to speak to."

"Great. Keep an eye on things while we nip in an' 'ave a word with 'im?"

Five minutes later the two roadies were hard at work, unloading the hearse. The Undertakers seemed to have about ten times as much equipment as we did but it didn't take them long to get it all set up on the stage. They'd obviously done it many times before. In addition to the usual drums and guitars there was a saxophone, propped up on its stand on the right hand side of the stage. After a quick sound check the driver announced he was leaving. His mate, who said his name was Frank, would be staying to make sure none of The Undertakers' expensive equipment went walkabout.

The driver shouted out of the window of the hearse as he drove off. "I'll be back about eight with the band. Put your stuff in front of ours. We'll give you a hand gettin' it out of the way as soon as you've finished your set. An' if there's any decent-lookin' girls hangin' about the place make sure Frank gets their phone numbers."

We were working with professionals.

By the time we'd got everything set up it was just past six o'clock. We had well over an hour to kill, so we decided to run through our set. It would do as a sound check and one last rehearsal.

A few youngsters drifted in and out of the hall as we were playing, some of whom stopped and listened to us. I noticed two girls in particular hanging about by the glass doors at the far end of the hall for most of the second part of the set. As we finished they wandered towards the stage and stood there.

"That sounded okay. Are you The Three Exiles?"

"If that's what is says on the drum kit, I suppose we must be."

I was trying to be laid back and cool, but the Reslo microphone was still switched on. My voice boomed out over the speakers.

"Jesus! Sorry about that. Give us a second and I'll unplug the mike."

The girls started laughing. "You've not been doing this long then?"

"No, er, well. We're based up in North Liverpool. Waterloo. We've, er, you know, done a few gigs around there. This is our first one down this end of town."

Attracted to the girls, like a moth to a flame, Steve wandered over.

"I was just saying to the girls, Steve. We're based up in Waterloo and we've done most of our gigs up that way 'til now."

I turned away from the two of them and gave him a quick wink. He leapt straight in.

"Yeah. That's right. Small places mostly. Like St Luke's in Crosby." He sounded so confident and convincing that I almost believed him myself.

There was an awkward silence. The two girls were smiling at each other and I took a good look at them. Even without make-up they were both very attractive. I guessed they were about sixteen, small and slim, one with long, blonde hair and the other with slightly curly, light brown hair which was cut a little shorter. I was trying hard to think of something else to say, to keep the conversation going, when Steve came to the rescue.

"Yer both gonna be comin' along to the dance then?"

"Yes. We came down to get a couple of tickets and heard you playing, so we decided to have a listen. It was good."

"You'll be bringin' yer boyfriends along, I suppose?"

I was lost in admiration. For Steve this was very subtle. The two girls blushed slightly.

"No. Don't think so. Just the two of us."

"Great. We'll see yer later then. After we've finished playin'. We're always ready for a few dances to help us wind down. That's right isn't it Tone?"

"Yeah, sure," I said. "That'd be good."

"Okay then," said the one with light-brown hair. "See you this evening."

With that the two girls wandered off, giggling and whispering to each other. I saw Frank, who'd positioned himself at the back of the hall, move towards them as they reached the glass doors. They ignored him.

"That was close," said Steve, who'd also been watching Frank. "For a minute I thought we was about to lose 'em to The Undertakers."

Dave finished off some adjustments to his drum kit and came over.

"What're you two up to?"

Steve licked his fingers and ran them quickly through his Elvis-style quiff. He was about the same height as me, a couple of inches under six foot, but his hair was thick and dark. He'd managed to grow quite a decent pair of sideburns as well. I was jealous. I barely needed to shave and my hair was much lighter, a rather nondescript sort of pale brown. Sideburns were completely out of the question.

"Just chattin' up a couple of new fans, Dave. That's all. Just keepin' 'em happy." He continued to work on his quiff as he spoke. "We've gotta be good tonight. Yvonne's comin' along, I suppose. Well, those two girls are too. Me an' Tone could be on if we play it right. So we need your drummin' to be spot on. Got it?"

Dave gave him a smile and shook his head.

"Don't worry, Steve. I'll be ace. Nothin' too flashy. Just solid rock'n'roll. So if you two don't get yer wicked way with the young ladies it won't be down to my drummin'. Okay?"

The two girls stood right at the front, up against the stage, for almost the whole of our set. The three of us had changed into the white shirts, fake-leather waistcoats, blue jeans and black Chelsea boots which we'd decided upon as our stage outfits. We'd even got a few cheers when we first walked on stage, although Dave said not to get too excited as it was probably just some of our mates in the audience taking the mickey. The numbers we'd chosen seemed to go well, though, and we got a good reception when we came to the end of 'Be Bop A Lula' which we'd announced as our last number. There were some whistles and shouts for more, led by Eric who'd turned up to make sure he got his ten per cent.

We'd kept Chuck Berry's 'Johnny B Goode' back as an encore and we launched straight into it without giving the shouts and applause time to die down. As we came to the end of the song, and more applause broke out, the curtains closed in front of us. Steve grinned and gave us both a big thumbs-up. It couldn't really have gone much better. But the gig wasn't quite over. With the help of the two roadies we still had to shift our gear to the side of the stage.

Fifteen minutes later, dressed in dark suits and wearing top-hats with funereal, black ribbons attached to the back of them, The Undertakers stood in a straight line at the front of the stage.

They opened with a rocked-up version of the '*Funeral March*', before going straight into the up-tempo, James Brown song '*Do the Mashed Potato*'. I watched as the toes of their Cuban-heeled boots moved up and down in unison, keeping perfect time with the beat. As expected, they were good. And the saxophone certainly made a difference. It filled out their sound as they played some less familiar, American numbers.

As The Undertakers continued with their set, Steve and I joined up with the two girls. Steve had made it very plain that he fancied the blonde girl, who turned out to be called Marilyn, leaving me with her friend, Louise. As far as I was concerned this was no hardship. Steve seemed to like blondes, but to my eye Louise, with her petite figure and light brown hair, was by far the prettier of the two. And now she looked even more attractive in a tightly-fitting, black leather skirt and a lightweight, cotton blouse, with her features enhanced by just the right amount of make-up.

"I thought you were really good," she said, smiling up at me as we danced. "Even better than this afternoon."

"Thank you, that's great. It's amazing what a combination of fear and adrenaline can do. I'm glad you enjoyed it." I looked up at the stage. "But this lot are in a completely different league."

As I was speaking The Undertakers came to the end of '*Money (That's What I Want)*' and the lead singer, Jackie Lomax, announced that they were going to play a couple of slower numbers.

"It's Saturday night, so we're gonna get you all in the mood for love. Okay then. Let's hear it for Brian Jones and his sexy sax."

A few people began to applaud as the saxophonist started to play a lazy intro to '*Unchain My Heart*'. I pulled Louise closer to me. She didn't resist and I could feel the soft warmth of her body against mine as we moved slowly backwards and forwards, surrounded by other young couples who were holding each other similarly close. I kissed her cheek gently and waited for her lips to move towards mine. She lifted her face up to me and smiled. Our lips met, and we remained locked together as 'Unchain My Heart' drew to a close and a second slow number, which neither of us recognised, followed. All too soon it was over and Jackie Lomax was shouting into his microphone.

"Okay everybody. That's yer lot for the slow stuff. We're gonna finish now with a song by an American rhythm and blues singer called Rosco Gordon. It was number two in the R&B charts in the States last year. It's called 'Just A Little Bit'. Take it away boys."

A faster beat started up, driven by urgent blasts on the saxophone. Louise drifted away from me a little, but I continued to hold her hand as we did our best to work out some jive movements while The Undertakers stormed through their last number.

As the dance floor started to clear we continued to stand there, both of us unsure what to do next.

"Come on. Don't look so serious." I bent forwards and gave her a kiss. "That was good. I enjoyed myself."

"Me too."

I looked around. There was no sign of Steve or Dave, but I could see the outline of several figures moving around on the stage behind the closed curtains.

"I'd better get off and help them pack up. Give me your number and I'll ring you next week. That's if you don't mind. Have you got a pen?"

Louise searched around in her handbag and pulled out a biro and a crumpled scrap of paper on which she quickly scribbled down a phone number.

"That's our number at home. I live with my Mum and Dad in Penny Lane. Just by the school playing field. If you ring, one of them'll probably answer."

"That's fine. I'll tell 'em I'm a scally from North Liverpool who picked you up at a dance. That be okay?"

"My Dad won't mind that," she said, laughing. "He lived up that way when he was a kid. In Crosby."

She gave me another kiss.

"I'd better go and find Marilyn. We've got to be home by ten-thirty or we won't be let out next weekend. I hope I'll see you again soon."

I gave her one last hug, and then watched as she hurried off to look for her friend. Once she'd disappeared I made my way up onto the stage to find Steve and Dave standing alongside our gear.

"Thanks for all the help, Tone," said Dave as he lifted the last of his drums into its case. "We'd better start gettin' this stuff into the van. Steve's Dad's outside and I've seen 'im happier. Ses he's got better things to do on a Saturday night than ferryin' would-be, bleedin' pop stars around the city."

Steve grinned.

"I told 'im we'll buy 'im a big 'ouse when we're rich an' famous, but 'e said pigs might 'effin' fly. 'E's got a cob on cos 'e's not at The Legion. 'E's usually down there on a Saturday with 'is mates."

We loaded up as quickly as possible while Steve's Dad sat with both hands on the steering wheel, revving up the engine. The message was clear, and in less than five minutes we were on our way, by-passing the city centre on Queens Drive then north towards Waterloo. Steve and I squeezed ourselves into the back of the van along with all the equipment, leaving his Dad to fume on his own up front. Dave and Yvonne were going into town with Eric and a few mates.

For the first part of the journey not much was said. I was going over the events of the evening in my head and thinking about Louise.

As we got nearer to Waterloo, I turned to Steve. "How'd it go with Marilyn then?"

"She basically told me to get lost," he said, giving me a grin as he leaned to one side and rested his right arm on top of one of the drum-cases. "I think I was a bit like, yer know, sort of too direct for her."

I shook my head.

"You've got no idea. You go at it like a bull in a china shop. You need to take things a bit more slowly."

"Yeah, well. She wasn't my type anyway. She was wearin' a crucifix which is never a good sign. Every time I tried to get near 'er she pushed me away." He shook his head and laughed. "Just my luck to pick a strict Catholic."

"Come on, Steve. Do me a favour. You can't blame The Pope. According to Dave Yvonne's a Catholic. And if they overdo it a bit she just goes along to confession and tells the priest all the details of what she's been up to. The way she looks in that blouse it's probably the highlight of the old geezer's week. Then he gives her a few Hail Marys or whatever and she's ready to go again. It's a great system."

"Brilliant," said Steve sarcastically. "I'll bear that in mind next time. An' I suppose you had a great time with 'er mate."

"Louise gave me her phone number. I'll be giving her a ring next week."

Steve slumped back in his seat.

"You jammy bugger." Steve gave the drum-case a jealous thump. "Anyway, I'm not bothered. Once The Three Exiles start gettin' well-known we'll be able to take our pick of the girls. We won't need to bother with all the faffin' around. It'll be straight in the back here, pants off, an' get on with it. The van'll be bouncin' up an' down like a pair of barmaid's knickers."

"You'd better not be saying that when Dave's around. Yvonne does a couple of evenings behind the bar at The Sefton Arms."

Steve grinned and shook his head. "No problem, Tone. Yer know me. Discretion's me middle name. Anyhow, if the way she leaves 'er tits hangin' out of that blouse is anythin' to go by, once Yvonne's pants've gone down they probably don't go back up again."

We both burst out laughing just as Steve's Dad pulled the van to a stop outside the garage of their semi-detached house and opened the back doors. "I heard that. Cut out the foul, bloody language or you'll be findin' yerselves another driver." He tossed the keys onto the floor of the van. "Get yer gear unloaded an' then lock up. I'm off to the Legion for a few pints."

Steve winked at me as his Dad headed off down the road. "I told yer that was the problem."

We dragged all the equipment out of the van and piled it up in the garage. Then it was into the house for a much needed coffee. We were both exhausted but it hadn't been a bad evening. The gig had gone well. And it looked like I might be seeing a lot more of Louise.

Four

THE MESSIAH

August 1961. The weather was hot. Despite the temperature the new football season was about to begin. I was sitting with Steve in the store-room at the back of the shop when Eric came rushing in. His face was flushed and his ginger hair flopped forwards over his eyes. His brown corduroy trousers and desert boots didn't really look right with the red football shirt he always wore at the weekend. Not the usual attire of a legal assistant. But it was the red of his beloved Liverpool. So he didn't care.

"Bill Shankly's signed a bleedin' mountain."

He held up the newspaper which he had in his left hand. He was clearly excited. But we knew from past experience that when it came to matters concerning Liverpool Football Club Eric was very easily excited.

"What on earth yer goin' on about, Eric? For God's sake calm down." Steve looked up from the News of the World which he'd borrowed from the shop. "Me an' Tone was just 'avin' a quiet sit down an' then you turn up an' shatter our peace."

"Honest to God, Steve. I'm not kiddin' yer. It's in the Echo. Liverpool have signed this centre half called Ron Yeats from Dundee United. Shankly's been sayin' to people 'e's a man mountain. 'E's told all the reporters if they want a bit of exercise they just need to 'ead down to the trainin' ground at Melwood an' take a walk round 'im. 'E reckons with Yeats at centre half Liverpool could play with little Arthur Askey in goal an' still win. 'Ere. Take a look."

Eric, who up to that point had hardly stopped for breath, thrust the Liverpool Echo into Steve's hands.

"See. There. The 'eadline on the back page. Liverpool sign Scottish colossus."

He paused for a moment to recharge his lungs. Then he was off again.

"Colossus. That means 'e's a bleedin' giant. An' we've got a new forward from Scotland as well. Ian St John. From Motherwell. They're sayin' with St John linkin' up with Roger Hunt in attack, an' Yeats in defence, we might even make it back into the First Division. You're gonna have to start comin' to Anfield again an' see what they're like."

"Fine, Eric. Whatever."

"We've got Bristol Rovers away on Saturday. Then there's two home games. Sunderland on the Wednesday evening, an' Leeds United the followin' Saturday."

One of Eric's rather sad party tricks was to learn Liverpool's fixture list off by heart each season. Just as it looked as though he might be about to reel off the next ten or fifteen games Steve held up his hand to stop him.

"Enough, Eric. We don't need to know any more. Wednesday evening's out as far as I'm concerned. But maybe we could manage the Leeds game? What d'yer reckon, Tone?"

"Sounds good to me. Dave'll probably want to come along as well."

With that it was agreed, and Eric left us in peace.

To our slight surprise Liverpool beat both Bristol Rovers and Sunderland to go top of the table and, at two o'clock on the Saturday afternoon, we all met up in The Albert on Walton

Breck Road. If you've ever gone to watch Liverpool at Anfield you'll know The Albert. It's a traditional pub not far from the Kop turnstiles and it's been one of the pre-match watering holes for years. That Saturday the main bar was packed. There was a real sense of anticipation and excitement in the air.

Eric got the drinks in.

"Just a quick one, lads," he said as he returned from the bar. "They're all sayin' it's gonna be full. I don't wanna risk bein' locked out."

We weren't in The Albert any more than fifteen minutes. But by the time we got through the turnstiles and up the steps the Kop was heaving. We pushed our way down the packed terrace to our usual spot and stood there, exchanging gossip with various of the supporters around us as we listened to the latest hits being played over the Tannoy.

At five minutes to three there was a huge roar as the Liverpool team, clad in the red shirts and white shorts which had been the club's colours for many years, emerged from the tunnel beneath the main stand and ran onto the pitch.

The tightly-packed crowd swayed from side to side and then tumbled down the concrete terracing in giant waves as people pushed forwards to get a better look at Ronnie Yeats. Not that we could have missed him. As he lumbered towards the Kop with what looked like a tiny football at his feet he towered over the other players. Just short of the penalty area he swung a huge right foot at the ball and sent it soaring high over the goal into the packed crowd. A loud cheer, accompanied by some ribald laughter, rang out from the delighted spectators.

"Nice one, Ronnie. But don't get any ideas about takin' penalties." Yeats looked up in our direction as the shouted comment ignited further laughter.

Ian St John, who had followed Ron Yeats out of the tunnel, slotted his ball straight into the top right corner of the goal from the edge of the area. There was a joyous roar which he acknowledged with a wide grin and a wave. That was more like it.

Yeats was as powerful and solid as he was tall. We looked at each other and nodded in approval. Bill Shankly's description of him as a man-mountain was spot on.

"You wouldn't want to bump into 'im on a dark night up a jigger, would yer?" shouted Steve above the noise of the crowd. "Let's 'ope Leeds think the same."

I'd be exaggerating slightly if I told you the Leeds forwards took one look at Yeats and ran off in the opposite direction. But they didn't look happy. And the five goals we put past their keeper without reply certainly didn't flatter us.

After a quick pint at The Albert we set off home along Anfield Road. There was just one question on all our minds. Was it possible that Mr Shankly might be the long-awaited Messiah? Could he make our dreams come true and lead us back to the Promised Land of Division One? That afternoon anything seemed possible.

"Have you done this with anyone else before me?"

Louise whispered into my ear as my hand moved slowly up the soft, warm skin of her back towards the clasp which held her bra in place. The worn cinema seat creaked as she moved forwards slightly. The Futurist, one of Liverpool's oldest picture houses, had seen better days.

"No," I said, keeping my voice as quiet as I could. "Have you?"

"No. Not as far as this anyway."

"Are you sure you're okay?"

"Yes. I want you to."

My fingers touched the clasp. I could feel her chest moving up and down as she started to breathe more quickly. How easy would it be to unfasten the bra with just one hand? My thumb slid under the elastic of the strap. We kissed, and I could taste the sweetness of her lips as I tried, without success, to release the fastening with my fingers.

"Pull the two clips together and they'll come undone."

I tried the whispered suggestion, but the clips remained stubbornly closed. I struggled for several more minutes but it was no good. The moment was rapidly passing, and we were both starting to giggle. I gave up and slipped my hand out from under her top.

"Sorry. I'll have to get some practice in."

"My fault really," she whispered. "I shouldn't have worn the Fort Knox bra."

The answer was so quick, and it was delivered with such seriousness, that the partially suppressed giggling could no longer be contained.

"That's brilliant," I said, still doing my best not to laugh out loud. "Real Scouse humour."

"No, seriously. There's a label on it which says it keeps your valuables safe." She leaned over and kissed my ear. "I'll give you the keys next time."

Angry murmuring noises started to come from the cinema-goers who were seated closest to us.

"Shhh. Some of us are trying to watch the film, even if you two aren't bothered."

"What are you doing anyway? Whatever it is, it shouldn't be allowed. You ought to be ashamed of yourselves. Do you want us to call the manager?"

I put an arm around Louise's shoulder and leant towards her. "The film's crap anyway. D'you want to stay til the end?"

She shook her head. "Not really. Come on. Let's go."

We stood up and crept along the row towards the nearest aisle, trying to make as little noise as possible, acutely aware that our exit was accompanied by a continuing groundswell of disapproval.

Once outside the cinema we made our way, arms around each other, along Lime Street, one of the city centre's main thoroughfares which was home to quite a few pubs and which had seen better days. It was still early evening, but men who'd probably started drinking when the pubs first opened at lunchtime were leaning for support against various doorways as we headed towards Lewis's Department Store which marked the end of Lime Street and the beginning of the shopping area in Renshaw Street. Above the main entrance of the store we could make out the bronze figure of a man. Stark-naked, and standing on the prow of a ship as it pushed through the waves, he had been grandly named 'Liverpool Resurgent'.

But for obvious reasons all the locals called him 'Dickie'.

We crossed the road and stood half-way up the wide, stone steps of The Adelphi Hotel, one of Liverpool's finest, from where we could see 'Dickie' in all his unclad glory. We giggled childishly as we gazed up at the bronze figure which was only just visible despite the street lights. There was mist and fog in the air.

"It's not very big," said Louise, grinning at me. "You can hardly see it. I don't know why The Echo's been getting so worked up about it."

The local evening newspaper, The Liverpool Echo, had been running a campaign, only half-serious and so far unsuccessful, to have the statue removed.

"Sells papers I suppose. But to be fair you do get a real eyeful if you're sitting upstairs on one of the buses going along Renshaw Street as it turns left onto Ranelagh Street."

In the early sixties a lot of the older citizens of Liverpool were scandalised by the naked statue. But for us 'Dickie' was just a bit of fun.

The times were a'changin'. Even if Bob Dylan hadn't yet got round to telling us.

I gave Louise a hug and we sat down on the steps leading up to main entrance of The Adelphi, closely entwined in our own little world. An expensively-dressed, older couple made their way past us, grumbling as they went, before disappearing through the big, glazed doors which led into the grand lobby of the hotel. I pulled Louise towards me and kissed her on the lips.

"Right, that's quite enough." I turned my head and looked up in time to see a uniformed attendant making his way smartly down the steps towards us. "I've been watching you two. This is a respectable hotel, not some sort of doss house, and you're upsetting our guests. You can move on. Right now."

The old couple must have said something.

"Miserable sods," I whispered. "They're just jealous because they're past it."

The doorman stood over us. He removed his peaked cap and placed it carefully under his left arm. His hands were gloved and his hair was cut short, military style. Between slightly blood-shot cheeks he sported a neatly trimmed moustache, while his expensive-looking, dark green uniform, topped off with imposing gold epaulettes, was immaculately pressed. It concealed a powerfully-built frame. He'd probably fought in the war.

"Did you hear me?" he said. "Move on. Now. Or I'll move you myself."

Now I don't much like being ordered about. So I did think about asking what harm we were doing. But almost as soon as the thought entered my head I dismissed it. The look on his face told me he meant business. And I quickly worked out that he'd make mincemeat of me if it came to a fight.

"Come on," I said to Louise, helping her to her feet. "Let's go."

The ex-soldier continued to keep a close eye on us as we hurried down the steps and over the road towards Lewis's.

"What're we going to do now?" I said as we stopped for breath beneath the statue. "D'you want to go home? Or would you sooner hang about in town for a bit?"

I waited for her answer. I certainly didn't want the evening to finish so early.

Louise looked at me, her soft, brown eyes peeking out cheekily from under her fringe, and lifted her left wrist to look at her watch. "It's only half eight. We could go back to mine if you like. My Mum and Dad are out with some friends. They won't be home much before midnight. My brother might be in, but he won't bother us."

Since our first meeting we'd been out a few times but we'd always met up in town. I'd never been to her house. Louise was very pretty and great fun, and I always looked forward to being with her. I wasn't altogether sure what falling in love felt like, but I had a feeling that's what was happening. She was my first real girlfriend and she was stunningly attractive. What if it turned out her brother wasn't at home?

The quickest way to her house was to catch one of the frequent buses from opposite Lewis's to the roundabout at the junction of Allerton Road and Penny Lane. The four mile journey from the city centre to the inner part of the southern suburbs would take fifteen or twenty minutes. Then it was just a short, five minute walk to her home.

In less than half an hour we were outside a small, terraced house, half-way along Penny Lane. Louise reached up and unlocked the front door which opened directly onto the pavement.

"Anyone in?" The hall light was on and she called out as she pushed the door open and stepped into the house ahead of me. "Andy?"

We both stood in silence, waiting, but there was no reply. She turned towards me and shrugged her shoulders. "Looks like we're on our own. What do you fancy?"

Steve would definitely have told her. But I decided to wait.

"I don't mind. You choose."

"If you're hungry we could grab something out of the fridge. Or I could just make us a coffee. Come on in, anyway, and shut the door. The kitchen's this way."

I followed Louise along the hall, past the stairs, into a small room which looked as though it was meant for sitting and relaxing. The floral wallpaper was rather tired-looking and old-fashioned, but the room had a friendly and welcoming feel about it. There was an open fireplace around which was arranged a slightly worn, but very comfortable-looking, three piece suite. Alcoves on each side of the chimney-breast had been fitted with wooden shelves on which were several bottles of spirits. In front of the shelves, to the right of the fire and in pride of place, was what looked like an almost brand-new TV set. Against the opposite wall, behind the couch, stood a radiogram upon which were displayed a number of family photographs, all in matching, black frames.

"Why don't you put some music on while I make coffee?" said Louise. "That be okay for a start?"

"Yeah. That's fine."

"If you move the photos onto the window ledge you can lift up the lid and get at the record player. Most of the records are on the floor behind the couch, but if you don't like them I've got some up in my bedroom as well."

I watched her as she made her way towards a door on the far side of the room, beyond which I could see a kitchen. As she went she slipped off her jacket, under which she was wearing a black skirt and thin, roll-neck top. She had an almost perfect figure.

"You're seriously attractive. You do know that, don't you?"

She turned her head round and laughed. "That's nice. And once you've had a bit more time to mature, and maybe start shaving, some girls might say you're not that bad-looking yourself."

She half-turned, hesitating for a moment as if she was about to come over to me, before changing her mind.

"Have a look through the records. I'll be back in a minute."

There were a few LPs leaning against the side of the radiogram, but they were mostly early fifties dance music. The rest of the records were 45s, piled up on top of each other on the floor. I picked up a handful and settled down on the couch with them.

If I expected the usual collection of hits by well-known names like Cliff Richard and The Shadows, Elvis, The Everly Brothers, Adam Faith and Billy Fury, I was completely wrong. I didn't recognise any of them. A lot of the songs were on labels I hadn't even heard of. Satellite Records, Chess Records, Vee-Jay, Imperial, Liberty. They all had large, central holes into which white, plastic inserts had been carefully fixed. Without them the holes would have been far too big for the spindle on a record player.

I picked half a dozen records at random and, after moving the photographs and lifting the lid of the radiogram, positioned them on the spindle, ready to be played. As I was doing so, Louise came back into the room carrying two mugs of coffee and a plate of chocolate biscuits.

"Coffee and biscuits for two. Music sorted?"

She handed me one of the mugs and turned towards the wooden shelves.

"Let's put a bit of brandy in the coffee. Dad'll never notice."

Taking a half-full bottle from one of the shelves she poured a generous slug into each of our mugs before giving me a grin.

"That should liven us up a bit."

As she stood beside me I switched the record player on.

"To be honest I'm not altogether sure what I've chosen. I don't know any of them. It's going to be a bit pot-luck I'm afraid."

"Don't worry. They'll be fine. They're mostly rhythm and blues. Come on, let's make ourselves comfy."

As we settled down on the couch, and started to sip our brandy coffees, the first of the randomly-chosen records dropped down the spindle and onto the turntable. The cream, plastic stylus arm moved slowly across towards the edge of the record and dropped into the groove. After a few crackles the music started and as we listened to the raw vocals and harmonica Louise allowed her head to fall gently onto my shoulder.

"I really like this one. It's Sonny Boy Williamson. *'Don't Start Me Talkin'.*"

As the very unfamiliar sound filled the room I slipped my arm around her.

"Where did these records come from?"

"They're mostly American. My Dad collects them. He works in the Cunard Building down at the Pier Head and the guys who work on the ships bring them back from New York. He started off by borrowing a few of them. Just to see what they were like. And now he's a massive rhythm and blues fan. They're not all as good as this one, but they make a change from the stuff that gets into the charts."

If you know anything about the music scene in Liverpool in the late fifties and early sixties it's a tale you might have heard before. Obscure American blues records arriving in Liverpool from New York. And groups then playing this very different music in the clubs that were springing up all over the city. Louise's Dad appeared to have a great collection of them, and I wanted to hear as many as possible. But maybe, for now, that could wait?

"Do you keep your own records up in your bedroom?"

Louise looked me in the eye and gave a little laugh. She had read my mind. I shrugged my shoulders as she paused for a moment.

"I'd like to, Tony, but we can't go upstairs. I've no idea when my brother'll be home. He'd be okay. But if Mum and Dad came back early and found us in my room they'd go spare. Dad usually has a few drinks when they go out. He'd probably kill you."

"Maybe you'd be worth dying for?"

"I doubt it. But he might've drunk enough to think about killing me too. And I'm not ready to go just yet. If you like I could bring some of my records down?"

I shook my head.

"Don't worry. You can teach me all about rhythm and blues instead."

The second record had just dropped down onto the turntable.

Like the Sonny Boy Williamson number it was a simple rhythm and blues recording with no unnecessary polish. And once again that wailing harmonica. It was a world away from most of the records which made it into the UK charts.

"What's this one then?"

"Muddy Waters. It's called '*Hoochie Coochie Man*'. Dad said it was recorded live at a jazz festival in America last year. Somewhere called Newport I think."

"This one's brilliant. Much better than the Sonny Boy Williamson."

"Mmm, yeah. I like it too," said Louise. "That rough, bluesy voice. It makes you feel very, sort of, sexy, doesn't it. And the harmonica as well. Apparently it's a guy called Little Walter playing it. Dad says he's one of the best harmonica players he's ever heard."

She moved closer to me. I took the hint and finished off my coffee, feeling the raw heat of the brandy on the back of my throat as I swallowed it down. Louise had already placed her mug on the floor.

"I suppose that's the rhythm and blues lesson over then," I said.

She laughed quietly and we began to kiss. We half-listened to the music as several more records dropped down onto the turntable, one after the other. But mainly we were concentrating on each other. Louise's body felt soft and warm to the touch, and I was just starting to wonder if she'd be giving me the keys to Fort Knox when I heard the sound of the front door opening.

A male voice called out. "Hello there. Louise?"

I jumped up from the couch, like a frightened rabbit, and stationed myself alongside the radiogram, as far away from Louise as possible, sorting myself out as I did so. To my amazement she remained perfectly relaxed and hardly moved, apart from straightening her sweater and tidying up her hair, while at the same time giving me a quick grin.

"It's okay. Don't worry. It's only Andy." She shouted a reply to her brother. "We're in the sitting room, Andy."

As I turned down the volume on the radiogram a figure appeared at the door. At just under five foot ten I thought I was reasonably tall, but Louise's brother outdid me by three or four inches. With short, neatly-brushed, light brown hair, and wearing corduroy trousers along with a white shirt, tie and heavy duffle-coat, he was good-looking in a rather traditional way. His general appearance was that of a typical, middle-class student.

Louise looked at him and gestured towards me. "Meet Tony." Andy nodded his head to me as his sister retrieved her coffee mug from the floor. "I've just made coffee. Would you like some? There's still a few biscuits left."

"No thanks. If the two of you don't mind I'm going to hit the sack. I've got to go over to the university library first thing in the morning to pick up a couple of books. See you again sometime, Tony."

Louise gave him a sisterly hug. "Okay. Sleep well."

Andy disappeared into the hall and we heard the stairs creak. He was on his way up to his room.

"Andy's reading medicine. At least he will be in September. He's got a place at the University here in Liverpool. He's lovely, my brother. We get on really well even though he's two years older than me." Louise glanced at her watch. "It's just coming up to ten. How long can you stay?"

Had we still been on our own I'd have been more than happy to walk the nine or ten miles back to Waterloo in order to spend more time with Louise. But her parents were due home. And with her brother in the house I didn't feel I could properly relax.

"I'd better be on the bus into town by ten-fifteen. The last train to Waterloo leaves Exchange Station just before eleven. Come on. Let's listen to one more record."

I turned the volume back up and we settled down again on the couch.

"It's been great, despite the film being useless," I said, giving her a kiss. "As always I've enjoyed every minute of just being with you."

Louise rested her head against my shoulder and let out a sigh. "Me too. It's been fun. It's just not been long enough. If Andy gets a place in hall and his bedroom's free I'll ask Dad if you can stay over sometimes. Mum'd be fine about it. He's the one who'll need persuading. He thinks I need protecting from all the men in the big, bad world who want to take advantage of me."

"And do you? Need protecting I mean?"

"Not from you I don't. You can take advantage of me any time you like."

As the next record dropped down onto the turntable and crackled into life Louise began to hum along with the lyrics.

"This one's '*Smokestack Lightning*' by Howlin' Wolf. It's one of the earliest records Dad's got. I love it the way he makes that hooting sound. Like a freight train whistle."

"It's a great song. A bit sad though as well."

"Mmmm. Dad's only had that record for a couple of months, but he says the song was written way back in the nineteen thirties. It's difficult to believe it's that old."

"I'm going to have to listen to all your Dad's records. If he doesn't mind, that is. We could use some of the songs in our set if Steve and Dave like them."

"I'm sure Dad'd be fine about it. He's just pleased when someone says they like the music as much as he does. The only thing is he won't let the records leave the house. So you'll have to bring your guitar over here and learn them." She smiled and gave me a wink. "I'd be okay with that."

"Me too." I said as she glanced at her watch.

"Hey. Look at the time. You'd better get going or you'll miss the last train."

We hugged tightly and kissed for at least two minutes and then, reluctantly, let each other go.

"Okay. Time to hit the road."

At the front door I gave her one more hug, and another long kiss, before hurrying off.

"Take care of yourself. I'll give you a ring next week."

I waved as I ran, but I didn't look back. At the end of Penny Lane, heading towards the bus stop, I caught sight of my bus in the distance. As I quickened my pace to catch it, I found myself singing a Liverpool folk-song.

'*In My Liverpool Home*', written not long before by Pete McGovern, a local folk-singer, celebrated our two cathedrals, our Scouse accent, and 'Dickie', our very bare statue. It took me back to the evening I'd just spent with Louise.

Life felt good.

Five

A SHOT OF RHYTHM AND BLUES

"Ever heard of Muddy Waters?"

Steve and Dave both shook their heads and looked blank, as if they didn't have the slightest idea what I was talking about.

"What about Howlin' Wolf then? Or Sonny Boy Williamson?"

"Chicago gangsters." said Dave. "Sometime around the nineteen thirties I reckon."

Steve started to laugh. "Spot on, Dave. That's what my money's on anyway. What odds yer offerin', Tone?"

"Give it a rest, both of you. Why does everything have to turn into a bloody joke? I'm trying to be serious."

"Excuse us for breathin'," said Steve, shrugging his shoulders and grinning at Dave.

"They're American rhythm and blues singers," I said, ignoring him. "Louise played me a couple of their records last night. They're amazing. The Undertakers do a few rhythm and blues numbers but most of the Liverpool groups seem to go for country and western. It'd be really great if we could start playing a few songs that the other Liverpool groups don't know."

"It depends if they're any good," said Dave, who suddenly seemed interested and who was now also ignoring Steve. "How come Louise was playin' you these records anyway?"

"We went back to hers after we walked out of a crappy film before the end on Saturday evening. Her folks weren't in and we got some of her Dad's records out."

"Wow!" said Steve. He too was suddenly taking an interest. "You jammy bastard."

"I know," I said. "Her Dad works for Cunard and he's got an amazing collection. All from America."

Steve looked at me as if I was simple.

"I'm not talkin' about the records, you useless bugger. I'm talkin' about you bein' on yer own with Louise. I hope yer not gonna to tell me you didn't make the most of it." He winked at Dave. "The thought just sort of flashed into me mind that maybe you and Louise might've … yer know."

"Well it can just flash right out again." I suddenly found myself feeling very protective about Louise. "There's no way I'm giving you the lowdown on me and Louise, so you can sod off."

Steve looked over at Dave and made a face. "What's got into 'im then? D'yer reckon this Louise business might be gettin' a little bit serious and our Tone's losin' 'is sense of humour?"

"Give it a rest, Steve." Dave had decided he'd better try and build a bridge over what were beginning to look like troubled waters. He turned towards me. "Look, Tone. These songs. How do we know they're any good? Okay, so you've listened to a couple of 'em. But it seems to me this girl you're goin' a bit crazy over. An' to be honest you're gettin' a bit touchy over as well. She tells you 'er Dad's got all these amazin' records, an' that's it. We've gotta start playin' 'em. Come on, mate. Me an' Steve at least need to 'ave a listen first."

To be fair I could see he had a point.

"Okay. But Louise's Dad won't lend the records out."

"So we'll 'ave ter sneak in there when 'e's not around." Dave looked at Steve. "What d'yer reckon?"

"Sounds good to me. You fix it up Tone. An' then we can see what we think of 'em."

"I'm seeing Louise on Saturday," I said. "I'll have a word with her."

"Okay," said Dave, "but don't forget the Scunthorpe game. If we beat 'em it'll be six wins on the trot. Shankly's some sort of genius. The atmosphere at Anfield's unbelievable at the moment. Things are really startin' to happen."

"It depends what Louise is doing."

Dave gave a sigh. "You're in trouble, Tone. I'm sure she's a great girl but I can't believe you can even think of missin' out on what's gonna be a brilliant match. Yvonne's great too. But she knows the score. On Saturdays she takes a back seat." He shook his head in disbelief. "You've got yer priorities all wrong, mate."

The Three Exiles got together for rehearsals as often as possible. If I wasn't with Louise that is. And if Steve and Dave weren't worshipping at Anfield. We'd agreed on several of the American rhythm and blues numbers and we soon had a nice, tight, little set to present to the waiting world.

"Eric can get 'is arse in gear an' line us up with a few more gigs," said Steve. "I'll let 'im know we're ready."

I wouldn't have put Eric down as a the world's greatest salesman, but within a few days he'd got us five bookings. With a promise of more if we went down well.

"I said you'd be playin' rhythm and blues," said Eric. "The real thing. American style." He paused for a moment. "I didn't crack on yer live in Waterloo."

Dave looked at him. "You 'aven't given 'em the idea we're from America, 'ave you?"

Eric smiled and shrugged his shoulders. "It'll be fine."

⁕ ⁕ ⁕ ⁕ ⁕

We got to see The Beatles playing at The Cavern a week or two later. It was a Saturday towards the end of October and they were doing an all-nighter with Gerry and The Pacemakers and The Remo Four. Although rock and roll was now by far the biggest draw in town Ray McFall had decided to hedge his bets. To ensure a full house he'd put three jazz bands on the bill as well.

I was with Louise, and Dave had brought Yvonne along. Steve and Eric were on their own but Steve was confident he'd strike lucky once The Beatles had worked their magic on the watching girls.

We joined the queue outside The Cavern in Mathew Street. We'd arrived early but it still snaked half-way down the narrow street. As we shuffled slowly forwards Paddy Delaney, the doorman whose job it was to keep out trouble-makers, looked us up and down. Having passed inspection we picked our way carefully down the steep stairway.

At the bottom of the stairs we paid an entrance fee which made us members of The Cavern Club for a year. Then, clutching our small, red and black membership cards, we turned right into the brick-arched cellar. It was already busy and the wooden chairs were all taken, but we found ourselves a good spot to one side, alongside one of the arches, a few rows back from the stage. Steve eyed up the girls and nodded approvingly at Eric.

"I reckon we could be in luck," he said. "I've got me Old Spice on."

"Yer wastin' yer time, Steve," said Eric, shaking his head. "The only thing the girls are gonna be able to smell down 'ere is Dettol."

When the time came for The Beatles to begin their set Louise could hardly contain herself. The four of them wandered casually onto the stage and plugged their guitars into the Vox AC 30 amplifiers, while at the same time chatting up the girls in the front row. Various requests were handed over, scribbled on scraps of paper. The requests weren't just for songs. It looked as though quite a few of the papers had names and telephone numbers written on them as well.

Turning their backs on the audience John, Paul and George checked that their guitars were in tune while Pete Best loosened up with a few drum rolls. Then, clad in the leather gear they had first started to wear in Hamburg, they took their places at the front of the small stage. Standing behind three Reslo microphones they were no more than fifteen feet away from us. And when they started to play, the noise they generated in the small, crowded basement was incredible.

Louise was transfixed as they started their set with ''Some Other Guy' before moving on to other rhythm 'n' blues and rock 'n' roll classics, as well as one or two of their own songs. She just stood there, her eyes wide open and breathing rapidly, as the band progressed through their set. All too soon it was over. As the last chord of 'Twist and Shout' faded away, and the audience shouted and applauded wildly, Paul leaned forward and put his lips to the polished steel microphone.

"Ta. Yer've been great. We'll see yer again in a couple of hours."

Sadly we we'd have to go. Louise's Dad had laid down the law. He wanted his daughter home by midnight. We'd be able to stay long enough to hear Gerry and The Pacemakers, who were due on next, but waiting for The Beatles' second set and spending the night at The Cavern was not an option.

Then quite suddenly, Louise turned to me. "I'm not leaving." Her cheeks were flushed and she was still breathing heavily. "My Dad can do what he likes. I don't care. That was just amazing. I've never heard anything like it. Sorry Tony. I don't care what happens. If we don't stay I might never see them again."

"And if we do stay you certainly won't see them again. I've promised to get you home on time. And if I don't, your Dad'll murder us."

"He can't do that. I'm sixteen. I can do what I like. You can go now if you want but I'm not moving. You can tell him I refused to leave and you couldn't do anything about it."

I tried to reason with her but there was no point. Her mind was made up. And if I left her in The Cavern on her own I'd be in even more trouble. In any case, the feeling that something special was happening was getting stronger all the time. I couldn't put my finger on it. I couldn't say what it was. But I knew it was there. And I knew I had to stay too. Whatever her Dad might have to say.

The Beatles' second set was just as sensational as the first, finishing in the early hours of the morning with an extended version of the Chuck Berry classic 'Rock and Roll Music'. John Lennon took the lead vocal and, after what had been a heavy session, his voice sounded exhilaratingly broken and raw. Louise was ecstatic. It had been quite a night.

We headed off, with Dave and Yvonne, along a deserted Mathew Street leaving Steve and Eric to see in the dawn. It was a slightly misty night, and the damp cobblestones glistened as we passed the one or two street lamps which were working and lit up. Yvonne and Louise, who didn't seem at all tired, chatted away as we made our way along the narrow street with the slightly forbidding warehouses looming over us out of the darkness.

"I was talkin' to a girl in the ladies," said Yvonne, holding Louise's arm tightly. "She was sayin' The Beatles made a record called 'My Bonnie' when they were in Germany in the summer. A lad she knows was at Hambleton Hall in Huyton last Sunday. The Beatles were on the bill and there was a DJ there called Bob Wooler. 'E was playin' some records in the interval an' Paul McCartney gave 'im a copy of it. 'E was sayin' it was their first record. Bob Wooler was playin it and tellin' everyone they must go and ask for it at their local record shop. The girl said it sounded great."

Louise turned to me. She was suddenly very excited.

"We've got to get hold of a copy, Tony."

"You could try," said Yvonne. "But it mightn't be that easy. The girl I was speakin' to said she went to a record shop in Bootle an' they 'adn't even heard of The Beatles. Mind you the assistant was dead old. At least forty the girl said. So maybe it's not that surprisin'. To be fair to 'er though she went through all the lists of releases from the big record companies an' 'My Bonnie' wasn't on any of 'em."

By this time we'd walked the length of Mathew Street and negotiated the maze of small, dimly-lit alleys which took us onto Williamson Square in front of The Playhouse Theatre, originally a nineteenth century music hall and subsequently Liverpool's repertory theatre. Then we cut through to Great Charlotte Street and passed a branch of N.E.M.S., one of the main record shops in Liverpool. Louise turned to me and pointed out the four, large letters which were fixed to some varnished, wooden boards above the window.

"Dad says Mr Epstein who runs the other branch of N.E.M.S. in Whitechapel is really helpful if you're looking for a particular record. If they haven't got it in stock he'll go out of his way to try and order it for you. He got hold of a recording by some French blues singer that Dad had been wanting for ages. Maybe we should call in there next weekend when they're open and ask him if he knows anything about The Beatles and their record?"

She was still speaking as we rounded the corner into Ranelagh Street. About thirty yards away, stationary outside Lewis's, I spotted a black cab with its orange *'For Hire'* sign lit up. The last bus had long gone so we ran over to it and jumped in, leaving Dave and Yvonne to head towards the Pier Head from where they'd be able to pick up a lift to Waterloo.

It was just after two o'clock when we opened the front door and crept into the house. Although we did our best to make as little noise as possible, every creak of the stairs seemed fraught with danger. Louise and I were both expecting the worst, but the door of her parents' bedroom remained firmly closed. All was quiet. And next morning nothing was said.

The following weekend N.E.M.S. in Whitechapel was packed. Groups of teenagers selected singles from the hit parade and crowded around the series of small, arched booths which were lined up on the wall along one side of the shop, each with rudimentary sound-proofing, to listen to their chosen records. The boys were dressed smartly in shirt and tie along with their best Saturday jacket or coat. Many of them boasted an Elvis-style quiff, held firmly in place with Brilliantine. Peacock-like, they chatted loudly to each other as they tried to attract the attention of one or more of the girls whose figure-hugging skirts and brightly patterned blouses had been carefully chosen to showcase their best attributes. The girls, acting their part to perfection, nonchalantly ignored even the best-looking of the young men, while at the same time making very sure any sign of interest did not go unnoticed. Quite often none of the selected records were purchased. It was just a way of passing a Saturday afternoon. None of the assistants in the shop seemed that bothered.

The Top Twenty Board, high on the wall behind the counter, had Helen Shapiro at Number One with '*Walking Back To Happiness*', a bouncy, cheerful number which was a typical early-sixties record. She would hang onto the top spot for a further two weeks before being replaced by Elvis Presley. '*His Latest Flame*' would climb above all the competition as soon as it was released. In October 1961 there was no doubt at all about who was 'The King'. Elvis ruled in England, in the U.S.A, and in much of the rest of the world as well.

Louise pointed towards the far side of the shop.

"I think that might be Mr Epstein over there."

I followed her gaze as she identified a smartly-suited, elegant figure, standing a little back from the counter and smiling to himself. He seemed to be keeping a close, almost fatherly and affectionate, eye on the youngsters who were packed into his shop. As I looked towards him I realised that I'd seen his face before.

"Yeah, that's him. Brian Epstein. I've seen his picture in '*Mersey Beat*'. The way he's dressed you wouldn't think he'd have a clue about pop music, but he's been writing a regular column about the latest releases for the past few months. He seems to know what he's talking about. Let's see if we can have a word with him."

We made our way towards the counter, squeezing past the groups of youngsters who were huddled together around the booths.

"Mr Epstein. Can we ask you about a record please?"

The suited figure approached the counter where we were standing.

"Indeed, yes," he said politely. "What can I do to help you?"

Louise was so excited that she could hardly get the words out.

"Have you got a record called '*My Bonnie*'? It's by a local group called The Beatles."

Brian Epstein looked over the counter at her.

"Well, young lady. It so happens that you're not the first person to ask for that particular record. A young man about your age was in here earlier. I've read about The Beatles in 'Mersey Beat', although I haven't actually heard their music myself."

Louise pointed at me. "Tony here says you write a column in 'Mersey Beat'. His Dad sells it in his newsagent's."

Mr Epstein smiled at me before continuing. With his very posh accent, he sounded more like a BBC newsreader than the owner of a record shop in Liverpool.

"That is quite correct. I am indeed their record reviewer. I had lunch the other day with Mr Bill Harry. He is, of course, the Editor of 'Mersey Beat', and he tells me that The Beatles are becoming very popular here in Liverpool. Apparently they have a regular spot at a place called The Cavern, just round the corner from here in Mathew Street. Mr Harry said he'd try and have a word with Mr McFall, who I believe is the owner of the club, and arrange for me to go down there one lunch-time so I can take a look at them. In fact we've had quite a number of requests for their record so one of my assistants has been looking into it to see if we can order some copies to sell here in Liverpool. We think it was released on the 'Polydor' label in Germany and produced by Mr Bert Kaemfert who is a well-known band leader over on the continent. It seems that The Beatles were acting as the backing group for a British singer called Tony Sheridan. The record hasn't been released in England, but if you'd like to leave your telephone number with the young lady over there at the cash till we'll let you know if we are able to obtain a copy for you from Germany."

"That'd be great. Thanks Mr Epstein."

"Is there anything else I can do for you in the meantime?"

"No, that's all. Thank you."

We left our contact details with the cashier and as we walked out of the shop onto Whitechapel Louise was grinning from ear to ear.

"I know Dad said Mr Epstein would be helpful, but I can't believe how nice he was. Do you think he'll really be able to get hold of a copy of '*My Bonnie*'?"

I gave her a quick hug.

"I've honestly got no idea. He sounded reasonably optimistic, so let's just hope he comes up with the goods. But didn't he say The Beatles were just the backing band for someone else?"

"Tony Sheridan."

"Yes. That's right. Have you ever heard of him?"

She shook her head. "No."

"So we don't know if the record'll be any good then." I was trying to damp down her expectations. "You'd better not get yourself too excited in case it's useless."

"Okay. But that girl in The Cavern did say to Yvonne that the DJ at Hambleton Hall got hold of it from Paul McCartney. He wouldn't be handing it out to a DJ if he thought it was useless."

"I suppose so," I said. "We'll just have to hope Mr Epstein strikes lucky."

It was just before five o'clock in the evening and the light was fading. It had been raining on and off for most of the afternoon, and black thunderclouds now filled the narrow strip of sky between the office buildings on either side of us. Heavy raindrops began to fall and I held my dark blue jacket over our heads in an effort to keep as dry as possible as we ran across Whitechapel towards the Kardomah Cafe, one of a typically nineteen-fifties chain of coffee bars which had been started up in Liverpool before expanding to cities across the country, and eventually as far afield as Paris and Sydney. It was the Starbucks of its day, and a popular meeting place for all ages. We'd arranged to meet up with Steve and Eric who'd been to Anfield to watch the match between Liverpool and Leyton Orient.

I was keen to know how the game had gone. Louise, to be fair, was rather less keen. She found our limitless passion for football incomprehensible and boring. But to her credit she pretended to take at least a passing interest in the fortunes of Liverpool Football Club to keep us happy.

All the Formica-topped tables were taken so the four of us perched on some tall stools which faced a large, curved window, overlooking the street. We watched as groups of wet, bedraggled shoppers made their way round the street corner and up the slight hill towards Exchange Station. Dry and warm, we sipped at the steaming coffees which sat on the polished, wooden shelf in front of us.

The news from Anfield was mixed.

"It ended up as a draw," announced Eric. "Three all. But really we was dead lucky to get away with it. The Orient went ahead in the second half an' it didn't look like we had a hope of gettin' back into the game. But the ball was dead slippery in the wet an' their keeper let a header from Tommy Leishman slide through 'is hands with about ten minutes to go. We didn't really deserve it to be honest but one point is better than nothin'. At least we're still top. An' with a bit of luck we'll still be back in the First Division next season."

• •·· ——— •·•·•·• ———— ··•

Exactly three weeks later Louise got a phone call from N.E.M.S. to say they'd tracked down the record by The Beatles and they hoped to have it available for her soon after Christmas.

Louise was thrilled. *'My Bonnie'* was on its way.

Six

THE JIVE HIVE

It was when Dave and I went along to see Kingsize Taylor and The Dominoes at The Aintree Institute that we realised we might not be the only band on Merseyside who could claim to know some of the more obscure rhythm 'n' blues numbers. Bob Wooler, who'd played '*My Bonnie*' at Hambleton Hall, and who was recognised as one of the top DJs in Liverpool, gave the band a typically Scouse introduction.

"The Beatles came here direct from Hamburg. And now, direct from the bar at The Black Bull, I want you to give a big Aintree welcome to Mister Edward 'Kingsize' Taylor and his fabulous band The Dominoes."

The introduction was warm and enthusiastic, but with just that little bit of edge. 'Kingsize' Taylor, clad in a very loud check jacket and loose trousers in the style of the American rocker Bill Haley, was a large man in every way with a huge number of fans. But nobody was allowed to get too big for their boots in our city.

Apart from a couple of slower sections, when a red-haired girl who called herself 'Swinging Cilla' White joined them on stage for songs like '*Fever*' and '*Summertime*', the evening was a non-stop rampage through a series of rock 'n' roll and rhythm 'n' blues classics, including most of the numbers which we thought nobody else would know and which we'd spent so much time rehearsing.

"Back to the drawin' board I think Tone," announced Dave gloomily as the evening came to an end with a thunderous version of '*Hippy Hippy Shake*.' "Kingsize has been listenin' to the same records as us."

When Eric heard the news he said he was going to contact all the promoters who'd booked us and cancel the gigs. "Listen lads. You told me you was goin' to be playin' stuff that nobody else round here knows. An' now it turns out that's a load of garbage. These guys've got bouncers. An' bodyguards. They're seriously hard. If they was to get the idea I was pullin' a fast one on 'em they wouldn't be pleased. An' some of 'em think you're from America as well. Which you're obviously not."

"Shut it, Eric," said Steve. "The America bit was your daft idea."

"Whatever. Anyway. I'm not gonna end up bein' taken to a bomb site an' concreted into the foundations of some brand-new office block just for the sake of you lot."

Dave laughed. "Jesus, Eric. What's up with yer? This is Liverpool. Not bleedin' Naples. These people who run clubs aren't soft, I'll grant you that, but they're not the Mafia for God's sake." Eric looked a little sheepish as Dave carried on. "An' even if they were they wouldn't waste a load of concrete on a dick'ead like you."

"Okay, Dave. 'Ave it yer own way. But it's not just the bouncers. There's teddy boys at a lot of these places. They'd be more than happy to give yer a goin' over with bicycle chains an' flick knives if they don't like what yer playin'. Just for a bit of fun. I'm supposed to be yer manager, so I'll be turnin' up at yer next gig to make sure we get paid our money. But if there's any trouble, I'm off."

We got together to talk things over. Without Eric.

Steve was definite we should carry on. This was mainly because he hadn't yet found himself a willing groupie. In fact, if the truth were known, he hadn't found himself any sort of groupie, willing or otherwise.

"If Eric wants out that's fine," he said. "We'll just carry on without 'im. We can easily fix up our own gigs. An' if we can't, we'll get ourselves another manager. There's no way we're jackin' it in after all the practice we've been doin'. We've got the gig at St Luke's comin' up on Saturday. I don't reckon anybody there's gonna be that bothered about what sort of music we're playin'. As long as we sound alright they won't care. We're heaps better now than when we did the gig with The Undertakers. Eric's talkin' a load of bollocks. With a bit of luck 'e won't show up. Then we can hang onto his ten per cent."

Dave nodded his head in agreement. "Sod 'im. I reckon we should hire a cement mixer an' 'ave it parked outside the church-hall. If he does decide to turn up it'd be worth it just to see the look on 'is face."

The audience at St Luke's were friendly. The Jive Hive, as the dance hall was known, was in Crosby, one of Liverpool's smarter suburbs. It tended to attract a less rowdy audience than many of the city centre clubs. The boys, who were gathered in small groups on the floor of the hall as they waited for the music to start, were wearing uniformly smart shirts, ties, sports jackets and grey trousers, while most of the girls were perched on seats around the perimeter of the large room. They were nearly all conservatively dressed in knee-length skirts and buttoned-up blouses, topped with knitted cardigans. A few of the more adventurous ones, standing up and eyeing the boys, were out to attract attention with revealing blouses and tighter skirts. But they were the exception.

We were the warm-up band so we didn't expect a large crowd to turn up for our set. But by the time we started to play there were about a hundred people in the hall. Including Eric. Not a bad turn-out, we thought, even though quite a few of them were friends who'd made the short journey from Waterloo to watch us.

Yvonne was there, but Louise couldn't make it. St Luke's was on the other side of Liverpool so she wouldn't be able to get home afterwards. And there was no way her Dad was letting her spend the night in Waterloo with me.

We went down well. A couple of the younger kids even asked for autographs. Then we cleared our gear to make way for the main attraction of the evening, Rory Storm and The Hurricanes. They were one of Liverpool's biggest bands and they had an enthusiastic following. By the time they got on stage, at about nine-thirty, the place was packed.

The three of us hadn't seen them before so we grabbed a spot near the front, just to one side of the stage. We wanted to watch them closely, and hopefully pick up a few tips. He had blond, rather than black, hair, but otherwise Rory Storm was a singer straight out of the early Elvis Presley mould. He swivelled his hips and directed his vocals at the girls who stood below the stage, staring up at him. He was kitted out in a white bomber jacket over a shirt which was unbuttoned to the waist, exposing a seductively-tanned chest to his adoring fans. With his Elvis quiff and classical good looks there was no doubt that he was a strikingly effective front man, as well as being a very useful singer.

The Hurricanes, though, were all good, old-fashioned rockers, kitted out in baggy jackets and trousers. Their ties hung loose and the collars of their black shirts were unbuttoned. They created a solid beat, driven along by Richard Starkey, their drummer, who was gradually establishing himself as being one of the best on Merseyside. To cement his burgeoning reputation he'd changed his name to one which he thought was more suited to his status as a top drummer. He now called himself Ringo Starr.

"If Ringo ever decides to move to another band we'll have him. What d'you reckon Steve?"

"No way. Dave's gettin' better all the time. Give 'im another couple of months and our problem's gonna be hangin' on to 'im. All the big name bands'll be comin' after 'im with amazin' offers."

Dave gave us a V-sign. "I dunno what's the matter with you two. If you carry on like that you'll find yerselves without a soddin' drummer. An' I can't think of anyone else who'd be daft enough to put up with yer. So pack it in or I'll be off."

Just then there was a drum roll, and Rory shouted into his mike. "Okay folks. It's 'Starr-time.'"

As he did so he handed the microphone and stand to Ringo who stood up behind his drums to acknowledge the cheers which were now ringing out from the audience. It was clear that he was very popular.

Rory put a finger to his lips. "Quiet everybody. Ringo's gonna sing."

Positioning the stand and mike so that he still had room to play his drums, Ringo sat down and counted in the rest of The Hurricanes before launching himself into an up-beat version of The Shirelles' big hit, '*Boys*'.

As the song came to an end, a loud, rhythmic stamping and shouting erupted in the hall.

"Ring-o. Ring-o. Ring-o. Ring-o."

He stood up again and waved to the crowd, laughing as he handed the mike back to Rory for the next number. He was a born entertainer. And he was enjoying himself.

While we had been concentrating on Ringo, a couple of girls had positioned themselves alongside us. One of them was an attractive blonde with a nice, petite figure. Steve quickly moved next to her. Her friend was taller, and rather less slim. She was wearing heavy, black mascara and her straight hair, reaching half-way down the back of an almost unbelievably tight red dress, was as black as her make-up.

Steve, who wasn't going to miss an opportunity, noticed them first.

"Fancy a dance, girls? I'm free. And so's me mate Tone here. Dave's girlfriend is down the back of the hall somewhere, so I'm afraid 'e's gonna have to behave 'imself. Aren't yer Dave?"

Dave proffered another V-sign, but said nothing.

The two girls looked at each other, communicating telepathically while they calculated their next move. Communications over, the blonde one spoke.

"Yeah, okay then. Don't mind."

The four of us moved towards the middle of the hall where most of the dancing was taking place. The area nearest to the stage was packed with girls, and not a few boys, who just wanted to watch the band. Within no more than a couple of numbers Steve was getting seriously close to his blonde partner. And she seemed to be responding in like manner. I carried on dancing with the girl I'd landed up with, moving from one foot to the other in a half-hearted and fairly non-descript sort of way. She seemed equally unenthusiastic.

"I'm Tone," I said, as a sort of ice-breaker.

"Yeah. Your mate said. I'm Mary."

"Are you from round here?"

"Yeah. Well close. Thornton."

"Been here before?"

"Yeah."

"Often?"

"Yeah. Most Saturdays."

"I'm from Waterloo."

She grunted. "Haven't heard of your band before. You just startin' up?"

"We've been going a few months," I said, but I could see she wasn't interested. Her eyes were scanning the crowd to the left and right of us.

"Are you looking for someone?" I asked.

"Not really. Just checkin' who's in tonight."

I sensed that, unlike Steve, I wasn't onto a winner. But I can't say I was bothered.

"Do you know many people here?"

"A few."

Then, quite suddenly, her eyes darted to the edge of the hall and she turned to wave at a heavily-built teddy-boy with ginger hair and luxuriant sideburns who was wearing a fashionably over-sized and bright, checked suit.

"Hiya, Johnny." Responding to her shouted greeting Johnny threaded his way across the crowded dance floor towards us.

"Hiya, gorgeous," he said, giving Mary a big bear hug. "I tried to get to speak to you earlier when you were with Tracey. I see she's with this bloke's friend." He looked at me. "Mary an' I go back a long way."

Mary nodded. "I'm done with dancin' now Tone," she said. "I'm gonna head off with Johnny here an' grab a Coke while we catch up. See yer."

Steve was still well entwined with his new catch, who I now knew was called Tracey, so I wandered back to Dave who hadn't moved from his position by the side of the stage. He was watching Ringo intently.

"No luck there then, Tone? I didn't think much of yours anyway. Bit of a scrubber I reckon. You're better off stickin' with Louise."

I nodded in agreement and continued to stand next to him as he raved about Rory Storm and The Hurricanes.

"Stay here with me an' watch. Yvonne's got a couple of mates with 'er so she's fine. These lot really know what they're doin'. Ringo's a brilliant drummer. Really tight. I wouldn't be surprised if they make it into the big time before The Beatles. Rory Storm's a proper entertainer, which is what people want. The Beatles've got a great sound, but they don't really do that much on stage. They mostly stand there an' crack jokes with their regular fans. An' that leather gear they wear looks dead scruffy. They need to get themselves some smart stage suits and sort out a proper act. Like The Hurricanes."

"Yeah," I said. "You might be right." But to tell the truth I didn't think for even one moment that he was. And I knew for sure that Louise wouldn't agree with him either. What she loved about The Beatles was that they were ordinary Liverpool lads. But at the same time they were totally extraordinary.

<hr />

"How did it go last night?" Louise was curled up alongside me on the couch.

"Okay, I think. We didn't get booed off. And we got some nice comments when we finished. A couple of kids even asked for my autograph which felt really strange."

"I wish you didn't live so far away. I know Waterloo isn't that far, but it's far enough to make it a bit awkward sometimes. Like last night. I wanted to be there and listen to you play. Did you get loads of girls throwing themselves at you?"

"Not exactly."

"So you did then."

"No. I had a dance with a girl called Mary who'd somehow managed to squeeze herself into a dress that was at least two sizes too small for her. She made it perfectly obvious that she wasn't the slightest bit interested in me. I only did it cos Steve fancied her mate. As soon as she could she dumped me and scarpered off with a big teddy boy."

"When you're famous you'll be able to take your pick of the girls. And then you'll dump me."

I gave her a kiss. "Don't be daft. Firstly it's extremely unlikely I'm going to be famous. And secondly there's no way I'm dumping you. Wherever I go, you're coming with me."

Her eyes twinkled and she hugged me. "I love you, you know."

"And I love you too. Okay?"

"Okay,"

My guitar was lying against the arm of the couch, and I leant over to pick it up. Louise knew that I'd been playing around with writing songs for a while. It had turned out to be much more difficult than I'd expected but finally I'd come up with something I wanted her to hear.

I started to sing, while strumming a chord of C in a slow, calypso type of rhythm.

Leaves are turning brown. Soon come tumbling down. I must go. I must go.
Now I must be movin' on again, like a swallow flying gracefully.
Far south, I go. Leaving you, I know. Come summer I may see you again.
Come summer I may see you again.

I stopped singing and Louise looked at me. "What was that?"

"It was supposed to be a song," I said, laughing. "Well, one verse anyway. I wrote it last week. What d'you reckon?"

"It's okay, I suppose, but it sounds sort of folky. It's not really a pop song." She paused for a moment. "It'd be worth trying to finish it though. If you can that is."

I put my guitar down and switched on the radio. It was Sunday morning and the theme tune to 'Two Way Family Favourites', an instrumental version of '*With a Song in My Heart*' filled the room, followed by the announcer's very proper, BBC-English voice. He sounded just like Brian Epstein.

"Hello everyone. Well, came the dawn this morning and, to borrow the title of one of the records I'll be playing in a few minutes, '*Down Came the Rain*'. But we won't dwell on that. Instead we'll get straight on with our first request which is from the Trensham family of Hartlepool, up in the north-east. One of their sons, Terry, is serving with the British Army On The Rhine and he'll be out there in Germany over Christmas. So, to remind him of home, his mother and father, and all the family, would like us to play him the song which was a big hit for Nina and Frederik this time last year when Terry was at home with them all in Hartlepool. It is, of course, '*Little Donkey*.'"

The Danish duo's folksy Christmas ballad was perfectly pleasant. I didn't dislike it. But the contrast between the nice, polite entertainment on the BBC and the sort of music that was being played in the clubs around Liverpool was unbelievable. And the best thing of all was that very few people outside the city had any idea what was going on. Even in Liverpool it was only the younger generation who really knew about it. It was our secret. We had it to ourselves. And we wanted to keep it that way.

"You know that song you just played, Tony." Louise interrupted my thoughts. "If you work on it a bit more it might suit Nina and Frederik. It's their sort of style and they don't seem to have brought anything out recently. Maybe they're waiting for the right song to turn up? If you can finish it you should take it down to one of the music publishers in London and see what they make of it."

I wasn't so sure. Did I really want to write songs for Nina and Frederik?

"I was just thinking it sounds a bit old-fashioned," I said. "You know. Compared with the sort of music Liverpool bands are playing."

"What if it is?" said Louise, shrugging her shoulders. "It sounds much like a lot of the stuff that gets played on the radio. It's what people want. Somebody's got to write the songs that get made into records."

Seven

END OF THE ROAD

The rest of the gigs went well. Nobody tried to slash our faces or bury Eric in concrete. So he got his ten percent. And he even said he'd do his best to fix us up with a few more bookings.

Then Dave fell off the back of his lorry at work.

"Dunno how it happened, lads. It was rainin'. I suppose I just sort of slipped."

"For God's sake, Dave," said Steve. "We've been waitin' months for something to fall off the back of yer bleedin' lorry. Yer know. Like some really smart guitars and amplifiers for starters. Straight into our grateful arms. Instead of that yer just go an' throw yerself off. What'yer playin' at?"

He could have been a bit more sympathetic, I suppose. But that's the Liverpool way. Turn everything into a joke. Steve didn't mean it. He knew Dave'd never go along with stuff being nicked off one of his lorries.

Dave looked down at his lower arm which was encased in plaster and supported by a triangular sling. "The doc ses I've broken both the bones in me arm, just above me wrist. So basically I'll be in plaster for about six weeks. Dependin' on the next lot of x-rays, that is. Then it's off to physio to get me arm movin' again." He stopped for a moment and did some quick calculations in his head. "I reckon it's gonna be a couple of months at least before I can pick up me sticks again. Yer'd better get yerselves another drummer. 'Til I'm right that is."

"Forget it, Dave," said Steve. "Eric's not got anythin' lined up for us at the moment. We can wait 'til yer in action again."

Finding a replacement drummer would be easier said than done anyway. Ringo wasn't available. And we didn't fancy the idea of starting over again with somebody new.

I was still trying to write songs and to be honest I was enjoying it. I was getting plenty of satisfaction from making music on my own. Steve, meanwhile, was spending pretty much every weekend with Tracey, the girl he'd met at St Luke's. And if the almost permanent grin on his face was anything to go by, he was getting plenty of satisfaction too. That had, after all, been his main reason for forming the group.

It's strange the way things work out. It had been fun. And we never actually made a decision to break up the band. It was just that by the time Dave's arm was fixed we'd sort of got out of the habit. We couldn't be bothered to start rehearsing again. Thanks to Dave's accident The Three Exiles had reached the end of the road.

Most of the other Liverpool bands, though, kept on going and, as 'Mersey Beat' continued to tell its rapidly expanding readership, the local music scene was getting bigger and bigger. It felt as though the city was about to explode.

How long would it be before the wider world discovered what was going on?

•—•————•—•—•—•————••

"It's 'My Bonnie'. N.E.M.S. have got it in. It's just been released in England today."

It was the beginning of January in 1962 when Louise rang me. Wednesday the fifth to be precise.

"I'm going into town to pick it up on Saturday morning. You could meet me at N.E.M.S. if you're free."

"Fine. What time?"

"Ten-thirty?"

"That's okay," I said. "The lads've persuaded me to go to the Chelsea game at Anfield this afternoon but we're not meeting up 'til one o'clock. Ten-thirty'll be perfect."

By the time I arrived at N.E.M.S. Louise had spoken to an assistant and arranged for her purchase to be played in one of the listening booths. I joined her, and together we listened to The Beatles on record for the very first time. Even though they were just the backing band we could hear them clearly behind the lead vocals of Tony Sheridan. Louise could hardly contain herself. She thought it was brilliant and she left the shop with her precious purchase tucked tightly under her arm.

I'd forgotten to grab a copy of '*Mersey Beat*' from the shop as I left home, so we picked up a copy from N.E.M.S. along with the record. Across the top of the front page there was a big headline.

BEATLES TOP POLL

Underneath it was a picture of the four Beatles, surrounded by their instruments. They were all wearing the trade-mark leather gear which the girls like Louise, and quite a few of the boys as well, found so seductive.

"Wow. Don't they look great," whispered Louise as she kissed me goodbye outside Lewis's. "Enjoy the match. Hope they win for you. I'll see you at home later."

She had a lazy afternoon planned. She'd play her new record time after time, occasionally flipping it over to listen to the B-side which was a rocked-up version of the traditional song '*When The Saints Go Marching In*'. And she'd read all about The Beatles in the paper. Perfect.

I headed for The Albert. It was the first Saturday of the year and Liverpool had been drawn against Chelsea in the F.A. Cup. We were riding high in Division Two, and looking increasingly like serious promotion candidates, while Chelsea were struggling in Division One. It was going to be an interesting contest.

The Kop was full to capacity. The atmosphere was electric. By half-time Liverpool were leading their illustrious First Division opponents by four goals to one. We thought it was all over, but in the second half things started to go wrong. Chelsea grabbed two quick goals to turn what had looked like an easy stroll to victory into a desperate, rear-guard action. The tension was unbearable and when the final whistle went, with Liverpool still clinging on to their slender lead, the roar from the crowd was a heady mixture of triumph and relief.

Mr Shankly emerged from the dugout and strode across the pitch. With his arms outstretched, in what was to become a very familiar posture, he stood in front of the Kop and saluted his adoring fans.

That evening, still on a high despite some persistent rain, I made my way into town and caught the bus to Louise's house. At the south end of Penny Lane, near the bus stop and the roundabout which marked the junction with Allerton Road, there were a few small shops, along with a bank. Above one of the shops the red, blue and white stripes on a barber's pole were lit up and revolving slowly, but the shop itself, along with all the others, was shuttered and firmly closed.

I hurried along the wet pavement, passing rows of the terraced houses with their front curtains tightly closed to guard their privacy, and quickly reached Louise's. I pressed the bell. After a short delay she opened the door. She was wearing a white cashmere jumper and a red, tartan skirt which just reached her knees. Over the previous couple of months she had let her hair grow a little longer and it was now swept back in a fashionable pony tail. She looked gorgeous, and I gave her a kiss as I stepped into the hallway.

"Mum and Dad have had to go and see my Nan over in Huyton. She's not well so they won't be back 'til late. I'm up in my room. '*My Bonnie*' sounds really amazing. Come on up and have a listen."

Her mottled cream, Dansette record player was on the floor beside her bed. On the turntable I could see the orange label of a Polydor 45 r.p.m. record. She lay across the bed, face down, and reached down to the Dansette to switch it on.

In a format which was very typical of the time, the record started with a slow, ballad-like introduction backed by just a gentle, acoustic guitar, exactly like the original folk song. Then, after a couple of lines, The Beatles, as backing band, broke in and the tempo changed to an out-and-out rocker.

Louise rolled onto her back and smiled up at me, lifting her arms up towards me as she did so. "Great isn't it. I couldn't wait for you to get here and listen to it with me. Have you missed me?"

I lay down and put my arms around her. "You know I have." The cashmere felt very soft. I stroked her back gently, feeling for the strap of her bra. "Have you got that combination number?"

"You won't need it."

I slid my hand under her jumper and ran it across her back. There was no strap to undo. Her skin was warm and smooth to the touch. As I continued to run my hand up and down her spine I could feel her breathing more quickly.

"I love you holding me, Tony. Kiss me."

I had already removed my jacket and, as our lips met, she started to undo my shirt before pulling it open to expose my chest. I lifted her pullover over her head and pulled her against me, pressing her body against mine. The record finished but neither of us moved to replace it. We just lay there with our arms around each other.

I brushed my lips against her cheek and whispered into her ear. "We won four–three."

She started to laugh. "Oh my God. You're a real romantic aren't you."

"I thought you might want to know."

"Perhaps not right at this moment."

I kissed her again. "Sorry."

She snuggled up to me. "It's a bit chilly. Let's get under the blanket."

We wriggled between the sheets and I could feel the warmth starting to build up.

"That's better," I said quietly. "Are you okay?"

"Yes. It's lovely being close to you like this."

I put my head under the blanket and kissed her, running my tongue slowly over her soft skin. I felt her shiver with pleasure.

"You'd better not do that again or I won't be able to control myself."

I moved up and pressed my lips to her mouth, while running my hand down her back until it reached the waistband of her skirt. I tried to slip my fingers under the band, but it was too tight.

She breathed urgently into my ear. "Try the other way."

"Sorry. I don't understand."

"My skirt only goes down to my knees, you idiot. In fact you'll probably find it's already half way up my thighs."

I moved my hand slowly onto a warm and very bare leg.

Louise gave a little murmur. "You're very gentle. I like that."

"And you're gorgeous. And getting more gorgeous by the minute. Are you sure you're still okay."

"I'm fine. Do you think all this is accidental? I want you to get to know me really well. Better than you've ever known anybody before."

I moved my hand up her leg, lifting her skirt as I did so. Beneath it she was completely naked.

I left before her parents returned home. We were worried the look on our faces would give us away. As I walked back along Penny Lane, away from her house, I could taste her lips, and the musky smell of her warm body seemed to surround me. Football was good, and music was great, but being with Louise was so very special. I couldn't imagine anything, ever, being better.

It was just after eleven when I arrived home and, even though it was late, I went straight to my room and took my guitar out of its case. All was quiet. I'd have to play very softly to avoid disturbing people, but my brain was too alive to even think of sleep.

Before I knew it two hours had slipped by and I was feeling tired. I placed my guitar carefully inside its red-lined case and got into bed, pulling the sheets up around me. As I did so, I wished that Louise was with me. How lovely it would be to wake in the morning and find her lying there. But, as I drifted off to sleep, I knew it would be a very long time before that was likely to happen.

Eight

GETTING BETTER

In the second week of February 1962 we heard that Brian Epstein had become The Beatles' manager. The band had previously been managed, on a fairly casual basis, by the Liverpool club owner, Alan Williams, who'd fixed them up with the work in Hamburg. But for some reason he'd fallen out with them.

According to an article in '*Mersey Beat*' Bill Harry had, as promised, arranged for Brian Epstein to go along and watch them perform at The Cavern one lunch-time just before Christmas. The word was that Alan Williams, still nursing a grudge, had advised him not to touch them with a barge-pole. But Brian Epstein could see there was something different and special about them. The way the lunchtime audience down in The Cavern reacted to their music, and the requests for '*My Bonnie*' at his record shop, suggested they had potential. Their leather gear, different though it undoubtedly was, would have to go. Audiences expected professional entertainers to be dressed smartly. One of the Liverpool tailors who made his own suits would be able to sort that out. Then, with his contacts in the music business, he was sure he'd at the very least be able to get them an audition for a recording contract with one of the major labels in London.

It was Saturday morning and I was sitting on my usual stool in the window of the Kardomah, waiting to meet Steve. I'd got there a bit early and by the time he drifted in to join me I was on my second cup of coffee. I pressed a couple of coins into his hand.

"Get yourself a coffee. I'm on my second already. I'll be buzzing if I have any more."

He waited at the counter while one of the girls put the coffee machine through its paces. Then he pulled himself up onto the stool next to me.

"How's things?" I asked him. "Tracey okay?"

"She's fine. We don't see much of each other durin' the week. It's just weekends mostly. But it suits us at the moment."

He paused and sipped at the white froth on top of his coffee. "What about you and Louise? Eric says the two of you are thick as thieves an' you practically live at her place. 'E never sees you up in Waterloo these days."

"Yeah, well, with her living down in Penny Lane it's easier just to stay over. Her brother's room's free. Her Dad wasn't keen at first but he seems to have got used to the idea of me being around. I give him a few bob in the way of rent each week which helps to keep him happy. We've had a big job on in Speke for the past month or two, so the boss picks me up on Smithdown Road, by the roundabout at the end of Penny Lane, on his way through. It means I get an extra half hour in bed."

Steve gave me a wink. "With Louise?"

"You've got to be joking. Her Dad'd batter me if he got even half a sniff of that sort of thing happening. He's okay most of the time but he doesn't stand for any nonsense when it comes to his little daughter."

"That wouldn't suit me an' Tracey," said Steve. "We 'ave a great time on a Saturday night. Her folks don't give a toss what she gets up to. I can spend the whole night in 'er room as far as they're concerned. We went to The Cavern last week to see The Beatles an' she couldn't keep 'er hands off me afterwards. Kept callin' me George. But I didn't mind."

He laughed and looked at me, waiting for me to say something. When I didn't, he carried on.

"Yer know, Tone, I used to think there couldn't possibly be anythin' better than goin' to Anfield an' watchin' Liverpool play football. But I'm tellin' yer. Even if we get promoted, an' all the top teams are playin' at Anfield next season, bein' in bed with Tracey's gonna run it pretty close."

I thought of Louise. And I knew exactly what he meant.

Just then the door to our left opened and three, leather-clad figures entered. We recognised them immediately. The Kardomah had been getting more crowded in the half hour or so since I'd arrived and, as we watched them, the three Beatles made their way over to the last empty table and sat down.

It was just after eleven in the morning.

Steve leaned over to me. "There must be somethin' happenin' for them to be out an' about so early." He thought for a moment before continuing. "They usually drink at The Grapes in Mathew Street. But that's when they've got a lunch-time session at The Cavern. They was playin' there yesterday, but I don't think there's anythin' on today."

Not wanting to turn round and stare we watched their reflections in the window. Three coffees appeared and they were soon deep in conversation but we couldn't hear what they were saying.

"N.E.M.S. is just round the corner," I whispered. "It says in '*Mersey Beat*' that Mr Epstein's just signed them up. Maybe they've got a meeting?"

"Maybe. But Pete Best's not with 'em. Surely 'e would be if they were 'avin' a meeting with Mr Epstein?"

"No idea. I'm just guessing. Somebody did say Pete had the 'flu' a few days ago and Ringo Starr from The Hurricanes stood in for him. Last Monday it was. They were doing a lunchtime session at The Cavern. Maybe he's still under the weather?"

"If we hang about 'til they leave we could ask 'em."

"Don't be daft. They won't tell you anything."

"Won't do any harm to ask, will it? Paul McCartney's supposed to be the one who's always happy to talk to people. An' if I tell Tracey I've bin chattin' with Paul in town she won't be able to control 'erself."

"I thought you said it was George she likes."

"I don't think she really minds to be honest. She'd 'ave any of 'em."

As we were laughing I saw in the window that the three guitarists had already finished their coffees and they seemed to be making a move.

"I think they're leaving, Steve. For God's sake don't make an idiot of yourself."

I could see that Steve was also watching them and as Paul McCartney passed behind him he turned round on his stool.

"Hi Paul. I was at The Cavern last Saturday with my girlfriend, Tracey. She really enjoyed the show. We both did."

Paul stopped. "That's great. Ta very much."

"Are you playin' there tonight?"

"No, we're over the water in Birkenhead. There's a dance in the Church Hall by St Paul's Presbyterian. The Zeroes are on at about seven-thirty, so we should be startin' our set around nine if you want to come over. I don't know if there's any tickets on the door, but you could give it a try. Maybe we'll see you over there?"

"Will Pete be back? Or is Ringo still standin' in for 'im?"

John Lennon was already out in the street. George Harrison was standing by the door, holding it open and waiting.

"Come on Paul. We'll be late."

Paul gave Steve a wink. "Sorry. George ses I've gotta go. See yer."

With that he followed George out of the door and they joined John on the pavement. We watched as they headed off along Whitechapel in the direction of N.E.M.S.

"Maybe they have got a meeting?" I said. "In the article it says Mr Epstein's hoping to get them a recording contract."

Steve scratched his head. "N.E.M.S must sell thousands of records every week. I suppose the record companies would 'ave to take a listen to 'em. Even if it's just to keep Mr Epstein happy."

◆·——·◆·◆·◆———··◆

Louise was very jealous when I told her about our brief meeting with the three Beatles.

"It's not fair. I wish I'd been with you. But I think I'd have been a bit disappointed Pete Best wasn't there. He's the good-looking one."

"Paul McCartney was great. Steve just asked him a question as he was walking past us. He could've ignored us but he didn't. He stopped and had a quick chat while George Harrison waited for him. But John Lennon just carried on as if we weren't there."

"He probably didn't even see you. Marilyn says he's very short-sighted but he hates wearing his glasses in public."

"Maybe. Anyway, what do you fancy doing this evening? There's a new Cliff Richard film called 'The Young Ones' on at the Futurist in town."

Cliff Richard was England's answer to Elvis Presley and, just like Elvis, almost everything he touched seemed to turn to gold. To be honest I wasn't a huge fan. I much preferred the type of music the Liverpool bands were playing. But Louise liked him so I didn't mind giving the film a try.

"Let's go," she said. "We can always leave if it's no good. There won't be anybody in at home."

I have to say I got pretty close to suggesting we should maybe give Cliff Richard a miss and head straight to her house. But I didn't. And the film wasn't bad. So we ended up staying right to the very end.

Looking back I think it was around then that I first felt certain that things were starting to happen. That Liverpool was changing. There was an unmistakable buzz about the place. At least as far as our generation was concerned. At first I thought it was just because of Louise, but it was more than that. There was a growing sense that The Beatles were something special. They were Liverpool through and through, and I couldn't see that changing. So if they were to make the big time it could boost the whole city.

Liverpool had suffered some terrible punishment in the war, and it was still struggling to get back on its feet. Maybe, at long last, things were about to get better.

On 21st April 1962 Liverpool Football Club were poised to end their eight year exile from English football's top division. A win against Southampton at Anfield would make the Second Division title secure. A capacity crowd was certain.

We couldn't possibly risk missing out, so we turned up at the ground four hours before kick-off even though it was raining heavily. There were a couple of hundred people standing outside The Kop turnstiles, waiting for them to open, but it was nowhere near as busy as we'd expected. We took our place at the end of the queue as the rain continued to pour down.

"Looks like we're gonna to get wet, lads," said Steve cheerfully as Dave and Eric headed off to fetch us some lunch from the chippy, a hundred yards away along Breck Road. Looking up at the thick, black clouds which hung low over our heads I could see he was right. A heavy rain soon started to fall, and we just had to grin and bear it. It would be at least two hours before we could get into the ground and seek shelter under the Kop's enormous roof.

At just before one o'clock the turnstiles were opened and we filed through before heading up the wide, concrete steps to grab our places for the big game. At first the terraces were fairly empty but as the crowd built up the accumulated body heat caused thousands of items of rain-soaked clothing to emit a steamy vapour which drifted slowly upwards towards the corrugated steel canopy high above our heads. We were wet and tired. We'd been on our feet for over four hours. But as kick-off approached we were too excited to care.

To our surprise, when the teams emerged onto the field just before the appointed hour of three o'clock, there was still quite a bit of space around us. The Anfield Road terraces behind the goal at the far end of the pitch didn't look full either. There couldn't have been more than forty thousand of us in the stadium, at least ten thousand short of full capacity.

Eric turned to me. "Bleedin' typical, isn't it Tone? The weather's put people off. We could've turned up at ten to three and walked straight in. All I can say is they'd better win."

He needn't have worried. Liverpool hardly had to break sweat. They scored twice without reply and when the final whistle went it was almost an anti-climax. Half-a-dozen youngsters scampered onto the still-sodden pitch from the direction of the boys' pen, but otherwise the crowd seemed subdued. We were back in the First Division. But it was as if nobody could quite believe it.

After a brief wave to the crowd the Liverpool team jogged past a line of clapping Southampton players towards the tunnel. As they were about to disappear from view a small boy who'd run onto the pitch reached up and placed a red and white straw boater on big Ron Yeats' head. Yeats leant down to thank him and as he did so the boy planted a big kiss on the skipper's cheek. It was that sort of afternoon.

The crowd all waited for something to happen, but the players had all disappeared and the pitch in front of us remained empty. It seemed there was to be no lap of honour. We would have no opportunity to show the eleven men how much their success meant to all of us.

The spectators in the main stand rose from their seats and began to make their way out of the ground, but hardly anyone left the Kop. Instead, as the realisation dawned that we really had won promotion, a chant began to build up until it was an unstoppable roar.

"We want The Reds. We want The Reds. We want The Reds."

All around us people were stamping their feet in unison, and the concrete steps beneath us seemed to shake.

"WE WANT SHANKLY. WE WANT SHANKLY."

As the chanting got louder and louder a thin, reedy voice made an announcement over the Tannoy.

"This is Mr T. V. Williams, the Chairman of the Club, speaking. I would like to thank all the players and you, the crowd, for helping us to achieve what many regard as the most difficult task in English football. Winning the Second Division Championship. Mr Shankly, the architect of our success, will now speak to you. Thank you."

The crowd fell silent as the unmistakable Scottish brogue of Mr Bill Shankly emerged from the loudspeakers all around the stadium.

"This is your manager speaking."

The crowd went wild.

"I want tae tell ye all there is no doubt at all in ma mind that today has been the happiest day o' ma entire football career."

His next words were drowned out by a deafening cheer, and the chanting and stomping which had died down momentarily started up again.

"WE WANT THE REDS. WE WANT THE REDS. WE WANT THE REDS."

It was becoming clear that nobody who was standing on the Kop that day was going to leave until they had seen the players again and given them the ovation which was their due. The big-wigs, who were already enjoying their usual tea and refreshments in the smart, dry lounge beneath the main stand, eventually got the message.

Mr Williams came back onto the Tannoy to explain that the team were all having a bath, but he assured the crowd that they would come back out onto the pitch as soon as they had changed. The rain continued to fall as twenty-five thousand people on the Spion Kop waited patiently to salute their heroes.

Then the players appeared, with Ron Yeats and Ian St John leading them out onto the pitch. There was a mighty roar and the front rows of the crowd began to pour over the touchline, followed by the rest of the Kop, all running in the direction of the men who had just made their dreams come true. The rest of the team, who were just starting to emerge from the tunnel, took one look at the tidal wave of humanity that was hurtling towards them across the muddy field and turned back. Ronnie Yeats and Ian St John were not so fortunate. Despite attempts by the few remaining police officers to hold back the front runners they were engulfed. We watched as the two players fought their way towards the safety of the tunnel, Ron Yeats holding out his massive arms and almost swimming through the crowd, while the much smaller figure of Ian St John could occasionally be glimpsed, clinging on to his skipper.

After a tense couple of minutes they escaped from the jubilant throng and fled down the concrete steps to join their team-mates in what would undoubtedly be an epic celebration.

The floodlights were turned off. That was obviously it. We made our way out of the ground, still very damp, but also very happy.

Eric was smiling to himself. "What an afternoon, eh, lads. Well worth gettin' soaked for. I'm glad we didn't miss that one."

Nine

LOVE ME DO

Over the next few weeks everything went quiet. In mid-April The Beatles returned to The Star Club in Hamburg for a seven week engagement which had been fixed up some months earlier by Allan Williams, before Mr Epstein appeared on the scene.

On Friday 4th May Liverpool lost their final game in the Second Division to Swansea, letting in four goals and netting just two. But it didn't matter. The season had effectively finished a couple of weeks earlier with the historic win over Southampton.

'Mersey Beat' came out once a fortnight and even our small shop was selling a lot of copies. The big national titles like 'New Musical Express' and 'Melody Maker' struggled to match it for sales on Merseyside. We kept an eye on what was happening in the city, but with The Beatles being in Hamburg, and it being the start of the summer, there wasn't much going on.

Then, on 2nd June and without any great fanfare, The Beatles returned home. They spent two days rehearsing behind closed doors at The Cavern Club before travelling down to London. On 6th June 1962, they walked into the E.M.I. Recording Studios in Abbey Road, via the back door, for an audition with a producer called George Martin who worked for Parlophone, a small label which was part of the E.M.I. Organisation.

It was possibly Brian Epstein's last throw of the dice. The Beatles had already been turned down by several of the big labels. Someone told me that one of Decca's A & R chiefs, Dick Rowe, a man with many years of experience who knew the music business inside-out, had offered what was intended as some friendly advice. "You're wasting your time, Mr Epstein. Guitar groups are on the way out."

If true, it was a historic misjudgement. But he managed to make up for his error a few months later when another unknown group, this time based in London, turned up for an audition. They called themselves The Rolling Stones.

Over at Parlophone The Beatles recorded one of Louise's favourites, the old standard 'Besame Mucho', along with three of their own songs, 'Love Me Do', 'Ask Me Why' and 'P.S. I Love You'. When they returned to Liverpool rumours flew around the city that George Martin had offered them a recording contract.

Then came a bombshell.

The late August edition of 'Mersey Beat' was delivered to our shop as usual. On an inside page they were running what was described as an 'exclusive' story.

BEATLES CHANGE DRUMMER!
RINGO STARR (FORMER DRUMMER WITH RORY STORM AND THE HURRICANES) HAS JOINED THE BEATLES.

According to the article Pete Best was being replaced by Ringo Starr. The Beatles were quoted as saying: 'Pete left the group by mutual agreement. There were no arguments or difficulties, and this has been an entirely amicable decision.'

I rang Louise to tell her. She couldn't believe it.

Nobody could.

After all the hard graft of the past couple of years why would

Pete Best want to leave the band just as they might be about to hit the big time? For many of their fans, particularly the girls, he was quite simply their favourite.

More rumours and gossip swept the city.

'The other three wanted to get rid of Pete Best because he was too good-looking.'

'There was a big bust up between the band and Pete's mother, Mona.'

'Brian Epstein wanted Pete Best and his mother out of the way because she kept trying to tell him how to manage the group.'

'George Martin at Parlophone wanted to offer them a contract but he wasn't impressed by Pete Best's drumming.'

'John, Paul and George had never been impressed by Pete Best's drumming.'

'Ringo just fitted in better.'

It was impossible to know which, if any, of these stories might be true. Pete Best had only joined The Beatles in August 1960, when they'd urgently needed a drummer for their first trip to Hamburg. He hadn't been with the band from the very beginning. But even so it was hard to understand why he had been cast aside so suddenly. The one thing that was very difficult to believe was that the split had been 'amicable and by mutual agreement'. That sounded like Mr Epstein speaking.

Eric and Dave went along to The Cavern the evening after the change of drummer had been officially announced. Ringo was due to be playing with the band and the two of them were full of it when we bumped into them a few days later.

"There was loads of girls just sittin' in Mathew Street at the top of the steps leadin' down to The Cavern. They were all cryin' an' sayin' they never want to see The Beatles again."

"An' then when we got inside it was like pandemonium."

"There was one gang of girls and lads standin' right in front of the stage shoutin, 'Ringo out. Pete in. Ringo out. Pete in.' An' then another lot of girls'd start screamin', 'Ringo never. Pete Best for ever. Ringo never. Pete Best for ever.' They wouldn't stop. The Beatles couldn' even start playin.'"

"Paul McCartney was up on the stage. 'E was holdin' up 'is arms and tryin' to get 'em all to quieten down. Then some bloke started shoutin' at George Harrison who wasn't doin' anybody any harm. 'E was just standin' there, tuning 'is guitar. The bloke accused George of bein' sarcastic cos 'e was messin' with 'is guitar when there was no way The Beatles were gonna be playin'. Then 'e just goes for George without any warnin' an' 'ead-buts 'im. Straight in the face. Honest. It was mad."

"John Lennon and Ringo didn't want anythin' to do with it, which I reckon was sensible. They just kept their 'eads down an' stayed in the band room by the side of the stage. They did eventually get started with their set, but everyone was sayin' they'd blown it an' The Beatles'd be finished without Pete Best. Completely effin' crazy it was."

A hard core of Pete Best supporters may have stuck by him and abandoned The Beatles, but over a period of months even Louise gradually got used to the change and convinced herself there must have been a good reason for what happened. Even if she couldn't understand it. She'd loved Pete Best's good looks, but she had to admit that Ringo was a great drummer. And he was already popular and well-known on Merseyside.

At about the same time yet another rumour was doing the rounds. John Lennon had been spotted outside Mount Pleasant Register Office with Brian Epstein. And a girl.

It was Louise who first told me. "According to Marilyn her name's Cynthia. Someone said she's pregnant and John had to marry her. Marilyn's devastated. John's her favourite."

There was never any confirmation of the rumour though, and John Lennon continued to play with the group every night. His so-called 'wife' was never seen with him again, with or without a baby, so everyone decided it couldn't be true and Marilyn returned to her dream of having a love affair with a Beatle.

With Ringo installed as their new drummer The Beatles got their recording contract, and on 4th September 1962 they were back at Abbey Road Studios. George Martin had lined up a Mitch Murray song for them called '*How Do You Do It?*' which he reckoned was an obvious Number One hit. Although the recording went well, John Lennon and Paul McCartney weren't happy.

They were keen to release one of their own songs, '*Love Me Do*', which had been recorded at the session back in June when Pete Best was still on drums. But George Martin didn't like the way it sounded. Further takes of the song, with Ringo on drums, still didn't satisfy him so a Scottish session drummer called Andy White was called in. Ringo was relegated to playing tambourine and, having burnt his bridges by leaving Rory Storm and The Hurricanes, some of his friends were saying he was more than a little worried that he might be about to suffer the same fate as Pete Best.

Louise got all this gossip from a girl she knew who was a member of The Beatles Fan Club. According to her, George Martin still thought '*How Do You Do It?*' was the obvious choice if The Beatles wanted a hit record. But there was no way The Beatles were going to agree. They could see that the Mitch Murray song was very commercial but it wasn't the kind of record they wanted to release. They were trying to do something new and different. They wanted to release their own songs. George Martin finally gave in and agreed that '*Love Me Do*', with Andy White on drums, would be their first single.

It reached the record shops on Friday 5th October 1962. We were at the head of the queue outside N.E.M.S. on the Saturday morning to pick up the copy which Louise had pre-ordered. On the B-side was *'P.S. I Love You'*, another song penned by Lennon and McCartney.

As we stood at the counter, waiting for the assistant to fish out our order, we looked up at the Hit Parade on the wall. *'Telstar'*, an instrumental number by a group called The Tornados, which had been inspired by the name of a recently-launched telecommunications satellite, had moved to the top from number three, pushing Elvis Presley's *'She's Not You'* and *'It'll Be Me'* by Cliff Richard and The Shadows down into second and third places.

When the assistant finally appeared with our record Louise told her she couldn't possibly wait until she got home to hear it. She begged her to put it on for us.

"Just *'Love Me Do',*" she pleaded, pointing to the far side of the shop. "There's a booth over there that's free. Please. So we can listen to it straight away."

With its open harmonies and repeated phrases on the harmonica it was completely unlike anything that was in the charts at the time. It used just two chords and, like the B-side, the writing credit was down to both Lennon and McCartney, although several people who knew him were saying Paul McCartney had written most of it on his own three or four years earlier when he was just sixteen. *'Love Me Do'* had certainly been part of their live act for quite a while, and the record captured the song's raw, almost primitive, character. It made the chart music of the day sound very ordinary and safe.

"It's really different isn't it," Louise remarked as we walked out of the shop. "It's much more like Dad's blues records than the stuff that usually gets into the charts."

She was right, but I did wonder if perhaps they should have taken George Martin's advice.

"It's not what people are used to," I said. "It might not even do that well here on Merseyside. Some of their fans have been saying they're not going to buy it. They're worried that if The Beatles have a hit record they'll move down to London and never play in Liverpool again."

"They could be right," said Louise. "About them moving to London, I mean. We'll just have to wait and see what happens."

Just over two weeks later it was looking as though none of us would live to find out the answer. The papers were full of doom and gloom as America and the Soviet Union engaged in a terrifying face-off, with no obvious way out for either side.

A U-2 spy plane had photographed Russian nuclear missile sites being constructed on the island of Cuba, just a few dozen miles off America's east coast. For the Americans this was unacceptable. The missiles had to be removed. President Kennedy declared a quarantine zone around the island which would be enforced by means of a naval blockade.

On October 22nd Louise and I sat in the sitting room with her parents and listened to the broadcast which President Kennedy had delivered to the American nation earlier that day. We looked at each other as we heard his grave voice say that he had chosen a path which was full of hazard.

"Let no one doubt that this is a difficult and dangerous effort on which we have set out. No one can see precisely what course it will take or what costs or casualties will be incurred. The cost of freedom is always high – and Americans have always paid it. And one path we shall never choose, and that is the path of surrender or submission."

As he spoke a convoy of Russian ships was already making its way across the Atlantic towards Cuba, carrying further military supplies. The President had made it crystal clear that America would not back down. If the Russian ships did not change course they would be challenged and, if necessary, sunk. And that would mean war.

The experts were all saying that Nikita Kruschev, the Russian leader, was volatile and unpredictable. It was a thermo-nuclear poker game. Would he be prepared to gamble, and risk everything? At stake was the future of the human race. The world held its breath, waiting to see what would happen.

The Russian ships steamed on for two further days and then, on 24th October 1962, when they were just five hundred miles from the eastern tip of Cuba, they saw ahead of them a vast American naval armada, including eight aircraft carriers. It was clear that sailing on would mean being sent to the bottom of the ocean. They reduced speed and stopped. And then slowly, very slowly, they turned and headed for home.

Premier Kruschev had blinked and thrown his cards down onto the table. Nuclear war had been averted and we could get on with our lives.

Looking back it's easy to forget just how scary those few days were. The whole episode later became known as The Cuban Missile Crisis. It was less than twenty years since World War Two had ended. In Liverpool the stark evidence of what ordinary bombs could do to a city was there to be seen all around us. We'd all seen the pictures of Hiroshima and Nagasaki. And what the papers were calling the theory of nuclear deterrence, of mutually assured destruction, had never really been properly tested.

As it turned out, the theory worked. But I'll tell you one thing. As we waited to see what would happen I couldn't help thinking it'd be a real pain if we all ended up being blown to smithereens just as things seemed to be on the up.

Four days later Louise and I made our way to The Empire Theatre alongside Lime Street Station in the centre of Liverpool. We'd managed to get tickets for the evening performance of 'Star Studded Sunday', a joint promotion by Brian Epstein and Ray McFall, the owner of The Cavern Club. Heading the bill was the vintage American rocker Little Richard, supported by Craig Douglas, Jet Harris, Kenny Lynch, The Breakaways and Sounds Incorporated. They were all very big names in 1962, and we were looking forward to a great evening.

The opportunity to see Little Richard was not to be missed, but almost as big an attraction was the fact that The Beatles were also on the bill. They'd played in a talent contest at The Empire several years earlier, when they were still called 'The Silver Beetles', but it was their first professional appearance at Liverpool's major theatre which seated over two thousand people on two levels. It was a clear indication that they were now the top band in Liverpool, and that they might very soon be heading for much bigger things.

The show was a sell-out. Louise and I were sitting halfway back in the stalls and, as The Beatles made their first appearance on the stage towards the end of the first half, the reception they received from the audience around us was ecstatic. The moment the curtains started to open two girls in our row stood up and began to scream and, as the band launched into their first number, they started to yell out the names of all four Beatles. They were quickly joined by others and the noise in the auditorium became louder and louder. The band were looking at each other and laughing. It was obvious they were going down well, and they were loving every minute of it.

All too soon they had completed their short set and, after acknowledging the rapturous applause, they moved to the back of the stage.

The compere for the evening appeared and walked towards the centre of the stage, trailing his black microphone lead behind him and smiling broadly. As he did so he half-turned, with his arm outstretched, and pointed towards the band.

"Okay all you pop fans. That was The Beatles, an up-and-coming act from here in Liverpool. I hope you enjoyed listening to them. Let's give them one more big round of applause."

It was a mistake. The theatre erupted once again and showed no sign of quietening down. Over the shouts of "Paul" and "John" and "Ringo" and "George" the compere began to introduce the next act. His smile had disappeared.

"Right. Come on, now. Quiet please. Quiet. I want you all to put your hands together, right now, for the fantastic, the one and only, Craig Douglas."

As Craig Douglas started to walk onto the stage there was a shriek from a couple of rows behind us.

"Paul. I love you. I love you. Paul. Paul."

From elsewhere in the stalls, on both left and right, came further cries

"George. George. Look at us, George. Look at us."

"John."

"Ringo. Ringo."

From the balcony above our heads all we could hear were loud screams and wails.

Like a true professional Craig Douglas smiled through it all and began to count The Beatles in for his opening number. But inside he must have been seething. Who are these upstarts anyway? And who on earth arranged for them to be my backing band?

As he worked his way through his hits such as 'When My Little Girl is Smiling' and 'Our Favourite Melodies' the audience gradually settled down, and when he came to the end of his last song he received a genuinely warm reception. The Beatles performed what would soon become their trademark, very deep bows before joining with the audience and clapping Craig Douglas off the stage as the curtains closed.

Little Richard did not make the same mistake. He had his own backing band and his whole act was energetic and wild. It was exactly what we had hoped for. He was the undisputed star of the show, and he went down a storm.

Louise's eyes were shining as we made our way to the station.

"Weren't The Beatles fantastic," she said. "I couldn't believe the noise coming from those girls. I was going to join in and shout for Pete Best, but I thought you'd probably disapprove."

"Dead right I would," I said. "You'd have been sitting on your own after the interval if you'd tried anything like that."

She laughed. "And Little Richard was pretty good too, wasn't he."

It was my turn to laugh.

"Little Richard wasn't just pretty good. He was amazing. I loved it when he was playing the piano standing on one leg. I hope The Beatles were watching him from the side of the stage. There's still a few things they could learn from someone who's been around as long as he has."

I paused for a moment and turned to Louise. "We should go down to N.E.M.S. next weekend and see if they've got any of his records in stock. It'd be great to have copies of *'Good Golly Miss Molly'* and *'Long Tall Sally'*."

"And *'Lucille'*," she added.

"We'll have to see what Mr Epstein can find for us then. That's if he's not too busy these days to put in an appearance behind the counter."

I was staying over at Louise's that night, and when we got home we played *'Love Me Do'* yet again. We both loved it, and we'd been playing it so often that the grooves were in danger of wearing out. But our feeling that the record's appeal outside Liverpool might be limited seemed to be right.

We watched its progress in the New Musical Express each week. The rumour was that Brian Epstein had ordered ten thousand copies to try and push it right up the charts. Even if it was true, it wasn't enough. *'Love Me Do'* entered the charts at Number 32, and finally peaked at Number 17 towards the end of December.

The Christmas Number 1 was *'Return to Sender'* by Elvis Presley. This was a welcome return to his earlier, more upbeat style and it had knocked *'Lovesick Blues'*, by a yodelling, Australian country-blues singer called Frank Ifield, off the top spot.

The Beatles had become recording artists, but not much had changed. At the end of 1962, Elvis was still very much 'The King'.

Ten

PLEASE PLEASE ME

Just before Christmas Louise told me she'd joined The Beatles' Fan Club. She already had her membership card, sent to her by Freda Kelly who was the Fan Club secretary.

"They're going to be bringing out a colour magazine each month," she told me excitedly. "It'll be all about what The Beatles are up to and so on. In the meantime if we want to know anything we can get in touch with Freda and she'll tell us. They've got another record coming out in a few weeks."

As soon as we heard '*Please Please Me*' we knew it was going to be much bigger than '*Love Me Do*'. '*Mersey Beat*' splashed it all over the front page and we scanned the charts in the New Musical Express each week to see how it was doing. By mid-February it was in the Top Twenty. And, at the beginning of March, it finally pushed '*The Wayward Wind*' by Frank Ifield aside and hit the top spot. According to the New Musical Express, The Beatles had made it to Number One.

Louise was now in regular touch with some members of the fan club who knew the band personally. She'd heard from them that George Martin had told The Beatles immediately after the recording session that '*Please Please Me*' was going to be a big hit, and he wanted to get an album recorded as soon as possible to cash in on their popularity before they faded back into obscurity.

His initial idea had been to record a live album in front of their fans at The Cavern, which would have been brilliant. But sadly it never happened. It was too complicated and expensive to set up. So, in early February 1963, The Beatles set off in their van after a show at The Empire Theatre in Sunderland, up in the north-east of England. They were heading south to London where arrangements had been made for them to put the necessary album together at E.M.I's Abbey Road Studios. The plan was to record all the tracks in just one day. That way George Martin hoped to capture the feel, and the excitement, of a live performance.

After an exhausting overnight journey The Beatles began their recording session at ten o'clock on the morning on 11th February and, by the time the second, and final, take of *'Twist and Shout'* was safely in the can, John Lennon was frantically sucking Zubes throat sweets and drinking ice-cold milk to keep his voice from going altogether. As everyone sat in the control room and listened to the tape it was just before eleven in the evening. The band had been recording non-stop for over twelve hours.

Recorded on an old-fashioned, two-track tape machine, their first U.K. album, also called *'Please Please Me'*, was in the can. Opening with the self-penned *'I Saw Her Standing There'*, and ending with John Lennon's unbelievably raw rendition of the Isley Brothers' classic *'Twist and Shout'*, it was destined to make history.

George Martin and his engineers knew that they had witnessed something extraordinary that day. It would still be some time before The Beatles would shake the whole world but deep beneath the surface the tectonic plates were starting to move.

Liverpool's secret would not remain hidden for much longer.

"I was speaking to Val the other day," said Louise. "She knows Les Chadwick, the bass guitarist with Gerry and The Pacemakers, and he told her that Brian Epstein has got them a recording deal with George Martin as well. They were down in London the other week. Their first single's going to be '*How Do You Do It?*', the song The Beatles turned down. It's coming out in March."

I was lying on Louise's bed. It was Valentine's Day, which also happened to be her seventeenth birthday, and her room was full of presents and cards from friends and various family members. Most of the gifts were clothes and I watched as the various items emerged from their colourful wrappers.

"Do you like this?" She pulled a heavy-knit, bright yellow 'Sloppy Joe' sweater from Wallis over her head and admired herself in the mirror. "It's from Mum and Dad."

'Sloppy Joes' were the height of fashion and Louise had wanted one for a while.

"It's really thick," I said. "It'll certainly keep you warm."

"Is that the best you can manage?"

"Okay. It suits you." I winked at her and grinned. "I like the colour on you. It looks good."

She gave me a look and shook her head.

"You men," she said, laughing. "You're hopeless."

She looked at the mirror again. "It doesn't really go with this skirt. But it'll look good with those skinny, blue jeans I got from Lewis's last week."

She twirled round to see herself from the back. "Yes. I'm happy with that."

As she turned away from the mirror I handed her a small box wrapped in gold paper. She gave it a shake. There was no sound.

"Go on then," I said. "Unwrap it."

She removed the gold wrapper to reveal a green box. She lifted the lid slowly.

"Wow. That's beautiful. Here. Put it on for me."

She held out her right wrist. The delicate gold bracelet fitted her perfectly.

"Thank you so much," she said, wrapping her arms around me and giving me a big kiss. "You really shouldn't have, but I love it. It must've cost a fortune."

"At least a week's wages," I said, giving her a grin. "But it's Valentine's Day as well as your birthday. And you're worth every penny."

She gave me another kiss. "I'll wear it when we go out tonight. It'll add a touch of class to the 'Sloppy Joe' and the jeans."

We sat on the bed together.

"I was talking to Mum earlier about what I'm going to do next year after school. She said it's time I started thinking about it."

"And?"

"I don't know really," she said. "Mum said I should think about nursing. It's been a good job for her and she still enjoys it." She paused. "I'm sure it wouldn't be boring, but I'm not sure I fancy doing something so serious. I might get too involved and start worrying about my patients and making mistakes."

"Okay. What about fashion or design then?" I suggested. "You've always been interested in that sort of thing. You could go to the Art College here in Liverpool. It's supposed to be very good. John Lennon was there for a while. And Stu Sutcliffe. He was a big mate of John's. He used to play bass guitar with The Beatles but he decided to stay on in Hamburg when they came back to Liverpool so he could carry on with his art studies over there. Someone said he'd fallen in love with a German girl who'd been hanging around with the band at The Star Club and taking pictures of them."

Louise turned and looked at me. "Wasn't there something in 'Mersey Beat' about him dying? It wasn't that long ago. It must've been around the time The Beatles went back to Hamburg last spring. I wonder if any of them got to see him again? He can't have been that old."

Stu Sutcliffe's death didn't mean much to us. Death doesn't when you're young. It's not something you come into contact with very often and you don't think about it. So, having very briefly remembered Stuart Sutcliffe, we just as quickly forgot about him. We were much more interested in talking about our future.

"Art College isn't a bad idea, Tony. It'd definitely suit me much better than something like nursing. I'll get on to them and find out how I go about applying for a place."

"Right then," I said. "That's you sorted. What about me?"

"What about you? I thought you were already sorted. You're going to be an electrician. What's wrong with that?"

"It's a bit repetitive and boring," I said, shrugging my shoulders. "I thought it'd be risky and dangerous. That's why it appealed to me. But in the end it's just like any other job."

Louise started to laugh. "All jobs are repetitive and boring some of the time, Tony. It's called working for a living. That's why you get paid."

I put my arms out and pulled her towards me. "Come on. I've just thought of something else that might be a bit repetitive, but according to Steve it certainly isn't boring. Your folks won't be back for at least a couple of hours. And it is Valentine's Day."

For a moment she hesitated, a little uncertain, as if there might be something wrong. Then she lay back on the bed and motioned me to join her. "Let's just lie here for a minute and talk."

"That's fine. There's no hurry."

She was silent for a few moments. "Are you sure you love me, Tony?"

For a couple of seconds I didn't know what to say. It was all very sudden and unexpected. "Of course I'm sure I love you. What's the problem?"

At first she didn't reply. She just lay there, thinking. "Mum's been asking about the two of us. Apparently it's obvious we're getting quite fond of each other." I took hold of her hand to show her I was listening. "She's been working in a maternity clinic for the past few months and she says she sees girls of my age who get into trouble all the time. You know. Get themselves pregnant. She said she wants to be sure we're being careful. Dad would go ballistic if I had to tell him I was having a baby."

I felt myself starting to panic. "You're not, are you? Pregnant I mean."

"No, of course I'm not. We haven't done anything. Well, not all the way."

I looked at her and started to laugh with relief. "So there's nothing to worry about then."

"That's what I said to Mum. And she just said if we ever needed some advice she'd be happy to have a word with me about it."

I wasn't quite sure where she was going, so I didn't say anything. She turned on her side and gave me a hug.

"I suppose I'm saying that if we, you know, wanted to go a bit further, I could speak to my Mum. There's a new birth control pill just come out, but she says you've got to be married to get hold of it. Officially that is. But the place she works at is doing some clinical trials. According to Mum the doctors want to try it out on some younger women who aren't married and haven't yet had children." She paused for a moment. "Like me, for example."

To tell the truth I was slightly taken aback. I suppose it was good that we were able to talk about it. Or at least that Louise and her Mum were. But I didn't know what to say.

We lay there in silence, both of us thinking. Eventually Louise spoke again. "Are you shocked?"

"No, no. Not really. I'm fine. I'm just a bit confused I suppose. It wasn't what I was expecting."

"Me neither," she said with a slight laugh. "I wasn't going to say anything to you but it just sort of came out."

I turned to face her. We put our arms around each other again and hugged very tightly. It felt good. A barrier had been broken.

I let her go and rolled onto my back again. I obviously don't need to tell you that the idea of being able to make love to her properly without any risk was great. But at the same time I was a little worried it might change things.

"If you want to give the pill a try it's up to you," I said. "It's fine with me either way. I don't want to influence you."

We both lay there, lost in our own thoughts.

At the beginning of 1963 even the younger generation like us were still struggling to shake off the idea that sex was somehow a bit wrong. These days everybody refers, either nostalgically or in shocked tones, depending on their attitude to such things, to 'the swinging sixties'. But it wasn't until the pill became freely available, half way through the decade, that things really started to change. That was when the sixties really started to swing.

I sat up and squeezed Louise's hand. "Come on. Let's go down to Sefton Park and take a walk round the lake. I need some fresh air. And it'll give us an appetite for tonight. I've booked a table at Ma Bo's."

It was one of those very cold, blue-sky days that usually happen just once or twice in February. The sharp frost which had greeted us that morning had melted away in the gentle warmth of the winter sun and we wandered hand-in-hand along the path which wound its way round the boating lake. Beneath the still-leafless trees one or two early daffodils and crocuses were cautiously poking their heads through the as yet unmown grass. We talked some more about what her mother had said. About whether it might be sensible to get some advice. Just in case.

"It wouldn't do any harm," said Louise. "I don't know exactly what Mum's got in mind, but I'll have a word with her."

———————————

That evening we were in the city centre. Nelson Street, the main road in Chinatown, was bustling with people, mostly local Chinese, heading for one of the many, small eating places which lined the slightly shabby street, almost all family-run. In most cases the restaurant and kitchen were on the ground floor while the upper floors formed the family home.

Ma Bo's was one of the most traditional of these establishments. Most of the customers at the half-dozen wooden tables were local Chinese, a sure sign that the food was good. Genuine Cantonese cuisine. We sat at a table for two, sharing various exotic dishes. Things were getting better all the time. The Three Exiles hadn't lasted very long. But without them I'd never have met Louise. And I knew for sure that she was very, very special.

Eleven

THE MERSEY SOUND

I turned to Louise and pointed at the copy of New Musical Express which I'd been reading. It was a Saturday morning in early June, and we were sitting in The Jacaranda Coffee Bar in Slater Street. We'd arranged to meet up with her brother, Andy, and his new girlfriend.

"Just take a look at the Top Twenty," I said, running my finger slowly down the records which were listed. "Number One – Billy J Kramer with 'Do You Want To Know A Secret?'. Number Two – The Beatles. 'From Me To You'. Okay, then there's Jet Harris at Number Three. But Gerry and The Pacemakers are Number Four with 'I Like It' and then there's another Scouser, Billy Fury, at Number Five. That's four of the top five records from Liverpool. We're taking over from London. Liverpool's going to be the music capital of England."

Louise frowned at me. "Billy Fury's not from Liverpool. He's been around for ages. He comes from somewhere down in London."

"That's what I thought too. But I was at Frank Hessy's the other day getting some new strings for my guitar and I got chatting to Jim Gretty who works there. He was telling me he sold Billy Fury his first guitar. He was called Ronald Wycherley back then. It was Larry Parnes, the guy who puts on the big rock and roll tours, who discovered him and came up with the name Billy Fury. He worked on one of the Mersey tugs before he hit the big time and moved to London. Jim Gretty said his family still live down in The Dingle. By the river, near where Ringo Starr was born. As well as changing his name, Larry Parnes told him he'd have to lose his accent and forget all about being from Liverpool if he wanted to make it as a pop star. That's why hardly anybody realises he's from round here."

Louise shook her head.

"Come on, Tony. Even if you include Bill Fury, having four records at the top of the charts is hardly taking over from London."

I ran my finger further down the Top Twenty.

"Look at the rest of the charts then. There's Gerry and The Pacemakers again at Number Thirteen with '*How Do You Do It*?"

She still didn't look convinced.

"Okay, " I said. "Maybe I am making a bit much of it. But all this publicity has got to be good for the city. The thing about The Beatles and the other local groups is they don't try and hide the fact they're from Liverpool. They make a big thing of it. It's like they're just ordinary lads having a bit of fun. And people love their Scouse humour."

Louise lifted her arms above her head in mock surrender.

"Stop. I give in, Tony. But to be perfectly honest, I don't really care. If it all turns out to be good for the city, that's great. But the only thing that matters to me is The Beatles. I reckon the whole world could easily go totally crazy about them." She gave me a grin. "Just like I'm totally crazy about you."

I gave her a kiss, and told her I felt exactly the same way, just as Andy and his girlfriend arrived. They were both slightly short of breath.

"Sorry we're a bit late." Andy bent down to give his sister a hug. "Our pathology lecture went on a bit longer than we expected. We didn't want to miss you so we ran most of the way here as you can probably see."

Still breathing heavily they sat down.

"Meet Sarah," said Andy, turning towards his girlfriend. "Sarah, this is my sister Louise. And her boyfriend, Tony."

With dark brown hair, cut straight across just above her shoulders, and wearing a knee-length tweed skirt and cream-coloured blouse, Sarah looked like a typical, and very sensible, future doctor. She gave me a smile as I hurried off to order four coffees. By the time I returned to the table Louise had already discovered that Sarah was in Andy's year at medical school and that she came from a small town on the north coast of Somerset, not far from Bristol, called Clevedon. The two of them were chatting away like long-lost friends.

"So, how's life in Liverpool suiting you?" said Louise.

"It's brilliant. I could hardly have picked a better time to come up here, could I? What with The Beatles and all the other groups, the whole place is buzzing at the moment. If I didn't have exams to study for I could very easily forget all about medicine and spend every evening in places like The Cavern and The Iron Door."

Andy, who had been quietly drinking his coffee, turned to Sarah. "Why don't you show Louise those letters? You know. The ones from Paul McCartney."

Louise looked at her wide-eyed. "Paul McCartney? How come you've been getting letters from Paul McCartney?"

Sarah reached into a leather satchel which she'd placed on the seat alongside her and pulled out two envelopes.

"I'm afraid I carry them round everywhere with me. I don't want to risk leaving them in my room at hall in case one of the cleaners accidentally throws them away. Getting them was all a bit of an accident, really. Back in December a group of us from our year went along to the Queens Hotel on the promenade in Southport. We were having a sort of get-together before we all went off home for Christmas and The Beatles were playing at a place called Club Django on the ground floor of the hotel. Apart from hearing 'Love Me Do' a couple of times on the radio I didn't really know much about them and I couldn't believe how fantastic they were. They were brilliant. Anyway, one of the girls happened to know that Paul lived in Forthlin Road in Allerton. So for some reason I decided to write and tell him how much I'd enjoyed the show. I don't really know what made me do it. I certainly didn't expect a reply."

She took one of the letters out of its envelope.

"This is the first letter I got. And he also sent a list of all his likes and dislikes. You know. Like they have in New Musical Express each week. My favourite colour. My favourite food. All that sort of thing."

Louise was staring intently at the two pieces of paper which Sarah had passed over to her. At the top of the typewritten letter was Paul's home address, 20, Forthlin Road, Liverpool 18. And at the bottom was his signature with three kisses.

"I can't believe I'm actually holding a letter from Paul McCartney," said Louise. "With three kisses." She pointed at the letter. "It says there's a signed photograph as well."

"Yes, well," said Sarah, "he didn't actually enclose the photograph. So, even though I wasn't expecting a reply I sort of felt a bit cheated and I was cheeky enough to write to him again to tell him he'd forgotten to enclose the photograph. And a week or two later I got the second letter. With a signed photograph."

She handed Louise the other envelope. The letter and photograph were very carefully removed.

"Wow. That's amazing. I wish I'd thought of doing that. I bet if you wrote to him now you'd be lucky if you even got a printed thank you note from one of Mr Epstein's secretaries."

Louise passed me the typed list.

"It says here his favourite colour's black," I said, pointing to the bottom of the list. "And his ambition is to make the band's music famous. Maybe that's about to happen."

"What do you mean 'maybe'?" said Louise, sounding very defensive. "They've already had a couple of hit records. What more do you want?"

I shrugged my shoulders. "You're the one who keeps saying they're going to take over the world."

Andy laughed. "My little sister's always been a bit of a dreamer."

Louise ignored him and continued reading the second letter which contained a brief apology for not enclosing the signed photograph. Paul ended the letter by saying that they had a few gigs fixed up in Blackpool, where Cliff Richard was doing a season, so they might try and get along to see one of his shows.

Like the first one it was signed '*Paul McCartney*', followed by three kisses.

"I think I must've put something about Cliff Richard in my second letter," said Sarah. "I might've said I'm a big fan of his. I can't really remember. I don't know why Paul would have mentioned him otherwise. Maybe he's a Cliff Richard fan too?"

Sarah returned the letters to their envelopes and put them back in her bag.

"I'm going to hang on to them. You never know. In fifty or sixty years' time, when everyone's forgotten The Beatles ever existed and I'm losing my marbles, I'll be able to look at them and think back to what it was like to be young."

A few days later I met up with Steve, Dave and Eric in The Liver, our local pub in Waterloo, and about the only thing we talked about was the way Liverpool bands seemed to be taking over the hit parade.

Steve looked down into his beer despondently. "We should've kept goin' with The Three Exiles." He shook his head and sighed. "Brian Epstein seems to be signin' up almost anyone 'e can find who's got a Liverpool accent an' a guitar, an' then fixin' 'em up with a recordin' contract. All the papers are callin' it 'The Mersey Sound.'"

Eric chipped in. "Yer can 'ardly get in The Cavern for suits from London. I bumped into Sam Leach the other day. You know, the guy who puts shows on at The Tower Ballroom over the river in New Brighton. 'E said all the clubs in town're the same. There's posh lookin' guys from down south, all flashin' their cheque books about the place. The Searchers and The Undertakers 'ave both got deals with Pye. An' Robbo says The Swinging Blue Jeans've got a recordin' session lined up with HMV."

I looked at Steve. Eric's comments weren't making him feel any better.

"An' meanwhile we're stuck 'ere with our borin' bloody jobs," he muttered, taking a sip of his ale.

"Come on, Steve," I said. "Be realistic. They're not signing everybody up. Brian Epstein's only taking on bands like The Beatles and Gerry and The Pacemakers who are really good. And singers like Cilla Black and Billy J Kramer."

"Yeah. But we played on the same bill as The Undertakers an' they've been signed up. I know they were good. But I didn't think they was that much better than us. Anyway it's not just Brian Epstein and N.E.M.S. When you was up at the bar Eric was sayin' there's a mate of 'is who's only just got 'imself a guitar. 'E's put together a group an' they've got an audition with a record label called Oriole. They're doin' an LP called 'The Mersey Sound' an' there's gonna be about a dozen Liverpool bands on it. It's bein' recorded live at The Rialto in Toxteth next weekend. That's right, isn't it Eric?"

Before Eric could say anything I decided to try and make Steve see some sense.

"So what?" I said. "An audition doesn't mean anything. As soon as they realise this guy and his band don't know one end of a guitar from another they'll be out on their ears. There's no chance of them ever making a record."

But Steve wouldn't listen. "We knew how to play though. People seemed to like us." He looked over at Dave accusingly. "It's all your stupid fault, Dave. Why did you 'ave to go an' break yer arm? If you 'adn't've fallen off of yer bleedin' lorry we'd probably still've been goin' as a band. We could've been famous."

Dave wasn't going to take that lying down. "I said you could get another drummer. Didn't I say that, Tone?"

I didn't want to get involved. But Steve now started on at me. "Okay then, Tone. You tell me why we didn't 'ave a real good look around for another drummer? We never even agreed about breakin' up the band. We just gave up. I don't remember us talkin' about it or anythin'."

I could see he was getting himself worked up.

"Look Steve," said Dave, taking him by the arm. "Be honest. You weren't that interested in the band once you'd hooked up with Tracey."

Dave had downed a few beers. He was trying to be helpful but he wasn't thinking straight. Things were definitely going in the wrong direction.

Steve shook his arm free. "Just you leave Tracey out of this."

"Why? It's true."

I sort of knew what was coming next. I tried to shut him up but Dave was into his stride. It was too late. "You were never really into music, Steve. All you cared about was gettin' into Tracey's knickers. Admit it, mate. It's perfectly normal. You're a good-lookin' bloke an' she's a good-lookin' girl. So you were doin' yer best to get 'er pants off. What's wrong with that? Sounds pretty normal to me."

In his less than stone-cold sober state Dave thought he was being witty. And I suppose he was in a way. But Steve definitely wasn't amused. He just looked at him, stony-faced, as Dave blundered on. "Anyway, mate, I'm sure it doesn't matter to Tracey if you're in a band or not. I could tell the first time I met 'er. She's a real goer. I reckon she'd been round the block a few times before she got together with you."

He smiled at Steve, then started to laugh.

"Please, Dave," I said. "Cool it. You've had too much to drink. It's not funny."

Eric had gone pale. Steve had just gone deadly quiet. For a few seconds he sat there, looking straight ahead. Then he stood up and took hold of his pint glass. It was still nearly full. Without saying a single word he emptied the entire contents over Dave's head.

"For Christ's sake, Steve. What the …" Dave tried to dodge to one side but it was too late. He was drenched in beer. "Jesus. What the fuck's up with you?"

"I just didn't think what you said was very polite," said Steve quietly. "Tracey's my girlfriend. She's not some cheap little scrubber who goes around the place showin' 'er tits off like your Yvonne. You just be thankful I'm not a violent person. Otherwise I'd be smashin' this glass over yer fuckin' 'ead."

He put the empty glass back onto the table. Dave still had a full pint sitting in front of him. He picked it up. Looking straight at Steve through the beer which was still dripping from his hair and running down his face, he downed it in one.

"I'm not gonna waste a good pint on a wanker like you, mate"

I glanced towards the bar. A couple of people on adjoining tables had turned round and were staring at us, but fortunately the room was full of regular Sunday lunchtime drinkers and there was a fair bit of noise. The landlord, who normally kept a close eye on all his customers, was in the middle of pulling a pint. He hadn't noticed anything.

Having put his glass back on the table, alongside Steve's, Dave stood up.

"I'm goin'."

He took a couple of paces towards the door then turned back and looked hard at Steve. "You might fuckin' regret what you just did."

Twelve

THE JACARANDA

It was a glorious day as Louise and I made our way up Mount Street in the old, Georgian area of Liverpool, about a mile southeast of the city centre and close to the University. We were heading for the Art College.

The street took us up a gentle slope from Rodney Street, where all the doctors had their private practices, towards the appropriately named Hope Street which ran from the very traditional, and still not quite completed, Anglican Cathedral to the site of the new Roman Catholic Metropolitan Cathedral about half a mile to the north. Building work had only just started on the new cathedral but the locals, who'd seen an artist's impression of the proposed, ultra-modern, pyramidal structure and couldn't help taking a sly dig at the Liverpool-Irish, were already calling it 'Paddy's Wigwam'.

If you've ever seen it, you'll understand why.

We walked hand-in-hand up Mount Street, passing a row of modest Victorian terraced houses on our left. Facing them was a large, sandstone building, its grand entrance blackened by years of smoke pollution.

"Here we are," I said as we reached the doorway. "The Liverpool Institute and College of Art. This entrance takes you into The Institute. Paul McCartney and George Harrison both went to school here. 'The Inny' they used to call it. The main entrance to the Art College is round the corner."

We reached the top of the street and made a right turn onto Hope Street where another very grand, sandstone portico greeted us.

"Let's take a look inside."

We tried the door but it was firmly locked. Louise looked disappointed.

"It must be closed for the weekend."

I too felt a little deflated and we stood there for a minute, deciding what to do. Having travelled all the way into town we both wanted to make the most of our trip.

"Come on, then," I said, taking hold of her hand. "Let's not waste the afternoon. We can take a look at the cathedral and go up to the top of the tower. On a day like this it must be open."

The massive sandstone walls of the Anglican Cathedral towered over us as we pulled on the handle of the heavy oak door which guarded the entrance. It swung open and we made our way into the fifth largest place of worship in the world. We felt tiny as we looked around, lifting our heads to gaze at the vaulted ceiling high above us. The carvings and the discreet decorations on the gigantic, sandstone pillars looked crisp and fresh. It was as if they had been done yesterday. And in many cases they had. Work on the building had started in 1910, when the city was hugely ambitious and wealthy. Now, over fifty years later, there were still a large number of carpenters and stone-masons toiling away on the vast undertaking. It would be another fifteen years before they would finally complete their monumental task.

We stood together in silence. Even in its unfinished state the space seemed infinite and truly awe-inspiring.

When we had finished gazing at the architecture we found a warden who showed us the entrance to the tower and, after an exhausting climb up seemingly endless flights of steps, we found ourselves standing on a wide, flat terrace, surrounded by a low parapet. We were over three hundred feet above the ground. It was a long way down. And the fact that the cathedral itself had been built on a hill made it seem even higher as we looked out over the city. It felt almost as if we were flying.

I'd been up the tower a couple of times before but it was Louise's first visit and the unexpected magnificence of the view took her breath away. We had chosen the perfect day and she had not realised it would be quite so spectacular. The air was slightly cool for the time of year but it was very clear. The River Mersey glistened to the west of us, giving it the appearance of a wide, silver ribbon in the bright sunlight. We could see the Pier Head and the many docks which stretched in a long line, both north and south of the city centre, along the eastern bank of the river. Many of the southern docks were unused and semi-derelict, but the more distant and larger docks to the north were still busy with shipping.

I pointed out an early Victorian terrace on the far side of the St James' Cemetery which lay alongside the cathedral to the east.

"That's Gambier Terrace. John Lennon and Stu Sutcliffe used to share a flat in one of the houses. His wife, Cynthia, and their little baby, now live in a place which Brian Epstein owns over there in Faulkner Street, by the Philharmonic Hall. John joins them there when he's not away on tour."

Louise shook her head and sighed. She and some of her friends still couldn't quite come to terms with the idea of John Lennon being a married man. Peering over the parapet she gazed down at the tapestry of small streets which marked the city centre.

"Where's The Cavern?"

I pointed almost due north. "You can't see Mathew Street. It's hidden by the big stores and warehouses. But it's somewhere in that direction. Parallel with Lord Street."

We did our best to identify as many as possible of the various landmarks of Liverpool. In the far distance, beyond the modern university buildings and the crowded houses of the inner city, we could see the massive roof of the Kop at Anfield. Looking south Louise tried to work out where her house was, nestling among the rooftops of Mossley Hill and Allerton on the far side of Sefton Park. Almost immediately below us, the slated roof of the Art College was broken up by several rows of glazed sky-lights on the Mount Street side.

"They must be for the art studios on the top floor," said Louise. "Northern light's supposed to be the best for painting. It's cool and there aren't any shadows."

We spent about forty minutes up there, gazing at the view, during which time nobody else joined us. Louise couldn't understand it.

"Why aren't there loads of people up here on such a perfect day?"

"Maybe they don't know about it?"

I walked to the edge and leaned out as far as I could until the soles of my shoes were only just touching the floor. Louise pulled me back.

"Don't. You're making me nervous Tony. Let's go. Before you slip and kill yourself."

Clouds were starting to cover the sun.

"Okay. It's getting a bit cold anyway. Let's go get something to eat. Where do you fancy?"

"How about The Jacaranda?" she said. "We can walk there in ten or fifteen minutes."

⚫··⎯⎯ ⎯⚫·⚫·⚫·⚫⎯⎯⎯ ··⚫

At two o'clock on a Saturday afternoon the coffee bar was comfortably busy, but not packed. We ordered coffees, along with a couple of ham sandwiches. I stood and chatted to a dark-haired waitress behind the counter while Louise grabbed a couple of places at a small table. When our order was ready I carried the tray over and joined her on a padded bench with our backs to the wall.

"That girl I was talking to works here part-time," I said, taking a bite at my sandwich. "Her name's Fiona and she's doing Fashion and Design at the Art College. She says it's a great place and all the students on her course are really enjoying it."

"So our little trip's been worthwhile," said Louise, giving me a smile. "Even though we didn't actually get to see inside."

I looked around the room. A few of the customers were Saturday afternoon shoppers, surrounded by their carrier bags and parcels, but mostly the clientele seemed to be students. Quite a few of them still looked half-asleep, having just emerged from their beds for a very late brunch. The current offerings of various Liverpool bands were being played over the music system, along with some more obscure rhythm 'n' blues and jazz records, most of which Louise and I didn't recognise despite our familiarity with her Dad's collection.

On the far side of the room a tallish young man with dark hair was taking photographs with a very smart-looking camera. His subject was an extremely pretty girl who was sitting on a cushioned stool next to him, leaning back against a painted brick wall. Her hair was straight and black, cut in a Mary Quant sort of style, and she was wearing a calf-length dress made from a deep-purple, velvet-like fabric with short sleeves and a decorated neckline.

"Maybe she's a model?" suggested Louise. "He wouldn't be taking photographs of her otherwise."

"She's not a model, love." There was a slightly older man sitting next to us on his own, slowly sipping at a coffee and reading a copy of 'Mersey Beat'. He must have overheard what

Louise said. "She works in one of the clothes shops on Bold Street. The guy taking the photographs is Paul McCartney's younger brother, Mike. 'E's a really good photographer. Never goes anywhere without 'is camera. 'E took some great pictures of 'is brother's band before they were famous. See 'is camera? It's a Twin Lens Rollei Magic. Paul got it for 'im in Hamburg."

Louise was slightly taken aback by the unexpected intervention. But at the same time she was fascinated by what he was saying. "Do you know him?"

"Who, Mike? No, not really. Only from seein' him in here."

"So he hasn't shown you the pictures he's taken of The Beatles?"

"'E let me take a look at one or two of 'em a few months back. But since 'is brother started gettin' better known it's like 'e prefers to keep a low profile. Someone said 'e's even been thinkin' of changin' 'is name. 'E's got 'is own life to lead an' 'e doesn't want to be known just for bein' Paul McCartney's brother. Good on 'im I reckon."

We didn't want to stare at Mike McCartney. But knowing who he was we couldn't help taking occasional glances in his direction as, having finished taking his pictures, he sat down and started chatting to the girl he'd just been photographing.

The chap next to us started to gather up his things. "Nice talkin' to the two of you. Take care."

"And you. 'Bye."

Louise and I looked at each other. It was the summer of 1963. We were young. And we were beginning to realise just how lucky we were to be living in Liverpool at this particular time.

Thirteen

DOWN THE CAVERN

"I've got 'em!"

It was a Sunday evening towards the end of July, and Eric raced into The Liver holding up five tickets bearing the magical words:

> *THE BEATLES. CAVERN CLUB.*
> *SATURDAY 3RD AUGUST 1963*
> *ENTRANCE 10/-. BY TICKET ONLY.*

They were our passports to what we all knew would almost certainly be the last time The Beatles would ever appear at the Liverpool venue which was once their home from home. They'd already moved on to bigger things, but a local promoter had a long-standing agreement for them to appear at The Grafton Rooms on West Derby Road on the Friday evening. Brian Epstein didn't want to let him down so, as well as playing The Grafton, the band he now referred to as 'his boys' would stay on in Liverpool and play one last Saturday night gig at the club where he'd first fallen in love with them and their music.

We looked at the precious pieces of paper.

"You queued for 'em, Eric, so we'll give yer twice what they cost," said Steve. "What d'yer reckon?"

"Sounds fair enough. They were ten shillings each. I only need one so there's four going spare. That's four quid."

Steve and I handed over eight ten shilling notes before he had time to change his mind. Eric seemed to be happy with the deal. And so were we. The touts would be asking for a lot more outside The Cavern on the night.

We hadn't mentioned it to Louise and Tracey until we knew for sure that Eric had managed to get hold of the tickets. I hardly need to tell you they were both over the moon when they got the news. It was a shame that Dave and Yvonne couldn't join us, but since the incident in The Liver they weren't speaking to Steve.

There were five hundred of us crammed into The Cavern Club that late summer Saturday evening. The show started at six and, with the heat generated by all the tightly-packed bodies, the walls were soon dripping with condensation. People were fainting and being carried out into Mathew Street to recover. As well as The Beatles, five other well-known Liverpool beat groups were on the bill; The Escorts, The Merseybeats, The Roadrunners, Johnny Ringo and The Colts, and Faron's Flamingos. Ray McFall didn't need to bother with jazz bands any more.

By the time The Beatles appeared on stage the condensation had started to form pools of water on the floor. The heat was stifling and part-way through their set the electrics blew, plunging us all into darkness.

Steve started chuckling to himself. "Good job you did on the lights, Tone. You'd best get up there an' fix 'em."

I kept quiet.

Some sort of make-shift, emergency lighting came on almost immediately and, as the power was being restored, we could hear John Lennon muttering to himself. He'd retreated to the band room at the side of the stage along with George Harrison and Ringo. Paul McCartney, meanwhile, had picked up a Gibson acoustic guitar. Ever the professional, he stood on the tiny stage and gave us an unplugged version of 'When I'm Sixty Four', a cute little music-hall-style ditty which he said he'd written a couple of years earlier for his Dad. It was the first time we'd heard it, and it was certainly nothing like the rest of the numbers which the band blasted out at us once their sound system was back in action.

After an unforgettable evening we made our way home along Mathew Street.

"I can't believe that's it," said Louise sadly. "I wonder how The Beatles are feeling? You know about not playing at The Cavern anymore." She thought for a moment, before answering her own question. "I suppose they're probably too excited about the future to care that much about the past."

We walked on in silence. It was the end of an era.

⸻

Although that was it as far as The Cavern was concerned, exactly four weeks later we saw The Beatles again. It was the last night of a series of four or five shows they were doing at The Odeon Cinema in Southport. As they ended their set with 'Twist and Shout' and the curtains swished smoothly across the stage to hide them from view there was pandemonium. They had gone down well at The Cavern, of course, but most of the audience there had seen them many times before. They were almost like old friends and the reaction was nothing like the one we were now witnessing in the cinema. Smartly-dressed girls all around us were pulling at their hair and screaming hysterically before collapsing into each other's arms, sobbing helplessly. Neither of us had ever seen anything quite like it.

"That was completely insane," said Louise as we walked away from the cinema after the show. "All that craziness at the end. I couldn't believe it. Did you see the girl in front of us? Her face was all covered with the black make-up she'd rubbed off her eyes and she was just sitting there moaning. Like she'd had a seizure or something."

"Or something!" I said, grinning and giving her a wink.

We were only about twenty miles north of Liverpool, but we could have been on a different planet. Southport was genteel and sophisticated. A seaside town. A place people moved to when they'd got together enough money to escape from the tough, multi-cultural port that was Liverpool.

Although autumn was approaching the evening air was still warm. As we made our way slowly along Lord Street, which was lined on its west side with numerous expensive shops and Edwardian, glazed arcades, I was still thinking about what we'd just experienced. I suppose the girls in the audience at The Odeon may have been genteel and sophisticated before the show started, but by the time The Beatles had finished with them they were helpless, completely at the mercy of the surge of hormones and adrenaline which the band's performance had unleashed within them.

Louise took hold of my right arm.

"I can tell you one thing. The Beatles don't belong to us in Liverpool any more. We've lost them. You know how I used to joke about them taking over the world?" She looked at me as I nodded to show I was listening. "I'm starting to think that might actually happen."

We didn't know it at the time, but the two of us would never go to a live Beatles' performance again.

◆·+————◆·+·◆·+·◆———·+·◆

"They'll be back in forty-two minutes."

Along with about fifteen million other people Louise and I were sitting in front of the television watching 'Sunday Night at The London Palladium'. We were at home with her parents. The Beatles were topping the bill, a sure sign that as far as Britain was concerned they were now very much in the same league as Cliff Richard and other big-name pop stars.

Bruce Forsyth, the regular compere, had brought John, Paul, George and Ringo with him onto the stage at the start of the show and, having had a brief chat with them, he was gently teasing the expectant audience who couldn't wait to hear them play.

Louise's Mum nodded approvingly at the black and white screen and turned towards her husband who seemed more interested in the pint which he was holding in his right hand.

"They look very smart, don't they dear? They could do with a good haircut, but otherwise they're a real credit to the city."

Mr Browne grunted a reply as he lifted up his drink and took a deep draught.

Like the rest of their generation Louise's Mum and Dad didn't listen to Radio Luxembourg. And because there wasn't that much pop music on the BBC they didn't really know what The Beatles sounded like. Even though they were now selling tens of thousands of records every week.

"They've got a song called '*She Loves You*' at Number One at the moment, Mum. I'm pretty sure they'll be playing that one," said Louise.

"Yes, dear. I think Jean Metcalfe may have played it on the radio last week when she was doing her Radio Requests programme on the Light Service. A lady down in Cornwall wrote in and requested it for her daughter-in-law who's from Liverpool. Quite a lively song, if it's the one I'm thinking of."

"Not blues then?" said Mr Browne, before draining his pint glass.

"No, Dad. But The Beatles sometimes do a song called 'Twist and Shout' which you might like. The Isley Brothers had a big hit with it in America. The Beatles finished their act with it when me and Tony saw them in Southport. It might be a bit too wild for a Sunday night TV programme though."

"Tony and I, dear."

Mrs Browne, who'd ended up as a nurse but who would really have liked to be an English teacher, was very keen on correct grammar.

"Sorry Mum?"

"It's Tony and I, dear. Not me and Tony. Quite a lot of people here in Liverpool seem not to agree, but the rule is you use 'I' when it's before the verb and 'me' when it's after the verb. If you're hoping to go to college you might as well get it right."

"Oh. Okay. Sorry."

As promised, exactly forty-two minutes after Bruce Forsyth had first introduced them to the audience, The Beatles opened their set with 'From Me To You', and followed it with 'I'll Get You'.

"This next one's our latest single. It's called 'She Loves You'."

As they sang the opening chorus Louise's Mum nodded.

"Yes. This is the one. Very nice."

By this time some of the youngsters in the theatre were starting to scream. It wasn't quite as hysterical as The Odeon, but it was gradually getting louder.

As the last vocal harmonies of 'She Loves You' died away John Lennon addressed the screamers.

"Okay then. We'd all appreciate it if you could shut up while we play our last number."

There was a ripple of applause from the older members of the audience.

"It's a song we do called 'Twist and Shout'."

For a couple of seconds he stood there, legs apart in front of the microphone, with his Rickenbacker in his hands. Then his plectrum hit the strings of his guitar and, together with George Harrison and Paul McCartney, he launched into those unmistakable opening chords before almost screaming the first line into his microphone.

The theatre erupted.

By the time he reached the end of the song The Beatles were no longer just pop stars. They were household names, and well on their way to becoming much loved, national treasures.

I must admit I enjoyed that," said Louise's Mum. "Now, who's for a nice cup of tea?"

Fourteen

YOU'LL NEVER WALK ALONE

In mid-October 1963, while The Beatles were engaged in conquering the nation and the Daily Mirror was announcing the advent of 'Beatlemania', Liverpool were just two points behind the First Division leaders, Manchester United. West Bromwich Albion were the visitors at Anfield. To maintain momentum and stay in touch with Manchester United victory was essential.

I stood on the Kop with Steve and Eric, waiting for the kick-off and listening to the usual records from the Top Ten being played over the Tannoy. Dave wasn't with us and, unless he was standing elsewhere in the ground, he was about to miss one of the most historic moments in the rise to glory of Liverpool Football Club.

"And now for our next record," said the announcer. "It's the first time we've played this one by Gerry and The Pacemakers which has just entered the Top Ten at Number Seven. So here it is. Gerry's version of a fantastic song from the musical 'Carousel'. It's called '*You'll Never Walk Alone*'."

The song could have been written for us. The words carried a message that instantly resonated inside the heart of every single Liverpool supporter and we all stood there, twenty-five thousand voices on the Kop, united in belief. Red and white scarves were held aloft between raised arms and banners were waved as we joined in with Gerry Marsden. It was the perfect anthem for a crowd.

The roar as the record came to an end was for Gerry and The Pacemakers. It was for Liverpool Football Club and the mighty Reds. It was for the city. And every one of us knew at that moment that we were part of the greatest football family in the world.

From that day "*You'll Never Walk Alone*' was our song. Nobody was going to take it away from us. Ever.

The Top Ten that week included some other great records – '*She Loves You*' by The Beatles. '*Then He Kissed Me*' by The Crystals. '*Do You Love Me?*' by Brian Poole and The Tremeloes – but for those of us lucky enough to have been there that afternoon a magical genie had been let out of the bottle. Gerry and his Pacemakers had stolen the show. The passion and energy that the anthem had generated was unbelievable. The whole stadium was buzzing by the time the two teams ran out onto the pitch.

West Bromwich Albion, said to have been nick-named 'The Baggies' by their great rivals Aston Villa because of the large, baggy trousers their fans used to wear at work to protect themselves from the molten-hot iron in the foundries and factories of the Black Country, never stood a chance. The final score was one-nil to Liverpool, thanks to a rare goal from midfielder Gordon Milne, in the thirty-second minute of the first half, but 'The Baggies' had been on a hiding to nothing ever since that glorious anthem had transformed Anfield. The passion that the song had unleashed on the Kop was transmitted to every single Liverpool player. The Reds would now be invincible. And I was in love with a wonderful girl. Could life possibly get any better?

That Saturday night Louise and I went out as usual but she didn't seem to be her usual self. We went to the pictures in town and although I can remember everything that happened that evening in the most vivid detail I haven't a clue what the film was called. I just wasn't concentrating on it.

When I talked to her she seemed to be miles away. I kept asking her if everything was okay, and she just said it was fine. But it clearly wasn't.

Then, as we were walking along Lime Street to catch the bus home, she stumbled and fell over. As I helped her up I noticed her eyes. They seemed to be blank, as if she was in another world.

"Louise?"

She didn't reply.

"Louise? What's wrong?"

She started to mumble. "I'm sorry, Tony. I don't know. I don't feel right."

Her voice trailed away.

"What do you mean you don't you feel right?"

"I don't know. I can't hear you properly." She paused. "You're going all blurred."

Her speech was unsteady. It was as if she was drunk. Or high on drugs.

"You haven't taken anything have you?"

"Only the pill as usual this morning. Oh, and a couple of Panadol. Earlier. Before I left home. I had a bit of a headache."

I was getting very worried about her.

"I think you need to see a doctor."

"No. I'm fine. Let's just go home. I'll see how I feel in the morning."

She started to walk on but after a few paces she stumbled

again. This time I was ready and I managed to catch hold of her before she fell.

About twenty-five yards away, on our left, was the main entrance to The Adelphi Hotel.

"Come on. Let's go into The Adelphi. You can sit down and rest in the lobby."

I helped her up the stone steps. As we reached the entrance a liveried doorman hurried over to us. I immediately recognised him, but if he remembered who we were his attitude was very different to the last time he had seen us.

"Is the young lady alright, sir? She looks very pale."

With one of us holding each arm we guided Louise into the lobby and laid her down on one of the brown leather Chesterfield settees.

"I'll call the duty manager, sir. He'll be able to help you."

I sat on the couch, next to Louise, and waited. Her eyes were closed and she seemed to have gone to sleep. After a couple of minutes the manager appeared and looked down at her.

"What's the problem, sir?"

"I've no idea. Honestly. We've just been to the pictures. At The Futurist. This is my girlfriend. She's not been right all evening. And then when we were walking along Lime Street she just fell over for no reason. I don't know what's wrong."

"She's not been drinking, has she, sir? Or taking drugs?"

"No. She's just told me she had a headache earlier and she took a couple of Panadol. But that's all. She's not had anything to drink this evening. I'm sure of that."

The hotel manager thought for a moment.

"I'm afraid she can't stay here, sir. In any case she's obviously not well. I think the best thing might be to call an ambulance. If that's okay with you, that is."

I nodded. My heart was pounding. All I knew was that Louise needed help. And she needed it as quickly as possible.

The manager disappeared to make his phone call and I knelt beside her, squeezing her hand gently. There was no response. I leaned forwards and put my lips to her left ear.

"Louise. Can you hear me? They're getting you an ambulance. It'll be on its way very soon."

She murmured quietly, but said nothing. I kissed her gently. Her forehead felt very hot but her hands, when I held them, were stone cold. Something was very wrong.

"I love you so much. You mustn't worry. Everything'll be alright."

Twenty minutes later I was sitting in the waiting area at the Liverpool Royal Infirmary. Louise had been rushed into the treatment room as soon as we'd arrived. I'd hardly had time to think, but now my mind was racing. What was happening? What was the matter with her?

I'd never gone much for religion, but as the minutes passed I found myself praying silently, promising God that I'd go to church every Sunday for the rest of my life. Or every day if once a week wasn't enough. I'd do anything. Just as long as Louise was okay.

I felt that up to now I'd done nothing to help her. Nothing practical that would make any difference anyway. Maybe I should try and get hold of her parents? But what would I say to them? That I was sitting in the hospital and their daughter had been taken away from me and I'd no idea what was wrong with her? But they needed to know so they could be here with her.

The thoughts were still swirling around inside my head when a nurse came into the room.

"Are you with the young lady who's just been brought in by ambulance?"

I nodded my head. "Is she okay?"

The nurse didn't immediately reply. She just sat down on a chair next to me and looked at me sympathetically. I sensed a quiet sadness in her manner.

"The doctors are with her now. I'm afraid she's not conscious."

She paused for a moment, maybe so I could take in what she had just said, before continuing.

"Do you mind if I ask you a couple of questions?"

"No. That's okay. Go ahead."

I felt numb and confused. What was going on? A few hours ago we had been happy and carefree. Everything had been fine. And now Louise was lying in hospital, all on her own. I couldn't even see her.

"You told us when you first arrived that as far as you know she's only had a couple of Panadol. Are you sure she's not taken anything else? She's not on any regular medication?"

I was about to say no when, all of a sudden, I could see Louise sitting on her bed, holding a packet of pills. In all the panic I'd completely forgotten about it.

"The pill," I said. "You know. The birth control pill. She's been taking it for a few months."

"Do you know which one?"

Louise had mentioned the name. In my mind's eye I could see her holding the small, oblong packet with the name of the pill printed on it. I racked my brains. Then it came to me.

"Anovlar."

The nurse wrote it down.

"It might not be important," she said, "but I'll make sure the doctors know. And there's definitely nothing else?"

I shook my head.

"No. Nothing."

"And you're quite sure she's had no alcohol this evening?"

"No. I mean, yes. I'm sure."

"Are you her next of kin?"

She's my girlfriend," I said. "But we're not engaged or anything."

"Does she still live with her parents?"

"Yes. In Penny Lane."

"They'll be her next of kin then. Do they know she's here?"

I shook my head. "No. We just went out to the pictures. Louise didn't seem right all evening. And then she suddenly got really ill. We went into The Adelphi and the manager called an ambulance."

"I think we should try and contact them. Have you got their phone number?"

I recited the number to her automatically. I'd dialled it so many times, and suddenly I found myself wondering if I'd ever dial it again. I tried to put the thought out of my mind but it wouldn't go away.

The nurse glanced down at the papers on which she'd been writing my answers.

"Before I phone her parents I just need to confirm a couple of things. Your girlfriend's name is Louise Browne? And her date of birth is the 14th of February 1946, which makes her seventeen and a half?"

I nodded silently and felt my eyes starting to fill with tears. I blinked them back.

The nurse looked at me.

"I'm sorry. Have you known each other very long?"

"Sometimes it feels like we've been together for ever. But actually it's just over two years."

It was strange but I could no longer imagine life without Louise. The nurse continued to look at me.

"You wait here. I'll go and ring her parents. Then I'll get you a cup of tea. You look like you could do with one."

With that she left, and I was alone with my thoughts. I stared at the double doors. Somewhere behind them was Louise, also alone.

The hospital was eerily quiet. Very occasionally a shadowy figure could be glimpsed through the opaque glass but the doors remained firmly closed. I wanted to walk through them and find her. I needed to see her. How come it was all taking so long? Surely they must have worked out what was wrong with her by now?

I glanced at my watch. It was nearly ten past eleven. Louise's parents would be expecting us home, and instead they would be receiving a sudden and unexpected phone call. They'd want to see Louise straight away. The roads would be quiet so they should be at the hospital in less than half an hour.

"Here's your tea." The nurse had returned. "I've added some sugar. I hope that's okay."

"That's fine."

"Mr and Mrs Browne are on their way."

"Thanks. I'll wait for them here."

"The doctors have said they'll have a word with the three of you about Louise as soon as her parents get here."

"How were they when you phoned?"

"Very shocked obviously. But we didn't speak for long. They just wanted to get here as quickly as they could."

"What about Louise? Is there any more news?"

"All I can tell you is that she was moved into a side room about ten minutes ago. I haven't seen her since then."

"Don't they have any idea yet what's wrong with her?"

The nurse shook her head. "By the time her parents arrive the doctors should hopefully be able to tell you something. Dr Campbell's with her at the moment. He's very good. She couldn't be in better hands."

The hot, sweet tea was very welcome. Wrapping my hands around the cup to feel the comforting warmth, I took occasional sips and waited.

When Louise's parents arrived I quickly told them what had happened. Her mother was crying, while her father just looked totally shocked.

"Where is she?" he asked, as I finished my story.

I pointed towards the double doors at the far end of the room.

"The nurse who rang you told me they've moved her to a side room somewhere through there. I've not seen her since we got here which is well over an hour ago."

"And they've no idea what's wrong?"

"They didn't seem to want to tell me much. They said they'd speak to us when you got here."

Even as I spoke a doctor appeared and beckoned us to follow him through the double doors. He took us into a small office. One of his colleagues was already sitting behind a desk and he extended his right arm towards three empty chairs opposite him.

"Please sit down. I'm Doctor Campbell. My apologies for not giving you some information sooner but we've been waiting for the results of some tests."

He addressed the three of us.

"You are the parents of my patient I believe. Mr and Mrs Browne?"

Louise's parents both nodded, but said nothing.

Dr Campbell turned to me.

"And you arrived here at the hospital with her?"

"Yes. Louise is my girlfriend. We were out at the pictures together when she suddenly seemed to get very ill."

"She was okay before that? It was all very sudden?"

"She had a headache earlier, and she took some Panadol before we went out. I told the nurse when we first arrived. She wasn't really her normal self all evening but she kept saying she'd be okay."

The doctor gave a little grunt.

"And you mentioned that she also takes Anovlar."

I nodded my head.

"Yes."

As I spoke I looked at Louise's father. He had no idea she was on the pill. Only her mother knew. But there was no reaction.

"We don't believe her present illness is linked to any medication she's been taking," said Dr Campbell as he turned back to face Louise's parents. Then he looked over at the other doctor who was standing by the door.

"My colleague here, Dr Brookes, performed a lumbar puncture upon your daughter earlier in order to obtain a sample of spinal fluid. We're still waiting for some of the results, but we are expecting they'll confirm that she has bacterial meningitis. The symptoms are typical. And since she arrived here at the hospital she has developed a red rash. A rash of that type is very common in such cases."

Louise's Mum gave a little gasp and her husband put his arm around her shoulders. I was just feeling numb. Dr Campbell continued to speak.

"Such a diagnosis is a matter of grave concern, of course, and we cannot be sure how things will develop. She has already been started on treatment with intravenous antibiotics. Time is of the essence in such a situation."

He paused for a moment.

"Is there anything you wish to ask me?"

Mr and Mrs Browne looked at each other.

"Will she be alright?"

"I'm afraid I can't say for certain what will happen. If our diagnosis is correct – and I'm fairly confident it is – then she is already receiving the most appropriate treatment. She is comfortable and I am hopeful that she will respond to the treatment." He paused for a moment. "I do have to advise you, however, that in someone of your daughter's age there is about a fifteen to twenty percent chance that the treatment will prove to be ineffective."

"So we just have to wait? And hope."

"I'm afraid so."

"Can we see her? My wife here is a nurse."

Dr Campbell looked at Mr Browne, who had been asking the questions, before turning to his colleague.

"Will that be possible?"

Dr Brookes had been leaning against the door frame. He stood upright to reply.

"That'll be fine. But I'm afraid she won't be able to talk to you. She's unconscious and her condition is being monitored by various devices. She also has an intravenous drip in place to deliver the necessary antibiotics."

He opened the door.

"Please come with me."

We followed him along a corridor and into a side room on the left. Even though we had been warned what to expect it was a shock to see Louise lying there, motionless and surrounded by medical machinery.

Her mother, who had managed to control her distress during our talk with Dr Campbell, began to weep again, very quietly. As a nurse, the scene can't have been unfamiliar to her, but when it was her own daughter who was lying there it looked completely different.

"Oh my poor little Louise. My little darling."

She knelt at the side of the bed and began to stroke the back of Louise's right hand which lay flat upon the white bedcover. I remained in the background as her husband moved forwards to join her.

Dr Brookes slipped quietly out of the door, leaving us alone with Louise. For several minutes nothing was said. We just watched her, breathing regularly with her eyes closed, her face almost as white as the pillow on which her head was lying.

Mr Browne held his wife's hand and did his best to offer some words of comfort.

"At least she doesn't seem to be in any pain. She looks so peaceful."

I could see tears trickling down Mrs Browne's face as she slowly nodded her head.

We stayed with Louise for a further hour before deciding that we could do nothing more that night. After receiving assurances that her condition seemed to be stable, and that we would be contacted immediately if there was any change, we left her to sleep. Hopefully the antibiotics would do their job.

I didn't want to go home to Waterloo, and anyway a lot of my things were at Louise's house. So I went back to Penny Lane with her parents. It seemed odd to walk into the house without her and look into her empty bedroom. I wondered how long it would be before she would be able to return home.

I lay on top of the bed in Andy's room, fully dressed. I was exhausted but I knew I wouldn't be able to sleep. The next day was Sunday, and we would return to Louise's bedside.

It was just after five o'clock in the morning when the phone downstairs in the hall rang. I heard Mr Browne answer it and then, five minutes later, there was the sound of a car engine being started in the road outside.

I hurried down the stairs. Mrs Browne was standing by the front door.

"It's Louise, Tony. The doctors at the hospital want me and her father there right away. They're very worried about her."

She was crying.

"Do you want me to come too?"

Louise's Mum shook her head. "They said just her next-of-kin. I'm so sorry, Tony."

Fifteen

ELEANOR RIGBY

The funeral was at St Peter's Church in Woolton, a leafy suburb in South Liverpool. As is always the case when someone dies so young, the old, sandstone church was packed and heavy with sadness. I sat in the limousine alongside Sarah, with Andy and Louise's Mum and Dad in front of us, and watched as the black hearse ahead of us came to a halt outside the church. I couldn't help thinking of The Undertakers, and the evening when Louise and I had first met. The hearse that day, packed with musical instruments, had seemed so full of excitement and daring. But now there was just an unbearable and overwhelming grief.

We stood and watched as Louise was carried into the church. We made our way slowly through the entrance and followed the coffin up the aisle watched by hundreds of pairs of sympathetic eyes. We were all past crying. Our faces were lined and drawn, and people remarked later that we all looked years older. None of us had slept very much over the previous twelve days.

Andy looked serious but, like Sarah, he seemed to be able to control his feelings. I suppose it was their medical training. They had learnt how to suppress their normal, human emotions, as they would have to in their future careers. Even though they were not yet fully qualified they had coped with the situation by switching into doctor mode. Andy, with Sarah's support, had busied himself organising everything. His parents were too grief-stricken to cope with anything. The service was heart-breaking, but it was also a beautiful tribute to a very beautiful person. What would we all do without her?

I couldn't bear to go to the burial. I just sat on my own in the churchyard, fingering the gold bracelet which I'd kept hold of ever since Louise's mother had given it back to me. It was a damp, autumn day with a threat of rain in the air. As I waited I looked at the names on the ancient tombstones and tried not to think about what was happening to Louise just a short distance away. Many of the inscriptions were too worn to read, but a few could still be deciphered. They had all once been living, breathing people, like Louise. Now they were just names, etched into weathered stone. Lily Liversage and her sister Mary. Thomas Woods, lying alongside his wife, Eleanor Rigby.

Who were they? Would anybody remember their names?

A sudden breeze blew a few dry, crumpled leaves towards me along the path by the church. It wasn't particularly cold, but I felt myself starting to shiver.

We gathered in the church hall across the road for tea and sandwiches. Now that the funeral service and the dreadful business of the burial were over everybody seemed just a little less tense and sad. Family and friends were chatting away, and from time to time there were even some smiles and the sound of wistful laughter. People were telling stories, recalling their happy memories of Louise, and I kept telling myself that she would not have wanted us to be too sad.

The food and drinks had been laid out on four white-clothed, trestle tables which stood in a line across the back of a wooden stage at the far end of the hall. Pinned to the wall behind the stage were photographs of some of the local bands who had played at the regular Saturday night dances which were held in the hall. There were also a few old posters.

As I stood there, pouring myself a cup of tea, I scanned the pictures and posters looking for names which I might recognise. Anything to take my mind off things. The Remo Four. Howie and The Seniors. I'd certainly heard of them. Even The Undertakers were there.

On its own, in pride of place, there was a slightly crumpled picture of a skiffle band called The Quarrymen who'd apparently played at the St Peter's Church Fete in the late 1950s. For a moment I was mystified. Then I read the type-written card which had been carefully pinned alongside it.

'This is an early picture of John Lennon and his Quarrymen.
At the Church Fete, John Lennon first met Paul McCartney.'

So Louise's final resting place was close to where The Beatles, the band she had loved so much, had been born. She would never know. But somehow it felt right.

I sipped at my tea as the hall gradually became less crowded. I watched people saying their goodbyes before drifting off home. Then it was time to get into the black limousine for the short drive back to Penny Lane.

As we drove away from the church and turned down Beaconsfield Road towards the junction with Menlove Avenue Andy pointed out a large, gothic building which was visible behind some trees and a high sandstone wall, through some elaborate cast-iron gates. Boys in grey shirts and shorts were playing on the neatly-mown areas of grass to each side of the long driveway.

"That's The Salvation Army Children's Home," he said. "They call it Strawberry Field."

The funeral had been like a dream. It didn't really seem to be happening, although I knew it was. At times it was almost as if we were taking part in a film. As if it couldn't possibly be true.

Reality soon started to sink in, though. The days and the weeks passed in a blur. I couldn't face going to work. I couldn't even bring myself to let the boss know what had happened until he sent a letter, threatening me with the sack. I didn't care, anyway. Nothing seemed to matter without Louise. My whole world had fallen apart.

I knew that if there was such a place as heaven Louise would be up there. She was such a good person. In those first few weeks I'd happily have joined her if I could. You see God had let me down. Sitting in the hospital on my own I'd prayed. I'd made promises which I'm sure I'd have done my best to keep if Louise had lived. He didn't take any notice. The way I saw it, He'd let her die for no good reason.

For days on end I just sat around, doing nothing. I felt empty. Then I got angry. Very, very angry. I felt like breaking things up. Destroying them. In a strange way the senselessness of such an action would have made perfect sense. It would have been violent. Physical. And cathartic. On one very desperate day I nearly smashed up my guitar but it was about the only thing that was stopping me from going completely off the rails. So I spared it.

The lads were great, as you'd expect, but they couldn't really get inside my head and they soon grew tired of trying to understand. I didn't blame them. It must have been hard for them, trying to connect with someone who'd gone off into another world and didn't seem to be making any effort to return.

Soon my guitar was my only friend. Hour after hour I'd sit in my room, caressing the strings gently and telling it all my troubles. Songs poured out of me. Mostly garbage. But in such a situation even garbage seemed to help.

The world basically carried on without me.

* * *

'We apologise for interrupting your programme but we are bringing you an urgent news bulletin from America. President Kennedy and Governor John Connolly of Texas were shot today as the President's motorcade left the centre of Dallas. President Kennedy has been rushed to hospital where his condition is being assessed by doctors. Witnesses say that when he arrived at the hospital he was slumped face down on the back seat of his car and they could see blood on his head, but there is as yet no definite news on the seriousness of his injuries. We will bring you further information as soon as it becomes available.'

It was Friday 22nd November 1963 and I was sitting with the boss in the front of the firm's van as we returned from a job. I was back at work. My parents had explained things to him and he'd persuaded them that it might help. He'd been very understanding, and he hadn't been pushing me to do much. I still wasn't right, but I'd managed to get in for three days that week and things were slowly getting better.

He took his left hand off the steering wheel and increased the volume on the car radio so we could hear the news bulletin more clearly.

"Holy cow!" he said. "It'll be those bleedin' Commies, gettin' their own back for Cuba. You just wait and see, son. I hope to God they haven't gone an' fuckin' killed 'im."

He didn't often swear, but under the circumstances it was perhaps understandable.

As soon as I got home I wanted to phone Louise and tell her what had happened. But of course I couldn't.

Why did this news seem to matter so much? It was all taking place a long way away, over on the other side of the Atlantic. It probably wouldn't affect us that much in England. Yet somehow it seemed personal, and incredibly important. Years later we would all be able to remember exactly where we were, and exactly what we were doing, when the news came through.

I'd not been near a radio since the initial bulletin but my Dad was able to tell me more.

"They've been saying on the news that President Kennedy is dead. And Lyndon Johnson's going to be sworn in as President sometime in the next few hours. What's the world coming to? I can't believe it."

Who would want to do such a thing? Was it the Russians? Or the Cuban communists? And if so, what did they hope to achieve, apart from revenge, by carrying out such an act? Or was it just some lone nutter? I couldn't make sense of it.

Over the next few hours and days, as the suspected assassin, Lee Harvey Oswald, was arrested, and then shot dead by a Dallas club owner called Jack Ruby while he was supposed to be in police custody, it became increasingly obvious that nobody else really knew what was going on either. Or if they did they weren't going to be telling us.

It was all very sad. Especially for his wife, Jackie, and the two little children. They were the ones who were really going to suffer. And I knew how they would be feeling. As I watched the little boy, on TV, saluting his father's coffin I felt I could understand the Kennedy family's loss and their awful sadness. And for some strange reason, that helped me to cope with losing Louise.

Sixteen

THE QUARRYMEN

Phillips Sound Recording Services at 38, Kensington, near the centre of Liverpool, was a small, and rather basic, recording studio. Mr Percy Phillips had set it up in the mid-nineteen fifties in the front living room of his terraced house. I'd decided to record four of my own songs and, carrying my guitar and a few sheets of paper with the lyrics and chords scribbled down on them, I somewhat nervously introduced myself to Mr Phillips.

He showed me into the sitting room in which stood a piano. The house was old, and a slightly damp, musty smell permeated the whole building. The carpeted room had been sound-proofed with heavy blankets which effectively cut off any outside ventilation. They hung over the door and window to keep out the traffic noise from a busy main road which ran just a few feet away from the front of the house. A speaker and microphone had been positioned inside an upturned bath to act as a home-made, but very effective, echo chamber.

The recording equipment consisted of a four-way mixing desk, a Vortexion tape recorder, an HMV ribbon mike, another Reslo microphone, an amplifier and loudspeaker, an electric spring reverb unit, and an acetate cutting machine manufactured by Master Sound Systems. Mr Percy Phillips, who looked well into his late sixties and was wearing a slightly worn, white shirt and dark blue tie beneath an everyday grey suit, looked me up and down.

"Four songs you say? Just you. Singing with your guitar. One take for each song and no mixing. That'll be seven and sixpence for each song. Thirty shillings in all. Payable before we start."

I passed him three ten shilling notes which he checked carefully before folding them in half and slipping them into his back pocket.

"There's been a few smart Alecs turn up here thinking if they don't pay me 'til the end, when the acetate's been cut, they can name their own price. I only fell for it once."

Within a couple of minutes he had two microphones set up.

"Okay son. You just start singing and playing your guitar. Into the microphones. Anything you like while I sort out the sound levels and balance. Then we'll be ready to go. Once I'm happy with everything it'll be just one take on each song. So you'll have to get it right first time. With it being just a voice and guitar it shouldn't take long."

He moved to the side of the room and plugged the two microphones into the mixing desk.

"Making records for these rock and roll groups who come in here and fill up the whole room with all their amplifiers and drums takes ages, I can tell you. I charge them a couple of pounds for each song. More sometimes if I don't like the look of them. So you're getting a good deal."

He continued to chunter away as he busied himself with the recording equipment.

"You know that singer Billy Fury? Nice lad, but a bit shy. He was in here three or four years ago. Just him and his guitar. Like you. He seems to have done alright for himself. These days it's all rock and roll groups. Like those young lads that everyone seems to be going on about at the moment. The Beatles. They've been in here as well. A couple of years ago it was. They called themselves something different then, though"

He stopped for a moment and trawled through his memory, scratching the back of his head as he did so.

"The Quarrymen. That's it. I remember telling them I thought it was a good name. I don't know why they changed it. The Beatles sounds bloody daft to me."

He shook his head as if it was all a mystery to him. Then, after making a couple of final adjustments, he took his place behind the desk and nodded to me.

"Right. Whenever you're ready we can get on with the first song."

As Mr Phillips had predicted the job was soon done. In less than an hour I was back out in the road clutching my precious 45 rpm record, a double-sided acetate with two songs on each side. I couldn't wait to get it home and play it. I wouldn't be saying anything to the lads, though. Even if they thought it was okay they'd feel obliged to take the mickey. And the way I'd been feeling I could do without that.

* * *

"The songs all sound pretty good bearing in mind it's just a demo disc and not a finished record," said my Mum approvingly. "I think I like the one about the swallows flying down south the best."

"Louise liked that one too," I said. "'*Come summer I may see you again*' it's called. I played it to her on my guitar just after I'd written it."

"You miss her a lot, don't you." She looked at me with her soft, blue eyes. "Even though you hardly ever talk about her."

I shrugged my shoulders. "It's easier that way. A lot of the time I feel like there's a big, empty hole inside me. It's really hard.

But she'd have been the first one to say life has to go on. She was the one who said I should try and do something with my songs."

"Play it again, just that one."

I put the acetate back on the turntable and lowered the stylus gently onto the track. My Mum, who'd always enjoyed singing, started to hum the tune quietly as it played.

"Yes. I definitely like the words, and it's a nice tune as well. It might even have passed The Old Grey Whistle Test."

I had no idea what she was talking about. "What's that?"

"It's how the New York music publishers tested out their new songs back in the thirties and forties. They'd play them to the grey-haired chaps they employed as doormen. And if the old guys could whistle the tune after one hearing it meant it was catchy enough to be a hit."

"How on earth do you know that?" I said. "I've never heard of it."

"The Reader's Digest. Your Dad brings me up a copy from the shop now and then. It's a mine of random information. Most of it useless. Anyway. Now you've got your songs on record you should get some people in the music business to listen to them. You know. Publishers. Down in London. They'll be able to tell you if they're any good."

"I wouldn't want to just send the record off to someone in the post though," I said. "I mightn't get it back. It's the only copy I've got, and Dad says they're all sharks down there."

"Your father has never trusted anyone when it comes to money. And I have to say he's probably right." She was silent for a moment or two. "Why don't you take it down to London yourself? You could call in on some of the music publishers and see if they'll listen to it. They can only say no, after all. Your Dad's sister, you know, Jeannie. She lives down in London. I'm sure she wouldn't mind you staying with her for a day or two. I could give her a ring. She lives in Chalk Farm. I've never been down there, but I think she once said it's not far from the West End on the tube. Do you remember her daughter? Your cousin Claire. She's a nice girl. Attractive too, judging by the holiday snaps Jeannie showed us when she was up here last year. Maybe she'd tag along with you? There's nothing like a pretty girl to help open doors and influence people."

I nodded my head. "That's not a bad idea. I might give it a go."

Rushworth's Music House, just off Williamson Square, had the largest selection of sheet music in Liverpool and I spent half an hour in there, jotting down the addresses of London music publishers. Alongside the racks of sheet music a huge selection of guitars and drums were on display. They'd taken over from pianos as the store's top selling instruments and I stood there, breathing in the smell of the newly-varnished wood.

On one wall, opposite the door, there was a framed, black and white photograph of John Lennon and George Harrison, each holding a very fine-looking, Gibson J-160E, electro-acoustic guitar. Looking to steal a march on Frank Hessy, who was Liverpool's other well-known musical instrument stockist, James Rushworth had arranged for a photographer from the local press to be present when John and George called in to pick up the guitars which had been flown in that morning from Chicago. It wasn't obvious from a distance, but a close look at the picture revealed that George was still sporting the remains of the black eye he'd received when he was head-butted at The Cavern after the sacking of Pete Best.

Most of the London music publishers seemed to be based in Denmark Street in the West End, just off Charing Cross Road. Hopefully it wouldn't be too difficult to visit several of them in the course of a day and get an opinion on the songs, with or without the added attraction of my pretty cousin Claire.

Seventeen

DENMARK STREET

On a frosty December morning, just a couple of weeks later, I found myself walking along Denmark Street. Claire, who was as attractive as my Mum had promised, had readily agreed to accompany me and I looked at her as she checked each door to see if it was a music publisher's office. At about five foot eight she was fairly tall which allowed her to wear light brown boots without heels. Her straight blonde hair reached down to the middle of her back and she was wearing a bright orange top with matching jeans. Just as we were leaving the house she'd added a thick, white sweater to keep out the worst of the cold.

Denmark Street, back then at the end of 1963, was London's Tin Pan Alley, home to most of the UK's biggest music publishers. Three and four storey, brick-built buildings, some dating back to the eighteenth century, lined each side of the narrow side-street which had received its name in honour of Prince George of Denmark, husband of the then reigning British monarch, Queen Anne. Most of the buildings had once been smart homes, but over the years they had been converted into offices, many of them now slightly run-down, with glazed shop-fronts on the ground floor.

The street was quiet. There were no pedestrians about. Just a couple of slightly grubby, white delivery vans parked with two wheels on the pavement.

We stood outside Number Four.

"It says here 'Essex Music'", said Claire. She tried the door, but it was locked. "Shall I ring the bell?"

I shrugged my shoulders. "No harm in trying, I suppose."

She pressed the very ancient-looking, ivory-coloured button on the door frame. We could hear a bell ringing inside but there was no sign of life. At Number Eight we found Southern Music but once again there was no reply. It was the same story at Mills Music, Box and Cox, and Campbell Connolly. I looked at my watch. It was just before ten.

"We might be a bit on the early side," I said. "Musicians aren't exactly renowned for being morning people. Maybe music publishers are the same?"

Over the street, at Number Nine, was The Gioconda Cafe. The door was open.

"Let's grab a coffee," said Claire. "They should be able to tell us what time the street wakes up."

The cafe was empty. A girl behind the counter told us that she'd been open since nine and we were her first customers. We sat on a couple of stools and ordered two cappuccinos.

"Where are you guys from?"

"I'm Tony," I said, "from Liverpool. Claire here is my cousin. She's a Londoner. Chalk Farm."

"Wow. Liverpool." Poor Claire was ignored as the girl turned towards me. "That's a pretty cool place at the moment." She carried on talking as she prepared the coffees. "I'm Tina. My boyfriend's in a band and he's been talking about taking a trip up there to see what's going on. It must be great actually living there."

Turning away from the Gaggia Coffee Machine, which was still dripping fresh coffee into the small cups she had positioned beneath two curved metal spouts, Tina placed a couple of saucers, each with a macaroon biscuit balanced on the side, upon the Formica counter.

"So what's brought you down to boring old London?"

"I'm just here for a couple of days," I said. "Staying with Claire. We're trying to get someone to listen to a few songs I've written."

The Gaggia started hissing and Tina turned away to finish off our drinks as the smell of freshly-prepared coffee drifted towards us. After dusting them with some chocolate powder she placed them on the saucers, alongside the macaroons.

"So, you're the next wave of The Mersey Sound then?" she said, giving us a grin.

Claire decided it was time she said something. "We don't know yet. The songs aren't bad. Tony played them to me last night. Hopefully someone might be interested, but unless he's very lucky I don't think he's going to create that big a wave."

They both laughed. What could I say? Claire was just being honest.

"Well, good luck anyway," said Tina. "Most of the music publishers won't be in 'til lunchtime so you might as well take a wander through Soho. With it being so chilly you'd probably be best carrying on to Oxford Street and nipping into one of the big stores for an hour or two. There's not much happening round here at this time of day."

When we'd finished our coffees we took Tina's advice and headed for Soho which was a few minutes away on the other side of Charing Cross Road. The early morning street cleaners were hard at work, picking up the debris from the previous evening and tidying the narrow alleyways. A few cafes and ethnic food stores were open, but the majority of the shops were locked and shuttered. Neon lights which twinkled above them told us that most of them, along with the nightclubs whose doors were also firmly barred, made their money from Soho's traditional trade. As I looked around I couldn't help thinking of Steve. He'd have been like a kid in a sweet shop. That's not to say I was completely uninterested, mind you.

As we made our way along Greek Street towards Soho Square we noticed a figure leaning against a peeling doorway. Thick make-up made it difficult to tell her age, but she was certainly no spring chicken. She was wearing a tight, leather skirt and a low-cut, black top which didn't leave much to the imagination, as was doubtless intended. She took a couple of steps towards us.

"You two youngsters look like you've got half an hour to spare." Her voice was husky and deep, suggesting many years' over-indulgence in both alcohol and tobacco. "I could give you a good time. Something a bit different. It'd only cost you a couple of quid."

I glanced at my cousin. "What do you reckon? It'd help pass the time."

She looked at me, horrified. I grabbed her arm and pulled her away.

"Sorry. Just kidding. Scouse humour. Honest. God knows what we might catch off her. We'd better not get too close."

Fortunately Claire got the joke and we hurried off, laughing, through Soho Square and onto Oxford Street.

"I don't know about you," she said as we stopped for breath. "It's a bit early for lunch, but I'm hungry. Why don't we grab something to eat? Then we'll have the whole afternoon free."

When we returned to Denmark Street a couple of hours later things were much livelier. The shops had removed the wooden shutters and most of the first floor offices were lit up. The door bells now produced a response, but when we got inside it was the same story every time. Even when we said we were from Liverpool.

"Unfortunately there's nobody available to see you now. But if you send us a tape or a demo of your songs we'll certainly listen to them. We're always on the look-out for new material."

We were about to give up and go home when Claire spotted a typewritten notice taped to the inside of a rather grubby, glazed door right at the end of the street.

SONG-WRITERS WANTED!!
OUR RECORDING ARTISTES ARE LOOKING
FOR SONGS!!
RIGHT NOW!! APPLY WITHIN!!

She looked at me. "What do you think? It doesn't look very professional, but we've still got a bit of time left. Do you want to give it a try?"

There was no bell, but the door was unlocked. We made our way up some ancient wooden stairs to a second floor office. A heavily made-up, blonde lady with startlingly red lips, who looked about thirty years of age and who we guessed must be the receptionist, was perched on a stool behind a small counter. Dressed in an extremely tight, white blouse, which showed off her ample cleavage to quite stunning effect, she was busily engaged in applying a fresh coat of black varnish to her long fingernails. She looked up and gave us a smile as we walked in.

"Hello there. I'm Sylvia. What can I do for you?"

"We've got a recording of some songs," I said, holding up the acetate. "We were wondering if anybody might be interested in having a listen to it."

"Well, that's what we're here for. Give me a minute." She gave her nails a quick blow before picking up an ivory-coloured telephone. "Isaac, love. I've got a young couple out here who say they've got some songs for us."

She listened to the reply, then gave us a smile and nodded her head.

"Mr Levy'll be with you shortly."

A couple of moments later the door behind her opened and a slightly overweight, middle-aged man in white shirt-sleeves and dark trousers appeared. His face was tanned and his receding, dark hair, neatly parted on the left, was plastered tightly to his scalp with what smelt like a generous application of Brylcream. He walked round the counter towards us with his right arm outstretched. Claire and I both shook his slightly damp hand.

"Good afternoon to you both. You've brought some songs along for me to listen to, I believe. What have you got with you? A tape?"

"No. They're on an acetate. It was recorded up in Liverpool."

"Liverpool, eh. In that case I definitely want to hear them. There's some good stuff coming out of your city at the moment. Come on in."

We followed him into his office and I handed him the acetate. He removed the cellophane cover then looked at the white cardboard sleeve which had a list of the songs typed on it.

"Two on each side?"

I nodded as he removed the sleeve.

"Before we make a start," he said, "let's get to know each other. My name's Isaac Levy."

"I'm Tony Cooper," I replied. "And this is Claire Phillips, my cousin."

"And the two of you write together?"

"No," I said. "It's just me."

Isaac Levy looked over at Claire. "While you provide encouragement and moral support?"

Claire nodded agreement. "I've listened to the songs," she said, sounding slightly nervous. "They're good."

After her slightly lukewarm comments earlier to Tina, her support was much appreciated.

"That's great to hear. Song-writing can be a lonely business unless there's someone to listen to the end results and make positive comments." He placed the acetate on a Garrard turntable which sat on his desk. "Right then, let's see what these songs sound like."

He turned on a Leak amplifier which was next to the turntable. A couple of expensive-looking monitor speakers were attached to the wall behind him. Very gently he lowered the stylus onto the groove and the first song started to play.

I saw you last night.

You were crying. It was my fault and I knew.

Crying. Crying.

Isaac Levy sat completely still, playing with his lower lip and listening intently, but offering no clue at all as to what he was thinking. The second song then followed.

Leaves are turning brown. Soon come tumbling down.

I must go. I must go.

Now I must be moving on again, like a swallow flying gracefully.

Far south I go, leaving you I know.

Come summer I may see you again. Come summer I may see you again.

He continued to squeeze his lower lip between his finger and thumb. He was thinking.

"I have to be honest," he said, after a brief pause. "I wasn't impressed by the first song." He paused again. "But the second one is more promising. Before I say anything else let's take a listen to the other side."

The acetate was flipped over. This time Mr Levy lifted the stylus off the record before the last song had even finished. He didn't waste any time in giving his opinion.

"The only song which I think might be of interest to me is the second one. I know Nina and Frederik's agent here in the U.K. and I'd very much like him to hear it. It's the type of song they might want to consider. Could you leave the acetate with me? Or would you be happier if I made a copy? That second song is all I need."

I looked over towards Claire. "What do you think?"

"A copy'd be okay. Mr Levy's got to have something to play to Nina and Frederik's agent."

What she was saying was obviously sensible. If I wanted to get the song recorded I couldn't just keep it to myself.

"Okay," I said. "It'd be great if you could get them to listen to it. I'd like to hang onto the acetate if you don't mind. But a copy'd be fine."

In less than ten minutes Mr Levy had copied the song onto a quarter inch tape and my original acetate was safely back in its sleeve. He stood up and shook us both by the hand.

"If you'd like to leave your name and address and a contact phone number with Sylvia I'll be in touch as soon as I've got any news."

As we wandered back along Denmark Street to Leicester Square and caught the tube back to Chalk Farm I felt slightly dazed. "Do you think he really knows Nina and Frederik's agent?"

Claire shrugged. "Who knows? Your guess is as good as mine. But I can't see why he'd say he knows him if he doesn't." She looked at me thoughtfully before continuing. "It's strange. I didn't say anything to you but I thought it'd be a good song for Nina and Frederik when you played it to me last night. Then Mr Levy comes up with their names without us mentioning them. Is that weird or what?"

"My girlfriend, Louise. The one who died. She mentioned Nina and Frederik too. When I played it to her on my guitar. Maybe it's an omen. We'll just have to wait and see."

Even though Claire was my cousin I'd not seen her for several years. Slightly to my surprise I'd enjoyed spending time with her. Perhaps the world could carry on without Louise? And at least my trip to London hadn't drawn a complete blank.

Eighteen

DOING THE RIGHT THING

Eric was sitting at his usual table in The Liver, enjoying a quiet pint on his own. He looked at me as I walked in and pulled up a chair. I had some news for him.

"Dave's being done for nicking records from N.E.M.S. The idiot had about half a dozen LPs under his coat. I was with him but I never noticed what he was up to or I'd have stopped him. One of the shop assistants pulled us up as we were walking out of the shop and called the police. They took us down to the Bridewell in Cheapside but they let me go after they'd asked a few questions. Dave's going to be charged though. Even though all he'd got on him was a few outer covers. N.E.M.S. aren't daft. They take the records out of the sleeves and store 'em behind the counter."

Eric looked concerned. "Where is 'e now?"

"Still down at The Bridewell. They're going to keep him in the cells overnight. To teach him a bit of a lesson I suppose. He'll be up before the Magistrates in Dale Street tomorrow morning."

"Does Yvonne know?"

"I've no idea. I suppose Dave must've told someone he wouldn't be home. If the police let him that is."

"D'yer think we should get in touch with 'er? Just in case."

I shook my head. "I don't really want to get involved. We might say the wrong thing. She's pregnant and I don't want to give her a shock."

"Who is?"

"Yvonne. Dave's got her pregnant. He was telling me about it just before we got stopped in N.E.M.S. He's not thinking straight. He said his folks went completely berserk. They've told him he's got to marry her before anyone finds out. The wedding's supposed to be at Mount Pleasant next week." I hesitated for a moment. "God knows what'll happen now though. The whole thing might be off. He'll have a criminal record by this time tomorrow. And I suppose if he's really unlucky he could even end up in jail."

Eric shook his head. "Poor Dave. His boss isn't gonna be impressed either. With it bein' N.E.M.S. it could easily end up in the Echo. Nickin' records off the guy who manages The Beatles would make a nice, juicy headline."

I stood up and pointed at Eric's almost empty glass. "Ready for another?"

"Thanks, Tone."

When I returned from the bar we sat there, supping our beers and talking about Dave.

"I still can't believe it," said Eric. "Are yer goin' along to Court tomorrow?"

"I don't have any choice. I've got to be there at ten. The police said the magistrates might want to ask me a few questions. Anyway Dave's been my mate for years even though we've not been seeing that much of each other since he fell out with Steve. The least I can do is go along and give him a bit of support."

"Be careful what yer say if they start askin' questions."

"Don't worry, Eric. I honestly didn't have any idea what Dave was up to. So there's nothing really I can say."

"All the same," he said. "They're crafty these lawyers. They twist things round an' put words in yer mouth."

I turned up at the Magistrates' Court as requested and sat around for a couple of hours waiting for Dave's case to be called. Just when it was looking like I might be there for the whole day one of the ushers came out into the corridor and told me the case was about to begin.

The walls of the court-room, which dated back to Victorian times, were lined with dark-coloured wood panelling. Around the perimeter of the room were long, wooden benches which matched the panelling, each with ornately-carved arms at the end. Above the panelling the walls were painted a stark white. Five large windows threw light onto the wooden dock in which Dave was already standing, holding tightly onto a brass rail which ran around the top. He looked very pale and anxious. It was pretty obvious he hadn't had much sleep.

I took a seat on one of the benches, but almost as soon as I had got myself comfortable a shout of "Be upstanding" rang out and three magistrates entered the room. They took their places on raised chairs, directly in front of Dave.

On the advice of the duty solicitor Dave pleaded guilty and, as a first offender, he got fined twenty-five pounds. It doesn't sound much now, but it wasn't far short of Dave's weekly wage back then. The stony-faced battle-axe of a lady magistrate, who'd taken a position between the two much smaller men making up the trio, was obviously running the show. She looked as though she'd gladly have sent him to the gallows. But she had to settle for a stern warning that any further similar offences would mean a definite prison sentence. After pausing to let her words sink in she told Dave he was free to go.

He still looked bewildered as we made our way along the wide, covered passageway which had been constructed back in Victorian times to allow magistrates to enter the building without having to alight from their elegant, horse-drawn coaches. It would take us out onto Dale Street. And freedom.

"Thanks Tone. I appreciate you coming. I won't do this to you again, I promise. I dunno what came over me. I've never tried to nick anythin' before. I was just flickin' through the LPs an' all I could think about was Yvonne bein' pregnant. I've no idea what made me put 'em inside me jacket. I wasn't even lookin' at 'em really."

"Come on. It's not a problem. Let's go and grab a bite to eat. And a stiff drink too. You look as though you could do with one."

We walked down Dale Street towards the river before turning right into Hackins Hey, a narrow, cobbled street which dated back at least two hundred and fifty years. We were heading for Liverpool's oldest pub, '*Ye Hole in Ye Wall*'.

"I rang me folks from The Bridewell yesterday afternoon," said Dave as we sat down with our pints. "I told 'em I 'ad to take a delivery across the Pennines to Leeds an' I'd be stayin' overnight. They know last minute jobs turn up from time to time so they didn't ask too many questions. They said they'd let Yvonne know so I didn't 'ave to speak to 'er myself. Good job really. She'd've sussed out straight away I was coverin' something up."

After a couple of pints and a cheese and tomato sandwich we made our way up Hackins Hey to Exchange Station and picked up a copy of that evening's Liverpool Echo. We were expecting the worst, but to our relief Dave's case wasn't mentioned. And that's how it stayed. It was mid-December, the season of good-will. The only thing the editor of the Echo wanted was stories about Christmas.

Dave had got away with it. But he still had to get married.

●-●━━━━●-●-●-●━━━━●-●

The wedding day was overcast and bitterly cold. Sleet was falling as we walked down the hill, past the side of The Adelphi Hotel, from Mount Pleasant Register Office where John and Cynthia Lennon had, not that long before, also exchanged their vows in almost complete secrecy. There was just a week to go before Christmas and we were making our way to the cafeteria on the fifth floor of Lewis's Department Store where a table had been reserved for us in one corner. The large room was packed with noisy office parties, and the atmosphere was very festive.

Yvonne was very quiet, even though she looked as attractive as ever in a loose, off-white dress which disguised her pregnancy. Her face was as white as a sheet.

"How's the bride?" I said, planting a kiss on her cheek which still felt cold from the short walk down the hill.

"Feeling a bit sick, I'm afraid. The midwife says it should start to get better in a few weeks. Once I get to about four months." She glanced towards the table and gave me a wan smile. "I don't think I'll be eating much."

I couldn't help feeling sorry for her. And for Dave too. Okay, he'd got her pregnant. And, just like John Lennon and Cynthia, they were doing what, in those days, was seen as the right thing by getting married. But even so it was a pretty miserable way to start their life together.

To round off what hadn't been the best of days, I got home to find a letter from Isaac Levy waiting for me. He'd played my song to Nina and Frederik's agent who didn't think it was right for them. The only slight consolation was that the letter said he'd still like his company, Levy Music Management, to publish the song. He was hopeful he could place it with somebody else and the necessary contract was enclosed for me to sign if I was agreeable. I posted it back to him, duly signed, but I didn't let myself get too excited. I wasn't expecting anything to come of it.

Over Christmas and New Year I couldn't stop thinking about Louise. They say the first Christmas and the first birthday are the hardest, so I just hoped that after Valentine's Day things would start to get better. But it wasn't at all easy to see how they could.

Steve took Tracey down to London to celebrate the start of 1964. Brian Epstein was putting on a 'Beatles Christmas Show' at The Astoria in Finsbury Park and they'd managed to get hold of a couple of tickets. When Eric and I met up with him after their return to Liverpool his verdict was lukewarm.

"Tracey enjoyed it, but most of it wasn't that great to be honest. Cilla Black was on the bill. She's the girl we saw singin' with Kingsize Taylor at The Institute in Aintree. She was called Cilla White back then but Brian Epstein changed 'er name when 'e signed 'er up. She's just released a Lennon and McCartney song called '*Love of the Loved*', which wasn't bad. The Barron Knights were okay too. But then we 'ad to sit through Rolf Harris doin' 'is usual stuff. You know. '*Sun Arise*' with 'is bleedin' wobble board, an' then 'im blowin' into that didgeridoo thing. I honestly don't get what people see in 'im.

"'E's a bit different, I suppose," said Eric. "An' with The Beatles toppin' the bill Brian Epstein knew the show'd be a sell-out. So I don't suppose 'e was that bothered about who else 'e booked."

Steve nodded his head. "An' I do have to admit The Beatles were amazin'. It was worth it just for the set they did at the end. Me an' Tracey was quite near the front an' a lot of the girls around us was standin' on their seats goin' crazy. One or two of 'em were even tryin' to chuck their knickers onto the stage. It was mental."

Eric downed a large mouthful of beer. "Bloody Norah, Steve." It was difficult to tell whether he was shocked or excited. "I can't imagine your Tracey doin' anythin' like that."

I placed my hand on top of Steve's pint.

"Just remember what happened to Dave," I said quietly.

Eric remembered. "Oh, yeah. I mean, er, no. Right. Sorry Steve."

Steve removed my hand from his drink and picked it up. "I said one or two of 'em, Eric. The girls didn't all take their knickers off. It wasn't compulsory."

Eric gave a nervous laugh as Steve took a couple of sips from his pint. "Sorry Steve. I didn't mean anythin' about Tracey. I'm sure she kept 'er knickers on. Well, at least while the two of yer was at The Astoria anyway."

Steve leaned forwards in his chair and looked Eric in the eye.

"When yer in a hole it's usually best to stop diggin', Eric. Yer a good mate, an' I like yer mostly. But yer can be a real dick'ead sometimes."

●·————●·●·●·●————··●

Valentine's Day would have been Louise's eighteenth birthday and I knew the only way I was going to cope was by keeping busy. After work I went to see one of my Dad's friends, Mr Simpson, who ran a small fruit and vegetable shop. I'd been thinking for a while about getting myself some wheels, and he was selling a Mini-van which he'd been using to transport stock. With the business expanding he needed something bigger and he'd heard from my Dad that I was after some sort of vehicle. With a black roof and red bodywork it looked really smart. And it had just twenty-four thousand miles on the clock.

"Your Dad's been a good mate to me, Tony. He's helped me out a few times over the years and it's a sound little van. I wouldn't even think of sellin' it to you if it wasn't. It's yours for a hundred and sixty quid."

After a quick drive round the block we shook hands on the deal. It was indeed a sound little van. Louise would have loved it.

On the first Sunday in April 1964 Steve and I were sitting in the flat looking at the newspapers which had been delivered that morning. Two months earlier The Beatles had flown to New York and appeared on the Ed Sullivan Show in New York. And now they were all over the front pages. American teenagers had gone crazy over them. Their records held the top five places on the Billboard Hot 100, and altogether they had a dozen singles in the American charts. Their first two American LPs 'Meet The Beatles' and 'Introducing The Beatles' were at Number One and Number Two in the U.S. album charts. Nothing remotely like it had ever been done before. Not even by Elvis. No wonder they were making headlines.

Everything had happened so quickly. It was just over three years since we'd first seen them at Litherland Town Hall and thought they were from Germany. And it was less than two years since we'd bumped into them in the Kardomah. Hardly anyone had given them a second glance that morning. Now they were well on their way to becoming just about the most famous faces on the planet.

"Four lads from Liverpool, eh?" said Steve. "Knockin' the socks off 'em in America."

Four days later we were at Anfield. It was all happening. The Beatles were conquering America and now our team was heading for the very top of English football. Our opponents that day were Arsenal. One more victory and the First Division title was ours.

We arrived at the ground very early and this time we got it right. The queues were long and the gates were closed an hour before kick-off. According to the official count from the turnstiles there were 48,623 happy supporters, including the three of us, in the ground. It was party time. On the Kop we all swayed backwards and forwards, up and down the terracing, singing and carousing as kick-off approached.

'*We're gonna win the league. We're gonna win the league*

Ee – aye – addio, we're gonna win the league.'

All the traditional chants were chanted and all the usual songs were sung.

Then, as the teams were about to emerge onto the pitch, the unmistakable voice of Gerry Marsden rang out from the Tannoy speakers far above the heads of the twenty-five thousand ardent home fans who were packed tightly together on The Kop.

The hairs stood up on the back of my neck as every Liverpool voice joined in with him and sang the almost unbelievably emotional lyrics of '*You'll Never Walk Alone*'. Thousands of red and white scarves were held aloft and huge flags were waved over our heads. It was an exhilarating, uplifting sound that echoed around the stands and filled the ground.

As the greatest of all football anthems reached its glorious finale the Arsenal players, standing in the tunnel beneath the main stand, must have been quaking in their boots. Like gladiators in ancient times they were about to face a packed stadium and an uncertain fate.

Arsenal won the toss and chose to defend the Kop goal. In the opening exchanges Liverpool were untypically anxious and nervy. The defence was not as solid as usual. Then, in the sixth minute, Ian St John raced like an arrow onto a through pass from Alf Arrowsmith and slid the ball into the Arsenal net. We were ahead, and you could feel the crowd relax. The title was within our grasp.

But it was not going to be that easy. After twenty-nine minutes, Ronnie Yeats, normally so assured in defence, was outwitted by George Eastham who flicked the ball up and over the giant defender's head. Yeats was beaten, and he was forced to handle the ball to prevent a certain goal. It was a clear penalty, right in front of the Arsenal supporters in the Anfield Road Stand.

We all watched from the Kop, holding our collective breath, as Eastham rotated the ball in his hands before placing it on the spot. A sweet, left-footed shot headed low towards the net, aimed just inside Tommy Lawrence's right hand post. The Liverpool goalkeeper looked beaten, but somehow he managed to fling himself across the goal and palm the ball away for a corner. Poor George Eastham held his head in his hands as Anfield erupted.

The close shave seemed to energise the Liverpool players. Arrowsmith scored a second goal nine minutes later, and three more goals in the second half, two from Peter Thompson and one from Roger Hunt, completed what was, in the end, a very comfortable victory.

The chants were now 'We won the league.' 'We won the league.'

The shouts were for 'Shankly' 'Shankly' 'Shankly' and 'Yeats' 'Yeats' 'Yeats'.

The two heroes eventually emerged with the rest of the players to a deafening reception from the still-packed stands. A lady who was standing close to the edge of the pitch joyously waved a magnum of champagne in the air and big Ron Yeats, ever the gentleman, strode over and relieved her of the weight of the bottle. The crowd roared as the players performed a victory lap, waving to their ecstatic fans.

Once his players had completed their circuit Bill Shankly made his way across the pitch towards the Kop end. Arms aloft, he stood in front of the sea of supporters as they surged up and down the terraces like a living tide. In just three seasons he had delivered exactly what he had promised when he moved from Huddersfield Town to become Liverpool's new manager.

His Liverpool team were the champions of England. It was no longer just The Beatles who were giving the city a name.

Nineteen

FIONA

It was a Thursday afternoon in mid-July and the Kardomah was busy. I'd been doing a wiring job in a lawyer's office in Stanley Street and it had turned out to be much more straightforward than expected. There was time for a quick coffee in town before heading home.

I sat on a stool by the window and listened idly to the conversations which drifted my way.

"D'yer fancy goin' along to Speke Airport tomorrow to see The Beatles? They're flyin' up from London for the Northern Premiere of this film they've made called 'A Hard Day's Night'. It's at The Odeon in London Road. They're sayin' in the papers there's goin' to be loads of people there to welcome them home to Liverpool."

"You've gotta be jokin'. If you wanna see The Beatles all you need to do is open yer bloody paper. That's all they seem to write about these days. Sometimes yer'd think nothin' else 'appens in the world. To be perfectly honest I'm gettin' a bit browned off with it."

"Me too. Me brother ses they're just four scruffy layabouts from Liverpool who struck lucky."

"Come on. That's not fair. Their records are brilliant. An' the way they're jettin' all about the place must be bloody hard work.

I don't reckon they're layabouts even though all this Beatlemania stuff is gettin' a bit out of hand. Ever since they made it big in America people seem to think they're prophets or somethin'. It's like some sort of new religion."

"What's all this crap about welcomin' them back home to Liverpool anyway. All they're doin' is flyin' in to Speke on some fancy private plane an' goin' to a reception at the Town Hall. Which we'll be payin' for with our taxes by the way. An' then they'll be goin' over to the Odeon to watch 'emselves in a film. After that it's back to London. They won't be in the city for more than four or five hours. Liverpool's not their home anymore. They've abandoned us."

"I shouldn't think many people'll be turnin' out to see 'em on a Friday evenin' anyway. I certainly won't. I've got better things to do with me time."

I didn't say anything. I was tempted to butt in and say what an amazing job The Beatles were doing, putting Liverpool on the map throughout the world, making the city famous. But I didn't. I just sat there and listened.

Why couldn't they see that The Beatles could be one of the best things that ever happened to Liverpool? All they wanted to do was make sarcastic comments and moan about them moving down to London. What they should be doing was making the most of the opportunity. '*The Birthplace of The Beatles*.' What bigger or better slogan could any city possibly have?

• •• ————— • •• • •• • ————— •• •

I've got to admit I might have thought about going along to the airport myself, just out of interest, but I'd already arranged to meet up with a girl who worked at The Jacaranda. We'd spoken briefly when I went there with Louise, after our visit to the cathedral, and for a couple of months we'd found ourselves chatting over the counter whenever I'd called in. As she'd mentioned to me when we first spoke, she was a student at the Art College, and I'd finally plucked up the courage to ask her if she'd like to join me for a coffee. I couldn't help feeling guilty about it, but I told myself that Louise would understand. Life had to go on. She wouldn't have wanted me to stay on my own forever.

As I drove past The Empire Theatre in my Mini-van the pavements were packed with people, and fifty yards ahead the traffic was stationary. Every vantage point was taken. A few youngsters had climbed up the old-fashioned street lamps and were clinging on for dear life, while others had found themselves a perch on top of one of the smoke-blackened Victorian statues which decorated the wide plateau alongside St George's Hall.

I slowed down to a walking pace, and as I reached the corner by Lime Street Station I could see that the road junction ahead was blocked by a line of helmeted policemen. Looking in my mirror as I brought the Mini-van to a halt I could see that three or four other cars were already lining up behind me. There was no escape. All I could do was sit there and hope I wouldn't be held up for too long.

I got out of the van and stood beside it, trying to get a better look at what was causing the problem. As I did so a smart, black Rolls Royce, escorted by half a dozen police out-riders, glided across the junction. The occupants were waving to the crowds who were all shouting and cheering.

The scruffy layabouts had arrived home.

Almost as soon as the Rolls Royce had disappeared down the hill, heading towards Dale Street and the Town Hall, the police cleared the road and I was waved through. The crowds were soon behind me and by the time I reached Lewis's the road ahead was clear. The Jacaranda was just a couple of minutes away, with a free parking space right outside.

Fiona, the girl I was meeting, was already sitting at a table in the far corner, looking very attractive. When she was working she hid her dark hair beneath a white cap, and she had to wear a rather unflattering smock. But as I walked up to her I could see her hair curling down over the collar of a black jacket which was tailored to show off her slim figure. Tight, blue jeans and a pair of polished, black boots completed her outfit. I took off my coat and put it on the bench beside her.

"You look great," I said, giving her a smile. "I'll get a couple of coffees in. You haven't ordered anything yet have you?"

She shook her head, and as she did so I opened the black leather jacket I was wearing to show her the small flask which I'd slipped into an inside pocket before leaving home.

"Brandy," I said. "To liven the coffee up a bit. I hope that's okay."

She grinned. "As an employee here I should really shop you to the management. But the wages here aren't that great so I'll look the other way."

I brought the coffees over to the table and slipped a generous portion of alcohol into each one. They tasted good.

"Sorry I was a bit late," I said, sitting down on the bench next to her. "The Beatles are in town for the premiere of their film and I didn't realise it'd be so busy. Lime Street was heaving with people. The police had blocked off the road by St George's Hall and I had to wait while their big Rolls Royce cruised past. It was all flashing lights and police out-riders."

"Hardly surprising," said Fiona. "They're like royalty now."

"You wouldn't have thought so if you'd been in the Kardomah with me yesterday. All you could hear was people moaning about the way The Beatles had abandoned the city and gone to live in London."

"What's their problem?" Fiona looked surprised. "That's where everything happens in the music business. They've got to be down there."

"It's probably just a few miserable old buggers," I said, nodding to show my agreement. "If today's crowds are anything to go by, most of the people in Liverpool still think The Beatles are great. Someone on the car radio was saying over two hundred thousand people have turned out to see them. It'll be all over the news in America as well as here. It's great for the city. Someone said if you go over to the States at the moment you get treated like a minor celebrity. Just because you're from Liverpool."

"You might," said Fiona, "but not me. I'm a country bumpkin from Kent."

"But you know what I mean. You could easily pass for a Scouser anyway. Nobody'd know the difference in America."

She gave me a smile. "I was really pleased when you said you'd like to meet up." She paused for a moment. "I'd been wondering why you were always coming in here on your own."

"To chat you up."

"Come on now. Seriously."

I hesitated before replying, not sure whether to mention Louise.

"I used to have a girlfriend," I said. "But last year she got meningitis." I glanced at Fiona's face but I couldn't really tell what she was thinking. "We were out together in town and she suddenly got very ill. There wasn't anything the doctors could do for her."

"You mean she died?" Fiona looked shocked. "I'm so sorry. I didn't realise."

I knew immediately that I'd made a mistake. Fiona and I hardly knew each other. It wasn't fair to her.

"It's okay," I said, looking down at my coffee. "I shouldn't have said anything."

Fiona didn't speak. I lifted my head and caught her eye. "Her name was Louise. She'd probably have been starting at the Art College herself in September if she hadn't got ill."

"She'd have loved it," said Fiona quietly, taking a sip of her coffee. "We can talk about her if you like. I don't mind."

"Maybe one day," I said. "But not right now. I want to have a proper chat with you. Instead of just grabbing a quick word between customers." I gave her an apologetic smile.

She smiled back. "Okay. That's fine with me."

"How long have you been up here in Liverpool?"

"It'll be a year when college starts up again in September. We're in the middle of the summer break at the moment so I'm working pretty much full-time here at The Jacaranda."

"Didn't you want to go back home to Kent for the summer?"

Fiona shook her head. "I've got a bed-sit up here. Out Aigburth way. The landlord told me I'd have to keep paying for it over the summer if I wanted it for next year. And I already had this part-time job. So I decided I might as well hang on to it and earn a bit of extra cash. I've lived in Canterbury with my Mum's sister since I was thirteen. She's been very good to me but I'm afraid we don't get on that well."

"What about your parents?"

"My Mum died from breast cancer six years ago. That's how I came to end up with my aunt. My Dad was a ship's steward, but I don't really remember him. When I was about two he sailed off to The Philippines and never came back. According to my Mum he'd got himself a girlfriend in Manila and he decided to stay there. After that it was just the two of us. And when my Mum got ill and died there was no way of getting in touch with my Dad. Her sister was the only relative I had left."

As I listened to Fiona's story it made me realise that perhaps I wasn't the only one who'd had to cope with some tough times.

"You haven't got any brothers or sisters?" I said.

She shook her head. "No. But I'm fine. You just have to make the best of whatever life throws at you, I suppose. And I've been having a great time since I came up north to Liverpool. I do feel a bit guilty about not going back home for the summer, though. My aunt's never married, and she hasn't got any family except me. But we're like chalk and cheese. We can usually get on okay for a few days, but then we fall out over something stupid and it all gets tense. It's better for both of us if we just keep in touch on the phone."

We continued to talk, and drink more brandy-laden coffee, and it was obvious that she understood what I'd been going through. And I could understand her too.

After that first meeting we saw quite a lot of each other. We enjoyed each other's company, and I found her very attractive, but there was an unspoken agreement that we were just good friends. It was still less than a year since Louise had died and I needed time to think. I had to be sure I wasn't just getting involved with someone on the rebound. I didn't want to rush things. And as far as I could see, Fiona was equally happy to let things develop slowly.

Apart from my guitar the Mini-van proved to be the best purchase I'd ever made. The late summer of 1964 turned out to be unusually warm and sunny and, having kitted out the van with a mattress and some blankets, I camped out in it from time to time. The addition of a Primus stove and a music system made occasional overnight stays in the middle of nowhere very comfortable, and with my guitar to keep me company I came to value the quietness and peace of the gentle hills in North Wales and the Lake District. I could sit and think. I missed Louise, of course, but I wasn't lonely. In fact, for almost the first time in my life, I began to understand the difference between loneliness and solitude.

Once her second year at the Art College got under way at the end of September Fiona and I saw less of each other, but when we did meet up I could see a change in her. She loved being at the Art College, and she was absorbing every new experience like a thirsty sponge.

"This guy Adrian Henri you keep talking about," I said to her one day. "What's he like?"

"He's great. He's a lecturer on the Arts Foundation Course, but I have a tutorial with him every Wednesday. He knows an amazing amount about poetry and painting, and he's involved with all sorts of things here in Liverpool. He writes poetry as well as being an artist. He's just finished a big painting called 'The Entry of Christ into Liverpool'. It's a sort of homage to a picture called 'The Entry of Christ into Brussels in 1889' by a Belgian painter called James Ensor. Adrian invited a couple of us over to his studio last week to see it. All his heroes and friends are in it. They're part of a crowd accompanying a sort of Jesus figure as he makes his way along Hope Street into Liverpool. Adrian's known The Beatles for a while, so they're right in the middle. And then there's jazz musicians like Charlie Mingus and George Melly, along with the New York beat poet Allen Ginsberg. Plus some local poets like Roger McGough, and an artist called Sam Walsh who's another of our lecturers. It's all a bit chaotic. Like a sort of mob scene. Adrian told us the underlying message of Ensor's painting is that if Christ were to return to earth he'd almost certainly end up being crucified again. But I can't honestly say Adrian's picture said anything like that to me. Maybe he's saying something different? It was interesting though. He got a bottle of wine out while we were talking about the painting. He said it was a good opportunity to get to know us a bit better."

"I'll bet it was," I said. Fiona looked at me. I'd thought it but I hadn't really meant to say it out loud. To my surprise I'd suddenly found myself feeling a little bit jealous.

"Is me talking about Adrian bothering you?" she said, a touch mischievously.

If she'd pushed me I'd probably have said yes. But she didn't. So we just laughed and she carried on talking.

"When Adrian's not lecturing or painting he puts on things called *Happenings* at places like Hope Hall and The Cavern. He wants me and a couple of other girls to help him out with his next one."

"What would that involve?" I said, trying to sound as casual as possible.

"It could be anything, I suppose," said Fiona. "We're getting to know each other quite well."

She grinned at me and her blue eyes twinkled. She was playing games. And I have to admit I was quietly pleased.

<hr/>

The next *Happening* was called '*BOMB*'. It was taking place at The Cavern Club at the beginning of December and Fiona was very keen for me to go along. She told me the theme of the event was the four-minute warning that we would get if Russian nuclear missiles were on their way to wipe us out. It didn't exactly sound like a recipe for fun, and I didn't think it'd attract much of an audience, but I persuaded a somewhat reluctant Steve to keep me company. To our surprise the place was almost full and we only just managed to find ourselves a space. We sat in the familiar cellar, looking up at an unfamiliar flat ceiling which had been added for some reason, and waited for something to happen.

Then, without any warning, the lights were dimmed and the performance got under way. There were a number of poetry readings, with Adrian at one point wearing a red and white Liverpool scarf, while a Liverpool band called The Clayton Squares played some great rhythm and blues in the background. The time passed quickly. Steve and I were both starting to get into it when The Clayton Squares stopped playing and all the performers gathered together on the small stage. Nobody moved. As Steve and I looked at each other, wondering what was coming next, the silence was broken by a vocal group called The Excelles performing an 'a capella' version of the Christmas Carol 'Silent Night'. As they were singing, a slow countdown began over the loudspeakers, initially almost inaudible but gradually getting louder and louder. The tension increased until, as the last notes of 'Silent Night' died away and the count reached 'Zero', there was a bright flash and the cellar was plunged into darkness. People began to scream in what seemed to be genuine terror. With a great crashing sound the ceiling collapsed onto us, showering us all with dust and plaster. Then, once again, everything fell silent.

"That'" said Steve, "was mental."

"Yeah," I said. "Interesting though."

"What were you three up to while it was all going on?" I asked when we joined a few of the participants for a post-performance drink in a pub called Ye Cracke, not far from the Art College. Steve and I were sitting with Fiona and a couple of her fellow students called Julia and Trish.

"As soon as the lights went out at the end we had to pull on some ropes to collapse the false ceiling" said Fiona, laughing. "It was great when everybody started to scream. We hadn't expected people to be quite so terrified. Adrian was really chuffed with how it went."

"The only thing I didn't get," I said, "was the Liverpool scarf. "I couldn't work out where that fitted in."

"I think that was just Adrian letting people know he's a big Liverpool fan," said Fiona. "He loves it at Anfield. Especially the crowd on the Kop. He goes as often as he can. He calls it The People's Theatre."

"And how about you two?" I said, turning to Julia and Trish. "What did you make of it this evening?"

"It was great," said Trish. "Me and Julia both come from the Cotswolds. It's beautiful round there, but it's pretty quiet and boring most of the time. So everything about being in Liverpool is astonishing. We're still trying to get our heads round it. Even just being at John Lennon's old Art College is incredible."

"He was a regular at this pub," I said. "He brought his wife Cynthia here for their first date. She was at the Art College too."

Julia looked at Trish. "I didn't even know he was married."

"It was all kept very hush-hush," said Steve, giving her a wink. "It was when The Beatles were just startin' to get well-known. John got Cynthia pregnant an' they had to get married. Brian Epstein was dead worried it'd upset the fans an' mess everythin' up so 'e made quite sure the press didn't make a big thing of it."

"I don't suppose anybody'd care much now," said Trish. "The Beatles are so big they can get away with pretty much anything."

Twenty

DON'T THINK TWICE, IT'S ALRIGHT

"Have you heard of an American singer called Bob Dylan, Tony?"

"No."

"Okay then. What about *'Don't Think Twice It's Alright'*?"

"Yeah, sure. The hit record by Peter, Paul and Mary."

"That's a Bob Dylan song."

Fiona pulled back the plastic shower curtain and stepped out of the small cubicle in the corner of the room, drying herself off with a towel as she did so. It was a couple of days after the *'Happening'* at The Cavern and I'd stayed overnight at her bed-sit in Aigburth. It was the first time we'd spent the night together and I was still half-asleep, lying in her warm bed.

Over a year had passed since I'd lost Louise, and being with Fiona at last felt right.

"Trish has loaned me one of his albums," she said, running her fingers through her wet hair before wrapping the towel around herself. "*'The Freewheelin' Bob Dylan'*. It's fantastic. It's been out for a while. She's got his first one as well. That's just called *'Bob Dylan'*. She said there's another one that was released earlier this year called '*The Times They Are A'Changin*'. He's supposed to be a folk musician, but it's not what you'd normally think of as folk music. He mostly writes his own songs and they're absolutely brilliant. I was going to put it on last night but we sort of got distracted before I had a chance."

I gave her a grin as she sat down on the bed.

"You've got to listen to it, Tony. Why don't you put it on now? It's down there by the wardrobe."

"I'd sooner just lie here and look at you."

"Well you can't," she laughed. "You keep telling me you want to be a song-writer so you really need to listen to this guy. The lyrics he comes up with are amazing. It's like he's writing poetry and music at the same time. He's a genius."

Fiona began towelling her hair dry. I put the album on and by the time she had finished Bob Dylan was singing track three on side one, '*Masters of War*'. She draped the towel over her shoulders and lay down beside me.

"Well," she said. "What do you think?"

"About Bob Dylan? Yeah. It's different. I like it."

"Put side two on. I love the first track."

I did as asked, and as Bob Dylan started to sing '*Don't Think Twice, It's Alright*' I stroked her bare leg with the back of my hand.

"Last night was great, but don't be getting any ideas, Tony. My first lecture's at nine-thirty and I'm leaving in five minutes."

"Make it ten."

"No. I can't be late. Anyway, aren't you due in work today?"

"If you remember I had to put in a couple of extra hours yesterday. The boss said I didn't have to get in 'til eleven. It's just so he doesn't have to pay me overtime. He's a tight bastard."

As Bob Dylan moved onto his '*Dream*', Fiona swung her legs over and sat on the edge of the bed. "It's called running a business Tony. You're what's known as an expense. And just like me your poor boss has to keep you under some sort of control."

She pulled a few items of clothing out of a drawer. I watched as she quickly stepped into a pair of pants and fastened her bra, before slipping on a sweater and jeans. After giving her hair a quick brush she leaned across the bed and gave me a kiss.

"Right. I'll see you. Have a good day."

Then she was gone.

I lay there and thought about her. And about Louise too. But it was okay.

I made myself a coffee while the album finished. Then I flipped it over and listened to the whole thing again. Second time through it sounded even better. The way Bob Dylan played the guitar on several of the tracks I was going to have to learn. I'd need to work out the chords he was using, and listen carefully to how he put words together and turned them into poetry. Fiona was right. Mr Robert Zimmerman could teach me a lot.

By the time I had to leave for work I'd figured out the chords and written down the lyrics of a couple of his songs. I'd also worked out most of 'Corrina, Corrina' which was another track I really liked even though it was a traditional, American folk song rather than a Bob Dylan original.

As I was driving to work I decided I had to get my own copies of Bob Dylan's albums so I called in at N.E.M.S. on my way home. It was the first time I'd been there without Louise and I stopped by the booth we'd shared to listen to 'Love Me Do'. I stood there for a moment, allowing bitter-sweet memories to drift through my head, before making my way to the counter.

The two most recent albums were in stock, but I had to place an order for the first one, 'Bob Dylan'. Over the next few weeks I played along with them, time after time, slowly getting used to the finger-picking style and the more unusual chords. My guitar playing was coming on.

Fiona, meanwhile, continued to be involved in the many 'avant-garde' events taking place in Liverpool. The Art College was at the centre of much of the activity. With painters and poets like Adrian Henri, Roger McGough and Brian Patten leading the way, the artistic life of the city was buzzing. Coffee bars and pubs would host poetry readings. And at the same venues there would be performances by The Liverpool One Fat Lady All Electric Show, a musical comedy revue group whose various members included Paul McCartney's brother. As predicted by the man in The Jacaranda, he now called himself Mike McGear, and along with Roger Gorman and Roger McGough he would quite soon go on to achieve fame in his own right as a member of The Scaffold with hit records like 'Lily the Pink' and 'Thank U Very Much'.

On the red side of the city's sporting life, though, things weren't going quite so well. When I bumped into him just before Christmas Eric was as despondent as I've ever seen him. After the heady performances of the previous season, his regular trips to Anfield were starting to send him into a deep depression.

"I still can't believe Everton put four goals past us at Anfield," he said dejectedly. "We're supposed to be the champions, not them."

He was living proof of how tough it can be for a devoted football fan. I wasn't as obsessed with Liverpool Football Club as Eric, but I was definitely a fan. So I understood how he was feeling. As a true fan you love your team. You can't bring yourself to be unfaithful. Even when they break your heart you can't abandon them. You're trapped. There's nothing you can do. As someone once said, you can change your job if it's not right. You can change your house. You can even change your wife if things get really desperate. But you can never change your team. No matter how hopeless things seem, no matter how deluded you might sound, you cling on to the belief that one day they will master the beautiful game and sweep all before them.

"The Kop was only about half full last week which ses it all," said Eric. "The real fans won't stay away. They'll keep on turnin' up even if we end up down in the Fourth Division. But the average punter isn't gonna shell out good money to watch 'em at the moment. 'Ave yer seen where we are in the league? Fourteenth. Fourteenth for God's sake!"

He paused to let the awfulness of the situation sink in. He looked totally dejected. But despite everything he was still a true fan. Still a believer. "It'll get better though, Tone. Shankly's got 'em wearin' this new, all-red strip. They 'ad it on for the European Cup game against Anderlecht an' yer could see it made a difference. After the game 'e said we're gonna be an unstoppable red tide."

I nodded to demonstrate my support. "I'm sure it'll work out okay in the end. And even if it doesn't, it's only a game."

He looked at me as if I'd finally lost the plot.

"Sorry, Tone. You've got it all wrong there. It's not just a game." I could see he was deadly serious. "D'yer know what Shankly said?" He looked me straight in the eye. "'E said football's not a matter of life and death – it's more important than that." He stopped to savour what he clearly regarded as a shining pearl of wisdom. "An' if Bill Shankly said it, yer can't argue."

⁕⋅⋅――――⋅⋅⋅⋅⋅⋅――⋅⋅

"Julia and Trish have got a flat in Gambier Terrace and I'm going to move in with them. It'll be so much easier, living right by the Art College. It's not exactly a palace so the rent's less than in Aigburth. And I won't have any bus fares to pay either. I didn't say anything to you before because we weren't certain we'd be able to get it. But Julia told me this morning it's all fixed up."

Fiona was very excited. It was the afternoon of New Year's Day and we were sitting in The Jacaranda. She had gone back to Kent for Christmas because she felt she ought to see her aunt but she'd returned to Liverpool in time for us to celebrate the New Year together. We'd had a very late night and it was a chilly day. Two large mugs of reviving coffee stood on the table in front of us and I circled both hands around mine in an attempt to warm them up.

"That sounds great," I said. "It'll be good to have a place right in the middle of town."

Fiona leaned over and gave me a kiss.

"It's a bit rough and ready, but it's furnished. And there's three bedrooms. Mine's got a double bed so you can stay as often as you like. It'll be perfect."

Outside it was starting to get dark and snow was falling. By the time we'd finished our coffee the cobblestones on Slater Street had turned from grey to white.

The flat was on the top floor of one of the 1830's terraced houses which overlooked the eastern side of St James Cemetery by the Anglican Cathedral. They'd been built as elegant family homes with spacious rooms, high ceilings and elaborate plaster-work, but the wealthy city merchants had moved out of the city centre in the latter part the century and their large houses had been split up for multiple occupation. Fiona's room was at the back of the house with a large window through which there was a breath-taking view of the cathedral and, beyond it to the west, the River Mersey. Further away, on the far side of the river, there was a distant glimpse of Birkenhead.

Fiona carried on working part-time at The Jacaranda and threw herself into student life at the Art College. We were both enjoying ourselves to the full and the new flat was brilliant. Spectacular sunsets would sometimes light up the sky behind the cathedral and we'd lie next to each other on the bed, watching the colours slowly change as darkness fell.

Life was good.

"Do you fancy going to a European match at Anfield on Wednesday evening?" I said. "It's the second leg against a German team from Cologne. The first leg was nil-nil but we'll easily beat them at home."

Fiona looked at me and began to laugh.

"Seriously," I continued. "Eric and Steve'll be there so there'll be three of us to look after you. I know football's not really your thing, but the floodlights'll be on so it'll be more like a theatrical performance than a football game. Adrian would be really impressed if you told him you wanted to experience the atmosphere standing on the Kop."

"No, Tony. Honestly. Football's boring. And I don't fancy being the only female in a huge crowd."

"You wouldn't be the only one. Quite a few girls go to the matches these days."

"I don't care. There's no way you're going to get me crammed in on the Kop and swaying around with twenty-five thousand men. You go and enjoy yourself. If I was there you'd just be worrying about me the whole time. I appreciate you asking. But no. And that's final."

So it was just three of us went to the match. Eric arrived late, having been held up at work, and by the time we got to the ground The Kop was full.

"Come on lads," said Eric. "We'll have to try the Anfield Road end or we're gonna miss out."

Dodging past several groups of fans who were headed in the same direction we legged it round the back of the Main Stand to the other end of the stadium and just managed to get in before the turnstiles closed. It was a capacity crowd.

Kick-off was at seven-thirty. But as we all waited expectantly for the teams to take the field large, white flakes started to drift down past the floodlights. Eric was the first to notice them.

"'Eh, lads, look up there. It's startin' to snow."

"Don't be daft, Eric. It's March for God's sake. It's not cold enough for snow."

"Well if that's not snow, I dunno what else it is."

The three of us watched as what were now quite obviously thick snowflakes swirled around in the wind before settling onto the pitch. The green turf slowly turned white and the lines which marked out the playing area disappeared. Several of the ground staff were soon hard at work with brushes, frantically trying to clear the playing area, but the wind was picking up and the snow was getting heavier. No sooner was it was cleared than it was blown back again.

Bill Shankly, dressed in his usual grey suit, came out to inspect the pitch with the referee, followed by the Cologne manager and his team. They all made their way to where the centre circle should have been, kicking a couple of footballs as they went, and stood there for a few minutes, looking up at the sky and discussing the situation. Then, having taken a few more desultory kicks at the balls, they disappeared down the tunnel. Shortly afterwards there was an announcement over the Tannoy.

"Can I have your attention, please? The referee has decided that the kick-off will be delayed because of the condition of the pitch. The situation will be reviewed in half an hour. If the snow can't be cleared the match will be re-arranged for a future date. A further announcement will be made at seven forty-five."

"There's no way they're going to be able to clear it, lads," said Eric. The snow's gettin' heavier. We might as well get off home."

Along with a few others we started to work our way towards the side of the terrace, pushing through the still tightly-packed crowd. We were making for a big, wooden exit gate which would take us out of the ground onto Anfield Road. As we were about to head down the wide concrete steps at the edge of the stand we saw that the gate was still firmly closed.

We were trapped. Getting home was going to be easier said than done. All we could do was stay where we were and await the seemingly inevitable abandonment of the match. The Tannoy finally crackled back into life just after seven forty-five.

"The match officials have unfortunately decided that the pitch is unplayable. Tonight's game has therefore been cancelled. Ticket holders in the seated areas should leave through the usual exits. All ticket stubs should be retained as they can be used to gain entrance to the re-arranged fixture, the date of which will be announced in due course."

We could still see the big, wooden gate, but there was no sign of it being opened. Steve looked at me. He was obviously thinking the same as I was.

"What about the rest of us?"

The answer came fifteen minutes later. A further announcement told us that all the fans on the terraces would be issued with tickets which would be valid for the re-match. To get them we'd have to file out through the turnstiles instead of using the big exit gates. But first they had to sort out the tickets.

By half past eight a few people were spilling out onto the pitch and having good-natured snowball fights to pass the time. Considering we were completely in the dark as to how soon we'd be able to get out, everybody was amazingly patient. There was no trouble. We just stood there and waited.

At last, after what had seemed like an age, the tickets were ready. The three of us hurried down the steep steps towards a passageway which ran along the Kemlyn Road side of the stand. Within seconds we found ourselves caught in the middle of a tightly packed scrum as more and more fans surged out of the stand. We moved forwards slowly, but it was already obvious that letting us all out through the turnstiles was not going to be straightforward.

The area ahead of us had been designed on the assumption that supporters would enter the ground gradually, in twos and threes, through the narrow turnstiles and then, after the game, flood out rapidly like a great tide through the wide exit gates. Reversing the process had been done with every good intention. But it was a recipe for potential disaster. The turnstiles were acting like a dam, restricting the flow of people, and the closer we got to them the tighter the crush became. The pressure increased and Eric, who had been carried a little way ahead of us, found himself being pressed against a high brick wall where the passageway was at its narrowest. Steve and I could see him struggling.

"Help me, lads. I can't breathe."

Steve and I tried to push our way through the crowd to reach him but it was impossible. Nobody was able to move. We were all jammed tightly together, and as people continued to try and get out of the stand behind us the pressure was increasing. I kept my arms to my side, pushing them out sideways away from my chest to create a bit of extra space which would allow me to get a little more air into my lungs. Then, quite suddenly, the pressure eased and, looking to my right, I could see that the exit gate had been opened. Or maybe it had given way under the strain.

Quite a few of the fans around us, shaken by their experience, gave up trying to reach the turnstiles and made straight for the gate. But there was no way we were leaving without our tickets. With the pressure off we were quickly through the turnstiles, and a few minutes later we stood outside the ground clutching the precious slips of paper which would guarantee us entrance to the replay.

Eric gave a sigh of relief.

"Jesus, lads. That was close. I thought for a minute I was a goner. Let's 'ope we don't 'ave to go through anythin' like that again. It's a good job Fiona wasn't with us, Tone. She'd never've made it."

We'd been inside the ground for well over two hours, but nobody complained. Nothing ever appeared in the papers, and the crush was never mentioned again. It was as if it was normal. And I suppose it was. That's the way things were back then. Tens of thousands of people were desperate to see Liverpool play. And with it costing no more than a couple of shillings to get into the ground everyone just accepted there'd be no luxuries.

●·•·————●·•·●·•·●————·•·●

The re-arranged match was another goalless draw and Liverpool went through on the toss of a coin after a third drawn match at a neutral ground in Belgium. That's how stalemates were decided then. The drama of penalty shoot-outs had yet to be invented.

In the semi-final we would face Inter-Milan, one of the giants of European football and the holders of the European Cup, but first there was the small matter of an F.A. Cup Final to be played. At Wembley.

There were two trophies that Liverpool Football Club had never won. The F.A. Cup, and the European Cup. And now we were very close to winning both.

Our opponents at Wembley were Leeds United. At the end of normal time both sides were goalless, but the Leeds defence was finally breached in the third minute of extra time. Liverpool's left back, Gerry Byrne, who had sustained an injury in a tackle very early in the game and had been playing with a broken collar bone for most of the match, delivered a perfect cross into the box which Roger Hunt headed home. Our wild celebrations were cut short when Leeds equalised after a mix-up between Stevenson and Yeats in the Liverpool defence. But it all came right in the end. Ian Callaghan sprinted up the wing and sent another cross fizzing into the middle. Ian St John threw himself at it and the ball was sent powering into the net. The football Gods had looked down kindly upon us. Leeds United were beaten.

Victory was sweet, particularly for Gerry Byrne. He had hidden his pain so well that not a single Leeds player had spotted he was injured and taken advantage of the situation. It'd be more than fair to say they don't make them like that anymore.

The homecoming was ecstatic. Eric, Steve and I joined the vast crowd which filled St George's Plateau in the centre of the city as Bill Shankly, arms aloft in his now familiar pose, stood before us on the steps of St George's Hall and acknowledged the grateful adoration of the faithful.

Less than a week later we were all back at Anfield as our still relatively unknown club from the North of England faced the biggest game in its long history. Inter-Milan, the defending champions and one of the great European teams, had arrived in Liverpool for the first leg of a tie that would decide who was going to be playing in the European Cup Final.

The turnstiles were closed nearly two hours before kick-off leaving thousands of unlucky supporters outside the stadium. The excitement on the Kop was intense, and Shankly's decision to parade the newly-won F.A. Cup around the ground just before the start of the match was a stroke of genius. All around us people were going wild as the precious trophy was held aloft in front of the Kop.

"Hang on, lads. Here we go!"

Steve shouted a warning and clung on to me as we felt the pressure of bodies building up behind us. Then the vast crowd started to move. We were swept down the terrace and from side to side as great tides of ecstatic humanity swirled around the wide, concrete steps. The steel barriers, dotted around at strategic intervals, were designed to keep the motion from getting completely out of control but even so, surrounded as we were by thousands of others, there was no way of resisting it. We just had to go with the flow. It was exhilaratingly dangerous, like surfing a series of huge ocean waves.

Then, as the voice of Gerry Marsden rang out from the Tannoy speakers above our heads, we all joined him, scarves held high and lungs bursting. A mighty choir once again filled Anfield with the joyous sound of 'You'll Never Walk Alone.'

As the last notes of our anthem died away the Inter-Milan team, sitting in their dressing room beneath the Main Stand and hearing the commotion, must have wondered what on earth was about to hit them.

We were ready.

The Italian players looked nervous as they emerged onto the pitch. And they looked even more nervous when Liverpool went ahead, courtesy of Roger Hunt, after just four minutes. This was not meant to happen. We were all expecting a master-class from the Italians. Instead it was Liverpool who seemed to be out-thinking and out-playing the champions.

Normality was restored though when a mistake by Ron Yeats allowed the visitors to equalise. For the rest of the first half we were treated to the anticipated exhibition game from Inter-Milan. But despite all their beautiful football they were unable to put the ball in the net.

Shankly must have conjured up some sort of magic spell in the dressing room at half-time because the second half was all Liverpool. They took control of the match and scored two more goals. As the referee blew the final whistle Eric's face was a picture. Cheering and laughing at the same time, with tears running down his cheeks, he was in paradise. This was what made all the pain worthwhile. The agonies of the earlier part of the season had been washed away by two memorable victories. One at Wembley and one at Anfield.

Shankly was indeed The Messiah.

Then, with the kind of cruel inevitability that football fans always half-expect, the pain returned. The second leg was at Inter-Milan's San Siro Stadium and the referee made several decisions that nobody could understand. Bill Shankly told the world that we had been cheated and robbed. Inter-Milan scored three goals without reply and went through to the final by four goals to three over the two legs. We were devastated.

And then, to make things even worse, Inter-Milan went on to beat Benfica in the final. We all knew the European Cup should have been ours.

But what an end to the season it had been. Shankly's all-red strip would definitely be staying.

Twenty-One

THE BLUE ANGEL

It was a Friday evening at the beginning of May 1965. I'd not seen Fiona for a couple of days and she arrived back at the flat from college full of news.

"Guess what, Tony. We were down at The Blue Angel in Seel Street with Adrian Henri last night. And Allen Ginsberg was there. He's over from New York and he's convinced himself that Liverpool is the centre of the consciousness of the human universe. He was really keen to come up here while he was in England. Adrian knows him from when he was visiting New York, so he's been showing him round. Isn't that amazing? Allen Ginsberg, just sitting in the bar with us all, drinking and chatting away."

I wasn't entirely sure what to say. I'd definitely heard of Allen Ginsberg. But exactly what made him so well-known was a bit of a mystery to me. And all the centre of consciousness and human universe stuff sounded completely bonkers.

"I'm sorry, Fiona, but you're going to have to remind me who this Allen Ginsberg is."

"Oh, come on, Tony. He's one of the American Beats. Like Jack Kerouac and William S. Burroughs. Only they're novelists and Allen Ginsberg writes poetry. He's one of the people in

Adrian's painting. The one I was telling you about. You know. *The Entry of Christ into Liverpool*."

I was still confused, but the easiest thing was to nod my head to give the impression that I knew exactly what she was talking about. "So what's he doing up here in Liverpool?"

"I told you, Tony. He wanted to come here because he thinks Liverpool is the centre of the human universe. I was chatting to him and he was telling me all about it. He's a bit like Adrian in some ways. They look a bit like each other too. I can see why they get on. Do you know what he said to me?"

"I don't think I could even begin to guess."

"He put his arms round me and said that in his experience a certain type of genius in attractive students is best brought out in bed." She began to laugh. "Isn't that just completely outrageous? But I don't think he was being serious."

"I think perhaps he was," I said. "They're all the same these poets. Throw out a line and hope for a lucky bite."

"Very clever," said Fiona, laughing. "He's far too old for me anyway. I just told him to behave himself."

"And did he?"

"Sort of. He was pretty spaced out by then to be honest. I don't think alcohol was the only thing he was taking. He just took hold of my hand and carried on chatting as if nothing had happened. He was saying he came over to England so he could go to the concert Bob Dylan was doing in London. Apparently Bob Dylan's a friend of his."

"It's a pity you didn't meet him last week," I said. "He might've been able to get us tickets for Dylan's concert last weekend at The Odeon."

Fiona nodded her head. "He probably would've. Adrian had a couple of tickets and he went down to The Blue Angel with Bob Dylan after the show. Roger McGough was there too." She shook her head and sighed. "Allen Ginsberg. I still can't believe I was actually talking to him."

"Bob Dylan's the one I'd like to meet," I said. "But I don't suppose he'll ever turn up at The Blue Angel again."

I looked out of the window. The sky was clear and the sun was just dipping down towards the river.

"Come on," I said. "It's a lovely evening. What are we going to do? I can't promise to be as exciting as Allen Ginsberg but I'll do my best."

Fiona put her arms around my neck and gave me a kiss. "I don't want Allen Ginsberg. I just want you. Exactly the way you are."

I returned her kiss.

"I love you."

"And I love you too." She gave me a squeeze. "How about a Chinese? Then we can come back here and find something nice to do."

⚫·⚫——⚫·⚫·⚫————·⚫

As we wandered back up the hill from Chinatown a couple of hours later, the huge cathedral glowed in the light of a full moon which hung over the river behind us. At the top of Upper Duke Street we turned right into Hope Street and cut through the gardens behind Gambier Terrace.

From Fiona's room, high up on the top floor, we could still see the moon, hanging in the night sky and framed by the French window. I threw myself onto the bed.

"Let's lie here and look at the moon. We can get undressed if you like. It's not cold."

The bed still felt warm from the earlier sunshine. Fiona undid her blouse and skirt. As she was about to take off her bra and pants I stopped her. In the soft moonlight the black lace made her figure look even more amazing than usual.

"Leave those on for a minute. You're really gorgeous."

She joined me on the bed and we gazed at the romantic, silvery moon. I propped myself up on one elbow and looked at her. Her skin shimmered gently. She was totally irresistible.

"Is the door locked?"

"I think so." She hopped off the bed and tried the handle. "Yes."

I got up and stood behind her, pulling her against me, before gently removing her bra and slipping her pants down over her hips. They fell to the floor and she stepped out of them.

"Now you're even more gorgeous."

When I woke the following morning the sky was a cloudless blue. Fiona was still fast asleep, lying with her head on the pillow next to me.

I kissed her, but at first she didn't stir. Then, as I continued to look at her, she turned her face towards me and smiled. At that moment I knew without any doubt at all that I was in love with her.

Leaving her half-asleep I crept out into the living room to find that Julia and Trish were already up and having a coffee.

"Good morning, you two. It looks like it's going to be a glorious day. What did you get up to last night?"

"We were down at Ye Cracke. We got back just before midnight."

"Fiona and I hit the sack early," I said. "She was tired after her late night with Allen Ginsberg at The Blue Angel on Thursday. She was telling me all about it. Were you there?"

"I was there," said Trish. "Julia was at the pictures."

"Fiona seems to have taken quite a shine to Allen Ginsberg."

Trish started laughing. "Oh my God, Tony! I hope you don't mean she fancies him. Even his best friends wouldn't call him good-looking."

"It must have been his mind she fell for then," I said, giving her a grin. "She kept saying he was very interesting."

"I suppose he was at first. But he soon got pretty stoned. After that he wasn't making a lot of sense." She lifted up a jug which was on the table. "There's still a bit of coffee in here if you need some."

I poured myself a cup. "I'll be shooting off in a minute. I think Fiona'll be having a lie-in but I've got work to do. The boss wants me to sort out a problem with the electrics in an old house in Aigburth. It might take an hour or two, but it's double time on a Saturday."

The house in question was a large, white stuccoed mansion on a private estate down by the River Mersey, five or six miles south of the city centre. It had been built in the 1840's by a wealthy ship-owner who'd decided to move his family out of the increasingly crowded, and unhealthy, city centre. Unlike the city centre properties the house was surrounded by well-filled flower-beds and tall, mature trees. There was space to breathe. And from a raised lawn at the back of the house there was a magnificent view of the river.

The current owner, Mrs Cheetham, was an elderly widow who now lived on her own in the six-bedroom house, making use of just a couple of rooms on the ground floor. The rest of the property had seen better days and, to be honest, it was slowly falling apart around her. Her late husband had set up the electrical business where I was working, so the boss still did little favours for her from time to time.

I was down in the basement taking a look at some ancient electrical wiring when Mrs Cheetham called down to me. "Steven's on the phone for you, Tony."

The only Steven I could think of was the boss. Why would he be ringing me on a Saturday morning?

I climbed the cellar stairs to the hallway and picked up the handpiece of an old-fashioned, black Bakelite phone which was sitting on a fine, mahogany side-table. I put it to my ear.

"Everything goin' okay, Tony?" The voice of the boss was unmistakable.

"It's just one of the sockets in the kitchen needs rewiring," I said. "The cables run through the basement so they're easy to get at. I'll have it finished in an hour."

"That's fine. Can you call in at the office for a few minutes on your way home? I'm there now. I'll wait for you."

That was odd. The boss didn't usually turn in on a Saturday. Something must be up.

•┄┄┄┄┄•┄•┄•┄┄┄┄•┄•

It was a fifteen minute drive to the office. Peter, the firm's accountant, was sitting at his desk with the boss alongside him. They both looked worried.

"Sit down, Tony. Bad news I'm afraid. The job I booked you in for at Henderson's next week is off. It looks like they're in trouble." He paused for a moment, as if he was trying to work out exactly how much he should tell me. "They owe us a few thousand. Peter here's been tryin' to get 'em to pay up for weeks. And now we're hearin' they're in hock to quite a few other people as well. I've 'ad to say to 'em that everything's off until their account's up to date. I wanted to let you know what was happening. I'll be telling the other two apprentices when they turn in on Monday."

"Telling them what, boss?"

"I'm afraid we're going to have to lay the three of you off, Tony. Hopefully it'll just be for a couple of weeks while we get things sorted. But if we have to write off what we're owed it'll hit us hard. Hopefully the bank might agree to extend our overdraft. If they don't, we could be in trouble as well." He gave a sigh and shook his head as if he couldn't really believe he'd been so foolish. "I blame myself for letting things get to this stage, but Henderson's have been good customers for years. They've never let us down before."

"Will you be giving us some kind of pay-off?" I said. "You know. To help us through."

"I wish we could, Tony, but as things stand there's no spare cash. If we can come to some arrangement with the bank, or Henderson's pay up, things might change. But we won't know the answer to that for a couple of weeks. That's why I wanted to be straight with you. Right now we can pay you every penny you're due. But in a week or two that might change."

Peter handed the boss a sealed wages envelope which he passed over the desk to me.

"That covers all your earnings," he said, "including today's overtime. You'll be due a tax refund at the end of the month. We'll send that on to you as soon as it's been worked out."

I looked at my name on the outside of the square, brown envelope and slipped it into the top pocket of my overall without opening it. The boss stood up and held out his hand.

"I'm sorry, Tony. I really am."

I took hold of his hand, feeling slightly numb and shell-shocked. And that was it. All very civilised and according to the rule-book no doubt. One minute I was earning reasonably good money. And then, bang. No job.

I headed back to the flat. Fiona was still in bed so I joined her. But it didn't help much.

I love you in the morning, with your body soft and warm beside me
Your head upon my pillow, and your hair uncombed and free.
There is nothing more to say or do, I only want to stay by you,
The sun comes up, it's shining, yes 'n' good morning, you're my life.

Last night we lay there with the full moon shining, you kiss me gently and you taste like wine,
Your body turns to silver, as you drift away to dream.
Now the morning light is soft and golden, your eyes are heavy for the night still holds them,
You know I love you, yes 'n' good morning you're my life.

My lady when we lay together, your body keeps me warm.
You're a shelter in the storm that tried to shake us.
My lady when we lay together, your body keeps me warm.
You're a shelter in the storm that tried to break us.

My lady when I looked and saw you, I could only love you more and more,
You've given me the morning, and you've given me your life.
Soon the time will come to kiss and wake you. You lift your head and in the time it takes you,
I'll whisper that I love you, yes 'n 'good morning, you're my life.
I'll whisper that I love you, yes 'n' good morning, you're my life.

It was exactly a week since I'd lost my job. As I came to the end of the song and put my guitar down Fiona clapped her hands together.

"That's good. It's easily the best song you've written. It's about that night last week, isn't it."

"How did you guess?"

"It wasn't difficult." She looked at me and gave me a smile. "The words sort of gave it away. Promise me you'll get it down on tape. It'd be awful if you were to forget how it goes."

"Don't worry. The lyrics and chords are all written down. But I'll get it recorded as well."

•·————————•·•·•·•————————•·•

A couple of weeks earlier, while I still had a few bob in my pocket, I'd spotted a Beocord reel-to-reel tape recorder as I was driving past Berry's, a pawnbroker's shop in Everton, a working class area a mile or so north-east of the city centre. It was propped up in the window and I stopped to take a look.

"If you want it, you'll 'ave to take it 'as seen', son. I've tried it out an' it works okay. I've got an old amp an' some speakers in the back, so you can plug it in if you want to 'ave a listen. They're no use to me so you can 'ave 'em if you think they sound okay. There's four or five seven inch BASF tapes which I can throw in as well. The bloke who owned it said 'e'd lost the microphone, so I don't know if the recordin' heads are workin' or not. 'E told me they were fine, but you'll 'ave to take a chance on that."

Bang and Olafson was top of the range kit so, once I'd had a listen, I decided to risk it if the price was right. The sound was good so it'd be useful for playing tapes even if the recording heads were no good.

"How much do you want for it?"

The pawnbroker reached under the counter and pulled out a battered notebook. Flicking through it he stopped at a grubby page with various items scribbled on it and scratched his head as he did some quick calculations.

"How does fifteen quid sound?"

I pretended to give his offer some thought, but I knew straight away it was more than I could afford.

"It's a bit steep. You're not even sure it'll record properly."

He shrugged his shoulders. "Okay. Name your price then."

"I was thinking more like five."

He looked down at his book and laughed.

"You gotta be jokin', son. That's less than I paid for it. An' I'm throwin' in all the other stuff for free. You've gotta leave me a little bit of a profit or I'm out of business."

"Nine then."

He closed the book and thought for a minute. "Twelve and it's yours."

"I'll give you ten. Cash. That's all I've got."

He laughed again and shook his head. "It's gotta be cash son. Nobody takes cheques round 'ere. They bounce higher than bleedin' rubber balls."

He closed the notebook slowly and placed it on the counter. A grimy hand was thrust out towards me.

"Fair enough. Ten quid it is. Cash. As seen. No receipt and no refunds."

We had a deal.

I pulled ten notes out of my pocket and handed them over before loading the tape recorder and speakers into the back of the van and heading straight for Hessy's to see if Jim Gretty could fix me up with a second-hand microphone. I was in luck. The manager of a local band, who'd just split up because of 'irreconcilable musical differences', had returned their equipment to the shop. One of the microphones was somewhat battered around the edges, the band's drummer having used it to try and beat a sense of rhythm into the lead singer's head. But it was perfect for my needs.

"There's no way I'll be able to sell it in that state," said Jim Gretty as he handed it to me. "But it still seems to be working okay. So if you think it'll do the job it's yours."

Back at the flat I set the machine up and everything was fine. As an added plus it had a double-tracking feature, which meant I could bounce one track onto another and build up layers of sound, as well as using reverb and echo effects. It wasn't quite Abbey Road, but it would certainly do until I could afford something better.

To hear recordings of some of the songs in this book you can visit www.blameitonthebeatles.com

Twenty-Two

RUBBER SOUL

The summer of 1965 drifted by. The Beatles continued to appear regularly in the papers but some of the crazy hysteria of Beatlemania, when you couldn't pick up a newspaper without reading about them, seemed to be calming down. Their records still sold like hot cakes, and every concert was packed out, but they no longer made the front pages every week.

To satisfy the huge demand for tickets to see them play live, Brian Epstein started booking the biggest venues he could find. The vast football and baseball stadiums in America allowed tens of thousands of fans to attend each performance and see them, which was great, but the problem was the amplifiers and the PA systems which were available back then simply couldn't cope. They didn't have the power to fill such huge, open spaces. Even the band could hardly hear themselves over the non-stop hysteria and screaming.

As I stood in our shop, reading about what was happening, I thought of Louise. In my mind's eye I could still see the two of us in The Cavern, standing with Dave and Yvonne just a few feet away from the band.

I could hear Louise saying, "I wonder just how big they're going to get?"

Would she have been surprised? Probably not. She knew The Beatles were something special the very first time she saw them. She'd have loved watching them as they conquered the world. I smiled to myself. And as I did so I realised it was getting easier. I could allow myself such thoughts without feeling quite so sad.

But I still missed her. So much had changed in such a short time. For The Beatles. And for me.

Almost before I knew it the nights were drawing in, and what had been an unusually warm summer was coming to an end. I hadn't been able to find another apprenticeship but I was getting by. I was helping out in the shop in Waterloo to pay for my keep, and making a few bob extra by cleaning cars for commuters who parked them on an old bomb site near the station. I'd thought about moving to London and looking for a job down there, but Fiona was still at the Art College and I definitely didn't want to leave her.

Friday 26th November 1965 was my twenty-first birthday and we'd arranged to meet at the flat after her afternoon tutorial. I'd spent the day helping to move some stock around at the shop. Despite the time of year it was hot and sweaty work.

When I let myself in Fiona was already home, sitting at the table. In front of her was a bottle of red wine, along with two carefully wrapped presents. And an envelope.

"Happy birthday!" she said, jumping up and flinging her arms around me before giving me a kiss. She'd obviously been home for a while because her hair was freshly washed and she'd put on more make-up than usual. She was wearing a loose, white sweater, along with the light-blue jeans which she'd been wearing when we first got together and which she knew I liked. Her feet were bare, and she had painted her toe-nails a deliciously dark red. She didn't really need to bother too much about her appearance as she always looked great, even without any make-up. She had one of those figures which look good in almost anything. And when she spent a bit of time on herself, the effect was stunning.

"You look really fantastic."

She smiled. "It's not every day your boyfriend has a twenty-first birthday so I thought I'd treat you. But thanks anyway. It's good to know I'm appreciated."

We stood there, arms around each other. She felt as good as she looked. As I held her I became aware of the perfume she was wearing.

"Mmmm. You smell nice."

"It's the Rive Gauche you gave me for my birthday last month."

I kissed her again and slid my right hand into the back pocket of her jeans. She laughed and pushed me away. "Open your presents. Then you can let me know what you think of them."

I didn't want to disappoint her, but it had been a very long day in the shop. "Give me a couple of minutes to have a shower. Then I'll be right with you."

I couldn't wait to see what Fiona had bought for me. In less than ten minutes I was sitting alongside her as she handed me the smaller package to open. Inside was a copy of The Beatles' new single *"We Can Work It Out"*. I turned the record over. On the B-side was a number called *"Day Tripper"*.

Fiona looked at me. "I picked it up this afternoon from N.E.M.S. It came out today."

"Let's put it on."

"In a minute," she said, passing me the envelope. "Open this first. And then the other present."

Fiona was obviously very keen for me to see what was inside them. The envelope could only be a birthday card, and the other gift was exactly the size of an LP. No mystery there. I wondered what it was that made them so special.

I opened the birthday card to find a written message.

'Have a very happy Twenty-First Birthday. Let's make it a really good one.'

Inside the card was another envelope on which Fiona had written *'I wanted so much to see The Beatles playing live in Liverpool – with you. xxx.'*

It contained two theatre tickets.

SUNDAY 5TH DECEMBER 1965
EMPIRE THEATRE LIVERPOOL
THE BEATLES – WITH SUPPORTING ACTS
SECOND SHOW. DOORS OPEN – 8.15 P.M.

I was unable to hide my astonishment.

"How on earth did you manage to get hold of these? They're like gold dust."

The Empire Theatre had just over two thousand three hundred seats and according to the Liverpool Echo at least a hundred times that number of fans had been trying to get tickets.

"Open the other present. You might like that even better."

I picked it up and began to remove the wrapping paper. It was definitely an LP. Fiona watched closely.

"Be careful with it. You'll really have to look after this one."

The front cover of the LP was slowly revealed – *'Rubber Soul'.*

Fiona gave me a big smile. "Like it? It was released today as well."

I looked at it carefully. Across the top left-hand corner, over a close-up photograph of the mop-topped heads of the four Beatles, was the title of the album, in large, red, sinuous lettering. Unusually the name of the band was missing.

"All they need these days is the picture," she said. "The whole world knows who they are."

I gave her a big hug. "Thank you so much. That's amazing."

Fiona nodded, but said nothing. I held the album in my hands and looked at it again.

"N.E.M.S. as well?"

"No. It's a special copy. Turn it over."

Scrawled in heavy, black pen, across the back of the album cover, were four signatures. I looked at her. "Are these genuine?"

She laughed. "I sincerely hope so. Someone who knows them got it for me. And the tickets as well. I said it was your twenty-first birthday and I wanted you to have something very special. He gave me the tickets for The Empire last week but he never mentioned anything about the album. Then he turned up at college with it this morning."

I gave her another, even bigger, hug. "I'm going to have to see if I can work out who your mystery man might be. They really are two unbelievable presents." I sat down and looked at the two tickets before moving on to the signed album. I was almost afraid to take my eyes off them in case they suddenly vanished.

"Come on. I think we should make a start on that wine and listen to some music," said Fiona, pouring a couple of glasses from the bottle of Rioja which she had already opened. Very carefully I took 'Rubber Soul' out of its sleeve and placed it on the record player. Then, as the gentle introduction to 'Norwegian Wood' began to play, I pulled her towards me and slipped both my hands inside her white sweater. I ran my fingers gently up and down her warm back and under the waistband of her jeans. This time there was no resistance.

Just over a week later we made our way along the dark, winter streets towards The Empire. Fiona had never seen The Beatles play live and we were both very excited. We were well aware that we were about to see something we would never forget, and the feeling increased as we got closer to the theatre.

Knowing the area around the theatre on Lime Street would be very busy we had cut through the University Precinct and made our way down Brownlow Hill, passing behind The Adelphi Hotel and using back streets as much as possible. Even so, by the time we reached Lord Nelson Street and turned down the hill towards the back of the theatre and the stage door, everywhere was so crowded that it was almost impossible to get through. It seemed that thousands of people had turned up, maybe hoping to buy tickets from touts, or perhaps thinking they could at least catch a brief glimpse of their idols as they were entering or leaving the theatre.

Ahead of us, at the end of the street, we could see a line of policemen blocking off the area outside the stage door. The first of the two shows had already finished so The Beatles would be relaxing in their dressing room and getting ready for their second performance. A couple of black Rolls Royce limousines with darkened glass windows were parked inside the police cordon.

"They must be in place for a quick get-away straight after the show's finished," said Fiona, pointing at the two vehicles. "The lads won't want to hang about and risk getting torn to pieces by crazy fans."

There was no way through, so we turned right and made our way along a street which ran directly behind the theatre towards London Road. We were able to make slightly better progress on this wider street and, after a further five minutes of good-natured pushing and shoving, we found ourselves outside the main entrance of The Empire Theatre.

A couple of hefty, crew-cut bouncers were stationed outside the wooden, glazed doors. They looked well-equipped to deal with anyone who stepped out of line so we tagged onto the end of what was a very orderly queue. As we reached the door I felt inside my jacket for the two precious tickets which I'd earlier placed securely in a pocket with a zip. I handed them to one of the doormen and they were closely scrutinised.

"Okay, that's fine," he said, tearing the two tickets in half. "Hang onto the stubs. There's another check inside so you'll need 'em to get to yer seats."

The foyer was tightly packed with people trying to buy programmes and refreshments. The show was due to start in twenty minutes, so we made our way straight to the stalls. I said nothing to Fiona, but I knew immediately that we were sitting very close to the seats which Louise and I had occupied for the Little Richard concert just three years earlier.

For what was to be their sixth and last appearance at The Empire Theatre, The Beatles began their set with '*I Feel Fine*' and included songs which were already becoming classics such as '*Yesterday*' and '*Help!*', before winding up with '*Day Tripper*' and '*I'm Down*'.

Quite a few of the audience for this second show seemed to be family and friends, so the atmosphere inside the theatre was in many ways affectionate rather than hysterical. Even so, the reaction was still a good deal rowdier than when they had made their final appearance at The Cavern. As the band took their bows we all knew it was the end. The Beatles would never perform in Liverpool again.

Fiona loved every minute of it. We both felt very fortunate to have been given this final opportunity to see them play live in the city of their birth.

So, who had got her the tickets and the album? I quizzed her, and named names, but she didn't give anything away.

⋯⋯⋯⋯⋯⋯

"Some bastard has nicked the Mini-van!"

It was the morning after the Empire concert, and I rushed back up the stairs to the flat.

"It was definitely there last night when we got back, and now it's gone."

Fiona, who was still half-asleep, looked concerned, but doubtful.

"Are you sure?"

"Yes. Of course I'm sure. It's not there."

"No. I mean are you sure you didn't park it round the corner on Canning Street. You sometimes do if you can't find a space any nearer."

"I'm sure. It was parked right outside last night. Don't you remember?"

"I'm afraid I was still buzzing after the concert. I didn't really notice."

"I'll check round the corner, just in case," I said, "but I definitely saw it last night."

Fifteen minutes later I was standing at the counter in the police station on nearby Hope Street, opposite the Philharmonic Hall, while the Duty Sergeant took details.

"A red Mini-van, you said?"

I nodded. "Yes. With a black roof."

"That's fine, sir. If you'd like to fill in the details of the vehicle on this form we'll see what we can do. My guess would be someone needed transport back home after seeing The Beatles last night and your van just happened to be sort of convenient. The older Minis aren't that difficult to start without a key. It'll probably turn up in a few days. I don't want to sound rude, but it's not the sort of vehicle the professionals would bother with. Not worth the trouble, you see. Now if it was a Rolls Royce or a Bentley, that'd be another matter. I wouldn't be giving you much hope of getting it back if that was the case. They tend to get fitted with false number plates and shipped off to the continent sharpish. Or the Middle East. The Arabs like the expensive cars. Not run-of-the mill motors like yours though. They're usually nicked by scallies who don't have their own wheels. If I was a betting man, I'd put my money on it being abandoned as soon as the petrol runs out."

I'd nearly reached the end of the form. To show I was still listening I made a few grunting noises as I finished it off.

"Make sure you put a contact phone number and your address down, sir. So we can get in touch. I'm sure it'll turn up before too long."

He was right. They found my Mini-van in Manchester two days later, parked in a small industrial estate near United's football ground. As expected the petrol tank was empty and there were a few extra miles on the clock, but the van itself was undamaged. The old mattress and the blankets were still there in the back, but the music system and Primus stove had vanished. The police-sergeant who took me over to pick it up said that some youngsters from Manchester had probably been over in Liverpool for the evening and borrowed the van to get home. The music system and stove were an unexpected bonus.

Eric, though, had another theory when I met up with him and Steve a couple of days later.

"Didn't you have a Liverpool F.C. sticker on the windscreen, Tone? I reckon some scallies from Manchester were upset we won the title last season and nicked the van just to get even."

"I'm not that bothered who took it. I'm just glad to have it back in one piece. The music system was on its last legs anyway.

And the pressure release valve on the Primus is jammed. It'll blow up on them if they try and light it."

"That'd be good," said Eric. "It'd serve 'em bloody well right. Make them think twice before doin' it again." Although he was a good Catholic he wasn't always the strongest of believers in Christian forgiveness.

The three pint glasses on the table in front of us were empty and he picked them up. "I'm gettin' three more pints in"

When he returned from the bar he turned to me. "Any joy with findin' yerself a job yet, Tone?"

I shook my head. "There's nothing going round here at the moment. I might have to think about moving down to London. They say there's loads of work down there. I only need another six months to finish off my apprenticeship."

Eric looked thoughtful. "Fiona's from down south somewhere isn't she?"

"Yeah. Canterbury."

Eric looked blank. He could find his way to most of the big football grounds in England, but otherwise geography wasn't his strong point. Any mental map of the country he may have had in his head was decidedly sketchy to say the least.

"In Kent," I added helpfully. "South of London. Near The English Channel."

Eric still looked blank. "I don't think there's much football played down that way, Tone. So if yer did decide on a move you'd 'ave to come back north at the weekend for the Liverpool games."

"There's always the London clubs," I said. "I could go along to White Hart Lane and watch Spurs. Or Arsenal. Probably Arsenal, I think. They play in red so it wouldn't feel that different."

"You couldn't do that Tone." Eric looked genuinely upset. "It'd be like, I dunno, treason or somethin'. Spurs I might just be able to cope with. They're a class act. But Arsenal would definitely be the end. I wouldn't be able to speak to yer again."

I started to laugh. "You daft bugger. It'll be a while before I do anything as drastic as moving away from Liverpool. Fiona's staying up here until she finishes at the Art College. And anyway there's a new recording studio opened in one of the old warehouses near Moorfields. I might shoot over there with a couple of tapes. They'll probably tell me to get lost. But you never know."

●・━━━━●・●━●・●━━━━━●・●

"They want to do a proper studio recording of six of my songs."

Fiona looked at me as I burst into the flat in Gambier Terrace. "Who?"

"The people at Moorfields Music. I told you the other day I was thinking of taking some tapes along to them. Well I went this morning. And they really like the songs. They're going to let me use the studio when there's nobody else booked in. There's a guy called Larry there and he wants to start writing songs with me. If we just use the studio when it's free it won't cost them anything. They've got a deal with one of the big, London music publishers. They reckon a couple of the songs are good enough to be released as singles."

"What? With you singing them?" She looked decidedly doubtful about the idea.

"No," I said, laughing. "Other singers. People who are already well-known. Larry had a big hit a couple of years ago when he was playing keyboards with a band. Since then he's been working as a freelance record producer down in London. He's moved to Liverpool because there's so much going on up here. He liked the way I'd arranged the songs on the Beocord and we're going to work on the recordings together and get some proper demos sorted out."

"That's brilliant! So they've got a copy of your tape?"

"No. They were very busy so I left my tape with them. Larry said he wanted to listen to it again. So he can decide who he should get in to record them. I think he means bands or singers from up here in the north-west. You know, to make demos. Not the records that are going to be released. I'm seeing him again tomorrow and he'll give me the tape back then."

Fiona looked a little worried. "And what if this Larry guy disappears to London with the tape and says they're his songs?"

"He seemed like a decent bloke," I said. "I don't think he'd try anything like that. Anyway, you've heard all the songs. You can back me up if I need to prove I wrote them."

"Yes, I know. But why take the risk? Wouldn't it be better to make a copy and hang onto the original? A hit song can be worth a lot of money."

I knew she was right. I could hear my father going on about the music business. "They're all sharks, son. Mark my word. You won't stand a chance. They'll eat you alive."

I returned to Moorfields Music the following afternoon. The studio engineer, James, greeted me with a smile. "Tony. How are you? Larry asked me to say he's very sorry, but he's had to go down to London. He's taken a tape of your songs with him so he can play them to a few people down there. He'll be back next week."

"My girlfriend was worried the tape might get lost," I said. "I haven't got a copy."

James turned towards the control room. "Don't worry. Larry wouldn't risk that happening. Come on through." Lying on the mixing desk was my tape in its red and yellow BASF box. "We made a couple of copies last night once the studio was free. Larry took one to London with him. If it's okay with you we'll hang on to the other. I suggest you lock the original away somewhere safe."

The following week, with Larry back from London, we got to work. He knew his way around all the equipment in the studio and within a few hours the recordings were complete. I took a copy of the master tape over to the flat and listened to it with Fiona.

"It doesn't sound like you," she said. I frowned at her and she laughed. "You know what I mean. It's much better than I expected."

"That's thanks to all the gear they've got in the studio. It's amazing what they can do. The vocals are mostly me and Larry. But he got four girls he knows from Manchester to do the vocals on the fourth track. The one called 'Love Isn't Always A Game'."

"That song sounds completely different from when you wrote it."

"We've added a whole load of extra harmonies and double-tracked the vocals which makes them sound much fuller. And Larry's put a lot of compression on the backing tracks. He's really pleased with how it's turned out."

"It sounds like a finished record to me."

"According to the recording engineer at Moorfields even a demo has to be as good as possible these days. The people listening to them are often the ones in charge of the money. They're not necessarily all that musical. Some of them struggle to imagine what a song could sound like unless it's handed to them on a plate. The girls are hoping they'll get a recording deal out of doing the demo."

"I reckon they should," said Fiona. "I'd buy it." She sat back in her chair. "So what happens next?"

"Larry goes down to London and sells the songs."

As it turned out it wasn't that easy. After a couple of weeks, and a number of fruitless meetings, Larry was back in Liverpool. He sat in the studio and scratched his head.

"I don't understand it. The people I played them to said they really like the songs. Particularly the one the girls did. But nobody's offering any definite deals. The only encouraging thing is that the publishers we're working with have said they'd be happy to publish the songs if we want and see what they can do with them. It'd be a joint deal with us here at Moorfields."

"That sounds fair enough," I said.

"The only downside is they'll own half the copyright. They'll do their best to place them of course. They won't make any money by sitting on them. But if they can't find anyone to record them we'll be stuck. We won't be able to offer them around without their agreement." Larry paused and looked at me. "It's up to you, Tony. Think about it for a day or two. The contracts are ready to sign but there's no rush unless we get a phone call to say someone is ready to record one of the songs."

It didn't take me long to make up my mind. When you're young you don't generally set much store by what your parents think. And I knew they'd want me to give it considerable thought before putting pen to paper.

So I told Larry I'd sign the contracts straight away.

Twenty-Three

LOVE IN THE SUMMER

The bright, morning light flooding into the room through a gap in the curtains woke me from a deep sleep. I glanced at my watch and placed my hand gently on the sleepy head lying next to me.

"Fiona. It's ten-thirty. It looks like it's going to be a gorgeous day."

She stirred slightly then snuggled back down under the bed-sheet. "Leave me alone."

"Come on. We've been asleep for nearly ten hours." I lifted the sheet from her head. "It'd be a shame to waste such a beautiful day. Let's drive over to Formby beach. We could find a sheltered spot in the sandhills and soak up some sun."

She rolled onto her back. Even bleary-eyed and squinting up at me she still looked gorgeous.

"Can't we just stay in bed?"

"No. It's too nice. I'm going to grab a quick shower while you wake up. Then I'll rustle up some coffee. If we get away by eleven we'll be on the beach by midday."

It was the end of May 1966. Julia and Trish had gone home for the Bank Holiday Weekend so we were on our own.

Formby was an affluent village about ten miles north of the city on the coast of Liverpool Bay, where the River Mersey flowed into the Irish Sea. There was a large nature reserve between the village and the sea which was a popular spot for a day out. An escape from the city.

By the time I'd showered Fiona was out of bed, standing by the wide-open window and gazing at the clear blue sky.

"Your coffee'll be ready in five minutes," I said as I filled the kettle. "I'll do you some toast as well to keep you going. I know what you're like if you don't have any breakfast."

She laughed and began to remove the white shirt which she'd been wearing in bed. Her breasts looked enticingly pale and soft as she pulled it up over her head. She turned away from the window and stuffed the shirt under her pillow. Her dark hair just touched her shoulders and my eyes traced a line down the middle of her bare back to where it met her slim waist.

I continued to gaze at her as she made her way towards the bathroom. She stopped at the door and looked back at me. "I thought you were making toast and coffee."

"I am," I said, and smiled at her. "I got side-tracked."

We breakfasted quickly and threw a couple of large bottles of cider into a small rucksack before hitting the road. We stopped at a small corner shop in Bootle to buy some sandwiches and twenty minutes later we were in Formby. The van bumped along a sandy track which led to the beach. To each side were tall pine trees, and ahead of us we could see some large sand dunes. After a couple of hundred yards the track petered out.

I parked the van on a flat, grassy area under some trees. "I guess we'll have to walk the rest of the way."

After adding a groundsheet and a couple of blankets to the contents of the rucksack we set off down a narrow path to the right which led deep into the woods. To each side a thick carpet of pine needles prevented weeds and other vegetation from getting a hold and, in the absence of undergrowth, we were able to leave the path and wander up and down some gentle slopes between the bare lower trunks of the tall trees. Suddenly I heard a rustling sound. Out of the corner of my eye I saw a movement high up in the branches. I motioned Fiona to keep still.

"Look. Up there." I whispered quietly and pointed up to her left. "See. Sitting there. About three branches from the top. A red squirrel."

We watched the cute, furry creature as it sat on a narrow bough, using its tail to balance as it munched upon a tasty nut. Then, quite suddenly, it scampered to the end of the branch and started jumping from tree to tree, moving swiftly through the canopy high above our heads. In just a few seconds it was out of sight.

Fiona looked delighted. "I don't think I've ever seen a red squirrel before."

"There's quite a few of them in these woods. I used to come here on the train when I was a kid."

"Lucky you. My aunt's idea of fun was a visit to Canterbury Cathedral. Or a trip to London to traipse round some museums or art galleries."

As we walked on the trees offered welcome shade from the sun and the pleasantly warm air carried a delicate scent of pine.

I slipped my arm around her waist. "I read somewhere that pine trees give off negative ions which can make you feel a bit high."

Fiona stopped and took a few deep breaths. "Well I'm certainly feeling good if that means anything. But that could just be because it's such a lovely day and we're all alone." She looked at me mischievously. "Where's the sea?"

I pointed straight ahead. "Over that way. Beyond the sand dunes."

"Come on then. I'll race you."

I followed as she ran towards the row of sandhills which blocked our view. The pine needles gave way to soft sand which felt warm and gave way beneath our feet as we scrambled up the final sandhill which was about thirty feet in height. Because I was weighed down by the rucksack and blankets Fiona was the first to reach the top. She lifted her arms in triumph. I quickly joined her and we gazed out over a wide, sandy beach which was completely deserted. In the far distance we could just make out some white breakers, marking the edge of the sea.

I stood alongside her and identified the landmarks which could be seen. The air was unusually clear and looking right, to the north along the beach, we could make out Blackpool Tower, standing erect and angular against the distant peaks of the Lake District. In the further distance would be Morecambe Bay.

"Can you see that hazy mountain over there," I said pointing to the north-west. "It looks like it's sticking straight out of the sea?"

Fiona peered along my out-stretched arm and nodded her head.

"That's got to be the peak of Snaefell on the Isle of Man," I said. "There's nothing else I can think of in that direction. I don't think I've ever seen it before."

To the south-west the mountains of Snowdonia, the tallest peaks in Wales, formed indistinct grey waves in the far distance. And finally, looking directly to our left, we could see the Wirral Peninsula, sandwiched between the River Dee and the River Mersey.

"My Nan used come over from Ruthin and stay with us in Waterloo when I was little and we'd go down to the beach at Crosby. She used to say if you can see the Welsh Mountains it's time to get your brolly out."

Fiona, who had been staring at the distant peaks, looked round at me.

"Why would she say that? You can see them today, and there's not the slightest chance of rain."

"I've no idea to be honest. She used to come up with all sorts of stuff like that. She was unbelievably superstitious. I can't even remember half the things she used to say. She spent most of her life throwing salt over her left shoulder and putting sliced onions in the bedroom to ward off colds. The first time I stayed at your flat I was getting a bag off the top of my wardrobe back home, so I could put a few things in it, and there were about a dozen onions up there. All wrinkled up and dry."

"Seriously?"

"Honest. I'm not making it up. We'd be walking along and she'd suddenly lift her arm and do a strange sort of salute. That meant she'd spotted a magpie. Which was a sign of bad luck. Or maybe it was two magpies. I can't remember. And then every New Year's Eve she'd stuff as many coins as possible into her purse. She said it'd make her wealthy."

Fiona looked at me as if I was talking gibberish. "And did it work?"

"No. Most of the time she didn't have two pennies to rub together."

"She sounds a bit crazy. But good fun. I'd like to meet her."

"You'd have got on really well with her. But she stepped off a pavement last year so she didn't have to walk under a ladder and got knocked down by a lorry."

Fiona looked shocked. "Oh my God!"

I grinned at her and started laughing. "Just joking. She's fine. I'll take you to meet her one day."

As I continued to laugh she gave me a gentle push. Unbalanced by the rucksack I tumbled down the soft, sandy slope onto the beach.

She ran down to join me. "Let's stop here and have a bite to eat. I'm starving."

We emptied the rucksack and covered the warm sand with the groundsheet before spreading both rugs out on top of it.

After we'd demolished the sandwiches and finished off one of the bottles of cider, I changed into a pair of shorts while Fiona stepped out of her short dress to reveal a red bikini. It hugged her figure tightly and left little to the imagination.

"I thought you'd probably approve of the colour," she said, turning from side to side.

I looked her up and down. "I certainly do. And what's inside it. You look gorgeous."

She smiled, and we lay down on our backs, soaking up the warm afternoon sun. After about fifteen minutes Fiona rolled onto her front.

"I'm glad we didn't stay in bed," she murmured. "The only problem is I'm going to have a bikini mark if we carry on sunbathing like this. Why don't we both strip off and get an all-over tan?"

The suggestion was a no brainer as far as I was concerned. "We'll have to move, though. It's quiet here for now, but if someone came down one of the paths through the sand dunes we wouldn't get any warning. It'd be better if we found somewhere a bit less public."

We collected our things together and headed inland along a slightly overgrown path which ran between some tall gorse bushes taking us deeper into the dunes.

"It doesn't look like this path gets used much," I said. "If we can find a nice, sheltered spot we should be fine."

After a couple of hundred yards the path widened out and we found ourselves in a flat, grassy area. It was almost completely surrounded by thick bushes which would give us some privacy without hiding the sun.

"This looks perfect. Let's make ourselves at home."

I spread the groundsheet and rugs over the grass while Fiona took her bikini off and stood with her arms outstretched, facing the sun, before spinning round several times.

"It feels really sexy, Tony. Give it a go."

I shook my head. "You carry on. I'm going to just lie here and take some sun."

Removing my shorts I lay face-down and watched Fiona as she continued to wave her arms above her head, moving slowly from side to side like a forest nymph, dancing in the warm, sea breeze. Then, laughing, she lay down on the rug beside me and closed her eyes.

"This is heavenly," she whispered, moving closer and draping her arm across my shoulders.

I stroked her thigh. "I really fancied you this morning. We nearly didn't make it here."

Fiona rolled onto her side to face me. "I'm glad we did though. This is much better than being indoors." Her warm, sun-kissed body pressed against me and her lips brushed against my ear. "It'd be a shame not to make the very most of a perfect afternoon like this."

It was the first time for both of us. Love in the open air. Afterwards we lay in each other's arms beneath a blanket, half-asleep and half-awake. It was blissful, but by mid-afternoon the sun had dipped behind the bushes and the temperature was starting to fall.

Fiona shivered. "We'd better make a move. It's getting chilly."

We dressed quickly and made our way back to where we'd parked the van. I opened the back doors and we piled all our things onto the mattress.

"Right then," I said. "Do you want to sleep in the van overnight? Or is it back into town?"

She gave me a hug. "Back into town I think. A night in the van'd be a bit of an anti-climax after this afternoon. I don't know about you, but I fancy snuggling up together in a nice, warm bed."

Funny how love in the summer used to be,
The world was only you and me.
One Sunday.

By the stream's bubbling water, gliding free,
The hawk found only you and me.
One Sunday.

Sunday's gone, and funny how
We made it now
Like it used to be
Sunday's gone, and funny how
We made it now
Like it used to be.

One Sunday.
One Sunday.
One Sunday.

Twenty-Four

BAYING AT THE MOON

No matter how hard I tried I couldn't get Fiona interested in football.

"I'm fine about you and your friends being obsessed with the game," she said, laughing. "It doesn't bother me. But I'm never going to understand what's so exciting about watching twenty-two grown men kick a ball around a field and maybe once or twice stick it into a net. Don't ask me to get worked up about football. It's not going to happen."

"What about this afternoon?"

"I'll watch if England are winning. I want to see The Queen hand that solid-gold trophy to Bobby Moore. You probably wouldn't appreciate it, but he's got really great legs."

It was Saturday 30th July 1966. Over 32 million people in England would soon be glued to their televisions, watching the biggest match that the country's football team had ever played. The World Cup Final was being played in London, at the national stadium in Wembley, and our opponents were one of our oldest adversaries, Germany. We had to win.

By three o'clock there were fifteen of us crammed into the flat. The players all looked tiny on the small, black and white TV which we'd perched on a stool by the window. The picture was a bit fuzzy but it was the best we could do with the indoor aerial.

The game seemed to be fairly even at first. Neither side were on top. Then, after eleven minutes, the TV picture dissolved into a series of jagged black and white lines and the sound went off. Adjusting the aerial made no difference until, after five desperate minutes, someone tried lowering it out of the window. Suddenly the picture reappeared and we could hear the commentary again.

"Don't move it. Leave the aerial right there."

A couple of hefty books on top of the lead held it in position and all seemed well. Then the score came up on the screen. During the loss of reception we'd missed a goal. The Germans were ahead. But we weren't worried. There was plenty of time to put things right. And so it proved. By half-time Geoff Hurst had equalised for England and the match was all square.

During most of the second half it looked as if things could go either way. Then, with thirteen minutes left, Martin Peters nicked a goal from just eight yards out. Fiona leapt into the air and cheered as the cameras zoomed in on Bobby Moore who was already organising the England defence for what would be one of their sternest tests.

The tension was now unbearable. Could England hang on? We all looked at our watches, willing the referee to blow his whistle and signal the end of the game. With a minute to go Germany won a free kick close to the England penalty area. This would be their last chance. A fierce shot hit one of the England players before ricocheting across the six yard box. For a moment it seemed the danger had passed but the loose ball was pounced upon by one of the German forwards. Time seemed to stand still as a German boot was pulled back and the ball was prodded into the net. The old enemy had levelled the match. It was two goals all. We were going to have to endure the agony of extra time.

After having been so close to victory we all feared that the England players might lose heart. Instead they began to play like men possessed. In the eleventh minute of extra-time Geoff Hurst thumped a shot against the underside of the crossbar which bounced down behind the German goalkeeper before being cleared by a defender. Hurst held his arms up in the air, convinced it had crossed the line.

For what seemed like an eternity we held our breath as the Swiss referee consulted Tofiq Bakhramov, the Russian linesman, who could be seen nodding his head vigorously. After a brief pause the referee turned away and pointed to the centre circle. It was a goal!

The German team threw caution to the winds. It was a blitzkrieg. Wave after wave of attacks were repulsed as the England defence held firm. In the final minute of extra time, with almost every German player in the England half of the field battling for an equaliser, Geoff Hurst picked up a booted clearance and found himself running unopposed towards the German goal with the ball at his feet. He reached the edge of the penalty area and blasted the ball towards the net.

"I hit the ball as hard as I could," he said later. "As far as I was concerned, it was either going into the goal or out of the stadium."

Wembley roared.

Kenneth Wolstenholme, the BBC TV commentator, shouted, "And here comes Hurst, He's got ... Some people are on the pitch ... they think it's all over!" Then, as the ball rocketed into the top corner of the net, he added, simply and memorably, "It is now."

England had won the World Cup.

We all watched as a triumphant Booby Moore received the Jules Rimet Trophy and, holding it with both hands, lifted it high in the air. Fiona turned her head and, smiling, gave me a knowing wink.

Years later, when asked why he had given the goal when he couldn't possibly have been certain the ball had crossed the line, the Russian linesman's response was brief and to the point. "Hitler," he said. "And Stalingrad."

That evening we all went down to Ye Cracke to celebrate. The bar was packed, and the evening finally ended when the landlord announced that we had drunk the place dry.

A few days later Fiona and I had another cause for celebration when she passed her final exams with honours.

***

"You can't live on fresh air, Tony. You've got to earn a living. It wasn't your fault you lost your job, I know that, and I appreciate your help in the shop, but you really need to finish off your apprenticeship. It'd be a waste to give up on it after all the hard work you've put in. Then maybe you can have a proper go at this song-writing business. You won't make any money at it. But if you need to prove it for yourself, so be it."

I was helping my Dad to clear some rubbish from the back of the shop. We were on our own and he had obviously decided it was a good opportunity to give me a reality check. I put down the stack of boxes I was carrying.

"Paul McCartney's father once told him he'd never make a living strumming away on a guitar. Look at him now."

"You can forget about Paul McCartney, Tony. Lightning's not going to strike twice in the same city. You might have some talent for music. I honestly don't know. But even if you're brilliant it's all a big gamble." He paused for thought. "I blame it on The Beatles. And Gerry and his Pacemakers. Thanks to them there's literally hundreds of kids here in Liverpool who think they're going to be big pop-stars with loads of money. Well I've been around long enough to know they're not. That sort of thing doesn't happen to ordinary people. For most of us life's about hard graft and a proper job."

"I am looking for a job. Honestly. But there isn't any work round here at the moment. I'm happy to help out in the shop whenever you need me. You know that. Spending a few hours down at the recording studio won't stop me finding a job." I paused for a moment before continuing. "Mum likes my songs."

My father closed his eyes and took a deep breath. The look on his face said that was the last straw. I really was scraping the barrel.

"Your mother's a wonderful woman, Tony. But as far as she's concerned your songs would be brilliant even if they sounded like a dog baying at the bloody moon. Mothers can't think straight when it comes to their own kids. It's the way their minds work." He paused for a moment, concerned perhaps that he might have overstepped the mark. "Don't get me wrong. I'm not saying anything against her. That's just how things are."

"What if I said I'm thinking of going down to London to finish off my apprenticeship? Would that make you happy?"

He stood there in silence. At least I'd made him think.

"Maybe that's not a bad idea, Tony. Spread your wings a bit and experience life in a big city like London. I once thought of moving down there myself. But then we got the chance to buy the shop." He shook his head somewhat ruefully, as if he still regretted not taking the plunge. "Your mother wouldn't hear of it. Too far away from the family she said." He paused and held out his hand. "London it is then. Come on. Let's shake on it. I don't want to fall out with you. It's just that you've only got one life. And I don't want to see you make a mess of it."

As I grasped his hand he looked at me. "Your mother won't like it, though. You moving away from Liverpool I mean. Don't say anything to her. At least not until you've got something definite sorted out."

Fiona was delighted.

"That's great. It'll be much easier for me in London. There's lots of work down there in fashion and design. I didn't say anything to you before, but my aunt almost stopped speaking to me when I didn't move straight down to London after my final exams. Particularly with me getting honours. She said it was a waste, me staying up in Liverpool." She put her arms round me. "We'll be following The Beatles. Heading down to the big city where the pavements are paved with gold."

I still wasn't sure. Leaving Liverpool wouldn't be easy.

"What about your friend Allen Ginsberg?" I said. "He thinks Liverpool's the centre of the universe. And that's without even going to Anfield."

Fiona laughed. "I know it's a big decision for you, Tony, but we can just go down there for six months while you finish off your apprenticeship. And then decide what to do after that. We can always come back if it's not working out. There's not much for either of us up here at the moment." She gave me a smile. "Let's at least give it a go."

She was right. Six months was no time at all. What did we have to lose?

Twenty-Five

LONDON - 1966

The recently completed motorways were almost deserted as we made our way down to London in the Mini-van. We'd left Liverpool at just after seven in the morning and, despite a slight hold up as we passed through the outskirts of Coventry on the dual-carriageway which linked the M6 and M1, we were there by eleven o'clock. The plan was to spend the weekend looking for somewhere to live.

I'd managed to fix myself up with a job at a small electrical firm in Camden Town. My old boss in Liverpool had given me a brilliant reference, so they were happy to take me on without an interview. The only problem was that I was due to start on 11th September. And that was only two weeks away.

I have to admit I was nervous. It had all happened much more quickly than I'd expected.

Fiona, though, thought it was brilliant. Quite a few of her friends from Kent had got themselves digs in Camden Town when they were students in London, and several of them were still in the area. It wasn't fashionable, so it was relatively inexpensive, but there was plenty going on. Camden Market, close to the Regent's Park Canal, was becoming increasingly popular. And a place called The Roundhouse, a disused turntable-shed alongside the main railway line out of Euston, was about to open as a creative arts and performance space. The area was definitely on the up.

A lettings agent in Camden High Street gave us a list of five bedsits which were available. The first two were hopeless. Dirty and damp. Then, when we arrived at the third one, we were quite sure we must have been given the wrong address. Alfreton Lodge, just five or ten minutes from Camden Town, was one of a number of large, elegant Edwardian houses on Haverstock Hill, the main road leading into the centre of London from Hampstead, one of the capital city's most expensive and desirable residential areas.

We rang the doorbell, fully expecting to be disappointed, but to our surprise the details were correct. The owners were two retired doctors whose children had grown up and left home. The house was now far too big for them but, having lived in the area for nearly forty years, they didn't want to move. Rather than sell up they'd decided to rent out three of their five bedrooms, each of which had been fitted out with a small kitchenette. The bathroom was shared, but it was spacious and everything was very clean and tidy. We had struck lucky.

Dr Robertson, who looked every inch the retired G.P. in his comfortably worn, tweed jacket, loose corduroy trousers and leather-soled brogues, was charming.

"If it's alright with you," he said, "we'll need a deposit of twenty pounds. Then we can let the agent know the last room's been taken. The other two have already been reserved by fourth year medical students at University College Hospital. To be honest we were rather expecting this last one would go to a medical student as well, but it'll be nice to have a young electrician and his fashionable lady living in the house rather than it being exclusively medical."

"Are you sure you don't mind us living together in your home?" asked Fiona, sounding a little anxious. "We're not married."

Attitudes were slowly changing, particularly in London, but the idea of unmarried couples living together was still slightly frowned upon. 'Living in sin' my mother called it. She had never really come to terms with me spending even one night at Fiona's flat.

Dr Robertson peered at her over the top of his small, gold reading glasses. "My dear young lady. I spent forty years as a G.P. And my wife, Anne, was a venereologist. That means she specialised in sexually-transmitted diseases. Between us we've seen and heard pretty much everything you can possibly imagine as far as people's relationships go. And probably quite a few things you couldn't even begin to imagine." He chuckled quietly to himself as if he was thinking back to some particularly salacious story. "We'll be delighted to have the two of you living with us. Whatever your marital status might be."

Fiona gave him a big hug. "Thank you so much. I just wanted to be sure."

Dr Robertson looked a little taken aback, but not unpleased, by her sudden and unexpected show of affection. The two of them continued talking as I removed some folded pound notes from my pocket and counted them onto a beautifully polished, mahogany side table which stood in the hallway.

"Eighteen. Nineteen. Twenty."

"Thank you Tony. That'll be fine."

Dr Robertson shook us both by the hand before opening the very solid, front door. "So, you'll be moving in two weeks tomorrow. Shall we expect you some time in the afternoon?"

"It depends how long it takes us to drive down from Liverpool," I said. "But hopefully we'll get here no later than five or six in the evening if that's okay. I start my new job at eight o'clock the following morning so I'll need to be away by about seven-thirty. I can't risk being late on my first day."

"That's fine. We'll give you a couple of sets of keys when you arrive so you can come and go as you please. My wife and I are up on the top floor so you won't disturb us whatever hours you keep."

I took Fiona's hand as we made our way down the slightly-worn, sandstone steps which led back to the main road. Dr Robertson gave us a wave. "I look forward to seeing you again soon."

He watched us leave, closing the heavy door very gently once we'd safely reached the pavement. As we made our way back to the Mini-van, which we'd parked near Belsize Park tube station a few minutes' walk away, Fiona squeezed my arm.

"What an amazing find. Wasn't Dr Robertson lovely?"

I took her hand. "It's a good job I wasn't on my own. If you hadn't been with me I'm not sure he'd have said yes to a Scouse electrician. I think he took a bit of a shine to you, though. It was you giving him that big hug that clinched it. He definitely liked that."

"Don't be daft. I'm sure he liked you too. Anyway, the important thing is it's a great start to our life in London. It'll be fantastic living in that lovely house after the flat in Gambier Terrace. Did you see the furniture? It was all antiques. Even the stuff in our room. We're going to have to look after it carefully."

The Mini-van was still parked where we'd left it. Unless we were going to head straight back to Liverpool we had a day and a half to kill.

"What do you want to do now?" I said to Fiona, giving her a hug. "It's nearly four o'clock and I'm starving. I've looked at the A – Z and Hampstead Heath's just up the road. Why don't we find a pub and grab a bite to eat? Then we can decide whether to drive back tonight or make a weekend of it and get to know London a bit."

"Sounds good to me. Let's go."

The next two weeks back in Liverpool were hectic as we got ready for our move to London. Julia and Trish were both staying on in Liverpool and Fiona offered them a month's rent to give them time to find a replacement flat-mate but they wouldn't take it. With the flat being so convenient for the Art College they were confident her room would be snapped up almost immediately.

We said our goodbyes to friends and family. My Mum in particular couldn't get her head round the idea of me going off to London, even for just six months. She'd never travelled much beyond Liverpool and North Wales. As far as she was concerned London was the other end of the world. I might just as well have been emigrating to Australia.

I phoned Larry to tell him what was happening and he said he'd let me know if there was any interest in the songs.

Eric's parting shot was very direct. "An' if yer turn into an Arsenal fan, Tone, I'll 'ave to disown yer. Nobody walks out on Shankly's Reds. Okay?"

"Okay, Eric. Keep a space on the Kop warm for me."

He looked at me. There were tears in his eyes. "Now bugger off," he said. "Before I start gettin' meself all upset."

Our first week in London seemed to fly by, and almost before we'd had time to catch our breath it was the weekend.

Almost six months earlier, at the end of April 1966, *Time Magazine* had coined the phrase 'Swinging London.' Carnaby Street was the place to see all the latest fashions and, having spent her first week in London sorting out the bed-sit and visiting various employment agencies, Fiona wanted to take a look. I'd been given a job re-wiring of a pair of 1930's semis in Hendon, a suburb close to the M1 which wasn't that different to South Liverpool. So I was equally keen to find out what 'Swinging London' was all about.

It certainly wasn't anything like Liverpool, where most of the shops were still determinedly stuck in the early nineteen fifties despite The Beatles and the explosion of rock music. Brightly-coloured men's suits and jeans were everywhere. Boutiques with names like '*Lord John*' and '*I Was Lord Kitchener's Valet*' overflowed with all the latest fashions while ultra-trendy youngsters thronged the pavements. As we threaded our way between Lambretta and Vespa scooters, which seemed to be parked in every available space, we passed wafer-thin girls, all wearing the most daring of mini-skirts and sleek, white boots.

Fiona was in her element. "We were studying all these London fashions towards the end my course. I wish I had a camera." As we were passing a shop called '*Lady Jane*' she grabbed my arm. "I've heard of this place. Let's take a look inside. I must see how the clothes are put together."

She spent ten or fifteen minutes studying jackets, skirts and blouses in minute detail, examining the stitching and working out how the garments had been cut and designed, until eventually an assistant came up to her.

"Can I help you with anything?"

"Oh. No. It's okay thanks." Fiona, who was about to turn an expensive-looking velvet jacket inside out to poke away at the lining, swiftly replaced it on its hanger. "I'm just looking."

"If you want to try anything on let me know. We don't mind people looking, but it's nice if they occasionally buy something as well."

Fiona turned to me. "We'd better move on. I think they're starting to wonder what we're up to."

"What's with all the 'we'?" I said. "Don't include me. I've just been standing around minding my own business."

"Whatever." She gave me a grin. "Let's go. It'd be embarrassing if they called the police."

We wandered on down the street, people-watching and taking in the atmosphere, before stopping for a coffee.

"Right," I said as we finished our drinks. "Where next? Your choice."

"Why don't we just do the sights. You know. Buckingham Palace. Big Ben. The Tower of London. That sort of thing. It's a while since I visited most of them. If we get them out of the way we can start behaving like normal Londoners. Most of them don't go anywhere near the tourist traps unless they've got visitors from out of town."

Twenty-Six

PENNY LANE

It was the middle of February 1967, and in less than a month my apprenticeship would be coming to an end. Fiona and I had a decision to make and it wasn't going to be easy.

She'd landed herself the perfect job with a small, but very up-market, dress design studio called '*Silver Peaches*', on the second floor of a converted warehouse near Covent Garden. She was getting some really valuable experience, and loving every minute of it. The business was expanding, with orders coming in from fashionable boutiques all over London, and she was one of a team of eight who had to do everything. It involved a lot of responsibility. And it suited her down to the ground. She definitely didn't want to give it up.

A rumour had been going round for some time that The Beatles were trying to put together an album about their home town, and in the middle of February 1967 they released a double A-side, '*Strawberry Fields*' and '*Penny Lane*'. It felt very strange. Living in London and listening to songs about places which I knew so well. '*Penny Lane*' in particular brought back so many memories. I just wished Louise could have heard it.

"I think maybe I need to go back home to Liverpool."

Fiona looked at me with a slightly puzzled look on her face.

It was Sunday afternoon and we'd just walked through Belsize Village and up onto Primrose Hill to get some air. The day was cold, and a pale, watery sun hung low over the centre of London which was spread out below us to the south. We were resting on a wooden bench which marked the highest point of the hill, gazing down at the city.

"The boss says he won't be able to keep me on once I'm qualified. So I've either got to look for another job down here or go back to Liverpool. I'm not sure I want to carry on being an electrician. Not down here in London, anyway."

The triangular kites which several people were flying from the top of the hill swirled and danced in the wind as their colourful tails traced circles in the sky. A chilly wind was starting to build up. I turned up the collar of my dark-blue, donkey jacket and pulled it tighter around me.

"What about me?" said Fiona. "Doesn't my job matter?"

I put my arm around her shoulders. "I'm sorry. Of course your job matters. That's why I said I need to go back to Liverpool, not we. I know you love being down here. There's nothing like 'Silver Peaches' in Liverpool and it doesn't look like there ever will be. I thought the city might start to go places with The Beatles taking off the way they have. But it doesn't seem to be happening."

Fiona just sat there quietly, without saying anything.

I kissed her cheek. "I've been thinking about it for a couple of weeks. Since 'Penny Lane' came out really. Every time they play it on the radio it makes me feel a bit sad. Homesick, I suppose. It's strange. Nothing's ever affected me that way before."

I looked at Fiona. I could see she was thinking. Eventually she spoke.

"You're bound to feel a bit unsettled with your job coming to an end. Maybe you could get yourself some sort of temporary job for a month or two? Maybe try something different. There's plenty of work down here even if you don't want to be an electrician. I might be able to fix you up with a job in one the fashion shops. I know quite a few people in the business now. And if that doesn't interest you there's always a bar job. You know. While you work out what you really want to do."

We sat in silence for a couple more minutes, staring at the view. On the exposed hill the wind was now distinctly fresh and I could feel Fiona starting to shiver.

"Come on," I said. "You're getting cold. We've had more than enough fresh air. Let's head back to Haverstock Hill. If you like we can stop for a coffee on the way. It'd warm us up a bit."

We hurried down the hill, hand-in-hand, following the path which led to Primrose Hill Road. The wind dropped as we reached the shelter of the tall trees and large houses. They reminded me of the wealthier parts of Mossley Hill, back home in Liverpool.

We linked arms and I turned to Fiona. "Did you ever go to Penny Lane?"

She shook her head. "No. I don't think so."

"It's not that far from where you had your bed-sit in Aigburth. Near Sefton Park and the University Halls of Residence. All the places The Beatles mention in the song are still there. The bank. The barber's shop. The roundabout at the end of the road." I could picture it all in my head as we continued to walk. "I suppose if you think about it, it's only about four or five years since Paul and John would've been wandering around that area without anybody taking a second look at them. It's not far from where they used to live. And George Harrison was at Primary School near there too. Just off Penny Lane in Dovedale Road."

At the end of Primrose Hill Road we turned right, along England's Lane, towards Haverstock Hill.

"Louise used to live on Penny Lane," I said. "So I got to know the area quite well."

Fiona stopped and looked at me. "I didn't realise. I suppose that must be why the song's affecting you so much."

"I know," I pulled her arm closely against my side. "Forget it. I shouldn't have said anything. It's my problem not yours."

She held my hand tightly. "There's no need to worry about me. If you want to talk, go ahead. It's not good to bottle things up."

We passed a small cafe which was open. Fiona peered inside. "It looks okay. There's a table free by the window."

The instant coffee wasn't anything to write home about. But at least it was hot.

"Maybe you're right," said Fiona, putting her cup down. "Maybe you should go back to Liverpool for a few days. Or even a week or two. See your old pals. And have a good think about what you want to do."

She was sitting opposite me. I leant towards her, with my elbows on the table, and cupped my chin in my hands. "You're very wise. And attractive. And understanding. You do know that, don't you."

"So you think it might be a good idea?"

I nodded my head slowly. "I don't like the idea of leaving you down here on your own. But you're right. It'd do me good. I thought I'd come to terms with losing Louise. That getting together with you would make it easy."

I sat there with my head full of memories. All the old sadness seemed to be flooding back. It wasn't easy at all.

Fiona reached out and took hold of my hands. "I really love you," she said.

"I know," I said quietly. "And I love you too. I'm just a bit messed up. The simplest thing, you know, when we started to see each other, was to let myself fall in love with you. I could tell myself that everything was fine. That it was what Louise would have wanted. And it all seemed to be working out. If The Beatles hadn't gone and released that song it probably still would be."

"You can't blame The Beatles, Tony. Even if 'Penny Lane' had never been written, something else would have happened to set these feelings off. It's you that's got to sort it out."

She gave me a few moments to take in what she was saying before she continued, very quietly. "How long was it after Louise died that we first got together?"

"I'm not sure. Eight or nine months. Maybe a bit longer."

She looked at me. "I remember thinking when we first started talking about her that you were obviously very much in love."

I nodded. I could feel my eyes starting to fill up. "Yeah ... we were."

"And yet you didn't seem as sad as I thought you should be."

"I was in pieces inside. I just tried not to show it."

Tears started to trickle down my cheeks. Fiona leant forwards and kissed them. "Sometimes it's important to cry. I'm sure Louise would have cried for you."

"I hope so."

"You know she would. So you need to cry for her."

I shook my head, and wiped my face with the sleeve of my jacket. "I've never even seen her grave. I went to the funeral but I couldn't face watching her being lowered into the ground. So I just sat on some old tombstones by the church and looked at the names, to take my mind off what was happening until it was all over."

Fiona leaned across the table and gave me another kiss.

"Perhaps if you went back home you could go and see Louise? Talk to her. Tell her what you've been doing. I used to spend hours at my Mum's grave after she died. I told her a lot more than I ever did when she was alive." Fiona laughed quietly to herself and smiled. "It really helped. And then one day, when I was standing there and everything was completely still, I heard her telling me I didn't need to visit her again. That was when I knew that everything was going to be alright."

I drove back to Liverpool as soon as my job in Camden came to an end. I'd been home for Christmas a couple of months earlier, when Fiona had popped down to see her aunt in Kent, but my Mum still greeted me like the proverbial, long-lost son.

"It's so good to see you home again, Tony. I'd almost forgotten what you look like." She gave me a big, maternal hug which seemed to go on for ages. "I'll put the kettle on. Your Dad's in the shop. Pop down and say hello. He'll be pleased to see you. I'll make a cup of tea for the two of you and bring it down."

Nothing much had changed. The layout of the shop was still the same. I looked around for a copy of '*Mersey Beat*', but none were on display.

"We don't sell it anymore," said my Dad. "Brian Epstein bought it and changed the name to '*The Music Echo*'. I think he reckoned he'd be able to shift more copies by combining the news about local bands with stuff from the rest of the country. But it didn't work. The kids didn't like it and sales were dropping off. So I gave up stocking it a couple of months back."

He paused and scratched his head.

"What brings you back home anyway? Is Fiona with you?"

"No. She stayed down in London. I finished my apprenticeship and we decided it'd be good for me to head back to Liverpool for a week or two. You know, so I can think about what I want to do next."

"Your mother'll be thinking you're home for good. Don't say anything to her about going back to London. Leave it 'til you know for sure what you're going to be doing with yourself. It's good that you got the apprenticeship finished though. There's always work for fully qualified electricians."

I didn't say anything. There'd be plenty of time to talk about my future once I'd got my head sorted out.

It felt very strange to be driving along Penny Lane again. There were little groups of people here and there, taking pictures.

The familiar street sign in front of the sandstone wall at the junction with Greenbank Road now carried the name '*Eleanor Rigby*', scrawled in purple felt-tip on the white background, while below the name of the road someone else had added '*MICHELLE IS COOL*' in blue.

I slowed down as I passed Louise's house. Perhaps I'd call in later.

Sitting at the traffic lights on Menlove Avenue, waiting for them to turn green so I could turn left into Beaconsfield Road, I watched a small group of girls standing in a half-circle outside John Lennon's old house, 'Mendips', about fifty yards further down the road. A lady seemed to be handing out cups of tea. Perhaps it was his Aunt Mimi?

A horn blared out behind me. I hadn't noticed that the lights had changed.

Quickly putting the car back in gear I accelerated up Beaconsfield Road, passing the heavy, cast-iron gates of Strawberry Field. A right turn at the top of the hill took me down Church Road.

I parked outside St Peter's and made my way through the lych-gate before following a path which led around the left side of the church, past the older section of the graveyard.

I could feel my heart beating faster as I approached the more recent graves.

And then I saw it.

A plain, white granite headstone.

I stood there and read the simple inscription.

IN LOVING MEMORY
OF
LOUISE MARY BROWNE
SORELY MISSED DAUGHTER OF PETER AND
MARY BROWNE
AND BELOVED SISTER OF ANDREW
14TH FEBRUARY 1946 – 20TH OCTOBER 1963
NOW AT PEACE

On the white gravel, surrounded by smooth, edging stones, lay a small bouquet. The roses were white, and still fresh. I placed a kiss upon the single red rose I had brought with me and, kneeling down, lay it alongside the bouquet.

"I'm sorry I left it so long, Louise," I said quietly. "I should have come to see you sooner but I wasn't brave enough. Please forgive me."

I could feel the tears coming, and I could hear Fiona saying it was alright to cry.

"I loved you so much. You knew that, didn't you? And I will always love you."

I knelt there for I don't know how long, the tears rolling down my cheeks, before finally getting to my feet again. Everywhere was quiet.

"I'll come and see you again soon. I promise."

I didn't want to tell her about Fiona on this first visit. I was sure she'd understand. But I needed to wait until it felt completely right.

I picked up the red rose and gave it one last kiss before replacing it on the grave.

⁕

The front door of the house in Penny Lane was still the same colour and, when I pressed it, the door-bell sounded the same.

It was all reassuringly familiar, even though everything had changed utterly. I stood there, feeling slightly apprehensive. Perhaps this wasn't a good idea after so long. I was about to turn and hurry away when the door opened.

"Hello Tony." It was Andy. Behind him stood Sarah. I took hold of his outstretched hand and gave Sarah a hug.

"I'm so sorry I've not called in sooner. I've just been up to St Peter's." I paused for a moment. "To visit Louise's grave. I've not been before. I couldn't face it. But I was speaking to someone who persuaded me it might help. So I finally plucked up the courage."

Andy looked at me sympathetically. "We were there first thing this morning. We still go every month."

I nodded my head. "I noticed the flowers. They looked lovely."

Andy moved backwards into the hall, holding the door open as he went. "We were about to make a cup of tea. Would you like one? We can probably rustle up a bite to eat as well if you're hungry."

"A cup of tea would be great. But no food thanks." I followed them past the familiar staircase and into the small sitting room. "How are your Mum and Dad? I feel bad about not seeing them but I kept finding reasons not to. I suppose I was worried they'd be too upset. And then I moved to London."

"They're not here at the moment. Sarah and I are looking after the house for them for a few days. They've gone up to Windermere for a short break."

"Are you sure it's okay for me to stay? I can leave if it's not convenient."

"It's fine, Tony. Don't worry. It's good to see you."

Sarah gestured towards the couch. Nothing in the room had changed.

"Sit down for a minute while we sort out the tea. Are you quite sure you wouldn't like something to eat?"

"No. That's really kind. Just a cup of tea'll be fine thanks."

Once the tea was ready the three of us sat together as Andy told me about his parents.

"Dad had a heart attack about six months after Louise died. Probably with all the stress. He didn't go back to work after the funeral. He just sat at home drinking. We tried everything to get him to stop but he wouldn't listen. Cunard were very good, but in the end their occupational health doctor said he'd never be well enough to cope with work and advised early retirement. That seemed to help a bit, but he's still finding it very difficult. I don't think he'll ever come to terms with losing Louise. Mum's having to be the strong one. She retired from nursing as well so she could look after him. He wouldn't have be able to cope without her."

He stopped, lost in thought. He too was clearly finding it difficult.

"So what took you down to London?" said Sarah, breaking the silence.

"The firm I was working for up here in Liverpool ran into some financial trouble and I got laid off. There weren't any jobs here in Liverpool so I had to finish my apprenticeship down there. I'm qualified now and I came back home to give myself a bit of time to think. Things are a bit up in the air at the moment." I decided not to mention Fiona. "And what about you two?"

"With a bit of luck we'll soon be qualified as well," said Andy. "Ideally we'd like to get jobs at the same hospital but that might not be so easy here in Liverpool. We'll probably have to move away. Mum and Dad have been talking about selling up and moving to The Lake District in any case. They love it up there and Sarah and I both think a change of scene would be good for them. This house has got too many memories. The Lake District's not far away so they can still pop down here whenever they want. You know, to see Louise. There's not really anything else to keep them in Liverpool, especially if me and Sarah have to make a move. And with The Beatles making Penny Lane so famous there shouldn't be any shortage of buyers if they do decide to put the house on the market."

I looked over at Sarah. "I hope you've still got those letters from Paul McCartney."

"I certainly have. Andy calls them his pension!"

"Quite a small pension, I think," said Andy, laughing. "But every little helps."

I sipped at my tea. "Someone I spoke to in London said The Beatles might stop doing live tours so they can spend more time in the studios at Abbey Road. He had a bootleg of the show they did at Candlestick Park in San Francisco back in August. Having listened to it I don't really blame them. With all the screaming you could hardly hear what they were playing. Paul McCartney finished the show with *'Long Tall Sally'*. It's funny, but that was the first song I ever heard them play. At Litherland Town Hall."

How long ago and far away that Boxing Day now seemed.

———————————

As we lay there, Sunday morning, on the seventeenth of April,
With The Sunday Times Review and cups of coffee on the
table,
I was trying to make some good sense of the pictures in
the paper,
While I tried to make some better sense of you.

That was Sunday morning and my hand began to stray,
'Til there was nothing left between us but the sheet on
which we lay,
And the birds outside were singing in another sunny day,
And it was Sunday and the seventeenth of May.

How you came to be there I'm not really all that sure.
But anyway we liked each other and we kissed a little
more,
While the milkman left a bottle and a bill outside the door,
And it was Sunday and the seventeenth of June.

We dispensed with Sunday lunchtime, with a joint and all
that stuff.
Why we only had each other, but it seemed like quite
enough,
We were too young then for eating, we were busy making
love,
And it was Sunday and the seventh of July.

As we lay there Sunday morning on the seventeenth of
April,
With The Sunday Times Review and cups of coffee on the
table,
I was trying to make some good sense of the pictures in
the paper,
While I tried to make some better sense of you.

I put my guitar down and looked at Fiona who'd been sitting on the bed listening.

"That's nice," she said. "Another one about us?"

"Well, sort of I suppose. Bits of it are. And then other bits aren't. I was playing around with some chords and thinking about last Sunday when I'd just got back from Liverpool and we stayed in bed pretty much all day. So it definitely started off being about us. Then a few things got changed here and there. So it's partly real, and partly imagined. Like most songs, I suppose."

"Get it down on tape before you forget it. I'll put some coffee on while you set things up."

On 1st June 1967, The Beatles released 'Sergeant Pepper's Lonely Hearts Club Band' and turned the musical universe upside down. As Fiona and I listened to it for the first time we could hardly believe what we were hearing.

"Do you remember me telling you about when I saw them at Litherland Town Hall?" I said as we were playing the LP for the third time. "When they'd just come back from Hamburg and we all thought they were a German band?"

Fiona nodded her head slightly but she didn't say anything. She seemed to be lost in the music as the opening sequence of 'Lucy in the Sky with Diamonds' started to play.

"I said it was difficult to describe to you what it felt like. Hearing them for the first time. Well listening to this album is a bit like being at Litherland Town Hall all over again. It's the same sort of feeling. Like it's something completely new. Something you've never really heard before."

"I know what you mean," said Louise as 'Lucy in the Sky with Diamonds' faded out. "The stuff everyone else is coming up with sounds pretty ordinary compared with this."

"Including the songs I've been writing," I added, giving her a wry smile.

She shrugged her shoulders apologetically. "I'm afraid so. But you can't compete with The Beatles. And that applies to pretty much every other musician in the world. Sergeant Pepper and The Lonely Hearts Club Band are in a league of their own."

A couple of weeks later we were sitting with four or five friends in a small flat in Belsize Park, trying to get a decent view of the rather grainy and indistinct images on a portable TV in the corner of the room. It wasn't all that easy to see exactly what was happening on the small, black and white screen, but The Beatles, dressed in what we assumed to be rainbow-hued, hippy clothes and surrounded by numerous coloured balloons, were perched on four stools. At their feet, like courtiers, were sitting various members of British Pop Aristocracy, including Mick Jagger, Marianne Faithfull, Eric Clapton and Graham Nash. It looked very much as if, for the time being at least, they'd all accepted that The Beatles were unassailable.

It was the last week of June in 1967 and The Summer of Love was in full swing. Fiona and I had decided to give it at least until the autumn before making a final decision on where we were going to live. I'd found myself some bar work in a Victorian pub called 'The Washington' in England's Lane, a short walk from our bed-sit, while Fiona continued with her job at '*Silver Peaches*'.

We were watching a programme on the BBC, called '*Our World*' which was using the very latest satellite technology to transmit television pictures to thirty-one different countries. Back then it was an astonishing technical achievement. Between 400 and 700 million people were expected to tune in and hear The Beatles, who were now four of the best-known people on the planet, playing live. No musicians had ever before been seen by so many people simultaneously.

The opening bars of La Marseillaise rang out as they launched themselves into the first ever public performance of '*All You Need Is Love*'. It was unclear if the song had been written specially for the occasion, or whether it was a number that just happened to be ready and available. It didn't really matter. The song was brilliant, and it chimed perfectly with the mood of the times.

It was about nine o'clock when the programme finished, and we all headed over to The Washington until last orders were called. Then it was back to the flat for more drinks. It was late when we finally staggered back to Haverstock Hill and crept quietly into bed.

When it was released as a single about a month later, 'All You Need Is Love' went straight to the top of the charts on both sides of the Atlantic. And in many, many other countries as well. The Beatles had truly gone global.

Twenty-Seven

THE LAST OF THE SUMMER WINE

Two months later Fiona and I were driving past Belsize Park tube station when a pavement sign outside a newsagent's caught my eye.

"My God!" I exclaimed.

Fiona, who had been leaning forward to retrieve something from the glove compartment in front of her, turned towards me. "What's the matter?"

"That billboard we just passed. I'm sure it said Brian Epstein's dead."

"Sorry Tony. I missed it."

"I'll pull in at the next paper shop."

We got hold of a copy of the Daily Mirror. The headline took up at least half of the front page.

EPSTEIN
THE BEATLE-MANAGING
PRINCE OF POP
DIES AT 32

According to the front-page story Brian Epstein's body had been found in his Belgravia home. His butler had been unable to wake him and had raised the alarm. There was some speculation in the article that his death might have been due to an accidental alcohol and barbiturate overdose, but nothing would be certain until after an inquest.

I recalled the charming gentleman behind the counter at N.E.M.S. who had been so helpful when Louise spoke to him about getting a copy of 'My Bonnie'. Just five short years had passed since that day when the future had looked so bright and promising. And now both of them were gone.

* * *

"You didn't come to Anfield at all last season, Tone," said Eric. "I suppose you've lost interest in what's happenin' up here now yer livin' down in London. I was beginnin' to think I'd never see yer again."

It was early November. I'd returned to Liverpool, just for the weekend, and had got together with Steve and Eric to catch up on their news. I'd meant to see them on my previous visit, back in February and March, but as it turned out I'd spent most of the time on my own. I hadn't even let them know I was in Liverpool. So it was twelve months since we'd last met up.

"I've been keeping an eye on Liverpool's results, Eric. But to be honest they didn't seem to be doing much last season. Where was it they finished? Sixth?"

Eric frowned at me. "Everton was sixth, Tone. We was fifth. That's two places ahead of Arsenal. So I hope you've not been wastin' yer time goin' to Highbury."

"No way," I said. "White Hart Lane turned out to be a much better bet. Spurs were in the top three for most of the season. They're really good to watch."

Eric shook his head and gave me a smile. "I may be a bit soft, Tone, but I'm not fallin' for that one again. Anyway, we're doin' much better this year. As long as we get at least a draw against Manchester United this afternoon at Anfield we'll still be top of the table. Me and Steve are both goin' along. You should come with us."

Steve grinned and gave me a thumbs up. "It'll be a crackin' game, Tone."

"Okay," I said. "You're on."

There were fifty-five thousand of us crammed into the ground to see the biggest game of the season, but for home fans the result was a disappointment. George Best, the long-haired, football genius with a rock 'n' roll lifestyle who'd been playing for Manchester United since he was a teenager, scored twice before half-time to put them ahead. Liverpool managed to scramble one goal back in the second half, but United hung on for a win.

Eric was downcast. As always he'd been banking on an emphatic Liverpool victory. "I can't stand that George Best. With 'is long hair an' fast cars all the press are callin' 'im the fifth Beatle. Well if 'e wants to be called the fifth bloody Beatle 'e should be playin' for us, not Manchester United."

It was good to spend time with the lads, but the main reason I was back in Liverpool was to visit Louise again. I'd asked Fiona if she wanted to join me, but she felt it'd be better if I went on my own. She said she'd pop down to Canterbury and say hello to her aunt.

Knowing what to expect I found the visit easier than the first time, but I could still feel my heart racing as I walked past the church and approached her grave. My single red rose was still lying there, withered and dry. Beside it, was another bouquet, looking fresh and white. I bent down and gently lifted my faded rose from the white gravel. The last few petals fell away.

I stood there, holding the bare stalk. All was quiet. The tall trees which surrounded the churchyard had lost all their leaves and the bare branches traced a delicate pattern across the cold, grey sky. There were a couple of wooden benches nearby and I sat on one of them, gazing at Louise's grave and thinking. My mind wandered slowly though all the memories I had of our time together. They were already becoming less clear, fading like the petals of the rose, but I was determined to hold on to them for as long as I could.

"I'll come back in the summer," I whispered. "In May or June. I'd like to be here with you when all the trees are green and the flowers are in bloom. It must be beautiful."

With me I had another rose. I brushed my lips against the delicate bloom before placing it alongside the bouquet. As I stood there silently, gazing at the bright red petals, they suddenly reminded me of a Flanders poppy. And from somewhere in the far distance the sound of a bugle playing the Last Post drifted towards me on the wind. It was Remembrance Sunday.

* * *

"Why don't we go and visit the E.M.I. studios in Abbey Road?" I said. "It's not far from here. I'd like to see where Sergeant Pepper was created, even if it's only from the outside."

Fiona and I were back in London and we had a Saturday morning to kill. After a lazy breakfast it was time to decide what to do. She drained the remaining coffee from her cup.

"That's fine with me. I'm pretty sure Paul McCartney lives just round the corner from the studios. In Cavendish Avenue. We could go and take a look at his house as well if you like."

A small group of fans were gathered outside the wrought-iron gates of the E.M.I. studios as we drove past before turning into Circus Road and then right into Cavendish Avenue.

Number Seven was guarded by high wooden gates. It had to be Paul's house because six or seven girls were hanging around outside waiting to see, or maybe even speak to, the great man. We parked the Mini-van about fifty yards away and walked towards them. Two were quite obviously Japanese, and the others sounded American.

"Any sign of activity?" I asked as we approached.

They shook their heads. "Not yet, but it probably won't be long. We were here yesterday and Paul came out to say hello. He said he'd be going over to the studios today. He should be leaving any minute. When you come here a lot you get a sort of feeling for what's going to happen. We heard a few noises from behind the gates about five minutes ago."

I looked at Fiona. "Do you want to wait? Or shall we wander over and take a look at the studios?"

"Let's leave the Mini-van here and walk. It'll only take a couple of minutes."

Just over five minutes later, after safely negotiating a zebra crossing almost opposite the studio entrance, we stood outside a slightly run-down, detached house. It had off-white, stucco walls and seven, evenly-spaced Georgian windows. Above the main doorway, at the top of a flight of stone steps, there was a glazed panel with the E.M.I. logo on it. The gateposts and front wall were festooned with multi-coloured, Beatles graffiti. It was proof, if any were needed, that we were at the right place.

As we stood there and looked at it I was surprised it wasn't more imposing.

"It doesn't look much," I said to Fiona.

I must have sounded disappointed.

"What were you expecting?" she said, laughing. "The Sydney Opera House?"

"Very funny," I said, giving her a gentle push. "You've obviously spent too much time in Liverpool coming up with a sarcastic comment like that. I sort of expected it to be a bit bigger, that's all. It looks like a rather large private house. You wouldn't think there'd be room inside for even one decent-sized recording studio."

"There's probably a lot we can't see from here round the back," said Fiona. She already had her camera out and she was shooting off pictures. "I'll bet it doesn't feel like a house when you get inside. Anyway, it's interesting to see it. Some great music has been recorded in that building."

We stood in the middle of the gateway, lost in our own thoughts, when suddenly we became aware of a car behind us. It was a white Rolls Royce which slowed almost to a halt as we moved to one side to allow it through. A uniformed chauffeur was at the wheel but the occupant of the rear seat was hidden behind darkened windows. Fiona snapped away as the car purred quietly past us and came to a halt right outside the main door. John Lennon stepped out and disappeared quickly up the steps.

A few minutes later Paul McCartney arrived, driving himself in an immaculate Aston Martin DB5. I turned to Fiona. "Make sure you get some pictures of the car as well as Paul. I've always fancied an Aston Martin. Apparently he's got a tape recorder and microphone built into the dashboard so if a song comes into his head while he's driving he can get it down on tape straight away."

Giving us a brief wave as he went, Paul too disappeared into the building.

We waited ten more minutes but nobody else turned up.

"I think that's enough excitement for one day," said Fiona. "Let's go and grab some lunch."

MOORFIELDS MUSIC LTD LIVERPOOL

20th November 1967

Dear Tony,
   Good news at last!
   There's been some interest in a couple of the songs, and it looks like we might have a recording deal on one of them.
   Please get in touch so we can discuss things further.
   All good wishes,
   Larry

I telephoned Larry and he filled me in on the details.

"We've got a deal for the girls from Manchester to record *"Love Isn't Always A Game"* on a new label called Alphagram. It's linked to one of the majors and they're going to be doing the distribution. Things were still touch and go when I wrote to you but it's now definite. We've got Trident Studios in London booked for Wednesday next week."

"That sounds great," I said. "I'm still working down in London. That's why I didn't get straight back to you. Your letter was forwarded to me from Liverpool."

"You'd be very welcome to come along to the recording if you'd like to. Since you're already in London you might as well pop along if you're free. It's up to you. We'll be making a start around midday."

"That'd be great," I said.

"The studio's in St Anne's Court. It's a little alleyway between Dean Street and Wardour Street in Soho. Look forward to seeing you."

Fiona was all over me when I told her. "That's fantastic. I'd love to go along with you but I've got an important meeting at work. Do you think you'll be able to bring a copy of the finished record home with you after the session?"

I put my arms around her. Her enthusiasm was touching.

"I've no idea. I don't really know how it all works. My guess would be probably not, but I'll see what I can do."

The main studio at Trident had only recently been completed and we were one of the first to make use of its state-of-the-art facilities. As well as a brand new A-Range mixing console, which had been designed and built by the two Sheffield brothers who owned the place, it boasted a vintage, Bechstein grand piano which was said to have a very special sound.

During the various stages of the recording I sat in the control room and watched. When the time came to put down the vocal track, the four girls gathered in front of a single microphone. Thanks to understandable nerves the first take was a disaster, but they soon settled down. After six takes Larry was satisfied. And when the final mix was played back over the four Tannoy speakers it sounded unbelievably good.

A London-based song arranger called Ray Dalkeith had done a bit of work on the song since the first demo had been recorded up in Liverpool. He hadn't changed it greatly, but there were some extra harmonies along with some minor changes to the words which meant Larry and I couldn't claim all the credit for the end result. We couldn't claim all the royalties either. They'd have to be split three ways. But if my Dad was right we were going end up with nothing anyway. So I wasn't that bothered.

Larry, who'd been listening from his seat at the Bechstein, gave me a thumbs-up as the play-back finished. I could see him through the control room window and he beckoned me to join him down in the studio.

"We've got fifteen minutes of studio time left. Do you fancy doing a couple of takes of that song of yours *'I Love You In The*

Morning' while we're here? This Bechstein is pretty special and if I can manage a Carole King type of piano arrangement I think it'd work well. Then if there's time we can do a quick run through of that other one I like, *'One Sunday'.*"

After a quick word with the recording engineer we managed to squeeze in all three takes. Larry took the master-tape back to Liverpool, while I headed to Haverstock Hill with a copy.

Fiona was already home from work. I handed her the tape.

"No joy with getting a copy of the record I'm afraid. We'll have to wait until it's released. But there was some spare time at the end of the recording session so Larry and I did a couple of takes of *'I Love You In The Morning'* and then a quick run-through of *'One Sunday'.*"

Fiona turned the tape over and looked at the two song titles which had been quickly written in black biro on the back of the BASF cover.

"How did the recording of *'Love Isn't Always A Game'* go?"

"Pretty well I think," I said. "Larry seemed happy with it. The next thing is to get it played on the BBC and Radio Caroline. And then, with a bit of luck, the punters might go out and buy it."

"When's it going to be released?"

"Sometime early in the New Year. There's too much competition around Christmas for an unknown girl group to get much in the way of radio plays. They've decided to call themselves 'The Manchester Girls' so we should get a few sales up there when it does finally get released. It won't do much in Liverpool though. Scousers tend to be a bit allergic to anything that comes from Manchester."

While we'd been speaking Fiona had taken the seven inch tape, secure in a clear, plastic sleeve, out of its outer cardboard box.

"Come on. Let's have a listen."

I took the cover off the Beocord and, after threading the thin tape between the recording and playback heads, I turned the metal switch to 'PLAY'. The sound wasn't anywhere near as impressive as it had been in the studio, but the piano arrangement certainly worked well. I stopped the tape at the end of 'I Love You In The Morning' and turned to Fiona.

"What do you reckon?"

"I like it. The piano sounds a bit like Carole King."

"That's the sort of thing Larry was aiming for. He thought it'd suit the song."

"Not just a pretty face, your friend Larry," said Fiona. "He obviously knows what he's doing."

I started the tape running again so we could listen to 'One Sunday'. As it finished Fiona nodded approvingly.

"That sounded really good too."

I gave her a hug. "Anyway, that's enough about my day. What about you? How are things going in the wonderful world of fashion?"

"Very well. We got some good news today. We've been working on a link-up with one of the big retailers in King's Road and it's just been finalised. Our profits should at least double if all goes well. The shops in Carnaby Street still generate plenty of business for us, but it's very competitive and the margins are tight. The young Chelsea Set are the ones who've got serious money to spend on clothes." She paused for a moment. "The directors want me to manage the new contract. We'll be taking on three or four extra staff and they'll be working for me. It'll mean a decent pay increase."

"That's great."

It was very good news, but Fiona looked uncertain. "The thing is, if I say yes I'm going to have to stay down here in London. At least for the next year or two. It wouldn't be fair to take the job on and then disappear after a couple of months."

I nodded. "I agree. If you're going to do it you've got to give it a proper go. You wouldn't be happy if you didn't."

"I told them I'd have to talk it over with you." Fiona paused. "They need an answer by tomorrow."

I glanced at my watch. "It's only seven o'clock. Come on. Let's go out and celebrate. We can give the whole situation some more thought over a meal and a bottle of wine."

A few hours later we made our way, a little unsteadily, down Haverstock Hill from a small bar and restaurant called The Holly Bush in Hampstead Village, leaving the Mini-van to be picked up the following morning. Two bottles of Chablis had slipped down very easily with our meal. I was definitely in no fit state to drive.

It had been an easy decision really. Fiona had to take the job. It was too good an opportunity to miss. I could always carry on doing bits and pieces part-time which would allow me to do some song-writing. And with a bit of luck there might even be some more recording sessions.

When we reached the house I fumbled with the door-key as I tried to insert it into the lock.

"If you're going to be the main wage-earner," I said, still working on the lock, "we'd better make sure you don't get pregnant."

Fiona laughed. "In your present state I don't think that's something we need to worry about too much."

I should have stopped at that but I was concentrating on getting the door open and I wasn't really thinking.

"No, seriously. We've got away with it so far, but maybe you should go on the pill? There are places where you can get hold of it now, even if you're not married. There's posters on the tube for a place called The Brook Street Advisory Clinic? It's up to you, of course, but maybe you should go and see them. I couldn't stand it if you had to have an abortion."

I finally managed to turn the key and stumbled into the hallway, holding the door open for Fiona as I went. I looked at her. She was no longer laughing.

"You wouldn't have to stand it," she said. "I'd have the baby."

A moment earlier everything had been fine. I couldn't understand what had happened. I tried desperately to clear my head.

"I'm sorry, Fiona. I didn't mean to upset you. It just occurred to me, that's all. You're right anyway. I've had too much to drink."

We made our way up the staircase to our room. I put my arms around her but she didn't respond.

"I'm really sorry," I said, "but I don't know what I've done."

"It's just a bit difficult for me, that's all."

"What is? The pill?"

She bit her lip and it looked as though she might be about to cry. "Look. Please, Tony. Just forget it. I'll be fine in the morning."

Once we were undressed and in bed I put my arms around her. "Are you sure you're okay? I won't be able to sleep if you're not."

She turned towards me and gave me a kiss. "I'm fine, Tony. Don't worry."

●·•————●·•●·•●————·•●

"I love you in the morning, with your body soft and warm beside me."

Fiona was still half-asleep, with her back to me. I stroked her gently, running my fingers softly up and down her spine. At first there was no response but then she turned and gave me a wry smile.

"I'm sorry about last night. I shouldn't have reacted like that."

"Don't," I said. "I've forgotten about it already. I'm sorry too."

I kissed her and pulled her towards me. She pushed me away gently. "I'd love to, Tony, but I've got to be in work for eight and let them know what we've decided. Wait 'til this evening."

"One more kiss then."

"One more kiss and I'm getting in the shower."

Our lips met for a couple of seconds then Fiona swung her legs over the far side of the bed, leaving me lying there thinking. When she returned from the shower and took her dressing gown off her face and hair were still wet. Little rivulets of water ran down her chest. She looked amazing but now that I was properly awake I could feel the after-effects of the previous night's alcohol. Fiona seemed to be fine but my head felt heavy and I badly needed some fluids. I went over to the sink and held a pint glass under the tap until it was full. After gulping the contents down I repeated the exercise.

"I need a coffee," I said. "I'll make a jug and we can both have some."

Having dried her hair and dressed, Fiona added a generous amount of cold milk to her coffee and downed it quickly. Then she was gone.

———

"This invitation arrived at work today." As she walked in through the door that evening Fiona took off her coat and gave me a hug before handing me a small envelope. "One of our directors used to do a bit of work with Apple, the company The Beatles set up to handle their business affairs after Brain Epstein died. With me having been at Art College in Liverpool he thought I might be interested."

I pulled a printed card out of the envelope and took a look at it.

THE APPLE BOUTIQUE 74 BAKER STREET
5TH DECEMBER 1967
COME AT 7.46 FASHION SHOW AT 8.16
ADMIT TWO

"It's the opening party of The Beatles' new boutique," said Fiona. "I've no idea what it'll be like. All I know is what it says on the invitation. Do you fancy it?"

I couldn't quite understand why she was even asking.

"I absolutely fancy it," I said. "Don't you? The Beatles might be there."

"They might be, I suppose. But I wouldn't bet on it. It's called The Apple Boutique, but I shouldn't think The Beatles themselves have necessarily had that much to do with it."

"Let's give it a go anyway. You might find the fashion show interesting. We can always leave if it's a waste of time."

Fiona took her shoes off and sat down. "Fine. As long as you're happy."

"I'm more than happy," I said. "It's not every day you get an invite from The Beatles – even if it's not addressed to us personally. We can frame it and bore the grandchildren to death with stories about how we once met them."

"By the time we've got grandchildren The Beatles"ll be long forgotten."

"I wouldn't bet on it," I said, giving her a kiss. "Anyway, how did it go at work? Have you got the new job sorted out?"

"Yes. Everything's fine. We're going to start advertising for my team next week."

"Brilliant. I'm really pleased." I looked again at the invitation. "I'm going to have to get myself something to wear. I can't turn up there looking like a scruff."

Fiona laughed. She seemed happy. It was as if the previous evening had never happened. I couldn't quite get my head round it. But I wasn't about to rock the boat by asking questions.

Twenty-Eight

MAGICAL MYSTERY TOUR

The Apple Boutique couldn't be missed as we walked towards it. Much to the dismay of some of the more traditional residents of the area, the brickwork of the elegant Georgian building on the corner of Baker Street and Paddington Street had been over-painted with a huge, psychedelic mural. A large crowd was milling around outside the boutique, many of whom seemed to be uninvited and were trying desperately to blag their way past two burly commissionaires who guarded the door. Anticipating that it might be busy we'd taken the precaution of arriving at least half an hour before the appointed time and it looked like it had been a wise decision. We made our way towards the doorway and our invitation was carefully scrutinised, after which a burly arm pushed the door open.

"That's fine. Go on in. The drinks are at the back. Soft drinks only I'm afraid. Someone never got round to fixing up the licence they'd need to serve alcohol." He shrugged his shoulders. "Takes all sorts. Enjoy yourselves anyway."

I followed Fiona into the building. Inside it was fairly crowded, but not packed. Above our heads the ceiling had been decorated with numerous white clouds while on one of the walls there was a brightly-coloured mural. The other walls were painted a very dark blue, dotted with silvery-bright stars and moons.

As we gazed around, taking it all in, we found ourselves standing next to a man with long sideburns and light-brown, collar length hair. He was wearing a cream-coloured jacket over a black, roll-neck sweater, and a pair of dark trousers. He seemed to be giving instructions to a couple of people who were paying very close attention to his every word. The moment he finished speaking they hurried off, presumably to carry out his instructions, and he turned to face us. As he peered at me through a pair of round spectacles which were perched on an oddly familiar, beaked nose I realised with a start that it was John Lennon.

I stood there, staring at him, as a thin-lipped smile crossed his face. Then, without saying a word, he headed off towards a curtained doorway in the star-covered wall and disappeared.

Fiona looked stunned. "I don't believe what just happened. That was John Lennon wasn't it?"

"I think so," I said, blinking. "Seeing him standing there right next to us took me completely by surprise. I was trying to think of something sensible to say but my mind went completely blank."

"Me too," said Fiona, still looking slightly bemused. "I suppose he's used to it. People must behave really strangely when they first meet him. Particularly if they're not expecting it. Come on. Let's take a look at the clothes."

"Fine. But no pulling them to pieces, please. I don't want you to get us chucked out."

She gave me a grin and started flicking through several racks of brightly-coloured jackets and trousers, removing the occasional item which caught her eye to inspect it in more detail. As she did so I stood and looked around the rapidly-filling room.

After a couple of minutes she shook her head. "They've got some nice stuff but it's not really my sort of thing."

"Let's grab a couple of drinks then," I said, taking her hand and guiding her through the crowd towards the tables at the back of the room.

Fruit juices in hand we stood together in one corner, people-watching.

"That looks just like The Casbah," I said, pointing at the star-covered wall.

Fiona looked puzzled.

I held up my hand in apology. "Sorry. It'd probably closed down by the time you were up in Liverpool. It was a sort of club. The Beatles used to play there when they were first starting out. Long before they played The Cavern or anywhere like that. It was in the basement of a big, old house in West Derby Village where their first drummer, Pete Best, lived. They'd smartened the place up and painted the walls themselves. Very dark blue, with stars all over them. I went there once with Steve and Dave."

As I was speaking Fiona suddenly tugged at my hand. "Over there, Tony. Look. Isn't that George Harrison?"

She pointed towards a pair of figures at the back of the shop. The lighting was quite dim, but I could just make out a person who definitely looked like George Harrison leaning against a small stack of unopened cardboard boxes. He was wearing a pale shirt and jeans, with a multi-coloured, striped jacket. A chiffon scarf hung loosely around his neck. Standing alongside him was a very pretty blonde whose face I recognised immediately. It was Patti Boyd.

"Let's go and have a chat," said Fiona. "He might be interested to meet up with someone who used to go to The Casbah."

I must have looked doubtful about the idea, and I was about to tell her again that I'd only ever gone there once. But she was already on the move.

"Come on, Tony. We'll probably never get the chance again."

George Harrison seemed to be deep in thought despite the crowds close by him but he gave us a brief smile as he saw us approaching. He was on his own. Patti had disappeared.

Seizing the moment, Fiona went straight up to him. "Hello George. I'm Fiona, and this is Tony. He's from Liverpool and he used to go and see you play at The Casbah."

George looked at me with a vague flicker of interest. "It was mostly friends, people we knew, who went to watch us there." His flat Liverpool accent was instantly familiar.

"I only went along once," I said. "On New Year's Eve a few years ago. With a couple of friends."

He nodded his head. He didn't seem that bothered about making conversation but Fiona wasn't going to give up. She gestured towards the star-covered wall. "Tony says that wall looks just like one in The Casbah."

George frowned slightly. It was as if he was trying to cast his mind back to a completely different life. Another existence. "Yeah, that's right. The dark sky and the stars. Someone said Paul noticed that too. I'm not sure he liked it. I think he wanted the whole place to be white. With stuff like china and furniture as well. Not just clothes. Everything white."

"Is he here?"

"Who, Paul?" George shook his head. "No. He's gone up to his farm in Scotland. With Jane." As he spoke his dark brown eyes were scanning the room. "Have you seen Patti? She was here a minute ago. I'd best go find her. Enjoy the party."

Our brief audience was over. We watched as he made his way towards the curtained doorway and slipped through it.

Fiona looked at me. "Poor George. He didn't look all that happy. I wonder if there's some sort of problem. He seemed a bit phased when he noticed Patti had disappeared."

"He probably just doesn't like having to make small-talk at parties. I've got some sympathy with him on that one."

"You didn't have to come."

I gave her a kiss. "Don't worry. Wild horses wouldn't have kept me away from this one. I'll be dining out on it for years."

I looked at my watch. It was almost eight-fifteen and people seemed to be moving towards some chairs which had been lined up in another part of the room. The fashion show was about to get underway and, after hurriedly topping-up our glasses, we settled down to watch. We stayed until the end, but it was all a bit surreal. Fiona wasn't greatly impressed.

"It'll be interesting to see how long this place lasts," she said as we were leaving. "I suppose with it being linked to The Beatles it'll attract plenty of customers. But I'm not altogether sure it works. It all seems a bit disorganised. It's certainly very different from the places we do business with."

"Maybe it'll work because it is so different?"

"Maybe," she said thoughtfully, but she didn't sound totally convinced. "I wonder what Brian Epstein would have made of it?"

***

For Christmas 1967 I bought Fiona a copy of '*The Mersey Sound*', a recently-published collection of poems by Adrian Henri and two of the other Liverpool poets, Roger McGough and Brian Patten. We'd gone along to a reading which the three of them were giving in a small room at the back of The Old Red Lion in Islington. Fiona had managed to grab a quick word with Adrian before the reading started and afterwards, while she was chatting to a couple of friends, I slipped away and got him to sign the book for her.

I explained who I was and watched as he wrote on the inside title page 'For Fiona. *A lovely student and very special friend. Adrian Henri.*'. He then added a couple of kisses.

He closed the book of poetry and handed it back to me. "Look after Fiona, Tony. She's a very special girl. I think one of these poems might be about her." He smiled. "But that was a long time ago."

Then, as he was turning away, pen in hand, to speak to a young girl who was waiting nearby, holding out a copy of his book ready for him to sign, he added, "I hope you've still got that signed copy of *'Rubber Soul'*."

When I gave the book to Fiona she was delighted. She immediately worked out that I must have asked Adrian to sign it at the poetry reading. I wanted to ask her about the poem. Did she even know about it? But I decided it was probably best to leave it for another day. If Adrian was right, it had, after all, been a long time ago.

※※※※

On Boxing Day we went round to some friends in Belsize Park. They had a colour TV and along with a few others we were going to watch the eagerly anticipated Beatles film *'Magical Mystery Tour'*. What we hadn't realised was that, although the film had been shot in colour, it was being shown on BBC1 which was only transmitted in black and white.

We all sat there and watched as a coach party of strange characters set off on a disjointed charabanc trip around the English countryside. It was the sort of uncomplicated day out that was still very popular in Liverpool and other northern cities. But on this psychedelic bus strange things started to happen at the whim of a group of magicians, played by the four Beatles and Mal Evans, their road manager.

It came across rather like a home movie. That may have been the intention, but if so it didn't really work. The only thing that made it worth watching was the music. The songs were as brilliant and inventive as ever.

As the only Liverpudlian present, who'd very happily been riding The Beatles' seemingly inexhaustible creative wave, I felt a strange sense of responsibility for the disappointment that filled the room. As the closing credits rolled up the screen I looked around at the bemused faces.

One of Fiona's friends from work was the first to speak. "Well, that was a load of garbage. It looks like the four geniuses from Liverpool have finally lost the plot, Tony."

Nobody disagreed.

I wanted to say the film might have been better if we'd been able to see it in colour, but I didn't bother. To be perfectly honest with you I didn't think it would've made that much difference.

The reaction of the newspaper critics was equally scathing. Hardly any of them had a good word to say about the film and I couldn't help feeling this was the opportunity they'd been waiting for. At long last they could bring the untouchable Beatles, and the bumptious inhabitants of Liverpool, down a peg or two.

It slightly worried me. The Beatles were big enough to shake off any amount of bad publicity, but their home city had spent the past few years basking lazily in the band's reflected glory. Not much effort had been made to harness and build on the worldwide attention which The Beatles had attracted. There'd be a lot of negative headlines. And Scousers weren't exactly good at coping with criticism. Two fingers to the outside world was likely to be their reaction.

The film was broadcast in colour on BBC2 a few days later, but as this channel was restricted to the London area very few people saw it. It was too late anyway. The damage had been done. The big American TV networks shelved any plans they might have had to broadcast it.

'*Magical Mystery Tour*' was probably ahead of its time. In some ways it was self-indulgent. But the type of surreal humour that had so bemused people that Boxing Day in 1967 re-emerged some years later in the form of 'Monty Python's Flying Circus'.

Okay. Maybe I'm just making excuses. But, as I said, we Scousers don't take criticism well.

The record by The Manchester Girls was released on Friday 16th February 1968. I travelled back to Liverpool for the launch party at Moorfields Music. Fiona was too busy at work to join me, so the plan was that I'd stay up in Liverpool for the weekend and take the opportunity to meet up with Eric and Steve again.

I drove up from London on the Friday morning and arrived at the studio to find that quite a few of the great and good from the Liverpool music scene had turned up for the launch. Larry had organised a buffet lunch, and complimentary copies of the record were handed out, all in specially-printed sleeves with a stunning picture of the four girls on the cover.

When it was played over the studio speakers the general opinion was that the record should do well. A definite hit. Mind you, as Larry said, our guests weren't likely to be negative about it after downing all our food and booze.

Everybody had drifted off by early evening so I headed to The Liver in the hope of bumping into either Eric or Steve. When I walked in, Eric was sitting at a table on his own. I joined him and got a couple of beers in. We chatted away, catching up on local news and generally putting the world to rights.

"We're playing Walsall in the F.A Cup tomorrow afternoon," said Eric. "Down in Birmingham. Me an' Steve's both goin'. Degsy was joinin' us but 'e's skint. So there's a spare ticket if you fancy it."

It sounded like a good idea. I had nothing else planned.

"If you like I could drive you and Steve to the match and then carry on home afterwards," I said. "Walsall's pretty much half-way to London anyway."

"That sounds good," said Eric. "We can get the train back to Liverpool. I'm sure Steve'll be okay with that."

"Has he been in tonight?"

"Who, Steve?" Eric shook his head. "No. 'E said 'e didn't much fancy a pint this evenin'. 'E's gone out for a bite with Tracey I think."

As he turned to pick up his drink I suddenly noticed that Eric's left cheek was slightly swollen and bruised. It wasn't that obvious, which was probably why I hadn't seen it sooner.

"What's up with your face, Eric?"

He put his hand up to his cheek and felt it. "Can yer still see it? I thought it'd gone down. It looked a lot worse last week."

"What happened?"

"It wasn't much really." He shrugged his shoulders as if it was unimportant. "Me an' a lad called Fletcher got into a bit of a barney with a gang of yobs who was out lookin' for trouble last Friday night. There was too many of 'em to fight off so we just 'ad to leg it. Fletcher got the worst of it. I was a bit quicker than 'im an' I managed to get away after the first couple of punches. The bastards scarpered when some coppers turned up, but by then they'd given poor Fletch a real good goin' over."

He looked at me as if he wanted to say more but wasn't quite sure about it. "Can I trust yer, Tone?"

I frowned at him. "What's up? Of course you can trust me. We've been mates for years."

"That's what I thought about Steve. But 'e went all strange on me when I told 'im." Eric went silent for a minute, then whispered quietly, "Just be grateful yer not queer, Tone."

His unexpected directness took me completely by surprise. For a few seconds I didn't know what to say. "Is that why they beat you up? Because they thought you were queer?"

He lifted his hand and motioned me to keep my voice down. "They didn't think it, Tone. They knew. I was 'avin' a drink with Fletch in The Magic Clock an' there's usually a few lads hangin' around in the street outside lookin' for trouble. They're well aware it's one of the places in town where men meet up. When you're leavin' the pub you know to keep an eye out for problems, but we was headed down to the Pier Head an' we just didn't notice 'em 'til it was too late. They must've watched us 'til they was quite sure what we was up to. Then they laid into us. It was our own fault really. We should've been more careful."

"Is that what you told Steve?"

Eric nodded. "Yer couldn't miss the bruisin' last weekend. Me face was really swollen. I suppose I could've said I'd fallen over or somethin'. But I didn't. I thought 'e'd be okay about it."

"And he wasn't?"

"'E just went all quiet. Then 'e said 'e 'ad to go an' meet Tracey."

Eric had been a good friend for years. I knew he'd never had a girlfriend, but I didn't for a moment think anything of it. I suppose I assumed all he cared about was football.

"What did the coppers do?"

"They weren't all that interested to be honest, Tone. They knew what we was up to. They're probably pissed off they can't arrest us and haul us down to the Bridewell anymore. Not since the law got changed last year. But I reckon they'd still like to." He looked sad then continued very quietly. "They probably thought we got what we deserved."

"I'm sorry, Eric," I said. "I really am."

He shrugged his shoulders and gave me a look of resignation. "Nobody's gonna be bothered if a few lads decide they're gonna 'ave a bit of fun with a couple of queers. It's a good excuse for a fight, I suppose. They can do what they like really. The coppers might even think they're doin' a useful job. Yer know. Clearin' us off the streets."

He gazed up at the smoke-stained ceiling as I sat quietly, looking around at the Friday night regulars enjoying their drinks. Then he took a drink from his pint and turned to me. "I don't suppose you can really understand."

I didn't say anything for a moment or so. I was thinking. "I don't suppose I can," I said. "But I'm glad you told me. You can be yourself now."

"Eh, take it easy, Tone." Eric gave a little laugh. "I'm not about to go all limp-wristed on yer. That'd definitely finish Steve off."

The tension had gone.

"Okay. But you know what I mean. I'm sure Steve'll be fine. He's not going to fall out with you after all these years." I paused. "Do you want me to have a word with him?"

Eric shook his head. "No. Let's just see how things go. As far as I know e's still comin' to the game tomorrow. It'll be okay."

We sat in silence, lost in our own thoughts.

"It's been a long day," I said. "Time to hit the sack."

I picked up my pint and drained it before placing it back on the table alongside Eric's already empty glass. We both stood up and I gave him a hug.

"Look after yourself, Eric. I'll see you tomorrow."

●–•–––––––––––•–•–•–•–•––––––––––•–•

Next day Steve was his normal self and Eric was full of beans. It was as if a weight had been lifted from his shoulders. We had a fantastic day out apart from the result of the match. Liverpool had put a full-strength team out against the lower-division opposition, but they could only manage a goalless draw. The replay would be at Anfield on the Monday evening, just two days later. By then I'd be back in London. But Eric and Steve would both be there. Liverpool couldn't possibly lose to Walsall at home. Could they?

After a curry at an Indian restaurant near the ground I dropped the two of them off at New Street Station in the centre of Birmingham and headed south. The roads were quiet so I was back at Haverstock Hill by just after ten. The house was in darkness. Fiona had said she might go down to see her aunt in Canterbury after finishing work, while Dr Robertson and his wife quite often went to the theatre on a Saturday evening, so it wasn't unexpected. I let myself in and went upstairs.

It was a cold, February night and the bed-sit was freezing. I switched on the electric heater and made myself a cup of coffee. I didn't know when, or even if, Fiona would be back, and there was no way of contacting her. I picked up my guitar and began to play around with a few chords while the room warmed up.

It must have been about an hour later, as I sat on the bed with the guitar still in my hands. A key turned in the lock and Fiona walked into the room.

"Oh my God! Tony!" She looked shocked. "I thought you were staying up in Liverpool for the weekend."

I gave her a grin. "Last minute change of plan. I went to watch Liverpool play at Walsall this afternoon with Eric and Steve. There was no point in driving all the way back up to Liverpool, so I decided to give you a surprise."

I stood up and was about to give her a hug when I caught sight of a figure just outside the still half-closed door.

Fiona's face flushed as I pulled the door fully open.

"I'm sorry," I said, "but who are you?"

The man, whose dark hair was flecked with grey, didn't reply. He was wearing what was obviously an expensive suit over a light blue shirt and tie. Fiona looked at me but avoided catching my eye.

"His name's David Saunders," she said. "We work together. We've just been out for a meal to talk about the new contract and he's come back for coffee. We didn't expect you to be here, obviously."

"Obviously," I said tersely. "Is he going to be staying?"

David Saunders, who had been standing silently outside the door, started to turn away.

"I think it's probably best if I go, Fiona. I'll see you in work on Monday."

I followed him as he made his way down the stairs and opened the front door. He stopped beneath the stone portico and turned to face me.

"I'm very sorry. It's my fault. I talked Fiona into inviting me back."

"Okay," I said. "I'll bear that in mind. Now sod off. Or I might have to hit you."

I shut the door and made my way slowly back up the stairs. Fiona was sitting on the bed.

"Has he been here before?"

She shook her head. "No. It's the first time we've seen each other outside work."

"So, what's going on?"

"We were going to have a coffee."

"And?"

"And nothing." She took a deep breath. "I don't really know what I was thinking of." She stood up and put her arms around me. "Tony, please. I'm so sorry."

I pushed her arms away. "What do you want me to do?"

"I don't know. Shout at me. Go mad. I missed you. I was on my own. And when David suggested a meal to talk about things at work I thought it'd be fine. Then we had a couple of bottles of wine. And he said he didn't want the evening to end. So I just said he could come back here for coffee."

We talked late into the night, trying to understand what was happening.

"If I hadn't come back early would you have slept with him?"

"David's married, Tony. He's got two young kids. He's at least twenty years older than me."

"Is that supposed to be a yes or a no?"

"No." She shook her head. "He's one of the directors of the company."

"In which case he should know better. He shouldn't take advantage of a member of his staff. What do you think he was expecting?"

"We had a meal together. To talk about work. His wife knew where he was going. We spent most of the time discussing how we were going to manage the new contract."

"Did he tell his wife how attractive he found you?"

"I don't know. For God's sake. No. Of course he didn't."

"I'm disappointed in him. He should be more appreciative when a very good-looking young member of staff agrees to go out for a meal with him."

"Stop it, Tony, please. Nothing happened."

"Obviously it didn't. I was sitting here on the bed. But that's not to say it wouldn't have if I hadn't turned up unexpectedly."

"Look. I don't even fancy him."

"You should have thought of that earlier. Before you started making offers which he was hardly likely to refuse."

I was starting to shout at her. At first I'd been too shocked to lose my temper. The whole situation was too sudden and unexpected. My mind was spinning round trying to work out what to do. I was getting angry.

Fiona began to cry. "I didn't think, Tony. I love you. Please believe me. I love you so much."

I stood there and said nothing. Her tear-stained eyes looked up at me from where she sat, on the edge of the bed. "Do you still love me?" she said miserably.

I wanted to believe I did, but I couldn't help comparing her with Louise. Had I ever loved Fiona as much as I loved Louise? Or even in the same way?

There was a long silence, broken only by Fiona's quiet sobs.

"I don't know," I said finally.

As she continued to cry I sat next to her on the bed and put my arm around her shoulders.

"What are we going to do?" I said.

I felt her wet cheek against mine as she started to kiss me and, despite everything – or maybe because of everything – I found myself responding.

She was still incredibly attractive and our love-making was even more urgent and passionate than usual. When it was finally over we were both exhausted.

We slept surprisingly well, but when we woke we both knew that the physical release hadn't really solved anything. We felt confused and uncertain. What did the events of the previous evening mean? We needed time to think.

I'd always known that what Louise and I had was very special. Maybe the romantics are right when they say it happens only once in a lifetime? Maybe it was different with Louise because it was the first time for both of us; and that could never be repeated?

Nothing had happened with David Saunders. I knew that. And Fiona said she was quite certain that nothing ever would. But if we were to stay together we had to be sure that we both wanted the same things out of life. That our relationship was heading in the right direction.

All of a sudden it felt as though I was growing up. And I wasn't altogether sure I liked it. You probably know what I mean. Life's a complicated business. Someone once said you live it forwards and understand it backwards. I suppose what I was starting to realise was that Fiona and I needed to try and understand it forwards.

Neither of us really wanted it, but we decided that it'd be best if we spent some time apart to see what would happen. Perhaps a bit of space might help us work out our real feelings for each other?

Was that sensible? Maybe not. But it seemed like a grown-up and sensible thing to do at the time.

The following week I said goodbye to Fiona and headed north. To keep me awake on the journey I listened to Sergeant Pepper at full volume on the radio-cassette player. Pop music was getting almost as complicated as life. It was difficult to believe that in less than five years The Beatles had progressed from a simple song like 'Love Me Do' to something as complex and many-layered as 'A Day In The Life.' Sergeant Pepper and his Lonely Hearts Club Band were unbelievably good. They were changing everything.

●‧•——————●‧•‧●‧•‧●————‧•‧●

As I drove into Liverpool along Edge Lane, with Sergeant Pepper still blaring out from the speakers, the city looked different. There seemed to be more bomb sites. And the nearer I got to the docks the more obvious the destruction became. Parts of London were the same, of course, particularly down in the East End, but I'd never noticed it quite so much in Liverpool before. When I was growing up the empty, rubble-strewn spaces had been part of everyday life. They were so normal you didn't really see them. They were just there.

The other thing I noticed was how quiet the streets were, even near the city centre. It was Sunday afternoon and everywhere seemed to be deserted. The shops were all closed and shuttered. Camden Town would still be heaving with life.

Liverpool had become world-famous. But it was still at heart a northern, provincial city. It was very different from London.

"I'm really sorry you and Fiona've run into problems, Tone. But it's good to have yer back. I've missed yer." Eric smiled and gave me a hug.

It was the following Saturday afternoon and we were standing on The Spion Kop watching Bill Shankly's Liverpool team, who were lying third in the First Division, as they took on Leicester City.

Eric had persuaded me to go along. "You'll enjoy it, Tone. They'll beat Leicester easy. It'll cheer yer up."

It was just the two of us at the match. Tracey had entered a competition in the Liverpool Echo and won what was described as a romantic night for two in Blackpool. Steve had filled me in the previous evening. "As far as Tracey's concerned that means a dirty weekend. They've given 'er thirty quid for spends an' she's told me she's got 'erself somethin' sexy to wear. She ses it'll be a big surprise. There's no way I'm missin' out on that. Sod the football."

The match went well, even though it wasn't quite as straightforward a victory as we'd expected. We were a goal down at half-time. Then in the second half we put three goals past the England and Leicester City goal-keeper, Peter Shilton. It was comfortable in the end, and it kept us in third position behind Leeds and Manchester United.

And Eric was right. It did cheer me up.

As we made our way over to The Albert after the game I started to feel at home. Liverpool was indeed very different from London, but its peculiar magic was working its spell on me again.

Twenty-Nine

LOVE ISN'T ALWAYS A GAME

Give me a little of the love you've been given,
Love isn't always a game,
Leave me a little of the life we've been living,
I don't believe you want me back again.
Last night you held me in your arms. I felt protected and I
*   whispered 'I love you'.*
And safe within my lover's arms, I thought it funny when
*   you didn't seem to say a word*
You seemed so very far away. So many things I couldn't
*   say to you.*
(I thought you had made your mind up. I thought you had
*   made your mind up.)*
Give me a little of the love you've been given,
Love isn't always a game,
Leave me a little of the life we've been living,
I don't believe you want me back again.

Following the launch party the north-west press, along with the
New Musical Express and Melody Maker, gave the record by The

Manchester Girls a decent number of column inches with plenty of positive comments. Several hundred copies were shifted by record shops in Manchester and there were some decent sales elsewhere in the UK, even on Merseyside. Not enough to break into the charts, but still respectable. The girls got themselves a Saturday night TV slot on The David Frost Show and there were quite a few radio plays.

I should have got some royalties, I suppose, but nothing ever materialised.

Fiona stayed in London while I signed up as an electrician with the city council in Liverpool, working mainly evenings and nights. The hours suited me as it gave me plenty of free time during the day.

It was no surprise to my Dad that the record hadn't made me a millionaire but, as he said, he could sleep easy now. As far as he was concerned, a steady job with a public sector pension was a much better bet than swimming with sharks.

I spoke to Fiona on the phone from time to time, but gradually the calls became less frequent. And at the end of May they stopped altogether. Our lives had gone in different directions and we no longer had anything to say to each other. We'd allowed ourselves to drift apart.

In June 1968 Jane Asher and Paul McCartney announced that they were parting.

Then, a few months later, John Lennon sued his wife, Cynthia, for divorce, alleging adultery which she firmly denied. She then counter-sued because of his relationship with Yoko Ono.

Splitting up was in fashion. Everything was changing.

●+———●+●+●+●———+●

The Cavern Club was also in trouble. Kids in Liverpool didn't have much spare cash and the club wasn't making money.

Because the club attracted mainly youngsters, Ray McFall hadn't been able to get a drinks licence to improve the cash-flow. So he'd sold it to a chap called Alf Geoghegan who'd converted an unused area at ground floor level into a late night piano bar in an effort to attract older punters with more money to spend. Moorfields Music was struggling too, so Larry had got himself a job playing piano in the bar. He was able to come and go pretty much as he pleased, which meant the two of us could meet up there during the day and work on our songs.

Towards the end of October in 1968 Larry and I were hard at work in the bar. It was the middle of the afternoon. Larry was sitting at the piano and I was perched alongside him on a stool, playing my guitar and operating the Beocord, which was sitting on the piano lid. We were half-way through making a rough recording of a song we'd just finished when a figure in a long, dark coat appeared at the door. The collar of the coat was pulled up high over his ears, and a wide-brimmed hat made it almost impossible to see his face. He wandered over to us, removing the hat as he did so.

"Hi Larry," he said. "It's been a few years."

The voice and face were instantly recognisable. It was Paul McCartney.

"Paul!" said Larry. "Silly question, I know, but what are you doing here?"

While they were greeting each other I switched off the tape recorder.

"I spoke to Alf on the phone earlier," said Paul. "I wanted to know if it'd be okay for me to call in this afternoon. No publicity. And definitely no press. Just a quick visit without any fuss."

Larry looked my way. "Paul and I knew each other when I was with Polydor in London. We used to hang out together from time to time." He then turned back to Paul who was unbuttoning his greatcoat. "When you first came down to London I introduced you and John to a few people in the business if you remember?" said Larry, smiling to himself. "Things have moved on a bit."

Paul laughed. "They have indeed. But I haven't forgotten those early days, Larry. They were exciting times."

Larry nodded. "They certainly were. For all of us. So what brings you down to The Cavern?"

"I'm on my way up to Scotland and I thought I'd call in for old times' sake. To see what's going on. I've left a friend outside in the car. I don't want to disturb you, but is it alright if I bring her in?"

"Sure." Larry turned to me. "This is Tony. We're just doing a bit of work on some songs we've been writing. But we're not in any hurry."

Up to this point I'd said nothing. My brain was almost completely scrambled. It was all so totally unexpected. Standing right in front of me, in the flesh, was Sergeant Pepper.

Paul looked my way. "Hi Tony. Good to meet you."

"Hi Paul." My mouth had gone dry and my voice sounded strange. Without thinking what I was doing I lifted up my right hand in a sort of salute.

Paul looked at me as if he wasn't entirely sure I was in full possession of my senses. Which at that particular moment was probably not an unreasonable assumption. In 1968, having Paul McCartney walk unannounced into The Cavern was a bit like coming face-to-face with God.

He turned towards the door. "I'll be back in a second."

Leaving his coat on he disappeared for a couple of minutes before returning with a very attractive, blonde girl. "Larry. This is a friend of mine, Linda."

Linda shook Larry by the hand. "Pleased to meet you, Larry."

"And this is Tony," said Paul.

Linda smiled at me. "Hi there, Tony. We just flew in from New York and Paul's been taking me round some of his old haunts up here in Liverpool. It's seems like a great place."

By this time my brain had unscrambled itself a little and I just returned her smile, keeping my right arm firmly by my side.

With her long, blonde hair and American accent Linda could have walked straight out of one of the Hollywood films we used to watch with such amazement. She turned to Paul. "Why not play us something? Here in The Cavern. Just for old times' sake."

He held out his left hand and laughed. "Now, hold on a minute. This isn't where we played. It's all new to me up here. We used to play downstairs in the cellar."

But Linda wasn't going to be put off. "Come on, Paul. The piano's here. Play 'Hey Jude'."

Paul shrugged his shoulders and turned to Larry. "Would you mind?"

Larry stood up. "It's all yours."

Paul sat down and placed his hands on the keys before playing the instantly recognisable, opening chords of 'Hey Jude' which had been released as a single just a few weeks earlier.

As he continued the chord sequence he turned to Larry. "Hey, this piano sounds nice, Larry. Not quite as good as the Bechstein at Trident which we used on the recording. But not bad."

We listened to the words of the already very familiar song which had first come to Paul as he was driving down to see John's wife, Cynthia, and Julian their son, after John had left the two of them for Yoko Ono. The very earliest version of the song may even have been sung onto the cassette player in his Aston Martin. The story was that he'd changed 'Hey Jules' to 'Hey Jude' because it sounded better, but I couldn't help noticing that several times, as he was singing, he looked up at Linda who was standing with her arms resting on the lid of the piano. Particular words and phrases seemed to hold a special meaning for both of them.

Larry also noticed the smiles and glances. To the two of

us there seemed to be little doubt that, while 'Jude' may at first have been 'Jules', and the initial inspiration for the song may have been John Lennon's young son, the first section had evolved into an expression of his feelings about the love affair with Jane Asher which had inspired some of his most beautiful early songs. And as Linda stood by the piano the glances which passed between them seemed to be saying it was no accident that she had asked for that particular song. For the second, and most important, part of the song was about a new love. It had to be about her.

All too soon the magical moment was over. Larry gave Paul a gentle pat on the back as the final chord slowly died away. "That song's a classic, Paul. It's going to be around for a very long time."

Paul stood up from the piano and took Linda's hand. "Let's go down and take a look at where we used to play."

Down in the cellar, from where The Beatles had set off on their journey to conquer the world, a Liverpool band called Curiosity Shop were rehearsing. After a few introductions Paul got up onto the old stage again. He sat behind the drum-kit and played a few rolls, surrounded by the young musicians, while Alf Geoghegan, who'd been watching the band as they rehearsed, passed his camera to Linda so she could take a few pictures.

Fifteen minutes later Paul and Linda were gone, heading for Scotland and his farm. The visit had taken place without any fuss, just as they had wanted, and the press never got to hear about it.

Many years later one of the photographs, showing Paul sitting behind the drum-kit on stage with the members of Curiosity Shop standing round him, was put on display in The Cavern. If you ever make a visit, take a look at the wall just to the right of the bar. The picture will probably still be there.

On 22nd November, a few weeks after Paul's visit to The Cavern, The Beatles' next album was released. The double sleeve-fold was entirely white with just the name of the band and a serial number stamped on each copy. Perhaps he'd managed to persuade the band that white really was a cool colour?

•••••••••••••

"I can't understand why John Lennon would want to take up with Yoko an' walk out on 'is poor wife an' little son. Why, for God's sake? Cynthia's really attractive."

"Yeah. But 'e got Cynthia pregnant. So I suppose 'e felt 'e had to marry 'er. Maybe 'e just wasn't happy."

"Me mate, Arthur, said 'e saw Yoko up here in Liverpool a few years ago. At The Bluecoat it was. The place in town where they put on all the arty stuff. Long before she took up with John. She just sat there on the stage, holdin' a pair of scissors, an' invited people from the audience to cut bits off the dress she was wearin'. It was mostly blokes who went up. They said in the Echo it was a very intelligent comment on the way men and women interact. Fair enough. But I'll tell yer one thing. If I went anywhere near me missus with a pair of scissors 'er comments definitely wouldn't be intelligent. An' I don't even want to think about what she might do to me with the bleedin' scissors."

With their 'Bed-Ins for Peace', protesting against the Vietnam War, John and Yoko were obviously on the same wavelength. And they'd soon be grabbing plenty of headlines. But a lot of people in Liverpool were unable to understand why he couldn't just stick to playing music.

The other three members of the band were also branching out alone. With Brian Epstein no longer around to keep them together, The Beatles were going their separate ways.

There would still be three more albums, '*Yellow Submarine*', '*Abbey Road*' and '*Get Back*', which gave the impression that all was well, but behind the scenes things were getting increasingly tense. They'd produced such fantastic music and given their fans so much pleasure over the previous six or seven years. People understood that their music had become more complex, and that they'd never tour again, but for The Beatles to break up was quite simply unthinkable.

Sadly, life isn't like that. We change. We get older. We grow up. And we move on.

Coffee at The Corner House, the crowds and the confusion,
But I might as well be drinking on my own.
The evenings when we laugh and sing are mostly an
*   illusion.*
In my mind I'm always on my way back home.

I never thought I'd miss you, like I never thought I'd hold
*   you by the hand.*
Isn't life just like a rolling dice, a spinning wheel, a played-
*   out poker hand.*

Last night there was another girl, another lonely evening
At another High Street Kensington address.
We sat around and talked a bit with neither of us feeling
*   much like making love*
It couldn't have meant less.

I never thought I'd miss you, like I never thought I'd hold
*   you by the hand.*
Isn't life just like a rolling dice, a spinning wheel, a played-
*   out poker hand.*

Tonight I'll sing another song, the money I will get
Could mean I'll send another cable home to you.
Now I know how much I needed you I don't know why I
     left,
But at the time it seemed the natural thing to do.

I never thought I'd miss you, like I never thought I'd hold
     you by the hand.
Isn't life just like a rolling dice, a spinning wheel, a played-
     out poker hand.

The songs I was writing seemed to reflect what I was feeling. Perhaps I'd made a mistake by leaving Fiona in London and going back to Liverpool? She was the one who'd suggested the break. But it was only because, as she said, I kept going on about that night.

"Why can't you just forget about it and move on, Tony? Nothing happened."

I knew she was right. That I should try and put it out of my mind. But I couldn't.

It wasn't going back to Liverpool that was the problem. It was just that, in all the weeks and months since I'd left Fiona, I didn't seem to have come across anyone who was remotely as attractive as her. No-one else seemed to be as interesting, or as much fun.

I missed her. I wanted the telephone to ring so I could hear her voice again, but it remained silent. And if I were to ring her, after so long, would we have anything to say to each other?

As Christmas got nearer, and the nights grew longer, the centre of town blazed with festive lights. All the stores were doing a roaring trade and Christmas revellers crowded into restaurants and pubs. The season of good cheer was in full swing.

December 3rd 1968 was just after my twenty-fourth birthday. Liverpool beat Southampton one-nil at Anfield to stay top of the league, but I didn't really care. I'd gone along to the match with Steve and Eric, more out of habit than anything else. We had a few pints afterwards at The Albert.

"Yer not seein' Tracey tonight then, Steve?" said Eric.

Steve shook his head. "'Er grand-dad died last week an' she's gone over to Manchester with the rest of the family to sort things out. They're stayin' over there 'til the funeral on Tuesday."

"'An' you're not goin'?"

"The boss wouldn't give me the time off. Said me girlfriend's grand-dad didn't count as close family."

"Tight bugger. You should go on the sick."

"'E was well ahead of me on that one," said Steve. "'E made a point of tellin' me I was lookin' really well, an' if there was any larkin' about with sick notes I'd get me cards." He took a sip from his pint. "It'd probably be way out of order if 'e tried to sack me, but I can't afford to take the chance. Tracey said she didn't mind too much if I wasn't there. All the family'll be with 'er anyway." He paused for a moment. "She was really upset though when she got the news. They were quite close, I think. She was 'is only grandchild. But she seems to be okay now. To be honest I get a bit spooked by funerals so I'm quite glad I don't 'ave to go."

At about nine o'clock we decided to grab a taxi and finish off our evening in town. Steve and I were all for going straight to the piano bar at The Cavern, which had a late licence on a Saturday night, but Eric wanted to call in at The Magic Clock first.

"Are yer sure it'll be okay?" said Steve, looking more than a little unsure. "I've never been in there before."

"Don't worry," said Eric. "It'll be fine. Babs'll be behind the bar tonight. She doesn't mind who turns up as long as there's no trouble."

Steve looked at me and shrugged his shoulders. "What d'yer reckon?"

"It's okay with me," I said. "After what happened to Eric it's probably best if we keep an eye on him anyway."

Steve gave Eric a grin. "We'll be yer minders then, Eric. Okay?"

It took us about twenty minutes to get to The Magic Clock which was just off Roe Street near the Royal Court Theatre, right in the centre of Liverpool. Eric pulled one of the glazed doors open and we found ourselves in a very small, old-fashioned pub with stained-glass windows and a copper-covered bar top. Behind the bar several magnificent brass pump-handles had been discreetly decorated with tinsel as a nod to the approaching Christmas season. The room was crowded and the warm air was heavy with the sweet smell of Ogden's tobacco.

As Eric had expected, Babs was there, busily collecting empty glasses from the tables. She greeted him with a wave. "Hiya Eric love. You've got a couple of friends with yer I see."

Her bleached, blonde hair was piled up into a tall beehive, and she was wearing black, diamante glasses, the frames of which curved up fashionably at each end. Having deposited a handful of glasses on the bar she came over to us.

"Meet Tony, and Steve, Babs," said Eric cheerfully. "They're me minders."

Babs looked us up and down. "'Is minders, are yer? Well you just make sure you look after him. 'E needs a bit of mindin' does my Eric."

She put her arms round Eric and clasped him to her ample bosom before letting him go and making her way behind the bar.

"What's it to be then?" She grasped one of the tall, pump handles.

"Three pints of Worthington's please Babs." Eric pulled a few coins from his pocket and turned to us. "The drinks are on me tonight."

Babs placed three glasses on the counter and continued to chat away as she dispensed the beer. When she'd finished Eric pointed towards a table where a young man with short, fair hair, and wearing a tight, black tee-shirt and dark-blue jeans, was sitting on his own.

"Come and meet Fletch, lads. I thought 'e might be in tonight."

We went over and joined Fletcher at his table.

"Fletch. This is Steve and Tony. Me Anfield mates. Remember me tellin' yer about them?"

Fletcher greeted us warmly and we chatted away until Babs produced a towel from behind the bar and draped it over the brass handles. The evening was at an end. As we finished our drinks people started to drift off.

"Are you and Fletch comin' down to The Cavern, Eric?" said Steve, looking at his watch. "The piano bar'll be open for another hour or two yet."

Before Eric could reply Fletcher shook his head. "I've had enough to drink for one night. Thanks anyway, Steve, but I think I'll just get off."

"Me too," said Eric, giving Fletcher a quick glance.

"Looks like it's just you an' me then, Tone," said Steve. He drained the last few drops from his glass and stood up. "Let's go."

As we walked away from The Magic Clock we were alert for any possible trouble but all was quiet. We crossed Williamson Square heading for Mathew Street, quickening our pace as a light drizzle began to fall.

"I hope Eric'll be okay," I said to Steve as we hurried along.

"Fletcher seems to 'ave 'is head screwed on," said Steve. "An' Eric's not daft. I don't reckon they'll make the same mistake twice."

Thirty

NEW YEAR'S EVE

I marked the last day of 1968 by visiting Louise's grave again. The weather was cold and bleak, with a light frosting of snow on the ground. This time there was no bouquet of fresh flowers. Nothing to indicate that anyone had been to see her. I placed another red rose in the middle of the empty square of white gravel and stood there for a while, telling her what had been happening and how I was now back in Liverpool. Possibly for good. It was a strange, sad feeling, but I was glad I had gone. I couldn't be sure, but there was a definite sense that something was changing.

That evening I went to a party. To be perfectly honest I wasn't much in the mood, but Steve and Tracey persuaded me to go along with them. The parents of a girl called Ruth, one of Tracey's pals from way back who she hadn't seen for several years, had gone to Spain for a couple of weeks so Ruth, along with her younger sister Lynne, had decided to invite some friends round to see in the New Year. The house was on the front, in Waterloo, overlooking the river, and a disco had been set up in a large conservatory which occupied most of what had once been the back garden. The DJ was an old friend, Carl, and I knew he had a good collection of records. With decent music, and a kitchen packed full of booze, it looked like 1968 was going to be given a memorable send-off.

Perhaps it was just because I was getting older, but time seemed to be passing ever more quickly. In only twelve months we'd be marking the end of the sixties.

As soon as we arrived Tracey went off to catch up with Ruth, leaving me on my own with Steve.

"Wanna hear the latest Tone?" he said. "Me an' Tracey's gettin' married. I asked her on Christmas Eve an' she said 'yes.'"

He looked very happy. And there was more.

"Don't mention it to anyone, but Tracey's grand-dad, you know the one who died, 'e's left 'er a bit of money. I didn't know about it 'til yesterday but it turns out 'e was a bit of an inventor an' 'e came up with an idea a few years back which did quite nicely for 'im. None of the family 'ad any idea 'e was well off. 'E never flashed it about. Accordin' to Tracey 'e was a lovely bloke. But when it came to money 'e was tighter than a duck's arse."

"It's not really any of my business," I said. "So tell me to bugger off if you want. But what's she going to do with it?"

"She seems to think there might be enough to get ourselves a house. Maybe with a little bit of a mortgage as well. To be honest it's got me a bit worried, Tone. I mean, she's really attractive. An' now she's got all this money. She might decide to fix 'erself up with someone who's got a bit more to offer than me."

"Bollocks, Steve. She's nuts about you. She wouldn't be agreeing to marry you if she wasn't. Stop worrying. It's great news."

Just as I finished speaking Tracey appeared. Wearing a figure-hugging, silver dress with black tights and heels she looked amazing. I put my arms around her and give her a big hug.

"Steve's just told me your news. Congratulations. I couldn't be more pleased."

She grinned and held out her right hand. The diamond ring on her third finger sparkled as she moved her wrist around.

"Aren't I lucky?" she said.

"You certainly are. And for that matter, so's Steve. If you ask me the two of you were made for each other."

Tracey grinned and took hold of Steve's hand. As she did so, 'Baby Come Back' by The Equals faded away and Carl picked up his microphone.

"This next record's for Tracey and Steve. Ruth's just told me they've not long got engaged. So here's Solomon Burke singing 'She Wears My Ring.'"

Steve looked around as if he didn't quite know what to do. I pointed towards the dance floor. "You'd better get out there and show us what it's all about."

There were loud cheers as they moved to the middle of the floor and put their arms around each other. Steve grinned and gave Tracey a big kiss.

Everything was going to be fine. The Three Exiles hadn't been Steve's passport to riches, but thanks to the band he'd met Tracey. It had all worked out in the end.

Leaving them to it I wandered over to see a couple of old mates from school. Ruth's sister, Lynne, was with them and as we all stood there swapping news I couldn't help noticing how attractive she was. Her hair was a pale, copper colour, reaching down almost to her slim waist. She was wearing a long, loose, light yellow dress with a plaited belt and her feet were bare. She looked as though she'd stepped straight out of one of the Pre-Raphaelite paintings I still remembered from school trips to the Walker Art Gallery in the city centre.

'Jumpin' Jack Flash' was playing on the disco and I turned to her. "You're Lynne aren't you? I'm Tony. Are you a Stones fan?"

"They're okay." She smiled at me as she replied.

"I was thinking if you did like them you might fancy a dance?"

She didn't answer, so I held out my hand. She took hold of it and I led her onto the dance floor, stopping on the way to ask Carl if he'd mind playing the Stones' record again. Lynne overheard and gave me another smile.

Her bare feet slid gracefully across the polished floor. She certainly knew how to move. The encore of '*Jumpin' Jack Flash*' was followed by '*Honky Tonk Women*', and then Martha Reeves and The Vandellas singing '*Dancing In The Street*'.

As The Vandellas faded out Carl picked up his microphone. A tall chap was standing alongside him. "I'm sorry about this, everybody, but I'm about to play a request for this gentleman who's standing next to me. He tells me his name's Vince Toscana, which may or may not be true, but apparently you all know him as Tosser."

There were some cheers and ribald laughter. Vince was obviously well-known.

Carl held up his hands. "Unfortunately his taste in music is as terrible as his nickname. He's asked for '*Congratulations*' by Cliff Richard."

As Tosser headed for the dance floor, to a loud chorus of shouts and boos, I turned to Lynne who was still laughing. "Let's go and get a drink."

We moved into the house and she guided me towards a brightly-lit kitchen.

"I've hidden the best stuff in here," she said, pulling the door of the fridge open and taking out a bottle of Dom Perignon. "I was keeping it for midnight, but I don't suppose it'll matter if we make a start now."

She handed the bottle to me. I pulled off the metal foil and removed the wire cage from around the cork. Keeping a tight hold on the cork I gently eased it loose and allowed the pressure to escape with a gentle hiss.

"Very impressive," said Lynne. "You've obviously done that before."

"Dom Perignon's far too good to waste," I said. "And anyway I wouldn't want one of your folks' expensive spotlights to be taken out by a flying cork."

She produced a couple of glasses from one of the pitch-pine wall cupboards and I poured a generous serving into each of them.

"Cheers!"

After raising her glass she emptied it in one. "More please." She held the glass out and I refilled it.

"Do you want to go back out to the conservatory?" I said.

"No. Let's stay here for a minute. It's too noisy to chat out there."

She moved over to a switch by the door and the bright spotlights dimmed. We perched on a couple of tall stools at a breakfast bar which ran along one side of the room.

"Haven't we met before?" she said, turning to me. "I'm sure I've seen you somewhere."

"My folks own the newsagent's by the station in South Road. I was down in London until about nine months ago but then I split up with my girlfriend and moved back here. At the moment I'm living in the flat above the shop. Steve and Tracey brought me along tonight."

"The couple who just got engaged?"

"Yes. Your sister Ruth said to Tracey it'd be okay if I tagged along with them."

"That's fine with me," she said, tilting her head to one side. "So you're originally from up here? How come you were going out with a girl from London?"

"I met her up here in Liverpool. She used to go to the Art College."

Lynne looked at me. "Maybe that's where I've seen you before then. Ruth was a student there. What's your girlfriend's name?"

"Ex-girlfriend," I said quickly.

Lynne laughed and gave me a slightly mischievous grin. "Okay. Ex-girlfriend."

She'd got the message.

"Her name was Fiona," I continued, smiling back at her. "Fiona Curtis. She finished a couple of years ago."

"That's when Ruth was there. Maybe they knew each other? I'll ask her."

I didn't want to waste the evening talking about Fiona so I changed the subject.

"And what about you? Are you at Art College? You look very chic and arty."

"No," she said, laughing again. "Ruth's the arty one in our family. I'm down at Bristol University. Doing Psychology. I finish my degree next June. All being well."

"Then what?"

"My boyfriend wants to travel and see some of the world, so maybe that's what we'll do. He's at Bristol as well, but he's in San Francisco at the moment doing some research for his Ph.D. Something to do with trying to predict earthquakes, I think he said, but to be honest I don't really know much about it."

"So you're on your own and fancy free."

"I suppose I must be," she said, finishing off her second glass of champagne.

"More?" I asked.

She shook her head. "No thanks. They're big glasses. I'll be on my back if I have another. Let's keep it 'til after midnight." She gave me a smile. "We can find somewhere quiet and finish the bottle off together."

In the background I could hear Carl announcing that he was going to play a few slower numbers and then take a break before starting the run-in to midnight.

"Let's go and have a couple more dances."

We moved back onto the floor and Lynne draped her arms around my shoulders as Joe Cocker began to sing '*With A Little Help from My Friends*'.

"I adore this record," she said.

"Me too. It's amazing. Ringo's version sounded great until Joe Cocker came up with this. It's either a work of genius or a really lucky fluke."

"I'd go for genius. I love his voice. It's so sort of earthy and real."

When the record finished we moved back into the lounge and flopped onto a big couch. As we did so I heard Carl announcing the next record.

"This next one's for Tony. It's by some girls from Manchester. It's called *'Love Isn't Always A Game'*."

The familiar record, which I'd not listened to for at least nine months, began to play.

"Why did Carl say this record's for you?" said Lynne as she leaned back and let the soft cushions envelop her. "This couch is one of the things I miss when I'm down in Bristol. It's so comfortable. And wonderfully decadent. I could easily spend the rest of the evening just lying here."

"I think he's probably taking the mickey," I said, but Lynne, lying back in her decadent comfort, seemed to have forgotten she'd asked me a question.

We listened to The Manchester Girls as they finished the opening verses and moved on to the chorus.

"I like the harmonies," she said. "I don't think I've heard it before. Have you?"

"Once or twice," I said, laughing. "I think Carl said it was for me because I wrote it. I was with the girls at Trident Studios down in London when they were recording it."

Lynne sat up and looked at me. "You're joking."

"Afraid not. It was released at the beginning of this year but it didn't do that much. Carl got hold of one of the promotional copies to play at his discos. We're mates so he wanted to try and publicise it for me. I've no idea how many copies were sold but I don't think it was a huge number. It certainly hasn't made me much money."

"That's a shame," said Lynne, raising her eyebrows. "Has it been on the radio?"

"It got a fair number of plays here in the U.K. And some in Australia as well I think. I got some royalties a few weeks ago. In Australian dollars. Just about enough for a couple of drinks. I should probably have got some UK royalties too, but they sort of disappeared. My Dad reckons the sharks in the music business swallowed them. They must've forgotten to snaffle up the royalties that came in from Australia. Better luck next time, I suppose."

"So you've got more records coming out?"

"Not at the moment. But we're still writing songs. Hopefully we might strike lucky one day."

"Who's we?"

The questions were coming thick and fast. Lynne was obviously intrigued. Maybe I was in luck.

"Me and a guy called Larry," I explained. "He's in the music business full-time. I just do a bit of song-writing with him on the side. We get together down at The Cavern in the afternoon when it's closed."

"Do you know a lot of people in the music business?"

"A few. Larry knows a lot more people than I do though. He was a record producer in London and I discovered not long ago that he used to hang out with Paul McCartney. He was with us down at The Cavern a couple of months ago."

"Who was?"

"Paul McCartney."

"Come on, Tony. Now you are having me on. It'd have been all over the papers if Paul McCartney had turned up at The Cavern."

"No. Seriously. He was wearing a long coat with the collar turned right up and a big hat which sort of covered his face. He was standing right next to me, but I didn't realise who it was until he took them off. Nobody would have recognised him outside in Mathew Street. I suppose he has to go round incognito if he wants to avoid being mobbed by fans. He told us he'd phoned Alf Geoghegan, the guy who owns The Cavern now, and said he'd like to call in but it had to be kept quiet. I didn't see his car but I think he must've parked it outside. He was with an American girl called Linda who seems to be his new girlfriend. They stayed for about half an hour. He even sat down and played '*Hey Jude*' on the piano."

Lynne lay back on the cushions and gave a deep sigh. "I used to be crazy about Paul McCartney. I suppose I still am in a way. You're so lucky."

We lay on the couch and continued to chat away. She was great fun to be with, and almost before we knew it the count-down to midnight had begun.

As the clock struck twelve Lynne snuggled up to me and gave me a kiss. "Happy 1969. I've always wanted to get to know a famous song-writer."

"Very slightly famous," I said. "And even that's probably pushing it a bit."

"That'll do me. Especially as you know Paul McCartney." She gave me another, longer kiss. "Come on. We'd better go and join in the celebrations. Then we can finish off that champagne."

Half an hour later, glasses and champagne in hand, she led me up the stairs to her room.

●·+———— ●·+·●·+·●———— ·+·●

Several of us had stayed the night and late next morning, as we all sat drinking coffee in the kitchen, Lynne turned to her sister.

"Ruth. Did you know a girl called Fiona Curtis when you were at the Art College?"

It was an entirely innocent question, as was Ruth's reply.

"Yes. We were on the same course. She was the one I told you about who had to have an abortion at the end of the first term because she got herself pregnant. She went to some back-street woman off Upper Parliament Street who made a real mess of it. The poor thing had to be sorted out in hospital afterwards. There were loads of rumours flying around but it was all kept very hush-hush by the college. Why do you ask?"

Lynne looked across the table at me.

"She used to be Tony's girlfriend."

I saw Lynne a couple more times but we both knew it was just a casual fling that would be over as soon as she returned to Bristol. We never mentioned Fiona, or the bomb-shell which Ruth had so innocently delivered.

We were enjoying ourselves. And while it lasted I was more than happy just to block everything else out.

By Saturday 11th of January Lynne was back in Bristol and we were all in The Albert, celebrating a one-nil victory over West Bromwich Albion which kept us at the top of the First Division. The pub was packed, as usual, and I was about to get another pint in when Eric climbed up onto a chair, waving a couple of tickets.

"Anyone want a ticket for the Chelsea game at Stamford Bridge next week? Robbo was gonna come with me, but 'e's cried off. One of these is mine, but the other's goin' spare if anyone can make use of it. I'm sellin' it for what it cost me. Ten bob."

Before anybody else had time to put in an offer I grabbed hold of his arm. "I'll take it, Eric. I've not been to a big away game in years."

He grinned and handed it to me. "Say no more, Tone. It's yours."

It was a bit of a gamble but, since Lynne's return to Bristol, I'd been thinking about what her sister had said. I wanted to go down to London and see Fiona. I wasn't entirely sure why, but I knew I needed to speak to her. And the Chelsea match was the perfect excuse. A last minute phone call would make it easier for her to say no if she didn't want to meet up. She'd almost certainly be in work on the Saturday morning so hopefully I'd be able to catch her at the office. 'Silver Peaches' had moved to Savile Row the previous May, just before we'd stopped speaking to each other, and she'd given me the number. As far as I was aware she didn't have a phone at Haverstock Hill. If she was still living there, that is.

The concourse at Euston Station was crowded as we made our way up the ramp from Platform Four where our train had pulled in, but the red telephone boxes were all free. I pulled one of the hefty, glazed doors open, leaving Eric waiting outside, and lifted the black handset. After feeding four pennies into the slot at the top of the black cash box I dialled Fiona's office. I waited with my finger on the protruding metal button marked 'A' and, after what seemed like an age, the call was answered.

"Hello. Silver Peaches."

It was Fiona's voice. I pressed button A and the four pennies dropped noisily into the cash box. She could now hear me.

"Fiona. It's Tony. I've only got a couple of minutes."

"Tony! How are you?"

"I'm fine. Sorry not to have given you more notice but I'm in London with Eric. We've just got into Euston. We're on our way to Stamford Bridge to watch Chelsea play Liverpool. Eric's heading back on the train tonight but I'm thinking of staying over 'til tomorrow. If you're not doing anything this evening it'd be great to see you."

For several seconds there was no reply. I could hear muffled voices discussing something in the background.

"Hello. Fiona. Are you still there?"

"Sorry, Tony. Somebody just came into the office. It'd be really nice to see you but I'm afraid I'm tied up tonight."

"Not to worry," I said, doing my best not to sound disappointed. "I thought you'd probably be busy. But I decided to give it a try since I was already down here. I'll get in touch if I'm in London again."

"That'd be great. Give me a bit more notice next time and I'll do my best to be free."

"Okay. Enjoy yourself this evening whatever it is you've got planned."

"I will. It's a Pink Floyd concert at The Roundhouse. Hope your team win. 'Bye."

"'Bye"

There was a click and the line went dead. I replaced the handset on its cradle. As everyone did back in those days I tried pressing button 'B' on the off-chance that I'd get my money back, but it remained stubbornly inside the machine.

"Any luck?" asked Eric as I emerged.

"No." I shook my head. "Fourpence wasted. She's going to see Pink Floyd at The Roundhouse."

"Lucky girl. No spare tickets?" said Eric mischievously.

"If there were she wasn't saying."

"It's probably for the best, Tone. If Chelsea beat us it'd be pretty miserable travellin' all the way back to Liverpool on me own. Now we can 'ave a few pints together afterwards whichever way things go."

"We'll be celebrating," I said. "There's no way we're going to lose to Chelsea."

By the time the match kicked-off Stamford Bridge was packed with about thirty thousand very noisy Chelsea fans but those of us in the away section of the ground gave as good as we got. It wasn't a great game but we left happy. The Liverpool Reds had beaten the Chelsea Blues by two goals to one.

Thirty-One

LET IT BE

It was the end of January 1969. The final year of the sixties. Larry and I were down at The Cavern when we heard on the radio that The Beatles were up on the roof of the Apple Building in Savile Row doing an impromptu concert. Traffic down on the street had come to a halt as people tried to see, and hear, what was going on.

"Brilliant," said Larry. "Those boys might be millionaires but they're still one hundred per cent rock and roll."

I could just imagine the scene, and I wondered if perhaps Fiona could see them from her office window. Four world-famous musicians perched between the chimney pots on make-shift planks and scaffolding, braving the bitterly cold, January wind. Their unexpected and unannounced appearance suggested that perhaps The Beatles had sorted out their differences. But it was not to be.

They'd been working on some new songs in a recording studio which John Lennon's electronics wizard, Alexis *'Magic Alex'* Mardas, had installed in the basement of the Apple Building. Paul wanted to put together an album which would take them back to their early Liverpool and Hamburg roots; maybe in an attempt to heal the increasingly obvious rifts which were appearing between the four of them. But the equipment in the new studio wasn't up to scratch. And while things were being sorted out they'd decided a brief, roof-top concert might provide some welcome relief from the tension which was building up.

Their final album, 'Let It Be', did eventually emerge from the basement sessions, but not in the raw, unpolished form that Paul McCartney had intended. Apparently without Paul's knowledge the American record producer Phil Spector, whose trademark 'Wall of Sound' had featured on many hits, had been invited by someone at Apple to take a listen to the master tapes. And, in typical Phil Spector style, some lush orchestration had been added to several of the tracks.

For Paul McCartney it was the final straw. He could not even control his own music. The rifts between the four Beatles would never be healed. That brief, glorious gig, high above the streets of London, turned out to be the last public performance by the best rock 'n' roll band the world has ever seen.

The Beatles were not the only ones who were having a tough time in the early months of 1969. Bill Shankly's Liverpool side were struggling to find any consistency in their performances and by the end of April the situation was simple. They faced Leeds United at Anfield on the evening of Monday 28th April. If Liverpool failed to win the match, Leeds would be the champions.

We got to the ground early and by seven o'clock the Kop was heaving. The gates were closed five minutes before kick-off with 53,750 people in the ground.

Don Revie, the Leeds manager, had declared to the press that even though his team only needed a draw his plan was to go for all-out attack and win the game. No one was fooled. Leeds were known for their stubborn defensive tactics and so it proved. Liverpool had all the possession and they launched numerous desperate attacks but they were unable to score. Leeds United had come to Anfield and, thanks to a boring, goalless draw, the First Division title was going back to Yorkshire with them.

The Leeds players stayed on the pitch for fifteen or twenty minutes after the final whistle as the Kop gave them a very sporting ovation. Bill Shankly announced over the Tannoy that Leeds United were worthy champions and that there'd be a crate of champagne in the dressing room for them.

Eric was couldn't understand it. "Why are we clappin' 'em for God's sake? An' givin' 'em champagne as well? They've just nicked our bleedin' title."

After a pint at The Albert he announced that he was going into town and that he'd see us at the weekend. It was almost closing time. Steve and I had to be in work next day, so we left him to it and headed home.

It had been a disappointing afternoon. And things were about to get much worse.

⬤·⬝⸺⬤·⬝⬤·⬝⸺·⬤

"Is Mr Tony Cooper in please?"

I was helping out in the shop the following evening when two police officers walked in. My Dad pointed to me.

"That's Tony. He's my son. Is there some sort of problem?"

"We just need to have a word with him if that's alright," said the older of the two officers. "It shouldn't take long."

I went over to them. "We live in the flat upstairs. We could talk up there if you like."

The two officers glanced at each other. "That'd be fine."

We arranged ourselves around the table in the living room. They younger policeman removed his blue helmet and placed a notebook on the table in front of him. The other man, who I presumed was the more senior of the two, then took off his peaked cap and opened the proceedings.

"I'm Detective Inspector Collingwood," he said, "and this is Detective Constable Warren. We're sorry to disturb you like this but I'm afraid we have what may prove to be some bad news for you."

I could feel my heart starting to race.

"Do you know a man called Eric Barstow?"

I nodded. "He's a friend. What's the problem? Has something happened to him?"

"We'll come to that in a moment." He looked at his younger colleague and very slightly nodded his head. "First of all can you tell us when you last saw your friend?"

"I went to the match with him yesterday. The Leeds game at Anfield. We were with another friend. Steve Grey. We went for a pint at The Albert after the game and then Eric said he was going into town."

"On his own?"

"Yes. Me and Steve went home."

"Did he say what he was planning to do in town?"

I shook my head. "No. I don't think so. As far as I remember he just said he was going into town."

"Can you recall what time he left The Albert?" D.C. Warren was taking notes.

"It wasn't that long before closing time. Maybe about quarter past ten?"

"Did he seem to be his normal self when he left you?"

"Yes. He was pretty fed up about Liverpool letting Leeds win the title. But that's normal for Eric if Liverpool don't win. I wouldn't have said he was any more upset than usual."

"And you've not seen Mr Barstow since then?"

"No. He said he'd meet up with us at the weekend."

Inspector Collingwood gave his younger colleague another nod and the notebook was slowly closed.

"I'm very sorry to have to tell you that your friend has been killed. He was knocked down by a bus at about eleven o'clock last night. In Roe Street. Just outside the Royal Court Theatre."

I could feel the two of them looking at me and I wasn't sure how they expected me to react. I just sat there stunned.

The inspector leaned forward. "Are you alright?"

I didn't know what to say. A million thoughts were spinning round and round inside my head.

"So Eric's dead. Is that what you're saying? I can't believe it."

"I'm very sorry," said the Inspector. "Your name and address, along with Mr Grey's, were in a diary we found on him. There were a couple of witnesses who saw what happened. We are obliged to make some routine enquiries, but at the moment it looks as though it was just a tragic accident."

"Does Steve know?"

"We've not been able to speak to Mr Grey yet. He's apparently away from home in Southport this evening."

I nodded my head. "He's getting married in a few months. Tracey – that's his fiancée – she's come into a bit of money and they've gone over to Southport to look at some houses."

I don't even know why I said it. Buying a house seemed totally unimportant after the news about Eric.

"I understand that this must have come as a shock for you." The Inspector looked me straight in the eye and held me in his gaze. "I presume you had no reason to think your friend might be planning to take his life?"

"No." I said firmly. "Eric'd never do anything like that. I'm sure he wouldn't."

"He'd not said anything to cause you concern?" The Inspector continued to look directly at me. "It didn't seem to you that he could be depressed for example?"

"No," I said. "No."

"Is there anything else that you think we should know?"

The way he was continuing to stare at me was making me feel uncomfortable. But that, I suppose, was his intention. I thought about mentioning Fletcher, and The Magic Clock. They'd said Eric was in Roe Street, so that's probably where he was heading. Or maybe leaving. But it didn't seem right to say anything. Not now he was dead.

I shook my head deliberately. "No. There's nothing."

The two policemen sat there, waiting. As if they knew I had something else to say. Then they stood up to leave.

"Thank you for your help, Mr Cooper. If you think of anything at all that might be of assistance to us please let us know. There'll have to be an inquest and the Coroner is likely to require both you and Mr Grey to attend the proceedings and give evidence. As far as we know you were the last people to speak to your friend before he lost his life. We'll be in touch once a date for the inquest has been set."

I showed them out through the shop where my Dad was busy with a couple of customers.

"Everything okay, Tony?" he called out as we passed.

"Fine Dad. I'll speak to you in a minute."

I sat in the little office area at the back of the shop feeling completely numb.

"What's up?" said my Dad as he wandered in. "You look like you've seen a ghost."

I lifted my head. "Eric's dead. That's what they came to tell me."

My Dad didn't know Eric that well, but I could see he was taken aback. I didn't wait for him to ask the obvious question. I just told him the answer.

"He got hit by a bus in town last night."

I got in touch with Steve as quickly as I could, but the police had beaten me to it.

"Did you tell them about The Magic Clock and Fletcher?"

He shook his head. "No. They didn't ask."

"Let's just keep quiet then. Okay? That's definitely what Eric would have wanted. Complicating things isn't going to bring him back. We'll just wait and see what the Coroner has to say."

Steve nodded in agreement.

The Coroner sat in his high-backed chair, upholstered in expensive red leather, listening to the evidence of the two men who saw the incident, one of whom turned out to be Fletcher. They both said that Eric just darted across Roe Street without looking and that he probably never saw the bus. The bus driver, who looked pretty shaken as he gave his evidence, said he'd had no time even to hit his brakes. Steve and I were both asked whether we knew of any reason why Eric might have wanted to take his own life. Obviously we said 'no'.

After a brief adjournment the Coroner returned to the Court and thanked us all for attending. Then, putting on a pair of steel-rimmed, reading glasses, he looked down at a sheet of paper which he was holding in his left hand. "The verdict of this Court," he announced, "is that Mr Eric Barstow lost his life as the result of an unfortunate and tragic accident."

Eric's funeral was held a couple of weeks later at Anfield Crematorium. And we joined his family at the ground of Liverpool Football Club as, with Mr Shankly's special permission, Eric's ashes were scattered in the Kop goalmouth.

It was where he would have wanted to be.

Thirty-Two

SLEEPING DOGS

During that last summer of 1969 I visited St Peter's several times, just as I had promised I would. With all the trees in leaf, and the flowers in full bloom, the churchyard was a quiet and peaceful place to sit and think. I thought about Louise. And I thought about Eric too.

Each time I took a red rose. But there were no more bouquets.

And then, one day in the autumn, just as the leaves were changing colour and starting to fall, it happened as Fiona had said it would. I was sitting quietly on a wooden bench which was dedicated to the memory of Elizabeth Draper when, quite suddenly, I knew that the time had come for me to move on. I gazed for what seemed like an age at the white gravel and the single red rose, but the feeling didn't change. Louise seemed to be telling me I was free to go.

For me she would always be just seventeen. Like the girl in the Lennon and McCartney song. And even if I never came back to see her again, I knew that not a single day would pass without me thinking of her. As I turned and walked away, past the church and through the lych-gate for what would probably be the last time, my eyes filled with tears. But I was certain that she understood.

I stopped at the house in Penny Lane. The new owners told me that Mr and Mrs Browne had moved to the Lake District the previous year. And they vaguely recalled two young doctors who had said they were making plans to emigrate to New Zealand.

•–•————•–•–•–•————–•–•

Then, out of the blue, I received a letter.

Alfreton Lodge
Haverstock Hill
London   *16th October 1969*

Dear Tony,

    I was speaking to a friend from Liverpool yesterday and she told me about Eric. I know it's quite a long time ago now, but I still wanted to write and tell you how very sorry I was to hear the news. He was a good friend to you, and you must miss him a lot. Please pass my condolences on to Steve and Tracey as well when you next see them.
Everything seems to be going well for me down here in London. Silver Peaches is building up quite a reputation. And I've been made a director which is good for the bank balance.

    The Pink Floyd concert at The Roundhouse was absolutely brilliant. I went with one of the girls from work. She's good company but it would have been much more fun if you could have been there. Do you remember The Beatles Concert we went to at The Empire? Exciting times!

    I've been hoping you'd ring again. Are you ever down in London? Please get in touch if you are. It's been a long time, but I'd love to see you again.

    With my love
    Fiona xxx

I showed the letter to Steve. "What do you think?"

He looked at me and gave me a smile, shaking his head as he did so. "I'll tell you what I think, Tone. If you don't get straight on the phone to that lovely, young lady you need your head testin'. She's tryin' to sound all London and cool, but she's desperate to see yer. It's obvious."

• • • • • • • • • •

"How about meeting up at The Washington at about six o'clock next Saturday evening?" said Fiona. "I'll be in work most of the day, but I can sort out a table somewhere in Hampstead. After we've had a drink or two we can grab a bite to eat and have a good chat."

I'd taken Steve's advice and phoned Fiona, giving her plenty of time to sort something out if she still wanted to get together. And it seemed that she did.

I drove down to London in the Min-van and got there in the middle of the afternoon which gave me plenty of time to freshen myself up and change into some smart clothes after the journey. At just before ten minutes to six I walked into The Washington and settled down at a table with a couple of glasses and a bottle of Fiona's favourite white wine. She arrived at exactly six.

She looked different. Her dark hair was cut short in a sophisticated, gamine French style which really suited her, and she was wearing very little make-up. Dressed in a loose mini-dress, together with a leather jacket and knee-length, laced cowhide boots, she looked even more attractive than I remembered.

I caught her eye and she made her way over to join me.

• • • • • • • • • •

The table she'd booked was in a small restaurant in Heath Street, up in Hampstead Village. The owner, Bernardo Stella, had left his native Italy in the late fifties to avoid having to do compulsory military service, while his wife, Androulla, was from Cyprus. Strangely, considering their backgrounds, the cuisine was mainly French. And this explained the unusual name they had chosen for their culinary venture, 'La Gaffe' – 'The Mistake'.

Bernardo greeted Fiona with a smile and a kiss on both cheeks.

"I've been here a few times with clients," she explained as he showed us to our table. "The food's good. And it's not expensive for this part of London. Bernardo's built up quite a reputation over the past few years so you occasionally see some well-known, show-biz faces eating here."

I looked around but didn't immediately recognise any of our fellow diners.

"Over there in the far corner," said Fiona as we were sitting down. "I think it might be Bruce Welch from Cliff Richard's backing band, The Shadows. He must live somewhere nearby. I've seen him in here several times."

By this time I had my back to the man she had spotted, so I couldn't be sure she was right. I didn't bother turning round as I wasn't even certain I could remember what Bruce Welch looked like. It was a year or two since a record by The Shadows had featured in the charts.

My fillet steak was as good as Fiona had predicted, and her rack of lamb looked equally appetising. Having had white wine at The Washington, we'd chosen a red Cotes du Rhone by Paul Jaboulet to go with our food and as we finished off the bottle with a shared cheese plate we were both feeling very relaxed. With the help of two bottles of alcohol the initial slight tension and uncertainty had completely disappeared. There was a lot to talk about and the time raced by. By the end of the evening it was as though we'd never been apart.

"It's lovely to see you." she said, leaning across the table and taking hold of my hand. "I've really missed you"

There was no point in playing it cool.

"I've missed you too. A lot. That trip to the Chelsea game with Eric was just an excuse to come down here and ring you. I was devastated when you said you were going to see Pink Floyd and couldn't make it."

"It's been a very long time." She gazed at me, and her eyes were as blue as ever. "But I still love you, Tony."

At first I didn't say anything. I just looked back at her.

"That's good. Because I don't know what on earth we think we've been playing at for the past eighteen months. I'm still mad about you too."

●·•————————●·•·●·•·●————————·•·●

In the middle of April 1970, shortly after Paul McCartney had issued a press release to say that he was leaving the band and that The Beatles were splitting up, Fiona and I moved into a garden flat on the ground floor of a large house which backed onto Hampstead Heath. 'Silver Peaches' was going from strength to strength, supplying clothes to shops all over the country. And there were plans to expand overseas. Our home had to be in London.

We'd had a quiet wedding up in Liverpool the previous month. At Mount Pleasant Register Office. It had seemed appropriate.

I never spoke to her about Lynne, or her sister Ruth. If it was true that Fiona had once had a difficult abortion it must have been dreadful for her. It was easy to understand why being reminded of it had made her so upset that evening. But as far as our relationship was concerned it was irrelevant. It didn't matter.

For her part, Fiona never chose to tell me how she got hold of that signed LP. Or mentioned Adrian Henri's poem. And I never asked her.

We both had our secrets. But they were now in the past. Sleeping dogs. It was best to let them lie.

I still played my guitar, and I still wrote the occasional song. But I lost touch with Larry and the song-writing was just for fun. I'd given up any thoughts of hitting the big time.

Walking down Camden High Street I was able to look up at an illuminated sign which told everyone who passed that *'Tony Cooper – Electrical Contractor'* was open for business.

The sixties were over. And, just like The Beatles, I'd grown up.

At noon on 12th July 1974 Bill Shankly called a press conference and, to the astonishment of all the club's fans, he announced his retirement. Everyone was shell-shocked. Like the break-up of The Beatles, it was the end of an era. But for Liverpool Football Club what Bill Shankly built in the sixties proved to be a beginning, not an end. I watched, mostly from afar, as the club dominated both English and European football.

His assistant, Bob Paisley, had spent many years in the Anfield 'boot room' with Bill Shankly, plotting and planning tactics. When he finally took over as manager he carried on where Shankly had left off. His Liverpool teams topped the First Division six times and won the European Cup three times.

Hopefully Eric was there, in spirit, to see it all.

People say it was the shooting of John Lennon in New York in December 1980, more than ten years after I'd moved permanently to London, which finally woke Liverpool up.

The worldwide reaction to what had happened shocked the city into action and The Beatles, who had seemed almost forgotten on Merseyside, were finally given the recognition they deserved. It was now certain that the band would never play together again. That simple fact, together with the huge number of people who turned up at Mathew Street to mark John Lennon's passing and pay their respects, meant that the proud city of Liverpool, with all its illustrious maritime and industrial history, at long last fully embraced its good fortune and global fame as '*The Birthplace of The Beatles*'.

In those early years of the 1980's, visitors to Mathew Street found that the original entrance to The Cavern Club had been demolished in the mid-seventies to make room for a ventilation shaft for the inner-city, underground railway. And the famous cellar, where The Beatles had played so many times, had been filled with rubble.

Paul had shown it to Linda just in time.

The ventilation shaft was never constructed so, to satisfy the increasing number of visitors who wanted to see The Cavern Club, a new entrance was built just a few yards from the original one. The rubble was cleared out. And The Cavern Club was reborn.

Since that day in 1960, when The Beatles first went off to The Star Club in Hamburg and turned themselves from a local, Liverpool band into the tightest rock 'n' roll outfit of all time, Mathew Street has changed. But, although the entrance is not in quite the same place, the brick-arched cellar is still The Cavern Club. It is still the place where four young Scousers first met Brian Epstein, and from which they emerged to become a world-wide phenomenon.

When Fiona and I visit Liverpool with our two children we always pop into The Cavern. Just for old times' sake. Nowadays, instead of wholesale fruit merchants selling their produce, and teenage office workers on their lunch break queuing to get into The Cavern Club, Mathew Street is thronged with tourists who are trying to imagine what it must have been like in those magical times. While, almost unnoticed, a life-sized statue of John Lennon leans casually against a wall opposite the entrance to the club, watching them.

A few hundred yards away, down at the Pier Head, all four Beatles are captured in bronze, as if it were still the early nineteen sixties, walking towards the River Mersey. Dreaming perhaps of America, and the world beyond.

And if you are a Liverpool fan you can visit the iconic Anfield Stadium, where you will be greeted by the figure of Bill Shankly, standing in front of his beloved football club with his arms high above his head in that familiar pose. You can even tour the ground and touch the sign which Shankly placed above the tunnel leading to the pitch to put the fear of God into visiting teams. It says, quite simply, 'THIS IS ANFIELD'.

For many years it has worked its magic.

It was all a very long time ago. A brief flowering of popular culture which lit up a provincial English city and made it famous across the world.

Now the world comes to Liverpool.

My heart still lives there.

And for that you can definitely blame The Beatles. And Bill Shankly.